SEVEN FLOORS HIGH

A Journey of Greed, Espionage & Deceit

STEVE GODDARD

UPSO

"The gulf between books and experience... is a lonely ocean."
WHITE TEETH by Zadie Smith, Penguin 2000.

"It has been a wonderful life."
MEMOIRS by David Rockefeller, Random House 2002

Seven Floors High © Copyright 2003 by Steve Goddard
Cover design, Copyright Steve Goddard 2003.
Front image: © Corbis Images
Back image: © David Nunuk / Science Photo Library

A catalogue record of this book is available from the British Library

First Edition: December 2003

ISBN: 1-84375-069-4

To order additional copies of this book please visit:
http://www.upso.co.uk/sevenfloorshigh

Published by: UPSO Ltd
5 Stirling Road, Castleham Business Park,
St Leonards-on-Sea, East Sussex TN38 9NW UK
Tel: 01424 853349 Fax: 0870 191 3991
Email: info@upso.co.uk   Web: http://www.upso.co.uk

For my family.
For everyone who worked at iaxis.
And for my friend Simon, who picked up the
phone and gave me a chance.

The Author

The author was born on June 29th 1971 and this is his first book.

Author's Note

The following is based on a true story. I would like to thank Simon, James and Alistair for helping to make this book possible. I am also indebted to 'Kathryn' and 'Seamus' who gave me permission to write about their backgrounds. Thank you.

There are many others who have known about this book and whose personal support throughout these past two years has been invaluable to me. I would not have got this far without your friendships and support. Thank you for being there.

Finally, the political and *espionage* material contained within this book is very real and everyone who provided me with detailed information for publication in *Seven Floors High* did so on the basis of remaining "*strictly anonymous*". You know who you are. Thank you.

Steve Goddard
7th January 2003

All text in smaller font, within brackets and double quotation marks, ie ["...."] is information supplied by a secret narrator.

There are always two edges to a sword.

"What I tell you in the dark speak in the light. And what you hear in a whisper, proclaim on the house tops."
Yehoshua ben Joseph

CHAPTER 1

'Blaady hell, Justin!' screams George, his blood-red face highlighted even more by his white hair as he looks up from his terminal.

Justin sits next to him in the hot seat and every day he wishes he didn't.

'What the *fucking* hell did you say, last time you were in Tehran?' shouts George in a savage tone. If he doesn't get an answer within three nanoseconds, he'll run outside and start pulling up the trees (again).

Young Justin looks sheepishly down at his PC screen. He can feel his chair starting to heat up once more as George is close to having a meltdown. Everyone is now looking over at his part of the dealing desk.

I work as a shipbroker with one of London's leading and most prestigious broking houses, 'Seamart Shipbrokers plc', and this is the start of my sixth year...

Today is the first real day of trading after the millennium celebrations. We have just been informed that the Iranians have chartered another two million-barrel oil tanker without using us as their broking channel to the owner of the vessel. Negotiating the deal between the shipowner and the oil company is how we make our money.

George's face now looks like somebody else has just eaten his dinner, and he eyeballs Justin hard for letting this happen. 'Justin! That's the seventh oil tanker those buggers have chartered in the last four weeks, and you've done one of them, *just fucking one!'*

George is one of the founders of the company; now he's losing his touch. Losing all his money from being a Lloyd's name hasn't helped matters either. Now he only takes home around two hundred thousand pounds a year, including his company share dividends and bonus. He might be fifty-seven, but he's as hard as nails. Nobody dares take him on.

From across the dealing room, careful not to catch his eye, I look up from my screen. After rubbing my tired eyes, I think to myself: 'after so many years in this industry, I hope to hell I don't end up like you, old boy.'

The Iranians have been chartering these ships for storage capacity in the Persian Gulf, and a single deal for a few phone calls can net us twenty-five thousand dollars commission here. Just now the market is low; if it were high, commission levels would be in the region of fifty thousand dollars or more. However, being cut out of a lucrative shipping deal stays with a broker like a trauma. And George has had his fair share of traumas over the years. Right now he is verbally beating a twenty-four year old broker in front of everyone. I should be feeling sorry for Justin, but since his arrogance takes the shine off his broking skills, I'm laughing to myself as he squirms. He can be a tosser, so this is payback time. He looks more stressed than I've seen him before.

'I just don't understand why the Iranians need so much storage capacity,' whimpers Justin, clearly now in a classic state of total shock.

On hearing this, George's grey eyes, which are usually colder than the brass plate outside the office front door, are suddenly on fire with rage. Within two seconds George snarls, draws a deep breath and then explodes.

'It's *simple*, you little *twat!* Their oil refineries are *shit!* If they turn off the taps to meet the OPEC quotas they've agreed to, they might not fucking start up again!'

Justin is squirming and flinching like hell and the whites of his eyes are now illuminating the entire dealing desk as George has sprung to his feet. Most of the twelve brokers bunkered up inside this dealing room are now shitting themselves in anticipation that George will do any of the following:

Throw Justin out of the office window.

Pick up his PC monitor and bury it in Justin's head.

Bounce Justin across the room to the telex machine, hit the Tehran number and ram his head through it.

George suddenly realises that we are all watching him and unfortunately he does none of the above. He now looks tired, and takes another deep breath in order to lower his heartbeat back down to one hundred and twenty beats per minute. He takes off his glasses and wipes away the condensation that has built up over the last fifty seconds. Then he takes a deep breath to get the simple words out of his mouth.

'Look here old boy, I've been in this industry since sixty-seven. Their oil industry is on its knees. BP, Shell and Total are going to invest tens of billions of dollars in the country in exploration and upgrading existing assets over the next eighteen months. The taps can't be turned off in a hurry,' says George, now making a serious effort to be patient.

I need to yawn, but think better of it when I see George's head turn viciously around to see who is not paying attention in today's lesson. He is of course right, but it's too close to lunchtime to care. And besides, it's not my account. Then suddenly our screens flash informing us that Marc Rich Trading has also chartered a two million-barrel oil tanker, for an Iranian shipment of oil going to the West. We'll have to check it out to see if it's correct, and if it is, what price they paid for the vessel. We have also been trying to get Marc Rich Trading to use us as their broking channel, but so far we've had very little success at trying to win this lucrative trading account.

On hearing this piece of market news, George goes berserk, and his voice rips through the dealing room. Everyone, including myself, buries their head behind their monitor just in case George takes it off.

I mentally break free from all the shouting and think about a Christmas present last year; it was my personal horoscope that had been worked out by *Equinox* in Covent Garden for the year ahead. My twenty-ninth year and the *Saturn Cycle of Responsibilities* spoke of big changes ahead in my life. I look around the tanker desk and I don't see too many changes. Most brokers sitting around this desk have been here for ten to fifteen years or more, all out of sheer loyalty to the firm. (Or rather the fat pay cheques we get every month.)

William is in his early forties. He runs the big Shell and Saudi Aramco accounts and is one of the most helpful and friendly brokers on the desk. He's working out how many days he's got to work before he retires, a "ritual" he does almost every day with his pension plans and shares as he charts and tries to forecast the stock market. Today he's looking at a ten-year stretch at his desk. Last year it was down to eight years, then his fund manager/pension planner got the market wrong after Greenspan put up US Federal interest rates. This added another two years to his sentence. Sadly this sentence is to be served in here without parole. Now he's on the phone telling his market maker he wants eighty per cent of his fund to be placed in the telecoms and technology sector. 'That's the future,' he keeps saying to us all.

Michael is in his mid-thirties, sits next to me and is the loudest person in the room and probably in London as well. As a child I'm sure his mother didn't feed him unless he screamed for his dinner. Now he loves the sound of his own voice and bellows loudly all day long. If it continues I could be putting in an industrial claim for my ears. He's also a top broker who brings in the big dollars. BP does not move its crude oil out of West Africa without checking with him on market conditions first.

Ned is one hundred per cent Norwegian and, like the rest of the desk, was educated at one of England's top public schools. He is the same age as Michael, but is only an average broker, which means he's always in Michael's shadow. This is probably why he never smiles. Even on the rare occasion when he brings in a good deal, he still walks around with a combined look of doom, sadness and anxiety haunting his face. It is as if his rollover, jackpot-winning lottery ticket has just blown out of his hand whilst crossing Vauxhall Bridge, never to be found again.

Henry is twenty-six years old and wouldn't look out of place driving a Bentley. (I think he owns one.) He is now on the phone enquiring about the new membership fees to his exclusive gentlemen's club. This is probably the same one in which various government ministers have their confidential "BOX 500" files read to them like a horoscope by *"representatives"* from the Cabinet Secretary ["...rather unpleasant business which we leave the 'Prefects' to deal with..."]. Henry and I get on well and take great pride in winding each other up.

Horace is in his mid forties, but looks fifty-five. He heads up the tanker desk. He has more money (family) than the rest of the desk put together. And he is completely thick. He joined the firm in 1977 (his father knows the chairman) and hasn't done much since. He has no respect on the desk whatsoever. This is because he gets paid a fortune and does very few deals to justify his position. Like George, he files his nails at his desk and both call other colleagues 'love' and 'darling', which are rather weird mannerisms but true...

Christopher and Rowland are both in their mid-forties and are two rather chubby chaps. Both are greedy as hell and have more money than calories. However, they do bring in lots of commission.

Justin is twenty-four years old and is usually sharp, bright and well respected. But sadly he's not today. He is being groomed to take over George's accounts after he retires from the desk to stand on display in the Natural History Museum alongside the dinosaurs. His main flaw is his bottom-kissing tendencies.

Billy is twenty-eight years old. He is a top bloke despite being a "Hun" from Glasgow Rangers Supporters Club. He even has a bank account with Ulster Bank, which in my humorous view is also known as 'The bank that likes to say Never!'. We worked in the offshore market together. He does a lot of crude oil shipments for Shell, BP and one or two others around the UK and Europe. He is not afraid to speak his mind to the elders and is well liked and respected in the market. The firm is lucky to have him.

Old Rupert is fifty-eight, but looks seventy. He is a skinny old boy who is more right wing than any BNP skinhead you'll find on the Isle of Dogs. Not only is he from the old school, he's its headmaster. He still thinks we have an empire and even has a picture of Mrs Thatcher and *The Heritage Foundation* in his wallet. He runs the Kuwaiti account. And the Kuwaitis he deals with have made him go mad over the years.

Richard is thirty-eight years old and an ex-law graduate. He is by far the most intelligent and friendly person on the desk. He deals with the Russians, Shell and BP, and is hugely respected in the fuel oil market. I've been under his teaching for the past year and he has helped me gain a solid grounding in the tanker markets. We both speak up for socialist issues, which in this office (the North-West Frontier of capitalism) means we both need to be closely monitored.

I am twenty-eight years old and this is the only firm I have worked for since graduating from university. It is more like a public school boys' dormitory than an office. Usually I tell myself I don't care about the way they carry on, but deep down I do, and it bothers me.

A short while later, our screens inform us that BP have a requirement to ship two million barrels of crude oil out of the Persian Gulf and we're one of the five leading London broking houses they've decided to give this cargo to.

'BP! Two million barrels Arabian Gulf to Rotterdam!' yells Michael, so loud that the shoppers in Harrods can now hear him.

We now have to quote this requirement to the owners of ships that BP find suitable to move the cargo, and a lot of the time it is a lottery whether you get support from the owners or not.

I call one of my Greek shipowners, but he's already got it. A polite way of saying, 'no can do this time, old boy, I'm giving it to another London broker to work'. I am not bothered since it is unlikely BP will take his ship due to the age restrictions on vessels, so I decide to wait for the next requirement. In the meantime I log onto the Internet, check my Hotmail and then read *Lloyd's List*.

This surprise BP cargo has brought George out of his savage depression. If we get support from one of our London based owners and fix the ship to BP, the company will stand to make a lot of commission for the sake of a few phone calls to cut the deal. The market has been low for months and our commission levels are well down from highs of fifty thousand dollars or more for a single deal. And everyone knows this. The pressure to get the deals "in the book" is on us all. However, we are also way short on our targets and we've just spent over one million dollars redecorating the small office and boardroom. The office doesn't even belong to us and we lease it year by year. *But we have to look expensive.*

George hangs up his phone and looks around the office. 'What we need is another fucking war out in the Middle East,' he says, speaking very loudly so the whole office can hear his statement.

We like wars in here. It's good for business. The chaps all actively agree with George's statement and start to zero their sights. This war talk is very frequent and there are casualties every day. Thousands have been shot around the desk over the years. (Old Rupert only goes to church on Sundays for one reason alone and that's to pray for Saddam to invade Kuwait again.) However, on this cold January morning Saddam is in their sights. Not to shoot him; he has his uses. And that is why oil companies love him. Word has it they all send him birthday cards thanking him for creating the "potential for instability" in the region. This in turn helps to push up the oil price every so often, and, importantly, controls production. *"Mr Rockefeller"* prefers the market to be twenty-five dollars per barrel, rather than ten. Saddam is very popular at the Houston Petroleum Club ["...especially with the former President of Zapata Offshore and a certain partner in its old legal firm, Baker and Potts..."] and a large private estate at Pocantico Hills, New York.

["...And why? In 1990, President George Bush Sr and his administration got Saudi Arabia, Japan and the Gulf States to effectively bankroll the Western alliance to fight the entire Gulf War with Saddam. Japan paid America thirteen billion dollars and the Saudi Finance Ministry initially paid out fourteen billion dollars. However, this Saudi sum was pretty much the first payment by King Fahd and the House of Saud, with their total cost to 'defend the Kingdom' adding up to almost sixty-two and a half billion dollars. The Saudis also got their neighbour Kuwait to pay twenty three and a half billion dollars, and the United Arab Emirates over six billion dollars.

However, additional payments were made up in secret cheap forward deals for oil shipments to the USA, oil exploration contracts in the Kingdom (and George W. Bush and Harken Energy in Bahrain) and, more importantly, on US military arms deals throughout the whole region. In the year 2000, oil from the Persian Gulf is effectively under US control as hard cash gets transferred from the Gulf to bank accounts in Wall Street. This overall Gulf War debt cash repayment from these proud Arab states is still being collected today. And tensions within Saudi Arabia against America have never been so high...and Saddam was left in power and exports cheap oil to America through the US backed 'oil-for-food' program..."]

Yet the Earth is round and spins at over one thousand miles per hour. And the oil within it keeps the whole world spinning around very nicely indeed. If there were complete peace and *harmony* in the region, oil would be a lot cheaper and vast areas of oil-rich desert would be opened up for exploration in both Iran and Iraq. With the region's oil taps fully open, what good is that for Gulf State economies and US corporate profits in the present? No American weapons would be sold to the Middle East, no American bases would be on Saudi soil ["...Saddam wouldn't have been left in power"], and ExxonMobil (ESSO) and Saudi ARAMCO would not be ringing up billions of dollars worth of profits every quarter keeping the Rockefeller family very happy indeed.

Chapter 1

And with the whole world spinning so fast, it is only natural that what goes around always comes around...

George now stands up again. Twice in ten minutes is always a dangerous sign that he could pull his shoulder-launched Stinger missile from his top drawer at any time. He shakes his head from side to side slowly, careful not to tilt the mercury switch in the back of his head.

Justin, in the hot seat, suddenly looks terrified as George walks past him to look at the map of the Persian Gulf's oilfields on the office wall (right next to the clock displaying the New York time zone).

'If only we could let Saddam know those Kuwaitis are stealing his oil again and increasing their production, the whole region might blow,' says George, with his hands on his hips, shaking his head dangerously.

'Next time he goes in, I'll personally give him the names of all those Kuwaitis who've been pissing me off over the last ten years,' grumps Rupert, flicking through his battered old Filofax for this month's Kuwaiti hit list.

During both the Gulf wars shipping rates went into "supermodel levels" and this firm was making more money on one shipping deal than we do in seven right now. Legend has it that we fixed a lot of oil tankers and some people in Seamart got very rich.

A short while later, after a few Kuwaitis have been shot, and Saddam is being left alone, the Iraq, Kuwait and Saudi Arabia war talk breaks up as the lunchtime dinner bell rings. This ringing is in the tone of our chairman ordering all forty-seven members of staff into the boardroom to toast in the new millennium. All the brokers of the various departments get up from their respective trading desks and walk down to the hallowed boardroom.

I get up from my chair and look around the room. I am convinced that there must be a better career in which to make a living. This office is the worst place outside North Korea to work in. I glance down at the book I have been reading on the tube. It is one of the best books I've read in years. What can I do that's challenging, apart from the scheming, wheeling and dealing I do everyday in here? I have thought about moving on, but the money here is very good.

Recently, a good *"friend"* of mine handed me the application forms for the graduate fast-track entry into Her Majesty's *"Foreign and Commonwealth Office"*. I started to fill them out and then I noticed the salary levels and I thought it was a joke (but they weren't joking!). I stopped writing and binned the forms, as it became apparent that I could probably earn more money working in a charity shop in Notting Hill. ["...But even so,

Steve, slipping into an anonymous grey suit can have its own unique challenges, dear boy..."]

Walking down to the boardroom, everyone is in a pinstriped suit, mostly from Gieves and Hawkes. I've just spent a fortune on a dark blue double-breasted suit from Alexandre's, further down Savile Row, and it looks the business, much better than anything one can buy from that shop at no1.

As we enter the room where deals are made to supply entire continents with oil for the next generation, everyone in tankers is stunned at what sacriligious audacity currently faces them on the grand teak boardroom table.

'Where's the fucking Krug gone!' screams George, as his ticker comes dangerously close to breaking free from his ribcage. Someone has changed the office champagne to an inferior brand.

'It's a blaady tart's drink!' bellows old Rupert, as he points to one of the full bottles of Moet on the boardroom table, looking terrified, as if he could catch AIDS from it.

Henry walks into the room, turns around and tries to walk back to his desk, but George stops him. The chaps at the club would have a good laugh at this.

A full-on row soon breaks out between George, Rupert and nearly everyone in tankers, and the person who is believed to be responsible for this shocking deed. He is a little man with glasses who works in operations. He just mutters the word, 'cutbacks', while shaking in his shoes like he's in a forest surrounded by snarling wolves that are ready to eat him alive.

After several tantrums, most brokers in tankers eventually pick up a glass and sigh 'oh bugger', as if this is a bad sign for the new millennium. Most continue to mix the Moet with fresh orange juice to hide the taste. The other departments just drink it without a second thought.

The chairman soon walks in and is followed by Horace. Horace is showing him the new watch one of his kids got him for Christmas. He is also trying to tell the chairman just how "proactive" he has been recently. The chairman, who is no fool, takes this like Horace is a pigeon that has just flown over from Trafalgar Square and deliberately shat on his new suit. And he's not happy about it.

'Just get me a glass of fresh orange, will you please?' the chairman asks with remarkable restraint.

On seeing the chairman, George's lips close tightly. This helps to conceal the frustration, but we can all see the steam escaping from those large red ears.

'This will be changed at the next board meeting,' says George very sternly, with controlled anger, knowing full well that this is not the time to discuss such serious issues. The next board meeting is two weeks away, but if he has to wait more than forty-eight hours to get this resolved there will be hanging internally for sure.

I glance at George. He might look old enough to claim his OAP bus pass, but he didn't get to be one of the best tanker brokers in the industry by being loving and sentimental. He can see the world as it really is and he doesn't give a shit. He has a job to do and that's that. Unlike the others, there are no personal belongings on his desk.

After picking up a glass of Moet, I talk to Billy. We are both drinking the new champagne, trying to work out what is wrong with the brand. (We both secretly come to the conclusion that there's nothing wrong with it at all.) I tell him about the thirty-two-inch Sony flat screen TV and DVD player I bought just before Christmas. It's now wired up to my TEAC 500 hi-fi system with B&W speakers for cinema surround sound. And the only reason I bought it is so I can watch the gunfight scene in the film *Heat*, which I bought on DVD as well. He looks at me as if I am mad.

Henry has overheard this conversation on his way over to join us both. 'That's a brilliant idea, old boy!' says Henry enthusiastically, as he mentally tries to work out how big a TV set of this size would look in his grand pad.

I tell them both that I was watching *Heat* last night and my neighbours and two people out jogging thought there was a large-scale gunfight somewhere near Bishops Park. In fact my ears are still ringing from how loud the whole system actually is. Both Henry and Billy laugh, Billy at the insanity of my purchase and Henry because he now wants one.

George, who looks like he's taken enough rounds today already, places his glass of orange juice on the boardroom table and wipes away more condensation from his glasses. He takes a deep breath and focuses on the surrounding dark blue pinstriped suits.

Shit, our eyes meet and we have an eyelock.

George struggles over the last few feet to speak to the three of us. 'Blaady hell,' he says with restrained wrath. His eyes, which look like they can bend steel, display what will be unleashed at the board meeting he's going to call as soon as this gathering is over.

Today's motivation speech is about to kick off as I see the chairman looking around the boardroom with a distinct lack of mercy in his eyes. Nobody knows how old he is, but he looks eighty at least. It is also of constant amusement to the office that he has a remarkable physical similarity to Mr Burns of *The Simpsons*. However, kids would have nightmares if our chairman were in a cartoon. And this is no fucking joke.

The chairman comes from a long established and distinguished family. His father owned coalmines in South Africa during the dark days of Apartheid. His wife, who seems to own most of the Isle of Wight, has more millions in the bank than my current girlfriend has pairs of shoes. Sadly, Mr Burns lost all his money as a Lloyd's name. And when Mr Burns found out about his Lloyd's losses, office legend has it that it was his outburst that triggered off the start of what we now call "global warming".

George might be a "psycho" during office hours, but at least he puts his heart back in when he leaves the office at 7 p.m. to go home to his family. Mr Burns, on the other hand, is on tranquillisers twenty-four hours a day, the size of which would stop wild elephants charging around the Serengeti. His heart has been in a deep freezer since he was eleven years old and when this old chap blows his top (at the slightest little thing) he goes completely wild with rage and raw fury. (George has been known to pick up a fax machine, throw it across the room and start kicking it to bits on the office floor and even he doesn't clash with our Mr Burns. And they started the firm together three decades ago.)

Before I joined tanker chartering, Mr Burns had an all-out *holocaust* of a verbal explosion at a young broker. All the poor lad did was cut somebody off the telephone line when he was transferring the caller to him. Approximately six polar caps melted after that stomper… The boy was asked to leave after his first six months probationary period and I'm sure he checked into therapy soon afterwards. (Another tanker trainee left after a senior broker gave him a verbal savaging in front of everyone at the desk. He threatened to sue the firm for bullying and was quietly bought off with six months' salary.)

Mr Burns removes a silver spoon from the breast pocket of his perfectly cut dark blue, double-breasted pinstriped Gieves and Hawkes number. To get everyone's unreserved attention he then starts gently tapping the side of one of the *St Clair* crystal glasses and everyone who is gathered in the boardroom knows exactly what this means… For the "*uniniatiated*", it means 'Shut the fuck up and listen' even if you are giving someone emergency mouth-to-mouth resuscitation.

'Silence please,' groans Mr Burns, as if he were a judge sitting in a courtroom at the Old Bailey and we are the defendants awaiting a swift retribution for our crimes against society.

'I would like to take this opportunity to welcome you all into the new millennium,' he says, trying to sound sincere, as it is almost an effort to get each word out of his mouth.

Chapter 1

I can feel my heart beating faster as Mr Burns starts to speak about *the future...*

'It is, without a doubt, going to be a blaady tough year for us all,' he pronounces with such seriousness that nobody dares move a muscle, twitch or flinch.

'We must meet our targets or the City will *crucify* us,' he says, as I slowly look down at my Church shoes. (Seamart has no assets apart from the brokers around the desks who bring in the commission. Last year we turned over nine million pounds and paid forty-five people over three and a half million pounds in total.)

'...If targets are not met, bonuses cannot be paid,' he says, as if he's a gillie stalking out the game to be shot. And bearing in mind that Mr Burns shoots anything that walks, runs, swims or flies, most brokers are now nodding slightly in agreement, but skillfully avoiding the demented glare radiating out from behind those black eyeballs.

That's done the trick, I can see him thinking, as people start to flinch, cough and scratch their noses. Mr Burns slowly takes aim and gets ready to squeeze the trigger.

'*Every single deal counts!*' he says, as his voice rises to beat the point into our heads while he looks sharply around the room, trying to shoot his eyeballs into as many slackers as possible. 'We do not take passengers on this ship,' he says, in a deadly serious tone, as his dark eyes scan the room for signs of movement.

The chairman might be an old goat who will probably be buried clutching a Charter Party in one hand and the handset to his landline in the other, but he has our complete respect. He founded the firm and still brings in huge deals that nobody else here has the foresight or vision to pull off. He has huge respect in the tanker market and this is well deserved.

'To the future!' he toasts.

'*To the future,*' I say, taking a sip of the Moet.

I leave the boardroom behind with its immaculate teak table and oil paintings of ships we've bought, sold and chartered to the world's richest shipping companies. This splendid room also contains items such as a teak drinks cabinet (rather large), Chesterfield leather chairs and very expensive wallpaper, all made to order. The room also boasts eighty thousand pound curtains to close off the back-end view of a certain Middle Eastern embassy. Although we have just entered the year 2000, you would not think it standing in here. The boardroom today looks like it could have once been used to run the opium shipments from India to China (on behalf of the world's first industrial globalists, Jardine's and the East India Company). This is part of our "glorious past" when the British Empire almost brought China to its knees by flooding the Chinese population with opium, after China's ruling elite objected to Britain's ambitions for "free trade".

Those were the "good old days" of the distant past. *The Present* is crude oil and a doomsday clock that measures time in nanoseconds. And after the motivation talk by Mr Burns the chaps are screaming into their phones for their lives. Mr Burns is stalking the desk and New York has just opened with a rush of post-Y2K orders for crude oil shipments from the American oil companies.

'*Fucking hell's teeth!!*' yells Michael, as our screens tell us Exxon, Chevron, Bay Oil and Texaco all want two million barrels of oil each from the Persian Gulf to America. Bay Oil of Texas ships and trades more Iraqi crude oil than practically any other player and these orders will require some of the largest and most modern tankers in the world. And day rates for chartering these tankers will go up. We'll see to that.

["…But at least the starving Iraqi children might get some food and medicine for selling America this oil."]

The phones are going crazy. All three of mine are ringing and have multiple lights flashing from them. I can hardly hear a word on the other end of the line, as Michael is trying to share his conversation with a park attendant at the far side of Hyde Park.

'*Exxon are out on the fucking market and I need your support now!*' he bellows to one of his shipowner mates who has a ship that could well be chartered through our firm.

It is just as well that they go back years. Anyone else would slam the phone down. In this industry punctuality really matters. If you don't pick up the phone after one or maybe two rings the line will go dead and the oil company will phone another broking house and give the requirement to them. Or the shipowner phoning you to give you their ship will hang up and give it to someone else. And if not picking up the phone after one second costs Seamart twenty-five thousand dollars in lost commission, then one's day tends to be ruined.

If Mr Burns hears about it, then one's natural life is over.

Mr Burns's raging face suddenly moves from a shade of dark red to deep-purple. He savagely breathes in, soaking up every last drop of oxygen in the dealing room. And then he detonates.

'*Will someone answer those blaady phones now!!*' he screams, so loudly that even the deafest corgi in the grounds of the large building on the other side of Hyde Park Corner must have heard him. And this time only one of his feet stamps repeatedly on the office floor.

Now all the brokers are shitting themselves. Everyone, including myself, hits whatever buttons are flashing to make it look like the calls are being taken, and never look up to meet those black eyeballs. If you accidently did and had an eyelock with him now, you might just burst into flames. But sadly it is all too much for Mr Burns and he has to leave the desk. Probably to go and pop two tranquillisers before the fuse ignites the C-4 explosives in the back of his head.

Seamart is not the only London broking house to be given these requirements. Right now other leading London brokers are all frantically phoning around the same owners whose support we are trying to get so they can put these ships into New York ahead of us. If they fix the deal they will stand to make a lot of commission for a few calls and maybe some tough negotiations.

A short while later, as the market winds down, I take a few minutes to read my newspaper, the *Daily Mirror*. I am trying to see if "The Boro" have got any more OAPs from Man Utd. I feel that there is not much hope for "The Boro" this year. Not to win the premiership: I stopped eating marshmallows a long time ago. But I still have a small amount of hope for them to at least make an impact and be considered a threat. After all, we've spent over sixty million pounds on players.

In the background I can clearly hear Ned struggling to get support from a tanker owner. It sounds like the owner is telling Ned that he is using another broker today, and Ned is trying his best to persuade the owner to change his mind. It is also rumoured that this owner is a homosexual who has recently left his wife for another man...

The phones are quiet now and most of the chaps are looking at Ned and are starting to snarl. This ship will be one that gets fixed to the Americans, but not by our firm. And we will lose about thirty thousand dollars commission. *'Ok, ok, right, yes I see, oh well, we can look forward to the next time...'*

The "homosexual" owner has just told Ned, 'No, not this time'.

I am still reading the *Daily Mirror,* waiting for my owners to get back to me to see whether or not they will give me a ship to market to the oil companies. However, the rest of the desk gets tooled up for the inevitable "mincer" shootout that is going to happen. In the meantime I think about that gunfight scene in *Heat*, which I'll be watching in a few hours time on that monster Sony TV, while the rest of Fulham listens to it.

Ned puts the receiver down.

'That fucking mincer!' he yells, not even trying to contain his frustration and anger.

Cries of 'poofy bastard' are heard from around the desk as people shake their heads and begin to feel sick thinking about what his alleged boyfriend and he get up to. In the long league of hates and prejudices that exist within the firm, gays are well and truly at the top, like a fairy on a Christmas tree. The chance of a gay broker being employed here is about as remote as the PIRA Command in South Armagh allowing the Portadown UVF to walk in and erect a statue celebrating "Oliver Cromwell 1599 - 1658" in Crossmaglen's town square. It just won't happen in this lifetime. Well, not in this office.

'Blaady back door boys!' shouts Rupert, who shakes his head with disgust. 'When I meet him I just can't look him in the eye,' he continues.

Justin keeps a low profile here. Not because he's gay, but because he could be a target for ridicule at any time. We all do and say things we regret. Justin regrets walking in to the office on day one wearing CK One aftershave. This is perfectly normal in any other company, but not in this office. He never wore it again.

Old Rupert looks over at me reading the *Daily Mirror's* sports pages. "The Boro" will be lucky to stay up in the premiership.

'Goddard!' yells old Rupert, 'I can't believe your lot want to reduce the minimum age to allow boy shafting!'

I look over to him. There is noise all around me, but I've switched off. Rupert makes this comment to me because I'm reading the *Mirror* and in his eyes I am part of the Soviet Bloc that has covertly moved into Downing Street since May 1997.

I just shrug my shoulders and remind him that the "darling" of the Tory Right, Mr Portillo, has a questionable past...

This cuts him up like a boy racer at a roundabout in Chelmsford, and I see him shaking his fist at me as I speed off. But around the desk, the bullets have been flying liberally and all the boy bands have been massacred. Elton John, George Michael and Dale Winton have all taken rounds and are no longer moving. Peter Mandelson is being verbally abused, strung up and is away to get a double tap to his stern.

'If that blaady "Mandy" and his Brazilian boyfriend try and adopt a kid like those queers did last year, then I'm leaving the fucking country!' yells Henry, who is now pacing around the desk like a caged beast.

'I wouldn't even let him own that fucking dog!' shouts Ned, who's shooting from the hip, trying desperately to save the face he has already lost today.

Rupert gets up to join in the shouting and to his surprise and utter embarrassment he breaks office protocol and etiquette by farting loudly. The desk erupts with laughter.

'That's it old Rupert, your secret's out now old boy, you were sexually penetrated at public school!' yells Michael, as Rupert tries to control his embarrassment.

George is filing his nails and has the handset between his shoulder and jaw. He is on the phone to another old boy shipowner he gets on well with. He is trying to get support from this chap for one of the American majors.

'Look here love, we have just been shafted by that shirt-lifter on the earlier cargoes, so please give us your support and we'll drive this crap market up.'

(Silence.)

'Splendid, thanks old boy,' says George as he gets the shipowner's vessel in and hangs up.

Ned's failure to get the "homosexual vote" is written across his sad looking face and this is made even worse by George's smugness at getting support. Ned then gets up out of his seat and leaves the room to get a fresh cup of coffee... and also a clearer perspective on what everyone now tells him he must go and do to win the gay guy's business!

A short while later I leave the office to go home. Walking up Knightsbridge towards the tube station, I realise that I have only been on the tanker desk for one year, but it feels like ten. And with every day pretty much the same, *my soul feels completely dead.*

International shipbroking is a very tight, close-knit community. *'Your word is your bond'* is the motto of the Chartered Institute of Shipbrokers. A Shipbroker's spoken word is legally binding, even if nothing is written down on paper. Step out of line and ranks will close. Your name, along with your word and reputation, will be something that dogs leave behind on the pavement.

Throughout a shipbroker's career (in offshore chartering, for example), many have done deals at the weekend and the ship has sailed within the hour. Nothing is in writing between the oil company and the shipowner. It is just our word and the integrity of the other two parties. The paperwork gets done on the Monday morning. And there are never any problems. This is how the system survives.

Oil is a global business, and there are no barriers in the office when it comes to "real politics". Billy, who sits opposite me, looks after the shipment of oil for the Libyans. They run their operation via a company registered in Cyprus. Their head office is in Italy, with an accounting office in Monaco, and their UK trading operations are all directed out of Curzon Street, Mayfair, London W1. Here their traders then sell the oil to UK oil companies. These UK oil companies ship it into their UK refineries, where it is then turned into petroleum-based products, such as paint and plastics, for the UK population to buy at DIY superstores.

I look after the Israeli account. I get on very well with the Israeli chartering manager, but I have yet to cut a deal with him. However, they are due to be changing the ship they've had on charter for the past year and he keeps me fully informed on their future oil shipments. The Israelis use an old two million barrel oil tanker (this ship was fixed through another broking house) to move the oil they buy from an American oil company (name withheld) who have an oil refinery in West Africa. This oil is then sold to Israel and shipped to their refinery every fifty days. These two million barrels of crude oil keep a small nation going.

We have approached the right owners who are discreet enough to charter their tonnage to Israel and they've given us their word that they'll support us. This means a lot of dollars for Seamart and I will be looking pretty good if we can pull the deal off. With the assurances we've got from our Israeli-friendly owners (not many, as ships get blacklisted by the Gulf States for going to Israel) I stand to make a good bonus if and when the deal goes through. I am now therefore counting the days down to April and bonus time.

Most of the desk gets in at 7:45 a.m. to check the overnight chartering activity from the Far East. This is in order to see what tankers are now going to Japan, South Korea, Singapore, Taiwan and China. But on this particular January morning, the desk is unusually quiet and I soon realise why. Rupert and Henry aren't at their desks and have probably been delayed on the trains. No doubt they are going to be pissed off when they eventually get in.

When the office door opens, I am not wrong. Both walk into the office with eyes charged with anger and faces blood red, as they take off their overcoats and pinstriped suit jackets and hang them up. We soon learn that it was not the trains that were the cause of the delay. They were listening to a news story on the *Today* programme about the banning of foxhunting. And although they live twenty miles apart, both were telepathically linked to the radio programme. I heard the news piece as well, but because it takes thirty minutes for me to get to work, I wasn't late in. However, Rupert and Henry have now both been arguing all the way up from Victoria Station to our office. Not with each other, but with the *Prime Minister*. Not that he was actually there to defend himself of course, but in their eyes, *he is to blame*.

Henry is far too angry to sit down now that he's seen that I'm reading page two of the *Daily Mirror*. I'll read about "The Boro" later on. I don't want to get depressed first thing in the morning.

'What *fucking* right has he got to ban it?' Henry shouts at me, barely able to contain his anger.

I can see Rupert getting tooled up with his trusty old Magnum 44 in anticipation of any "bleeding heart, liberal townie" response from myself.

'Well, how about having the majority of the population on his side?' I say calmly and with a smile.

Rupert's brain explodes and for a few seconds he's unable to speak. Henry, his face shuddering with anger and frustration, suddenly bangs his fist on the table and shouts, 'Look Goddard! If we want to hunt foxes it's none of his, yours, or anybody else's blaady business!' He says this with such a snarling expression on his face that he can almost taste the fox's blood in his mouth.

'Look, we pay our taxes to live in a civilised society. And in a civilised society foxes should not be chased by fifty dogs across the English countryside and ripped to pieces when they've run out of breath and are too exhausted and frightened to move.'

Rupert and Henry's brains are struggling to solidify at the speed of thought, so Horace, who's just off the phone to his stockbroker, now fancies his chances. He steps in and sticks his neck above the trench.

'Oh, that's blaady nonsense Goddard. Foxes are vermin and you and your "Mirror reading army" just don't want to see people having fun.'

'Horace! The majority of the British population does not want to see grown adults charging after a fox across the countryside and having fun watching it being savaged to death by dogs. That is not fun in a civilised society.'

Richard claps.

Horace is now lost, and has gone from being out of his depth to not even being able to see the beach.

'Good point Steve,' says Michael, nodding in agreement.

'Thanks Michael,' I say, as I see Horace still trying to understand what I've just said.

'Steve, why don't you ban fishing and golf as well? I got hit by a fucking golf ball once!' says Billy, laughing away and trying to stir the shit even more.

Rupert and Henry's brain cells have regrouped and old Rupert retorts sternly, 'Your "Cool Britannia" lot are wrecking this country's heritage.'

'Well, if it means saving a few foxes from a savage death at the hounds' teeth, then it's a national heritage we, as educated and civilised people, should be ashamed of,' I say, in an even and educated tone.

'That's another good point, Steve!' says Michael, with a massive spoon in his hand. It usually goes in his mouth with his cornflakes, but now he's using it to throw salt in everyone's wounds.

Christopher, who owns an estate in the Home Counties, suddenly screeches into action. (If he ever sat on a horse it would finish the beast off.) 'Goddard, do your lot ever think about the impact this would have on the countryside communities when it comes to these peoples' jobs? Let's say about twenty thousand of them old boy, now what do you say about that, then?' he asks, folding his arms. (The other chubby chap, Rowland, is far too busy eating his packed lunch to talk.)

Right, time for that little Exocet to come out of the toy box, I think to myself. Rupert, Henry, Horace, Michael and Christopher are the players in today's crossfire, and are now waiting for me to top that statement.

'That's a fair point, Christopher. But twenty thousand is nothing compared to one million job losses now, is it?'

They all look more perplexed than ever at where I'm going to pull one million job losses from...

Horace looks like he is well out to sea now and is trying to catch the attention of a passing car ferry.

'What the blaady hell do you mean about one million jobs?' barks Henry, trying like hell to catch up with me.

'Well, let's see, shall we chaps?' I say, as this gets me their unreserved attention and their eyes are focused with me firmly in their sights. 'What about the shipbuilders, the steelworkers, the coal miners, the motor industry and all the others? Did anyone in here ever care about the unemployment in their communities in the 1980s when they were all put out of work?'

'*No!*' yells Rupert.

'And why not?' I ask, as my posture drops.

'Because they were sacked by Maggie, for being commie bastards out to destroy the country!' yells the old duffer who is now reaping in the widespread applause he's getting from around the desk.

'Blaady hell Goddard! That lot was the "enemy within",' shouts Henry, as everyone's phones start ringing like a fire alarm going off in the building.

The Kuwaiti Petroleum Company has just come out on the market for a two million barrel cargo of crude oil to be shipped from the Persian Gulf to America.

I look at the London timezone clock on the wall. It has just gone 9:15 a.m. and it is just as well KPC came out; this "debate" could've gone on until lunchtime. There is no doubt that I have lost this one. Everyone switches into work mode and begins the frantic calls to owners who have the right ships for the job.

I get support from a London-based Greek owner who joined the tanker market the same time as I did. We share information and trust each other, and now I've got a ship that nobody else would've got. (And the Kuwaitis have used this ship before.) I could bring in a large amount of commission here. This should please me, but the unfinished debate of foxhunting and Maggie wiping out the manufacturing backbone of England, Scotland, Northern Ireland and Wales is still ticking away in my mind. This thought stays with me all the way up to lunchtime, slowly ticking away...

It is a tradition that everyone from the tanker desk goes down to the pub at lunchtime for a few drinks, and what you have to drink at lunchtime is of paramount importance. This is not up for debate, dissent or even a meek discussion. The lunchtime drink is a pint of bitter, as 'a real man does not drink anything else'. I drink pints of Caffrey's, and this is tolerated; it's strong and served in a pint glass. A pint of fizzy lager is not an option. A bottle of "designer beer" with a piece of lime in it is completely out of the question, and if it were ever chosen would call for a full sitting of the Privy Council.

The pub conversations are usually about any of the following: who's got the biggest and therefore the best tits in the pub right now, which female has got the best ass in the pub right now, the market activity this morning, and any other colleague who is not present. (This comes under "pub rules" explained to me by Horace when I first joined. 'A pub rule, old boy, is that what is said in the pub stays in the pub. It's good for teamwork,' he said this as if he had once learned it from a management semester at INSEAD or Harvard.)

This lunchtime, I walk in to one of "our" pubs, The Star Tavern in Belgravia, and I'm still pissed off from this morning's scrap. I see and hear them at the bar, which is relatively full today. All of the chaps have their backs straightened as if they've just left Sovereign's Parade at Sandhurst and are now speaking to visiting dignitaries from one of the colonies. As I approach the group, I think back to our Christmas night out at a resturant on the Kings Road. Against Richard's advice, I ordered a prawn cocktail starter and steak and chips for the main course. It went down well with me, but like an oil tanker during the Iran-Iraq war with the chaps.

'That's such 1970s cuisine. You should have ordered beer and blaady sandwiches Goddard!' said Rupert, who was scoffing away with pretentious disgust as the young waitress took my order.

Inside the bar as I move through the pack to get served, I catch Rupert and Henry's eyes as I pass them. They haven't finished this morning's foxhunting shootout either, and want another go. Both look at me suspiciously. I want to show I can be different if I want to be. I never went to boarding school and I thank my lucky stars for this every day I walk into the office. The comprehensive down the road was my introduction to education. And I have no recollection of what the school tie looked like, but I did wear it.

George greets me as if he's an old housemaster and I'm his pupil who's just done well on the sports field. He missed the foxhunting sniper attack. He was at the dentist, probably getting his teeth sharpened for his meeting with the Iranians this afternoon.

'Well done old boy, getting that ship in for the Kuwaitis,' says George, reaching into his inside pocket.

'Thanks George,' I say, as my heart beats around the inside of my ribcage at what I plan to do to unsettle Rupert, Henry and the rest of the chaps.

George offers to get me a drink.

'Pint of Caffrey's is it, Goddard?' he asks, as he gets a crisp ten pound note out of his leather Dunhill wallet.

My intuition is screaming at me, telling me to be the "grey man" and not to stand out by doing this.

'Don't do it Steve!' I can feel my friends and ancestors all telepathically telling me. This is a big deal. The other thought is 'fuck it'. I don't care what the chaps think anyway. And besides, I already know what I want.

The barman arrives and is waiting for me. I have one last look around at the chaps and turn to face the barman. Inside I can feel my heartbeat beating away and I need to take a deep intake of air through my nose just to steady my voice and get the simple words out.

'I'll have a gin and tonic, please,' I say calmly, as if it is the most natural thing in the world to order at lunchtime.

As soon as the words leave my mouth, the damage is done.

George flinches.

I look at him and we have an eyelock. He is horrified. Never in thirty years has he experienced this before and it has chilled him to the bone. I am convinced he's having an out of body experience, as he hasn't said a word. He just stares and stares at me, as if this is one of his life's experiences he will remember when the Almighty switches his lights off and stops his clock.

I can see that the barman is now smiling to himself as he gets out a sheet of paper to look up its price. No doubt he'll be on the phone to his area manager telling him or her about this as soon as we leave.

All of the chaps are frozen in shock. I am being eyeballed from all directions. Horace is wearing his Seiko kinetic watch and his shock at my order has stopped it from working. It is almost one o'clock. He's now got the thing off his wrist and is nervously fiddling with it.

The barman approaches us both and is still smiling. As he puts the drink on the counter, he winks at George as he hands over the six pounds change. I inhale deeply through my nose, but without making it obvious, as I notice George's hands are shaking when he takes his change. I toast him. 'Cheers George!' I say, optimistically, as a line of sweat runs down the centre of my spine and I struggle to control my heartbeat.

George looks at me as if I've just pissed all over his shoes.

As I turn around to face the chaps, I take a sip of the gin and tonic and my ears feel like they're on fire.

Richard raises his eyebrows as if to say 'you're in trouble now mate.'

William's face looks like the stock market has just crashed. Horace and Justin look like they're going to be physically sick with food poisoning. Billy has to excuse himself and goes to the toilet to have a good laugh. Both the chubby chaps have stopped eating their crisps, and Rowland's hands are now wobbling as well. And Rupert and Henry's mouths are aghast with horror. They are staring at me with a shocked look on their faces. It is as if in the last few seconds, before their very eyes, I have been beamed up into the far side of outer space, had a quick sex change and suddenly reappeared in front of them, drinking a gin and tonic in a tall thin glass!

Because this has never happened before, nobody knows what to say about it. There is still a look of shock and disgust in their eyes and a haunted look on everyone's face. Several nervously bite their bottom lip while they check other people's eyes for their reactions. After a few minutes the conversation starts to pick up, but it's only about our targets and how quiet the market has been recently. However, I have been sidelined and I'm not part of the general conversation.

Who cares about foxhunting now?

All of the chaps are immaculately dressed in their hand-cut pinstripes, cufflinks and Thomas Pink shirts, with TM Lewin silk ties and Church shoes (and with their lunchtime pints of bitter in their hands). Then there's me in my Alexandre pinstripe number, light navy-blue Burberry cotton shirt and Richard James hand-woven silk tie and drinking a gin and tonic at lunchtime. And this is pure quality that you just can't buy in the shops.

I catch Henry's eyes. Total disgust looks back and he looks away. Bless him, today has all been a bit too much. Now I really don't care. I've made my point. I'm not one of the chaps. I look around me and they can see I'm looking, but they just ignore me. The fact that I am not making a joke of it and just drink it as if it's totally natural only makes them even more pissed off.

I walk over towards Billy and our mobile phones start to ring. The market is too busy for the chaps to be drinking bitter today, so we head back.

During the afternoon word has spread around Seamart about my lunchtime "drink". The other departments think it's hilarious. However, tankers are outraged. In the scheme of things, this is worse than buying a Take That album and bringing it in to the office to say how good it is, drinking herbal tea at the desk, or breaking the "sanctions" the desk has against Harrods. (The chaps will not shop there until Fayed is deported and forced to sell his "corner shop".)

A strange feeling of anxiety comes over me. The deed has happened and it's now out of my control. There are no debates, no wars and nobody's even getting shot. But the long silver knives are out and if I lean too far back, I can almost feel them touching my back.

After a couple of hours the Kuwaitis and Saudis withdraw all of their chartering requirements and it's not that busy. This makes me think that we could've stayed in the pub for another drink. Then I could've really gone for it and ordered a bottle of Hooch.

Later on I arrive home and feel completely drained. I put on the gunfight scene in *Heat*. But after today's open display of revolt with the breaking of a sacred protocol, my head is far too full to enjoy it and I go to bed early.

...During the night I don't sleep very well and I have strange dreams about being lost in a cold, dark forest, and finding shelter in a small wooden cabin.

In the morning I wake up and I have that familiar feeling in the pit of my stomach that I do not want to get up and go in to work. Only this morning it is more intense, and when I walk in to the tanker room I can feel something just isn't right. Everyone nods and smiles politely at me when I walk in. I remember being told by a *"friend"* once, 'Always look for a change in a pattern of behaviour that is out of the norm. That is the time to be really suspicious.' And I am now very suspicious...

The day goes slowly, marked only by George fixing his ship to BP for yesterday's cargo. This deal will make the firm just under thirty thousand dollars commission. Strangely, nobody is really talking about politics today. And there's no sign of any foxes (just this young one).

I check my Hotmail and there's an email from one of my best mates,

Wacko. He wants to meet me for a few drinks at the weekend. Fantastic, I'll call him later.

After I've read my newspaper, I think about my first performance review with the tanker department six months ago. During the middle of 1999, Horace decided to take me out for lunch for a one-to-one pep talk. He said nothing to me about the way I conducted myself with clients, my professionalism as a broker or all the dollars I'd brought into the firm over the years. That aspect was fine. It was more important things, which he felt just had to be addressed...

'Look Steve, you're just not loud enough, you don't make any sexist comments and you enjoy keeping a low profile. You must do more to fit in, old boy, be more like Henry. *We just can't work you out...*', he said in a desperate tone.

This kept me amused in the sense that Horace still has trouble trying to solve *Scooby Doo* when he watches it with his kids. However, at the time, I just smiled politely and left it at that. I like Henry a great deal, despite being poles apart on any political issues which we frequently debate, or rather argue. In the past, he has helped me understand the oil tanker market. And more importantly, he has also stuck up for me in my absence when the knives have been out. But I'd rather keep my own identity, thank you.

The next morning after my chat with Horace I started to bring a newspaper into work for the first time; it was the *Daily Mirror* and it caused widespread indignation among the elders who saw this choice of paper as being on a par with the *Morning Star*. The young brokers saw it as a useful target and slagged it off remorselessly once they'd read it (wearing surgical gloves). And I have brought it into work every day since. The fact that I'd worked in the company's offshore division for four years was the only saving grace that stopped me getting binned there and then.

That was almost six months ago.

This afternoon as I am reading an OILSTOCK report, one of my phones suddenly starts to ring and I pick it up at lightning speed. On the other end of the line is Seamart's managing director. I look at my Omega watch and the time is now 5:44 p.m.

'Steve, let's have a little chat. Can you come down to the boardroom, please?'

'Er... Yes, sure.' My heart is pounding as I put down the receiver. He didn't sound angry. But this is well and truly out of the norm. It sounds like another pep talk, or maybe they want me to take on a new account. There has been talk of me looking after the Venezuelan account. Or he might simply ask me to stay in the office at lunchtime if I'm going to start drinking gin and tonic and other "tarts" drinks. *But why the boardroom?* There are lots of other meeting rooms to have a discussion in. I am nervous as I get up. I've always got on well with the MD and it was he who prised me out of the offshore department to join tankers.

I walk out of the dealing room with my coffee mug in my right hand. This clever use of office PSYOPS helps make it look like I'm casually leaving the dealing desk to go to the kitchen for another coffee refill. Not going downstairs to have my horoscope read to me in the boardroom.

As I walk into the boardroom, the MD and our Horace are waiting to greet me with two of the longest faces I've ever seen. Horace's presence sets off my ESP siren like a 1950s four-minute warning as I start to feel nervous.

'Steve, please take a seat,' says the MD, not holding eye contact.

The situation doesn't feel right at all. Their body language is official and the MD's usually smiling face looks sad. Horace looks at his watch and is probably wondering why it's working again, since he hasn't wound it up.

I take my seat and look at them both. They have pre-written notes on their Conqueror writing pads, which are at an angle, making it difficult for me to read. There's also a white A4 envelope under the MD's left hand and I can't see who it is addressed to. But I am very suspicious. The MD glances down at his solid gold Rolex. I can see the time on it. It is 5:50 p.m. He takes a very deep breath and starts to say a few words.

'Steve, there's no easy way to put this, but we are terminating your contract of employment with Seamart and making your position redundant.'

I flinch and then swallow hard as my shoulders drop. The blow those words have made is like a punch to the kidneys and my heartbeat races up with shock as I say 'What?'

He continues. 'You must understand, we are not making you redundant, but your position. Unfortunately you were the last one on the desk and therefore you are the first to go. We've checked with other departments and in the current climate, they're all struggling to meet their budgets as well. So there are no other opportunities for you within this company.'

I look disappointed and I just can't hide it as my throat goes dry, while my heartbeat pounds away. Horace starts to speak and the MD looks down at his sold gold Mont Blanc fountain pen. 'Look, old boy, being made redundant is nothing to be ashamed of,' he says, as a false smile of total insincerity escapes and runs across his face.

A rare rush of anger goes off inside me as my ears pop at the sound of his ignorant voice.

The MD flinches, realising that Horace is just being a bit dim and quickly adds, 'Steve, you'll easily find another job in this industry and we'll write a splendid reference for you. And your redundancy package is very good. We're giving you three months' tax-free salary.'

I am too shocked to think. In five years I have done over two hundred shipping deals and brought in an outrageous amount of commission. My mind focuses sharply on the sums involved. Legally they only have to give me a nominal sum, which probably wouldn't even get me a new Ermenegildo Zegna cotton shirt and silk tie. I feel I'm not in a position to argue and I just nod my head in acceptance.

'You can go back to your desk and take any personal belongings when you leave tonight. There's no need to come back tomorrow,' says the MD with a sincere tone, while eyeballing Horace hard.

I check the MD's watch. It is still working and the hands on this fine piece of Swiss craftsmanship look like they've hardly moved as my five successful years with the company have suddenly ended.

We shake hands and I take the envelope.

Still in shock, I go back to my chair and prepare to leave the desk for the last time. Most of the chaps are on the phone to New York. I switch off my PC and put on my suit jacket and Burberry cashmere overcoat and scarf. There are no photos or personal belongings to take with me. I only have my black Cross fountain pen, which was a birthday present last year, and my book. I pick up *In Harms Way* by Martin Bell, which I finally finished this morning and put today's copy of *Lloyd's List* in the bin.

As I pass their chairs, I say goodbye to Richard and Billy and walk out as usual. Both, as always, reply genuinely, 'see you tomorrow, mate'.

Outside on this dark January evening, it is very cold.

CHAPTER 2

'The wankers!' Natasha says, when I tell her about being made redundant.

I have the best sorry dog look on my face and for once I am not even trying. But in my depression, the Sony TV seems even bigger by the hour and has now lost its appeal. It now looks like a big silver elephant that is just staring back at me and is now laughing at my recent folly. On the TV is Jon Snow of Channel 4 News. He's doing an interview about the Millennium Bug "fiasco" to some prick who is trying to say that fifty billion dollars spent on software upgrades saved the day. My oldish PC still works and I spent jack shit on upgrading it. However, technology, media and telecoms stocks on the NASDAQ are booming and anything now seems possible.

'Can they just do that after you've been there for all those years?' asks Natasha.

'Yes, it's easy for them; I was last on the tanker desk and therefore first out. There's also no room in any other departments, the market's crap and the firm is way behind its budgeted targets.'

I turn the TV off, as I'm not really listening to it. Natasha is still shocked and has yet to take off her coat. (I don't tell her about the lunchtime drink as the sympathy is coming thick and fast. And she knows how set in their ways these people can be.)

'Oh, poor you, Steve. Do you know what you want to do?' she asks caringly.

'I have no idea. I haven't even got an up-to-date CV. But I don't want to go back to chartering oil tankers. This is a sign to move on and do something better,' I say, with my head spinning at not having a job while playing with a TV remote control that looks so big it could change the orbits of passing satellites.

'Would you like me to ask if my company has any trading positions coming up? Also, Bloomberg's are recruiting for European sales managers. I know people there and I'll give them a call as well, if you want?' she asks, full of enthusiasm.

At twenty-seven Natasha is a top fixed-incomes trader with a leading global investment bank. And she doesn't take crap from any other mortal sharing this planet.

'Thanks, that would be great,' I say. After all, it's the only bit of encouraging news I've heard all day.

'Look, I'll cook us both some dinner and you switch on that PC and start dreaming up your CV,' she says, showing yet another moment of generosity from a woman whose deals can affect whole nations' debt repayments.

'Would you like a glass of wine, Steve?' she shouts from the kitchen.

'Yes please, I could do with a drink.'

Waking up the day after you've unexpectedly lost your job for the first time in your life is one of the most confusing things a person can go through. You feel like part of your identity has been stolen from you and you are now nothing. Well I do, now that it has happened to me. I got up at the usual time for a shower, then quickly realised that I had nothing to get up for.

Natasha was out of bed and through the door at 6 a.m. And by now most of the governments in South America will be filling their pants.

I breathe a small sigh of relief. At least I don't have any debts. There's no wife and kids to support. No university fees to pay off, just number one and a big fuck off Sony TV to look after. Maybe I'll go on holiday. I'm not long back from trekking and could do with another break. Pakistan's North-West Frontier is where I want to head for next, but the Karakoram Highway is snowbound at this time of year.

After a couple of hours, a major attack of rationality takes over and I decide it's more sensible to get a job first and then go on holiday. But what am I going to do? And how do I conduct myself in interviews? I haven't got a clue. More anxiety hits as I realise that, although the money front is okay for the time being, money can run out very quickly living in Fulham with no income. Four pounds for a cappuccino and croissant can't go on for ever.

I compromise with my better judgement and get up at nine feeling surprisingly good. The stress of not going into battle during office hours has left my mind like aching pain that disappears after a massage. I take a hot bath and think how great it is that I will never see the desk again.

This chilled out state of mind stays with me until I see the TV set and I realise just how big it looks this morning. I switch it on and then turn it off just as quick when I see the crap that is on at this time of day. My Visa card statement arrives with the morning post. The TV is on the bill and it's just as well there is a good few grand soon to be coming my way. I put on a CD I've recently bought which is a fantastic piece of remixing: William Orbit's *Barber's Adagio for Strings*. I listen to it along with the neighbours, who are all now too scared to venture out of their houses after the recent gun battles in Bishops Park.

Later I phone up some friends who are all at work and get some moral support. The friends I can't reach, I just leave some messages and tell them I've been binned. I walk out of the front door to go and get the morning papers. (There's no need to get the *Daily Mirror* any more.)

A short while later Natasha phones while I'm sitting back on the comfy sofa reading the sports and jobs pages in *The Times*.

'Hi Steve! How are you feeling this morning?' she shouts.

In the background is her trading floor where whole countries have been bled dry. This morning it sounds like a feeding frenzy is taking place. It is almost as if some zoo animals have been deliberately starved and now there's a good feed going down. However, the reality is that some Third World country is bleeding.

'Not bad thanks, how's the floor doing this morning?' I ask, listening to the noise.

'Oh, the market's quiet so far, but listen, I've spoken to HR and they've said no chance in here. You've got no SFA qualification and have no financial trading experience and you're too old for our graduate course. Even if you did pay to sit the SFA exams yourself, it is unlikely anyone will take you on at your age.'

'*At my age!* I'm twenty-eight years old,' I say, dumbfounded, as I can suddenly feel the rest of my career potential slipping through my fingers like grains of desert sand.

'Yes, I know, Steve, but in this game, we get them young, starve them, humiliate them and beat them senseless. Then they're ready to kill anything on the floor, with no silly afterthoughts of guilt,' she says, as she starts shouting over to somebody.

'But I've just had five years of combat and done multimillion dollar deals,' I say, as all the sand has now drained from my hands, and I have a mouthful of bottled water. I take a deep breath and try to say something optimistic, but she spots the two-second delay. If I were still at my dealing desk with a screen, three telephones and my direct line to the Israeli chartering manager, that wouldn't have happened. It's only my first morning without a job and already I'm going slack.

'Look Steve, this existence is shit. It's worse than anything you could wish for,' she says, as some shouting increases in her background.

She picks up this little silence once again.

'Steve, consider Bloomberg's, they're a top company with a great working environment. They also have a very well respected name and product. And they are global.'

'Yes, I've just put the finishing touches to my CV and sent it off to them. They've got a big ad in *The Times*.'

'Great....' she says, as louder screaming engulfs her in the background, and then the line goes dead. An order came through and either she had to take a shot or take cover.

This job with Bloomberg's is the only thing that remotely interests me in the whole job section and this has me so concerned that I contact the local Job Centre to enquire if it's okay to sign on.

'Of course you can sign on, it's your right! You have to make an appointment though, but you're lucky, there's been a cancellation this morning. We can see you in twenty minutes if you like? Here's our address,' says the lady on the other end of the line. I could almost hear her having a laugh to her colleagues as I put the phone down... 'Hey, get this girls, some out of work yuppie wanker is coming in to sign on...!'

The Dole Office, or Job Centre, is not even ten minutes' walk from my flat. It is still bitterly cold and as I approach the entrance to the building, three single mums walk out. All are wearing shell suits, ski hats and scarves and are pushing prams. I think they're single mums, as none looks older than sixteen.

I walk inside and quickly feel that this is one of the most depressing places in West London. A few seconds later I spot the two noticeboards with the words, "latest jobs" on them, so I go and have a look and see what's on offer. While I'm looking to see if HMG are still offering any *"interesting"* and *"challenging"* overseas career opportunities, my heart briefly stops beating as the only careers I can see on offer are dog catcher, hairdresser and park attendant, all paying around four pounds fifty an hour.

Then I suddenly notice that some of the regulars are now walking past me and eyeballing me up and down and it is not long before I realise my mistake. I'm wearing my Mulberry wax jacket with Hugo Boss chinos and Timberlands. They look at me and they're not happy. Not because they are out of work, but because some tosser (me) has just walked into the Dole Office for a laugh.

One of the desk girls (probably called "executive recruitment analyst", or something similar) is sitting watching me. Her elbows are on the desk and her arms upwards, with her chin resting on her clasped hands. It's a frightening look she's giving me as I walk up to the New Claims Desk and sign on... And then I leave the building as fast as possible.

As soon as I am outside and across the street I look over my shoulder to see if anyone has followed me out; not in order to beat me up but rather to see if an "executive recruitment analyst" is trying to drag me back inside and turn me into a fucking dog catcher!

Outside my mobile rings; at least it never rang in there, as that would've upset the regulars for sure. I breathe a sigh of relief as I answer it. It is Natasha.

'Hi Steve! I spoke to a mate at Bloomberg's and their HR say they've got your CV and they'll be in touch soon,' she shouts. The "animals" are still screaming away in the background as she hangs up. (And these ones are not "lambs".)

'Fucking dog catcher!' This is more like it, I say, to reassure myself as I walk the short distance home... already planning out my new career with Bloomberg's.

I get home and I look again at Bloomberg's website. I'm more used to Reuters, but here financial information and charts scream out at you at full volume. While I am in the middle of trying to find out what a forex, fixed income, derivative junk bond, equity-linked swap is and what has been the average price for one in London, New York, Hong Kong and Tokyo over the last seven milliseconds, my mobile rings. It is a lady from Bloomberg's.

'Hello Steve, thank you for sending in your CV, could you make it in for an interview at three this afternoon? It won't take long, we're interviewing lots of people,' she asks, sounding sincere enough.

'Yes, that's no problem at all. But I do have an interview at six at Canary Wharf.'

'Oh, we'll be finished in plenty of time for that, Steve. Now, do you know where the office is?' she asks, relaxing her tone slightly.

'Yes, I've seen the Bloomberg building.'

'Good. We'll see you at three,' she says warmly, as we both say goodbye.

Of course I haven't got another job interview at Canary Wharf, Catford or any place else... It is essential that you never let a company think or, worse, know, that they are your only option. If you do you've just lost a few grand on your salary, respect, and some firms might not even ask you back, even if they're trying to headhunt you... Natasha's words of wisdom, which I remember her saying to me following our meal last night, which suddenly stick in my head.

I phone Natasha with my "success" and leave a message on her voice mail as I quickly get ready for my interview.

Before today, I never realised just how lonely and depressing a journey on the London Underground is during a workday when you haven't got a job to go to at the other end. In the past, I've only used it to go to work and wherever else. But now with no career to focus on at the end of the journey, it can very easily be one long dark tunnel without a light at the end.

At the end of this tunnel, walking up Finsbury Pavement towards the Bloomberg's office, I realise that I haven't got a clue what to expect from this interview. My last one was over five years ago and even then it only went on for a few minutes and the elders at Seamart did all the talking. Their mouths were dribbling at my university course and they couldn't get enough of it. I was also asked my favourite wine, what newspaper I read and that was about it.

I arrive in good time for my interview at the Bloomberg's office, which from inside actually looks more like an MTV studio, but without the music. I make myself known to one of the receptionists, take a seat and wait to be called for my interview. While I am waiting I look at the share graphs on the Bloomberg TV news and note that some telecoms and Internet companies almost look vertical. Then my name is called.

I quickly realise that there is no need for nerves as I've been through dozens of far tougher business meetings and complex negotiations over the past five years. I can answer all their questions apart from the in depth ones on the global finance markets. The NASDAQ and technology stocks are booming for sure, but that's about all I know about global finance. If the interview were on The Gulf War (1991), the world oil markets and the balance of power in the "Cold War" period, then I'd be laughing. But it isn't and the best question one American corporate fires at me is about the Austrian politician, Jorg Haider, and the "horrors of fascism". I am asked whether or not I thought it was "disgraceful" about "that fascist in Austria" being elected, while she looks at the second and last page of my CV.

I basically say that the process by which he is being elected is called "democracy" and that fascism is what the working and lower middle classes tend to vote for in industrialised Central Europe. This is when the population feel that their social class and economic well being is being undermined and therefore destabilised by the influx of poor immigrants who are then irrationally blamed for the region's economic decline.

This throws them!

'Oh… so er… what about Pinochet? Surely you'll agree with *Tony Blair* in detaining him for a possible trial in Spain for being a "war criminal"…?'

After a few thoughts I tell them that the whole issue smells of *hypocrisy.*

'Really…?' they ask, as they exchange nervous glances to each other and take a closer look at my CV.

I continue to "enlighten" them on the historical fact that during the "Cold War" it was a fundamental part of US covert foreign policy to install and fund fascist governments in South America ["...after training at the US Army's School of the Americas (SOA) in Panama."] In 1973 Pinochet came to power with *"direct assistance"* from the CIA who illegally overthrew a democratically elected foreign government, and Pinochet's domestic policy to 'defeat terrorism and stamp out subversion' was part of US covert foreign policy in South America at the time. So why detain Pinochet now? Why aren't living members of Gerald Ford's administration being arrested over *Operation Condor* as well? ["Track 2 deniability..."] This covert policy took shape under President Ford ["...via Bill Nelson and William Well's Directorate of Operations at CIA Langley"], and after his term in office was over, he awarded his Secretary of State, Dr Henry Kissinger, the US Presidential Medal of Freedom. This award was given with full White House knowledge about Henry Kissinger's covert foreign policies in South America and elsewhere ["...and Dr Kissinger also answered to his 'mentor', the Chairman of the Board at the Council on Foreign Relations, Mr David Rockefeller"].

I say this to two executives from one of America's largest and finest financial news organisations, whilst looking for a level of understanding about covert White House South American foreign policy "directives" and a challenging response about *"war criminals"* from them...

Silence.

["...Under President Ford, it was US covert foreign policy to train and coordinate South American military regimes. In 1976 it was known as *Operation Condor* in Langley, Meade and the Pentagon. It was engineered in Chile with full Washington support. Ford, N. Rockefeller, Bush Sr, Eagleburger, Dr Kissinger, Gen. G. Brown, Scowcroft, Clements, Cheney and Rumsfeld all embraced Operation Condor and none of them tried to have it halted... The SOA was to stay open for General Videla."]

'Er... well I'm sure if America had done wrong it would have been out by now, Steve.'

["...The White House stayed silent and the killing of civilians continued throughout the region. Langley and the Pentagon still hold the documents detailing their actions and Dr Henry Kissinger's files are locked away with David Rockefeller at Kykuit, Pocantico Hills."]

I let it go, but I could've also mentioned the histories of IBM, Rockefeller's Standard Oil/IG Farben and the historical fact about Prescott Bush's Union Banking Corp business dealings with Nazi Germany ["...the German Steel Trust and Fritz Thyssen's Consolidated Silesian Steel Corp."] when Britain faced Adolf Hitler alone... But I am not getting the right vibes from them. After this, they cough, shuffle some papers and move quickly on to salary levels.

Despite their lack of knowledge about fascism, "Project FUBELT" and

US corporate history, Bloomberg's overall questions are fairly standard ones. All of which are fired at me by two brainwashed corporate robots, who clearly believed that Bloomberg's created God Himself. I quickly sense that the Bloomberg's "production line" is a very slick, well-oiled operation, turning bright graduates into a well-polished product, ready to wave the corporate flag at the world's leading financial institutions. And they are very good at it. And they love it.

It is just not me. I prefer a far more low profile approach and feel uncomfortable being the centre of attention. The freedom to keep my individuality is paramount. Being "encouraged" to visit the company's tattoo parlour is about as appealing as being a dog catcher in SE1.

Walking out of their building I know that I don't want to end up working in there. (And I also know that I haven't got a hope in hell of getting a job in there anyway!) A few minutes after my interview, I am relaxing my politically charged brain whilst having a cappuccino in Starbucks on Finsbury Pavement. From my window seat, I look at all the successful-looking suits quickly passing by and notice the way they are all focusing on their career and what deals they are doing. And I miss it. I don't miss working for Seamart any more than I miss having my kneecaps drilled. What I miss is chasing after and cutting the deal.

I phone my Israeli friend who does the Israeli chartering and tell him that I've been binned. He is shocked and vows to support me if I join another firm, which is very reassuring to hear from such a good bloke. I hear back a few minutes later that Seamart announced to everyone in the firm and the Industry, that I had 'decided to resign'.

Back to reality, and I am not looking forward to getting on that tube again. I look down into the murky cappuccino and think about the Israeli oil shipments that I'm no longer going to be involved with. As I walk out of Starbucks, psyching myself up for the inevitable dark journey back to Fulham, my mobile rings and I answer it. On the line is Wacko, one of my best mates. He must be calling me back to offer me some moral support and to arrange a few drinks this weekend.

'Steve boy, got your message about the old boys finally binning you. Sorry to hear that!' he says, having a laugh as I cheer up.

'Yes, cheers mate, but I feel better already as I've just had an interview with Bloomberg.'

'Fucking hell, that was quick. How did you get on?' he asks, sounding surprised.

'It went really well and I'm optimistic. But I'm also going to give Control

Risks Group a call. I've got a friend who works there and they're going to be expanding in their political risk and analysis section.'

'Right, there's a position going at the company I work for. I'm the Director for Network and Business Development for an Internet/telecoms start-up company. What do you know about the Internet, Steve?' he asks, sounding in a hurry.

'Well, I surf it quite a lot,' I say, trying not to sound thick.

'Good. What do you know about e-commerce?'

(Shit, these questions are getting tougher now!)

'Well I bought a few books and CDs from Amazon before Christmas, and I also got some camera gear online as well,' I say as I'm trying to sound as knowledgeable as possible.

'Excellent!' he says enthusiastically. 'What do you know about fibre optics and telecoms networks?' he adds, well and truly boxing clever now.

'Er... well I did some legwork on "Project Oxygen" for my management when we were looking at supplying cable ships for the building of a global sub-sea fibre optic cable network.'

'Steve! You're almost a fucking expert!' he says, laughing. 'Right, I've got a meeting in one minute. Are you interested in a career in the Internet and telecoms world?'

'Yes, of course, *that's the future,'* I say, convincingly covering up the fact that I'd never previously thought of it.

'Good, let's have you over for an interview. Are you okay later on?'

'Yes, sure. What time is best for you?' I ask, looking at my watch. It's just gone 4:27 p.m.

'Say seven at All Bar One, Cambridge Circus on Charing Cross Road? I'll be on my own, so we'll sink some drinks and I'll tell you about the role.'

'That's great,' I say, with my faith in human nature restored after a two-minute phone call.

'Right, see you at seven.'

'Cheers Wacko... Oh, Wacko, before I forget, what's the company's name?'

'iaxis,' he says as the line goes dead.

I have known Wacko for a few years now. He's a chartered accountant with over ten years' experience with firms such as Coopers and CSFB. He was a specialist in Eastern Europe and spent eight years living and working out there. He's also very well connected in the City and a few other places. When it comes to complex numbers and advanced accountancy, this boy knows his stuff. He is also anything but an "old boy" in attitude, nature and vision. He wouldn't have lasted three days at Seamart. I lasted a year on the tanker desk, mostly out of determination not to surrender to them. But what he's doing in charge of "network developments" with a telecoms/Internet start-up company I have no idea. Last time I spoke to him, he was going for a job interview at the ITN building.

I arrive on time and he's already at the bar. With no hair, standing over six feet tall, wearing a black leather jacket and black jeans, he is quite easy to spot in a crowded area. He hasn't changed at all, apart from looking a bit more tired.

'So, the old boys finally binned you!' he says, laughing away. He knows all about the *Daily Mirror* and my lack of willingness to 'fit in with the team'.

'I don't miss it at all and it's only been twenty-four hours,' I say, as he's trying to catch the attention of the barmaid. The young looking attractive barmaid turns up and smiles at Wacko.

'What do you want to drink?' he asks.

'I'll have an orange Bacardi Breezer, please.'

(He doesn't flinch.)

'Two Breezers, please.'

'Cheers!'

We grab a table and I tell him about having a gin and tonic at lunchtime with the chaps, just to wind them up, before I was binned. He's practically on the floor laughing with tears in his eyes.

'If it's on CCTV, I'll pay to see it!' he says, coughing loudly.

'There's no CCTV in that place, so I'm sorry mate.'

'Pity. So what was the redundancy package like?' he enquires, genuinely interested.

'Just three months' basic, tax free,' I reply, sounding very close to spitting out my dummy.

'You should've asked for six months at least, after all the deals you did over five years.'

'Should've asked for twelve months after all the crap I put up with.' I reply taking a sip on the Breezer. 'So what's this job at your place?' I ask, casually.

'There's a position going in my department that will require someone to look after getting other Internet backbones to "peer" or connect with us at the European Neutral Internet Exchange Points. These peering contracts need managing and I'll maybe try and get you to sell some Internet transit capacity and look for co-location facilities around Europe if you're interested.'

My heart sinks as quickly as his Breezer is going down. I am now looking around for a passing ship, feeling well out of my depth. I didn't understand a word of what he's just said. He could've been speaking an *"ancient pyramid"* type language only recently discovered and yet to be *"deciphered"* for all I know.

'Wacko, look mate, I'm being completely honest with you here. I know nothing about telecoms and the Internet. You can write my knowledge of that stuff you've just said on the back of a postage stamp,' I say, looking despondent.

He laughs. 'Don't worry Steve, we were all in the same position one time or another. When I started I knew fuck all. You'll be amazed at how much you'll learn in that place. Just ask lots of questions, everyone's friendly and helpful, make mistakes, which we all do, and learn. The most important thing in there is being able to blag it out and wing it like fuck. Just read the "techie manuals", there's plenty of them, and also check out "whatis.com". Right now we're all winging it. There are only about forty people out of one hundred and twenty with real telecom backgrounds and experience. And only about three people know about this Internet peering bollocks! But everyone works really hard. Last year people were working seven days a week, till 11 p.m. sometimes, trying to build the network.'

'Sounds *challenging!* When did the company start?'

'I think it was April 1998, but we only started being called iaxis in April 1999. But we're looking to float on the NASDAQ in the third quarter this year. After this I'll be retiring with about one and a half million dollars after I've cashed in my shares. I've bought a load of shares to the value of my salary. We're all going to make a shit load of money,' he says, dropping this in just to make me realise something big is going on with this iaxis company. 'One thing though, Steve, if you join, you must put the hours in and learn fast. But the partying is full-on,' he says, as I contemplate all of what he has been saying, and he takes his fourth gulp of his Breezer and practically finishes the bottle.

'Two more Breezers please,' he says to the passing barmaid.

I have been listening intently, thinking what a great place this is to work and I've hardly touched my drink. In a desperate bid to catch up, I take a massive swig on the Breezer, trying my best to finish the bottle. Wacko is now on to his second and I'm sure that last gulp has fizzed up to the back of my head and is now dripping out of my ears. They seem to be popping like hell as I try and refocus on Wacko's TAG 2000 Chronograph watch. I think it is 7:25 p.m.

'So the atmosphere's pretty good in the office then?' I ask, trying to breathe through my nose in order to stabilise my head.

'It's fantastic. Everyone sticks together. There's no bitching and backstabbing and the girls especially are hardcore party animals. They're all good lookers and mostly single too. The chairman has told them all that he doesn't want to see any married women on his staff! But it's also a very multicultural and dynamic office. Leave all that old boy crap behind; it's a different world in iaxis.'

By now I'm seriously interested and want the job.

'So what assets do you have?' I ask, sounding more focused.

'We're a telecoms start-up. All iaxis has is a couple of fibre optic cables linking a few European cities. The fibres are as thin as a single strand of hair on your head. We sell capacity on that fibre and the space in our co-location facilities. We will also be selling Internet transit from the IP backbone which we're building on top of the fibre optic network,' he says, starting to lose me again with his *"ancient pyramid"* type talk.

'And IP means Internet Provider, yes?' I ask, sounding like I'm learning fast already.

Wacko laughs. 'That's what I thought until three weeks ago! Don't worry about it. If you decide to join, Nathan and Merlin will tell you all you need to know about Internet Protocol and Internet backbone connectivity, known as peering. But don't tell me about it because it's well complicated and I'll fall asleep!' he says, as he finishes his drink again. 'Right, come on, let's go to a good resturant in Covent Garden and have some frozen margaritas and some food. We should get a table,' says Wacko, as he gets up from his chair.

I take another massive gulp of Breezer and have to wipe my nose as it tries to escape again. We get outside the pub and the cold air hits us hard.

'Are you still seeing that sexy City chick?' he asks, with a dirty grin on his face, while trying to keep warm.

'Yes, but she's due to be posted to her New York office at the end of the month,' I say, feeling bloody cold.

'Pity, Steve, she'd get a job in our place if she just walked in and asked for directions!' he says, shaking his head.

'Not even your company could afford to pay her.' I say, as we both have a laugh about it while we're trying to cross Cambridge Circus and wondering which direction the traffic is coming from.

Three frozen margaritas later and our food finally arrives, which is then wolfed down.

'So, are you interested in joining iaxis then?' he says, as he eyeballs me.

'Yes,' I say, nodding my head slowly, keeping eye contact with a couple of Wackos that are now spinning in front of me. 'It sounds like a career I'll do well in.'

'Good, but understand, you'll be working for me. And if it doesn't work out I'll be the one who sacks you.'

'That's okay, I won't let you down,' I say, as a fourth frozen margarita arrives.

'So what package were you on as a shipbroker?'

He doesn't even raise an eyebrow as I tell him. (Bloomberg's just laughed when I told them. Their posture said they wouldn't be matching it!)

Wacko nods his head. 'Okay, I'll increase it by twenty per cent and our bonus is twenty-five per cent of your annual salary, plus pension, life insurance and you'll get some pre flotation/IPO share options. I think you'll be joining too late for buying into the share participation scheme.'

(Fantastic!)

'What's the share participation scheme?' I ask, feeling like I'm now missing out on a straight path to instant riches.

'One of the investment firms backing iaxis has lent the iaxis staff money to the value of their annual salaries. This is so we can buy pre-flotation shares in iaxis. We've all got five years in which to pay this loan off. However, when we float in the third quarter of this year, even the secretaries who've taken this salary loan will stand to make at least three hundred thousand dollars. It's even been in the *Daily Mail*. We're all going to be *fucking millionaires!*'

'Bollocks! I should've ordered that drink before Christmas!' I say as we click margarita glasses. (But I am just very thankful for a good job and a change in career direction.)

'Right now Steve, Wall Street is out of control. WorldCom is worth one hundred and fifty billion dollars, Global Crossing fifty-two billion dollars, GTS is worth about six billion dollars and when Carrier 1 floats on the NASDAQ, they'll be worth about two and a half billion dollars. iaxis was started by an ex-senior WorldCom/MFS person and we reckon we're worth at least one billion dollars, maybe even one and a half, but it depends on whom you speak to and what mood they're in! Everybody knows that telecoms and dotcoms are the future. That is a certainty after death and taxes, so nothing can go wrong. You see, all the investment houses and VCs are demanding to see us, all looking for a piece of the action. They can't get enough of us just now,' he says, with eyes hardened from recent experience.

'What did you mean by VCs?' I ask quickly, as in my steaming alcohol brain an AK-47 flashed across my mind!

'It stands for venture capitalist. These are basically investment firms with too much money and no ideas apart from balance sheets. But they are where iaxis gets most of its funding from,' he says, as his own eyes now look like they are flashing back to some of his recent skirmishes with these VCs.

'So what's the downside?' I ask, as right now it sounds better than a holiday in Club Med's complex in the Virgin Islands.

'You won't get much sleep, and you'll spend a fortune in the Blue Lion across the road and a few other places. I spend about two hundred pounds per week on drink! My card is always behind the bar. Rumour has it that the owner of the Blue Lion has bought a new villa in Tuscany since we've moved in across the road!'

'That's fine. I think I can handle the work and the partying.'

'No it's not fine. Are you sure you know what you're letting yourself in for?'

I look blank as Wacko brings me up to speed.

'You will wake up every morning at about three or four o'clock, with your head buzzing about IP, fibre-optics, co-location, peering, routers, switches and long legs.'

I nod my head in acceptance. (It still sounds good to me!)

'Okay, just never forget that we're a start-up and anything could happen, but its unlikely, old boy!' he says, now taking the piss out of my recent career history. I know where he's coming from. After ten years in the City and throughout Eastern Europe, he's seen it all.

'So do you want the job then?' he asks seriously.

'Yes. When do you want me to start?' I ask, thinking I might go to Indonesia trekking for a month and do some travel photography with the Leica R8 camera which I bought online last year.

'Tomorrow morning 9 a.m.'

I'm trying my best poker face not to look surprised, but I smile broadly as my head feels like it's a champagne cork that's just smacked off the ceiling above. 'Excellent! My holiday will have to wait a while,' I say, while I'm grinning away at the future, which now looks fantastic.

'If this works you'll be on a holiday for the rest of your fucking life!' he adds as we both shake hands on the deal. 'Just ask for me at reception. I'll take you to HR and get you to sign the contract. You might as well bring in your CV for their records.'

'Fine. Where are your offices?'

'We're in the ITN building at 200 Gray's Inn Road. We're on the seventh floor, right at the top. Take the Piccadilly line to Russell Square tube station and it's a little more than five minute's walk from there. Word has it that the chairman wants to buy the whole ITN building and call it the "iaxis building"! He just might do it as well. It is one of the best office locations in London,' he says, gulping down the last of his margarita, which I am just about keeping up with.

'Right, let's go,' he says, looking around for the waitress as I can't believe my luck.

'Okay, but I'll get the bill,' I say, as I'm getting my leather wallet out with my head spinning.

'No, put it away. I'll get this one in. It's an interview and I'll wing it through on expenses.'

He pays with his company's AmEx card and we leave. Once we are outside, every cell in my brain feels like electricity is charging through it.

'Well, I'll see you tomorrow morning. I'm off back home to work on my laptop,' he says grinning away, wondering if I'll make it in on time.

'What, tonight, just now?' I ask, trying not to sound too incredulous as I look at my watch; it is 10:12 p.m.

'Yes, we're buying Internet transit capacity from a couple of Tier 1 US backbones in New York and they're emailing over the contract about now. I'll get you started on that as well, you'll be dealing on the phone with Kathryn from time to time. You'll find her helpful on Internet Protocol, peering and transit connections. She sounds nice,' he says, speaking in that *encrypted* language once again.

As we get to *Great Queen Street* we say goodbye and go our separate ways. I'm now feeling a lot happier than I did after I walked out of the "Bloomberg factory" several hours ago.

After what seems like a lifetime's wait for a taxi, I eventually arrive home. Sobering up after a hot shower and a litre of water, I look up the website for my new company, which I see on Wacko's business card. It looks impressive, but I don't understand a word of it.

I log out and switch off the PC when I hear the front door open and slam shut. Natasha walks in and she is crying. She's had a bad day and it turns out between her sobs that she made a wrong call and the floor lost a lot of dollars. After closing, all the chaps got up and gave her a mocking standing ovation. She tells me this while we are hugging each other, as I get her to slowly calm down.

'I've got a job starting tomorrow morning,' I whisper into her ear as her tears stop flowing.

'That's fantastic! I got your message. I can't believe Bloomberg's took you on after just one interview,' she says, wiping her tears away.

'It's not with Bloomberg's, it's a telecoms/Internet start-up company called iaxis. I'm working for my mate, Wacko. So there's no old school tie for me any more! But not only this, I even got a salary increase and they're going to train me up!' I say, smiling at this prospect and smelling her Chanel Allure perfume on her warm skin.

'Brilliant! I'm so pleased for you,' she says warmly as I feel her heartbeat pounding.

'This means that I'll be winging it for a while, but you get nine lives *and one chance,*' I say, looking into her dark brown eyes.

'I knew you'd be fine, you've always been a jammy bastard!' she says, as her hands move up from my neck into my hair and we both start to kiss and laugh our way into my room.

CHAPTER 3

I'm in a post-sleep, pre-awake trance-like state and I feel slightly rougher than usual. And then it hits me; I realise that I start work in a couple of hours for an Internet/telecoms start-up company in an industry I know nothing about. Did Wacko really offer me a job, with that package? I think he said so, but my head does feel a bit heavy as I look at my watch; the time is 6:54 a.m. and the *Today* programme will switch on in just under one minute.

I see a little note Natasha has written for me. *Good luck Steve! Love Natasha xx.*

That's sweet. I'm going to need some luck. Loads of luck, come to think of it.

Then the *Today* programme starts and a wise and friendly-sounding female voice (friendly that is until it is turned loose on some scheming politician) will tell me that today is a Friday and it is therefore time to get up and go to work.

After a long hot shower, I look and feel a bit more like a human being once again. I put on my Alexandre pinstripe number, with a Bagutta white shirt and a silk tie from Gieves and Hawkes. This should make me look the business. It is raining outside, so the dark blue Burberry raincoat and my *black umbrella* will have to do.

Breakfast is a short walk away at the Starbucks coffee shop on the Fulham Road. I have a large cappuccino, with a couple of croissants. Some food and a shot of caffeine sharpens the senses, but does little for the nerves as I walk to Parsons Green tube station. There is a nice rainbow in the sky and I think to myself that this is a pleasant sight.

On the tube the journey today feels much better than the one I made to Bloomberg's not even twenty-four hours ago. As the tube pulls out of Knightsbridge, I breathe a sigh of relief that I don't have to get off there any more.

Last night Wacko said it was only a few minutes walk from Russell Square tube station to the ITN building. But this morning the rain is pissing down and the walk seems to take forever. While I'm walking down Gray's Inn Road, I look back on my interview with Seamart. I was one of over sixty who'd applied. It was on my CV that as part of my university degree course in politics and international relations I'd done a large essay on whether there was a link between military rule and fascism. The elders couldn't get enough of this, and I was offered the job the following day!

Sadly, they weren't too up to speed on the US government's Third Reich "rehabilitation" program in 1945 ["...Project Paperclip was coordinated by General Alexander Bolling and his assistant, Mr Henry Kissinger. Paperclip was overseen by Allen Dulles of the Zurich OSS office"]. But once I was in, they said the company could do with some more fascists. Although I think they were disappointed that I wasn't one, there was no doubt that this course helped me get the job. That interview was over five years ago and it now seems like another lifetime that I once visited. But surely this place won't be the same. Wacko works here and seems to love it. No matter how much I try and use this thought to reassure myself, inside my stomach churns.

I arrive at 200 Gray's Inn Road and from the outside the building looks very impressive. Inside the reception area, I see that the morning security shift isn't checking security passes as I walk past them, looking like I work here every day. As I move quietly inside the building, I can see that this is one big *glasshouse*. Natural light penetrates it from all angles and most of the light is coming from the huge glass ceiling *above*. The centre of the building is hollow, with a canteen on the lower ground floor. I get into the lift which takes me to the seventh floor. From up here the people down *below* in the canteen seem like ants moving in an organised manner, going to and from their eating tables.

I walk into iaxis through the glass doors and arrive at the reception desks. Two very attractive blondes are sitting at what appear to be two separate, silver, space-age-looking hot seat terminals. There is a TV screen facing me from each terminal where they are sitting.

This morning the TV is showing the world according to CNN.

Behind the girls is a glass wall with the six-foot high letters 'IAXIS' sculpted into it, which looks like it cost a lot of money, as if it's been made to order and *created* to last. 'I just hope this lot don't throw any stones,' I think to myself, feeling pleased that I've seen no cold brass plates anywhere in the glass office building.

'Can I help you sir?' asks the receptionist with piercing blue eyes. She has just finished taking a call on the most modern telephone system I've ever seen.

'Er... yes, Mr Jackson, please. I'm Steve Goddard.'

'Is he expecting you?' she asks, as she prepares to hit a button on the phone system.

'Yes, well I hope so, I start work for him today!' I say, a bit nervous.

'Oh excellent, Steve! Please take a seat over there and Wacko will be with you shortly,' she says in a Hertfordshire accent. She doesn't look a day older than twenty-one.

Wacko's number is then called.

'Can I get you a tea or coffee, Steve?' asks the other receptionist.

'No, I'm fine thanks, I've just had one,' I say, as they both smile and start taking more calls.

I study the large glass goldfish bowl type room within the reception area. A sign on the glass wall says the words 'Network Operations Centre'. Inside the room on the wall are six large plasma screens with funny lines on them. All nine young-looking employees are behind huge flat-screen monitors with high-tech terminals. They are all typing frantically into their keypads, monitoring the plasma screens, or are on the phones. This room looks very technologically advanced. In fact it's more like one of the many "*Overall Command Centres*" deep underground in GCHQ, Cheltenham ["Country…"].

However, in this "*Overall Command Centre*" it doesn't look like there's a "Richard" or a "Brian" sitting behind any of these monitors. Nor is there a "Ma'am" walking about wearing a cashmere cardigan, drinking a cup of Twining's Earl Grey tea and calling the shots as a storm begins to brew in her china teacup.

Inside this goldfish bowl, the personnel look like if they weren't sitting here, they'd all be off snowboarding together in a pack somewhere in Canada, trashing McDonalds and Starbucks during a riot, or hacking in to the mainframe supercomputer system of the Pentagon's DoDIIS for kicks!

I take a seat on the leather sofa facing the two receptionists and it feels like it is the most comfortable sofa I've ever sat on. Then I notice that there's a little stain on it, and think that this is probably where some clumsy tosser has carelessly spilt their drink and just left it there.

In front of this leather sofa there is an expensive-looking glass table that would look very good in my flat. Lying on its well-polished surface is a copy of today's FT and an iaxis brochure. The front page of the FT is practically shuddering with a dotcom Internet/telecoms orgasmic high, telling us that we are in the middle of a "New Age Revolution". This "revolution" has nothing to do with "Swampy", who incidentally looks like he has finally climbed down from his tree house and found a proper job in the "*Overall Command Centre*" to my right. (Well it's him or his twin brother!)

In January 2000, according to the media, "paper Internet millionaires" are being created every ten minutes. The anticipated success of these sudden millionaires is now the envy of the City. The feared "Y2K Bug" has failed to strike and in the "Techie Bubble" anything is now possible. The "Masters of the Universe" on Wall Street and the City dealing floors have decided the way ahead to instant wealth and glorious riches lies within the telecoms, media and technology sector. Now the media and the City can't get enough of it. The figures being invested are big enough to collapse whole nations. Respected global institutions are now valuing certain Internet and telecoms companies at tens of billions of dollars and this all helps to drive up the market hype. Everyone can see where the gold is. It is clearly marked on the City map. And right now I am sitting on a leather sofa, in a space-age-looking glass reception, on the seventh floor of the ITN building, right at the end of the rainbow.

And from where I am now sitting, nothing is more seductive than a financial dead cert and I wholeheartedly believe the hype. However, nothing is more desirable than something you cannot have and a wiser person would realise that when paper burns it destroys the perception of what was once on it. No matter how many zeros. All that remains is some black stuff and a lingering smell of fire and smoke. *And the blacker the smoke, the clearer the hindsight...*

Dizzy after scanning the FT's front page, I pick up the iaxis brochure and quickly read it. It doesn't contain much detailed information, but it says they've got a five-gigabit pan-European Internet backbone, which sounds big and looks impressive. I have no idea what a gigabit is, but I think this experience is going to be fun. The photos look nice and glossy.

Then I hear Wacko before I see him.

'Stalker, I need an update on all our Spanish Projects by mid-morning please,' he says, as the guy just nods his head and keeps on walking. 'Steve! You made it in! It's not too late to leave. You haven't signed anything and you've still got your sanity!' says Wacko, as he shakes my hand.

We both laugh and I take off my raincoat.

Wacko suddenly looks startled.

'*Steve!* What the Dickens is that?' He shouts out as he points to my pinstriped suit trying not to wet himself laughing. 'You look like "Mr Benn". Where's your bowler hat?' he asks, laughing and rubbing his eyes.

I look down at my City suit and realise my first mistake of the day.

'So what would you like to be today, Mr Benn?' He asks, laughing and shaking his head.

'A dotcom millionaire,' I say, catching on to his humour.

'Right then, you've come to the right place mate. Here, put this on!' he says, as he hands me my contract of employment in an A4-sized envelope. The envelope feels heavy. 'Read it, sign it and look forward to the rest of your life slipping away. But from now on, wear jeans. For the rest of the day everyone's going to think you work for Carlyle or Rothschild's! Don't worry, it's my fault, I forgot to mention it.'

'Yeah, thanks mate!'

We walk past the *"Overall Command Centre"* with the plasma screens, monitors and operators. 'This is our Network Operations Centre or NOC and it's run by a bloke called Amen. The dudes in it are all NOC engineers who help to keep the network alive and kicking. They sort out any problems, which are tracked in real time on the plasma screens. Those lines on the big screens that look like a tube map are our two pieces of fibre. That's all we've got apart from a good deal of blag.'

Two of the screens no longer have maps on them. One is now showing Sky Sports 1 turned down and another screen has MTV with sound turned up and it's beating away.

'They weren't watching that a few minutes ago, when I was hovering around,' I say to Wacko, who laughs.

'Well they probably thought you were an investor!' he says, grinning as he waves back to Swampy.

As we walk into the main open-plan office I sense that there is a buzz, but it's not a buzz like on a City trading floor. I see that there are about eighty people in this big open plan office. Everybody is sitting four to a large desk, facing one another. There are no separation boards blocking views around the office. Everyone is busy talking or walking about, looking relaxed, happy and focused. There are also lots of good-looking girls, who seem to be equal in number to the lads, and there's plenty of ethnic minorities all working together enjoying the banter. Everyone is casually dressed: jeans, fleeces, GAP sweatshirts, T-shirts. And then there's me in my pinstripe suit. This fine piece of tailoring now feels like a new school uniform on day one of a new term, which in this office means I now look as out of place as a zebra trotting down the M4 motorway.

We walk past an attractive girl who's playing a CD from her terminal. It's one of Robbie Williams's albums and 'Angels' is beating out of the little speakers on her desk. Not only this, but the phone on the desk next to her is ringing and nobody bothers to answer it, or cares when it rings off. Both of these capital offences would've got you skinned alive in my last place.

I look very closely at everyone and weigh up the place as fast as possible. And shit, I am not used to this! I cannot see anyone jumping up and down, screaming wildly like an action madman after their pin has just been pulled. In here nobody is shouting at anyone, or even screaming at somebody down a phone.

(I thought all offices were like my last place.)

We get down to where HR, accounts and the directors are all located. Glass windows give a truly panoramic view. Out of the windows to my left we can see the Post Office's Mount Pleasant complex, straight ahead of us is the Serious Fraud Office (SFO) and across the horizon in the distance is the City of London.

The SFO building is eyeballing everyone in here, but nobody seems to either know whom the grey anonymous-looking building belongs to, or remotely care. We walk past three people throwing a softball across the room (at high speed) to each other. Judging by their accents one is Australian, one is South African and the other hasn't spoken yet as he's just jumped out of his seat to try and catch a high ball thrown from the Aussie.

He catches it.

'Hey, not a bad catch for an English boy!' shouts the Aussie, as the department laughs.

'This is the accounts department, they're used to juggling balls,' says Wacko, as we walk past a woman's desk with a plaque on it that says 'Fit In or Fuck Off'.

We walk into Personnel's office which is more like a glass box and Wacko introduces me to Claire, one of iaxis's senior HR staff. She looks about twenty-four, has a fantastic body, with jet-black shoulder-length bobbed hair, and is far too good-looking to waste away in Personnel.

'Steve's going to be working for me, starts today in Biz Dev (Business Development),' says Wacko, looking impatient.

Claire looks at Wacko as if he's just landed from Mars.

'Yes, I know, I've just printed off his contract for you. It's probably still warm.'

'Good. Glad to see someone's doing some work around here!' says Wacko playfully. She pulls a smile and sticks her tongue out at him and laughs. 'Oh Wacko, can you sign Mike's holiday release form? He's taking the family to Euro Disney.'

'What! Tell him to bring his kids in to work; it's like Euro Disney in here most days!' he says, as we both laugh at the statement. Wacko signs the form with a squiggle, which seems to be enough.

'Right Steve, you're in Claire's hands. Claire, get him sorted and go easy on him. Show him around and make sure he doesn't do a runner before he signs up,' says Wacko, as he walks off before I can say thanks. As long as I've known Wacko he can't sit or stand still for longer than thirty-three seconds or else the grass might start growing under his shoes.

I hand Claire my CV.

'Thanks, do you smoke Steve?' she asks, as if it's been a tough morning already. I look at her watch as she picks up her latest Nokia mobile phone and Marlboro Light cigarettes from her desk. It's 9:20 a.m.

'No sorry, I never got started,' I say, as I notice her screensaver is a pair of sexy looking lips with a lady's forefinger pressed gently against them.

'Well I need a ciggie, so let's go down to the smokers' area on the second floor. That is where most of the work seems to get done around here. Well, down there or at Manhattan's outside. You can read your contract down there. I'll just phone the *Office of Technical Support*,' she says, as she picks up the phone and hits a button.

The phone is on speaker mode and it's the IT department who pick up the line.

'Hi Thomas, we've got another new start who starts this morning. See that he's sorted out for a PC, phone and a desk space. He's going to be next to Wacko, Nathan and Merlin on that quad.'

'Grunt.'

'And he's full time staff, not a contractor, so make sure he gets a Sony flat screen for his terminal, yeah?'

'Grunt.'

'And I'd like it fixed up ready within thirty minutes, please.'

'Grunt.'

'Thanks Thomas.'

She pushes the button on her phone to end the call, and I get the impression that she would push the button in the same manner to end his life if my gadgets weren't ready on time. I look on her desk: there's no personal photos, no postcards, nothing that gives anything away. This is one foxy, but very cool lady. I'll try not to cross her.

'Right Steve, let's go down for a smoke. You can leave your jacket in here.' she says as she takes my jacket from me and lays it on top of her desk.

'So why don't contractors get these flat screens as well?' I ask, as we get into the large lift which takes us down to the smokers' area on Level 2 in the ITN building.

'Well, most of them are on between six hundred and eight hundred pounds per day. We don't want to spoil them too much,' she says, shaking her head in disbelief.

'Certainly not,' I say, while I digest this amount of money.

In the smokers' area I grab one of the silver metallic-type tables while Claire goes to the drinks machine and gets two coffees in. I notice that there's only one other person down here, as I open my envelope and quickly review my contract. Everything is in it that was agreed last night. Top salary, great bonus with twenty-five days' holiday. Reporting to Mr Jackson, Director of

Network and Business Development, and my job title, "Business Development Executive", which sounds good.

Claire returns with two steaming hot plastic cups filled with coffee and lights up. 'Is everything okay with the contract?' She asks, with a look of intelligence in her eyes.

'Yes, it's perfect thanks.'

'Good, have a good read of the small print accompanying the letter. I've got to make a phone call. Speak to the boyfriend time…' she says, with a face that implies she might just be in a little bit of trouble.

She spots the puzzled look on my face.

'I didn't make it home last night,' she says with a cheeky little smile, as she walks off to use her mobile.

My mind suddenly goes on to autopilot, thinking about what she got up to last night!

I read the small print very carefully, and I have never seen a contract of employment like this before. It spells out equal opportunities, race relations, bullying, and respect for sexual orientation. I laugh at that one, remembering the boy band massacres! There are also clauses on grievance procedures, copyright, confidentiality, holidays, sickness days, warnings, pensions, health insurance, dismissal procedures and bonus schemes etc.

I quickly sign both copies with my black Cross fountain pen.

Claire clicks the button on her mobile and walks back looking a bit happier.

'Is everything okay?' she asks.

'Excellent thanks, I've signed both copies. Here's your one.'

'Thanks Steve, welcome to iaxis.'

'Thank you.'

I take a sip of coffee, which is shit, and out of genuine concern I ask how her boyfriend is.

'I've just ditched him,' she says bluntly.

'Really?' I say, not doing a good job at hiding my shock, while thinking that my feelings were right not to get on the wrong side of her.

'His time was up. He didn't like me going out partying with the crowd here and he was boring. But that's personal,' she says, raising a finely plucked eyebrow.

'Yes, sure,' I say, as I notice four out of the ten smoking tables down here now have people sitting at them, smoking away and chilling out.

'Do all these people work for iaxis as well?' I ask to get the conversation away from her love life, interesting though it seems to be.

She carefully looks around the other tables.

'Only him at the back.

I look over at 'him'. He was in before we were, and hasn't moved much since. His ashtray is full and he seems to be in a stressed out, deep thought trance. He looks like an older relation of James Hewitt with his reddish hair. He is also an "old boy", as I've spotted the gold signet ring on his little finger, proudly bearing the family name crest. Until I went into tanker broking I'd never previously seen these rings before. There, most of the chaps wore them...

I was grass green and completely soaking wet behind the ears (no excuse) when I asked the tanker broker next to me if his star sign was *Capricorn*. His face just screwed up and he looked at me as if I was a large pile of dog shit that had just projected itself from the heavens and landed on his desk!

'No I'm not a fucking *Capricorn*, Goddard!' he snarled, now aware that most of the desk was taking an active interest in the developing conversation. (By now I was shaking in my Hush Puppies.) 'Why'd you ask, anyway? You don't fancy me, do you?'

'*No!* Not at all, it's just that you're wearing a ring with a little goat on it,' I said, as he exploded with undisguised anger and embarrassment.

The desk erupted with laughter at him, thinking I was sticking my neck out and taking the piss out of his family name. It turns out it wasn't even a goat. My ignorance was kept hidden and I never asked him or anybody else a single dumb question ever again. (George refused to let me sit next to him when I joined tankers. He didn't want some silly dickhead asking him any questions whatsoever!)

'Be careful with him Steve, we all call him "Psycho". He's a senior director of iaxis and is responsible for market research and international marketing strategy. He spends a lot of time overseas and he is fucking mad. He frightens everyone in iaxis, especially all the girls. He's been bombarding quite a few with emails, love letters and personal invites to the theatre and to stay with him on his yacht. He's also got the hots for his PA, but she's having none of it and it's winding him up,' says Claire, staring away at him.

'Thanks for that,' I say, nodding my head slowly, ever careful not to catch his attention as I think to myself that I won't be asking that fucking nutter his star sign!

'The Indian-looking man over there is a presenter for Channel 4 News, he's down here quite a lot,' she says, motioning her eyes over to the coffee machine, where he is standing smoking a fag.

'Yes, I recognise his face, but I've got no idea what his surname is.'

'Neither do I,' she says warmly, as we both smile at this little piece of common ground.

The other tables are starting to fill up. I notice from her watch that the time is now 9:50 a.m. She says hello to the people that are starting to fill up the area. Most, I am told, are from Granada Media.

She takes out my CV and looks at it.

'So how long have you worked here, Claire?'

'About fourteen months now. I was with iaxis when we were called Telemonde. We moved into the old offices in Aldgate last April and those were wild days,' she says as she takes a draw on her cigarette, nodding slowly and smiling at the obviously fond memory. 'So tell me, what does a shipbroker do in tanker chartering? I've never heard of that career before,' she asks with interest.

'Well, in basic terms, a shipbroker negotiates the buying and selling or the chartering of a ship between the vessel owner and the company wishing to charter or buy it. In simplistic terms it's a case of a proud shipowner wanting lots of money for his/her ship in the current market, and the oil company who wants to pay as little as possible for the ship whatever the market conditions. The broker is in the middle of these two principles, assessing the market, which can change at any time depending on the level of deals being done in the market, and then negotiating between them both to get an agreement on the price and cut the deal. I tended to be more of an owner's broker and always tried to get the best deal for the shipowner. But you've also got to know the oil markets and global politics very well.'

'Sure. So is the negotiating quite difficult?' she asks, as she looks a bit more closely at my CV.

'Yes, too right it is. You have got to use a lot of psychology and pay attention when you're negotiating, because even the sound and tone of a person's voice on the phone can let you know a great deal more than they think they're giving away. In the tanker market it's almost like poker, but you can't read their faces down the phone line.'

'That sounds really cool,' she says innocently, as she can't see any battle scars since none are flesh wounds. 'How many deals did you do in five years?'

I am suddenly impressed that she noticed the dates on the CV. It is something that I always scan and don't bother to register.

'More than two hundred, I even did seven mad deals in one day back in ninety-six.'

'That's excellent. Why did you leave?'

Now is not the time to speak about the *Daily Mirror*, foxhunting and gin and tonics!

'The market went downhill and the firm had to make cutbacks. I was the last to join tanker chartering. It was a case of last in the department and first out. But before tankers I was with the firm's offshore division. There I looked after the towing of oil rigs, supplying oil rigs and construction support ships.'

Still impressed and genuinely interested, she goes for the kill.

'I would have thought your firm would've had a lot of money being based in Knightsbridge?'

(This is a very good question and I feel that she's asking it in order to satisfy her own intelligent curiosity as she builds up her overall picture of my situation...)

'Well, Seamart did have a lot of money, but the chairman's wife and her friend, who is an interior designer, both have a massive appetite for hard cash and gullible minds. So they did up the office and in the process they ran up a bill over one million dollars on carpets, wallpaper, curtains, paint and furniture. The Lord Chancellor might have been impressed, but nobody could spot the difference! The firm doesn't even own the property, it's on a lease, which means they could be out within twelve months!' I say, as my mind flashes back to the long faces in the old boardroom, while Claire laughs at the situation.

'Anyway, come on, Steve, let's get back up to the seventh floor. Your desk should be ready. But take off that tie and you'll look more casual,' she says, as she stubs out her second cigarette.

I do this right away as I notice that this Psycho chap is still in a deep trance and is now staring at the coffee machine.

Mr CH4 News's pager went off a while ago and he bolted.

We get in to the lift and she hits the button for the seventh floor. I notice just how much light is coming into the building from the glass ceiling high *above* as the clear morning sunlight breaks through the dark clouds and begins to penetrate 200 Gray's Inn Road down *below*.

'You'll fit in well here and I'm sure you'll pick up the techie jargon pretty quickly. Everybody else did. It's not that difficult, just wing it like everyone else and you'll do well,' says Claire, looking happy.

I nod my head and smile. It's not the first time I've winged it. When I was twenty-three years old, I decided to go backpacking. I'd just completed my post grad in business management and I'd never travelled on my own or even outside Europe. I went to Trailfinders and booked a one-way ticket to Bangkok with Aeroflot with a view to hitching a lift back home from

Singapore on a ship. I got the jabs, bought The Lonely Planet's *South East Asia on a Shoestring* and left within a few days. I didn't actually start reading the guidebook until I was on the plane. The flight was uneventful apart from spending six hours in Tashkent, which looked like it was either half built, or half destroyed.

Once I'd safely landed in Bangkok, I got a taxi into the city's Khao San district. After one hour in South-East Asia, experiencing the intimidating heat, humidity, smell and noise of Bangkok, I think in all honesty had I had a return ticket I would have got a taxi back to the airport! But I didn't have one, so I headed south and out of Bangkok. I lasted for six weeks, and spent most of it in the Malaysian jungle on my way to Singapore.

In the past I've put my faith in the unknown, taken chances, and it's always paid off. Here, I got by without a single scrape. But I ran out of money in Singapore and decided to fly back to the UK and start looking for a career. The FCO doesn't loan money to backpackers so they can stay in the sunshine.

The morning after I returned home, Seamart's advert was in the paper. It was quite small and anonymous looking. But on offer was a career as a "Trainee Shipbroker".

I started work a couple of weeks later.

We get back to Claire's box-like glass office and I collect my jacket off her desk and notice the dark clouds closing in overhead as the sun disappears.

'Any problems, Steve, and you just give me a little tinkle,' she says kindly.

'Of course I will. And thanks for the coffee,' I say, as we hold eye contact, smiling. I'm still in shock that she's just liquidated her boyfriend. I bet he didn't know that was going to happen when he woke up alone this morning.

'Come on, I'll show you to your desk and make sure you don't run out of the building,' she adds laughing, as if she knows it's a long walk from her office to my desk when your stomach is yet to calm down. (For Thomas's sake, or whatever his name is, I just hope my PC and phone is all set up and working. She's broken one heart already this morning and it's not even 10 a.m.)

Walking to my new desk I notice nobody reads any newspapers. There are a few editions of this morning's *Metro* sitting on desks, but that's it. The *Daily Telegraph* is nowhere in sight. I now like this place even more and I haven't even got to my desk yet.

Thankfully my computer is already set up within the quad. Thomas is just switching on the PC with a Sony flat screen, and it works. He doesn't look happy about being in the office today. He's got a mobile phone attached to his trouser belt and has a green T-shirt with "PRIVATEER" stamped on it. His hair is longish but thinning on top, and probably hasn't been washed since the day he graduated from techie school somewhere near Tolworth. He looks to be in his late thirties and if he weren't here would probably be working in the backroom of Radio Rentals in Croydon.

'Thomas The Techie' (TTT) picks up a techie-looking *red* book with the words "C2" and "CT-130 ANSI C" on it and in a few grunts tells Claire that my PC is now live.

'Good, there's four more starting on Monday,' she says, like he's got a lot more work to do.

TTT nods, but offers no small talk and just walks away back to his den in the *Office of Technical Support* or Techieland.

Claire smiles at me as she sees it's the first time I've seen a real techie.

'He's a bit stroppy and highly strung, but since his mum tried to tell him to get a place of his own, he's just got worse!' she says, as she shakes her head at his situation.

Wacko and two other blokes are walking back towards the quad. Both have longish trendy bobbed hair down to their shoulders. One is about twenty-five and tallish. The other looks in his fifties, has round glasses and looks like an older version of John Lennon with greying hair. Both look chilled out and very switched on.

'He's signed,' Claire says to Wacko as the three of them approach.

'Good, you've done your job then. Now go and get some more people to sign!' he says, laughing as he sticks at least one finger up at him.

Wacko turns to me and looks at me as if I'm mad for listening to him last night and we shake hands. I'm now in and part of the iaxis "Biz Dev" team. And I work for him.

'These are your two workmates. They've just been told they'll be responsible for bringing you up to speed on Internet connectivity with other backbones and anything else Internet related. And you'll be responsible for listening. Do you know what you'll be doing?' he asks, like he's having a laugh to himself.

I shake my head, trying not to look thick, as I remembered something about the initials IP from last night, which now feels like last week.

They introduce themselves as Nathan and Merlin, just as Wacko walks off. (I think he felt the grass under his shoes.)

Nathan is the young, very intelligent looking one and Merlin is the older, wiser one.

Nathan goes to his PC and clicks off his "SENIOR SMART" news ticker screensaver, while I check out the position of my desk within the room. There's no cityscape panoramic view for me, just the inside hollowness of the ITN building. I do get a good view of the SATCOM dishes on the roof, which I can see through the glass ceiling. I also see that the rain is now suddenly beating down onto it as well. This office does look good. Everything is up to date and the latest modern gizmo gadgets seem to be available if you want them. The atmosphere still isn't charged and there are more Robbie Williams vibes coming out from that girl's desk not too far away. And more importantly, there are attractive girls walking around freely who are not being harassed, intimidated and taunted.

In Seamart actually seeing a girl walking around the tanker desk was about as rare as seeing a panda having a stroll along the Great Wall of China. They viewed coming to the tanker room with as much trepidation as one would have regarded climbing over and covertly crossing the old Berlin Wall in 1982. Apart from one highly talented female broker in offshore, all the brokers were male. Rather sad, but true. (There were no black or Asian brokers whatsoever...)

Merlin has a mouthful of coffee and subconsciously scans me up and down while trying to mentally size me up in under half a second. After four seconds he suddenly asks, 'So you are going to be our peering guru?' He is not too sure how to take me, as I'm dressed like a City merchant banker.

I nod slowly and laugh slightly apprehensively, while inside I feel terrified.

He then informs me that I'm going to be setting up peering contracts for Internet connections. Not only this but I'll be putting together a strategy for Internet peering with the other members of Neutral Internet Exchanges (NIXs) around Europe and liaising with Kathryn who is our big Internet supplier for our US interests.

My face doesn't give away my ignorance of this *hidden* new world.

'Merlin, I know nothing at all about this Internet peering/Internet network connectivity, but I learn quickly.'

Merlin learns at lightning speed and looks at me like I'm training to climb K2 by going for a walk in the Lake District in July. He smiles, and thinks for another second. 'Don't worry Steve, if you can understand the very basics of what's involved and if you get on with people, then you're laughing.' He says in his Scots accent with a Morningside, Edinburgh dialect, sounding very much like that of Sean Connery. This reassures me.

'Do you get on with people, Steve?' he asks curiously.

Although this seems like an ordinary, everyday question, I cannot remember ever being asked it before.

'Yes,' I say automatically, as my mind refocuses on a few wankers I wouldn't mind seeing shot.

'Good. *That's the most important thing in the world.* Not just in here. If you can get along with other Internet companies' peering and connectivity managers, they'll connect with us because they like not only our network, but also you as a person. The Internet is a very small industry and Internet peering is like an elite club. In the future it will all get much more complicated than this with rules and procedures, but at the moment it is relatively informal. You look and sound like a friendly person, so let's see how you do.'

I'm thinking to myself, 'Yeah that's okay; please just tell me what it means…'

'What were you doing before you walked in here?' he asks politely, as if he's about to put the final few pieces into his seven-hundred-piece jigsaw of me, which he's assembled in the last two minutes.

'I worked in shipbroking as a tanker broker. I used to charter oil tankers to oil companies and trading houses.' I say this as I notice the time on his Timex watch.

It is close to mid-morning and I still haven't heard anybody scream, bellow, snarl or slam any phones down. More importantly my eyes haven't clocked anyone swaggering around the office floor with an ego from previous deals that says they have the biggest dick in the jungle. Nor is anybody loudly informing the rest of the office and downstairs that they have actually got the biggest dick in the jungle regardless of what deals they've done!

'A tanker broker, that's impressive. So why do oil companies use brokers and not just do the deals between themselves and the shipowners?' asks Merlin, sounding surprised. (This is the most full-on question you can ask a broker.)

'Well, brokers fix shipping deals and access the markets in the world's oil regions, the Black Sea, West Africa, Persian Gulf, North Sea, Mediterranean, South East Asia and the Gulf of Mexico all day long. We know the market intelligence and charter rates of various ships. But we are also used because we have good negotiation skills and can consult and advise on pricing levels in the market and on various contractual issues. If the two principals were negotiating directly it could easily become a battle of wills and nobody would ever back down and compromise for fear of losing face and flinching first. A broker removes this aspect and encourages compromise and mediation.'

'Good. I didn't realise brokers actually got involved in chartering ships,' he says, looking happy that he's learning something new.

'Neither did I until I saw the small job advert in the paper,' I reply truthfully.

'So why did they choose you?' he asks, still eyeballing me as he sizes me up.

'Well, I studied politics and international relations at university and that helped,' I say convincingly, as tales of fascism and office warfare can wait a good while longer.

'Ah yes. And you're obviously bright and there's lots of politics in oil,' says Merlin, understanding why the elders of the firm had chosen me just as he's about to place the final few pieces into his jigsaw puzzle.

'There's also a lot of oil in politics,' I remind him, as I think back to the politics behind the 1991 Gulf War with Saddam, where the cost of every single allied soldier, bomb, bullet and missile was backcharged to Saudi Arabia and the Gulf States.

["...This was after the House of Saud had been told by the Bush administration and the Agency which 'engineered' Operation Zapata using vessels called *Barbara* and *Houston* that Saudi Arabia was next on Saddam's invasion list of August 1990..."]

'*That's correct,*' he says, looking pleased.

'What about you, Merlin, what do you do here?'

'I'm the architect of the IP backbone, which K-Net are constructing for us.'

'So how long have you been here?' I ask, as I notice that his wise old eyes haven't left mine just yet.

'About ten months now.'

'And before that, were you doing IP design work for BT's Internet network?' I ask, as that's the only company I associate the Internet with.

Merlin is momentarily stunned. He gasps and looks at me like I've just trashed his completed jigsaw.

'*B-R-I-T-I-S-H T-E-L-E-C-O-M!!*' he says incredulously, and is now seriously concerned at my sudden naivety as the whites of my eyes start to dazzle him.

'I'm *really* sorry. I never meant to insult you!' I say quickly, bracing myself for a frenzied verbal assault that I am sure is going to leave his mouth and hit its target standing just two feet away.

'No, no, not BT! We only laugh at them; we don't ever talk about them in a good light,' he says laughing, seeing the funny side.

'Why not? Don't they make a few billion pounds profit every year?' I ask, really interested in his response and trying like hell to cover up my ignorance.

'They're an elephant, Steve. A big pink and white spotted elephant that could well come to the end of its corporate life within three, maybe four years. Nobody in this industry takes them seriously any more. You know, if it wasn't for their own arrogance and incompetence, BT could've ruled the Internet and telecoms world. But they couldn't move quickly enough and they got beaten. If anything, they've held back the advancement of the Internet in this country.'

'Really?'

'Oh yes. You see, back in the early/mid-Nineties, none of the thousands of BT's internal management committees could agree on whether or not the Internet was the future. And BT still thought they were magnificent, so BBN, UUNet and Level 3 and the other big American players took over and now rule the Internet world instead. BT has been left to eat the dust. It is hard to believe this, but in the year 2000 they use the same copper wires at their telephone exchanges that have been there since the 1940s. Some copper wires have been in place earlier than that! And they try and sell the idea to the British public that they are world leaders in the Internet. Don't believe it Steve, it's all *smoke and mirrors*.'

'So do you think they will get their act together?' I ask, as I think about some of the "sensitive" work they do for HMG at Oswestry and Martlesham Heath, which really is world class.

'We shall see. It will take change right at the top and a whole new cultural climate and that is pretty challenging, even in this boom market,' he says, as I also remember that I nearly once bought some shares in British Telecom.

'Okay, so, if you weren't working for BT, which company was it?' I ask thinking it must've been one of the major American Internet/telecoms companies that taught him his obvious worldly wisdom.

'I am a doctor in nuclear physics and I worked for the European Organisation for Nuclear Research, or CERN, based in Switzerland. I worked there for a good few years,' he says casually.

I nod my head and hope that he didn't spot my jaw dropping onto the office floor, which of course he picked up before he'd even spoken.

My head goes into a tailspin. If this guy ever wanted a job in shipbroking, the chaps at Seamart would bite his hand off. Old Rupert would end up taking something a bit more than spare clothes and his teddy bear in his suitcase, next time he visited Kuwait. Henry would just take his suitcase to any country that's pissed him off that morning. And after listening to the

Today programme this morning, I think he would be at Waterloo by now checking on to the Eurostar after buying a return ticket for Brussels!

'I read the EA-168 manual on Multiplexing Technology and afterwards I started studying Internet Protocol just for fun. Now I design Internet networks and get paid a fortune for doing it. So that's why I'm here, Steve,' he says, as he answers his desk phone which is now ringing. It is his wife.

I am contemplating Merlin's intelligence. If E.T. ever came back, this guy would be playing chess with it, for light entertainment.

Nathan, despite looking tired, has been watching and taking all of this in. Then Wacko walks up to us and he now looks somewhat downbeat.

'Steve, let's go to the boardroom and have a chat,' he says, just as I've noticed he's carrying a white A4 envelope and is looking down at his new Timberland desert boots. The envelope has *"P-2"* written on it. *My heart sinks.* The blood in my body has drained from my head and torso and is now concentrated in my legs, which both seem a lot heavier to move now than they did ten seconds ago. The memory of being called down into the last boardroom is still raw.

My heart is beating and my throat is dry as I walk behind him. I look down at my well-polished *Church* shoes, while trying not to make eye contact with anyone. I am also carrying my raincoat with me. I don't want to walk back in here to pick it up if I'm going to be binned before I've even sat down at my desk.

We walk past the two pretty blondes on the reception. Both are speaking about a party last night, while I am once again suddenly looking forward to being a dog catcher with a London council. We open more glass doors, and then another set of glass doors and see the immaculate sculptures on the glass walls of the boardroom. No brick walls in here, just glass. As we walk into the boardroom, which is another goldfish bowl type design, I quickly see that it is the most modern, chic, technologically advanced boardroom I have ever seen. The table is solid glass, an expensive, heavy, smoked-type glass. The glass forming the boardroom walls again does not look cheap. This whole room has been professionally designed with taste and no expense was spared.

'Take a seat Steve,' says Wacko as he takes a call on his Nokia mobile.

On the boardroom table there are three laptop connection points that mechanically rise up from within the centre. There is a digital phone system, with twin matching cameras monitoring the table for realtime conference calls and board meetings with the iaxis offices in New York's Chrysler building, Germany, France, Italy, Holland, Switzerland and Spain. At the far end of the table on the wall is a six-by-six-foot plasma screen, backed by a major piece of computer hardware that links a DVD, CD stereo and other futuristic looking gadgets with which I am not familiar.

All twenty-four chairs are black leather and are presidential in style. On the ceiling above the spotlights look like little diamonds as they shine away illuminating the glass table and all those who sit below them.

The view from this room is of West and North London with the BT/GCHQ Tower, CentrePoint and Euston Tower dominating the near skyline. There is no view of the glass ceiling or the grey SFO building from any seat at the glass table. Very quickly one sees that there are no cobwebs in this room. This room was clearly designed with the next century in mind, and not the "glorious past" of the last two.

Wacko clicks off his call.

Both my hands are now sweating and leave a clear forensic imprint on the immaculate surface of the glass table. Looking at Wacko, I am now mentally prepared for the worst. I am thinking his vice-president has said 'no chance' to my employment with iaxis. This would be down to my lack of knowledge about Internet and telecoms. I would of course understand, be thankful for the insight and leave gracefully.

'Steve, I've just checked with my VP, you're not eligible to buy into the iaxis company's share participation scheme. *Naturally* it's a bit of a shock, yeah?'

My ears were tuned to hearing totally different words altogether and he picks up the confusion on my almost *Albino*-white facial complexion.

'One of the main shareholders (name withheld) of our Dutch holding company, iaxis NV, has lent almost all of us in here one hundred per cent of our salaries in cash. This was lent to anyone who wanted to buy shares in iaxis. At the time, in November 1999, we could buy shares in iaxis at roughly forty dollars per share. Some people here have extended that and ploughed in seventy-five per cent of their savings, and some have taken out further bank loans. My vice-president and the chief financial officer have both put in over one million dollars of their own savings, to buy shares in iaxis. Now iaxis is worth between four hundred and eight hundred dollars per share, up from forty dollars, which means nearly everyone at iaxis is going to be a *fucking millionaire!'* he says, as he takes a deep breath and doesn't hide it.

I hide mine.

'Some people are going to be walking away with several hundred thousand pounds. Others will walk away with several million pounds. The ex-chairman's even had *The Sunday Times* researchers on to him. He's going to be in their "Rich List", number one hundred and forty-one or something, with over two hundred million pounds to his name. He's so proud of his rating, it makes me feel sick! But it did make me laugh how pissed off he was that some bloke from WorldCom is going to be ahead of him in the rich list! He wasn't happy about that!' he says, laughing away at the iaxis version of "big boys games, big boys rules".

(I do have money to invest and if I were being asked if I would like to invest in iaxis, then I would say 'Yes'. In this, there is no doubt at all.)

'So what can go wrong in this market?' I ask, as the imprints of my palms have now dried up on the surface of the glass table.

'Fuck all, really. The board is adamant that iaxis is worth a minimum of one billion dollars after flotation and the chances of us floating for less than this are remote. If we did float on the NASDAQ for less than one billion dollars, iaxis would just get "lost in the noise!" he says, laughing.

'So is everything still going according to plan?'

'Yes it is, but you should be aware that the chairman wants the shareholders to sell now. "Build fast and sell quickly" is one of many phrases you'll hear. We'll all make tonnes of cash and run off to live some dreams. His dream is this sub-sea fibre optic cable going round the Med, which he wants to build at a cost of nine hundred million dollars. There's some history to this and there's trench warfare going on right here in the boardroom over selling the company.'

'So have you had any offers yet?' I ask, thinking of the huge sums of money involved in this glass outfit.

'We have had whispers of offers from the boards of other telecoms companies, but they've all been for around five hundred million pounds. One of the main investors even picked up the phone and screamed at them to read the newspaper articles... *"iaxis is worth billions so fuck off!"* And they all walked away licking their wounds!' he says, as we both have a laugh at this.

(He laughs at the very close memory of the incident. I laugh because I still have a job and don't have to leave the ITN building and buy a dog lead from the Fulham pet shop!)

Wacko opens up the white envelope with the iaxis logo and "P-2" on the front of it and pulls out a few newspaper articles. It's very obvious that the market hype is in full swing and the iaxis PR department looks like it can work better than a mid-nineties Media Management Unit, ["...CCITT Group 3"] at Hercules House ["...Dreamland"], Hercules Road ["...Wonderland Road"] London, SE1.

'TELECOMS CARRIER PLANS £2 BILLION FLOAT'

Daily Telegraph

'IAXIS PLANS IPO TO FUND MEDITERRANEAN NETWORK'
Wall Street Journal Europe

'IAXIS PLANS £1.5 BILLION FLOAT' *The Times*

'TELECOMS BOOM GATHERS PACE AS IAXIS UNVEILS £1.5 BILLION FLOTATION PLAN' *The Independent*

'IAXIS LAYS PLAN FOR £1 BILLION FLOAT' *Daily Express*

'IAXIS SEEKS £600 MILLION VALUE IN FLOTATION'
Financial Times

'SECRETARIES TO GET £60K BONUS IN IAXIS WINDFALL'
Daily Mail

I've checked all the dates and they are the same, 13th October 1999, apart from the *Financial Times*. They broke the story the previous month.

'So I'm really sorry about this, Steve,' says Wacko, with genuine regret at seeing me missing out. 'But we'll give you a few thousand extra share options at ninety dollars per share, just so you don't miss out too much on the party.'

'Thanks! But I'm still happy to have a new career opportunity in front of me.'

'No probs, but you can't actually sell your share options until three years after we arrive on the NASDAQ.'

'That's okay. I'm more than happy to take all these share options and I'll cash them in as soon as I eventually see them!'

'Sure, but time moves very fast in here and never forget that anything can happen. Three years is a hell of a long time away. And in this industry, for a start up like iaxis, three months' survival is almost one calendar year,' says Wacko, who has just checked the time on his watch.

(Harold Wilson once said that 'a week is a long time in politics'. Looking ahead, three years in iaxis seems like a very long time indeed.)

'Too right, time moves fast!' I say as I contemplate the week so far, and we both get up to leave.

'Do you remember that newspaper called *The European* which went bust last year?'

'Yes I do, but I never bought a copy.'

'Well iaxis is now working in their old offices. They used to be up here on the seventh floor.'

'I hope we do better than them!' I say, looking across the skyline towards the old-looking 'BT/GCHQ spy tower' with its nine spook dishes ["including the CIA microwave relay dish..."] on it. ["...The Russians, French and Chinese still take a considerable interest in that huge spy tower."]

'You can say that again! At iaxis, everyone is looking at increasing their investments a minimum of tenfold. And we've been working like dogs to make it happen,' he says, as he shakes his head at the madness of the market as we leave the glass boardroom and walk towards the reception area.

(...There may well have been method in the madness of the expenses of the glass boardroom. The boardroom has to look the business. iaxis on the seventh floor of the ITN building has to look like it is worth over one billion dollars. If iaxis had the same product, but a boardroom in a prefabricated caravan in the car park, who would have taken us seriously? Would Rothschild's, coming into iaxis in December 1999, value the company at hundreds of millions of dollars if this were the case? No chance. On Wall Street, it is all about "perception", "confidence" and the "management of expectations" by the telecoms analysts. This keeps the Internet/telecoms hype going skywards, glass ceiling or not.)

We walk past reception and Wacko asks Charlotte, the blonde who greeted me this morning, if my office landline and mobile number are on the main telephone list.

'Yeah, they are already on it,' she says, as she files her nails and tries to see what Swampy is up to in the Network Operations Centre (NOC).

It looks like Swampy is showing everyone how he landed after a couple of police officers from Thames Valley picked him up by his arms and legs and threw him out of his tree house and told him to get a haircut and a fucking job!

'So don't you want your own private glass room?' I ask Wacko, as we walk back into the office, which I am so grateful to see once again.

'No, I like to be seated on the main floor and see things from the centre... from the inside, if you like. I'm hardly at my desk, so I don't give a shit about nice views. At Enron, even their VPs sit at desks next to their colleagues. It's good for teamwork.'

As we pass other people's desks I notice a lot of magazines with fast cars on them. Most seem to be on the desks belonging to the attractive girls working here. And back at our quad I see Wacko is reading a glossy yachting magazine. I now know what he plans to spend some of his cash on. I pick it up and look at the photos, which look very good.

He spots me looking through the pages.

'I'm going to buy a Warrior 40. It's basically a poor man's yacht for someone who wants to look good. It doesn't cost much, but it's okay. After this, I'm thinking about keeping it off St Kitts and not working again!'

'That sounds good,' I say as I place my suit jacket on the back of my chair and walk over to the other side of the room to hang up my raincoat.

As I return to the quad I can hear a classic tune vibrating rather loudly out of Nathan's desk speakers, which I recognise straight away.

It's 'A Final Hit', by Leftfield.

Nathan clearly sees I appreciate his music taste.

'Steve, let's go downstairs to Manhattan's and grab a coffee. We can have a chat and I'll try to bring you up to speed on Internet backbone connectivity/peering,' he says in a chilled out London accent.

'Okay, sounds good,' I say, as I still haven't sat down at my new desk yet.

Merlin is in deep thought and is staring at a highly advanced and seriously complicated looking set of Internet *(nuclear)* circuits on an A3 sized piece of paper. As Merlin scratches his head, I notice that the header of his project has the title '*Telecommunications Infrastructures (EA-049)*' and I begin to wonder just what I've got myself into. He also has "CLARINET MERLIN" on his very large flat screen as a screensaver and if he has noticed my presence he doesn't show it at all. He is far too focused on his super advanced IP network, which he is putting together. And he seems to be doing it faster than I would be completing the crossword puzzle in the *Daily Mirror*!

The music ends as Nathan picks up his battered-looking leather wallet and we leave the room to go downstairs for some coffee.

CHAPTER 4

The Manhattan Coffee Co. is right next door to the ITN building. After we get our drinks in, we take a couple of seats by the window. From my chair I see that most of the cars seem to have their headlights on as I watch them splash their way in the pissing rain. The rainbow I saw this morning as I left my flat is now nowhere to be seen.

'So how did you land this job?' I ask Nathan, whose eyes display an intelligence most of us can only look at in awe.

'I was studying electronics and telecommunications engineering at Cambridge University and graduated within the top two per cent of my year. iaxis had an advert in the vacancy lists recruiting undergraduates. Over four hundred applied and I was one of six taken on. They interviewed me in the pub twice and that was it. A week later I was taken on as the executive assistant to the chairman who was ex-WorldCom/MFS.' I nod my head as I absorb this with relative ease, thinking about my interview in the pub last night.

'What was he like to work for?'

'He hardly spoke to me!' he says, laughing.

'Why, what was the problem?' I ask, looking puzzled.

Nathan gives a knowing smile. 'Well, I think it had a lot to do with me not being female, wearing a short skirt and having a good pair of legs! But it's great fun. I joined last year and from being a poor undergraduate who was not long back from travelling and looking for a career, I was suddenly an executive assistant to this guy who's in charge of a telecoms company worth over one billion dollars! Soon afterwards I was working on special projects, such as web-hosting, co-location, IP networking, peering and streaming media.'

I hope my face doesn't display the blankness that just ran through my mind. But from what I've seen of iaxis so far, all credit to the chairman for having the balls to set up iaxis in the first place.

Nathan takes a draw on his Marlboro Light and exhales.

'So are you happy you joined iaxis?' I ask as he coughs out fag fumes.

'Too right I am! When I was at Cambridge I spent two summers working away in this fucking awful engineering factory in Wolverhampton. I thought that was a normal place to work and that was going to be my future career. And then iaxis pulled me in to telecoms and I've never looked back. I've been all over the USA on web hosting and streaming media jollies. And not long after I joined I was sorting out some dodgy telecoms business that iaxis was doing down in Italy. Dealing with Italians is a real experience. Nothing is ever straightforward with them... And it takes forever to get sorted out.'

'So what were you up to with the Italians?' I ask inquisitively.

Nathan suddenly looks very edgy and is a bit uncomfortable speaking about it.

'Back in the third quarter of last year, iaxis was looking at some deal in Rome involving Telecom Italia, Olivetti, Technost and Serti and a ten billion dollar debt transition. That's all I'm going to say on it,' he says as he draws a line with his forefinger across his throat. 'Have you heard of a chap called *"Mr Luciani"*, Steve?'

'No.'

'Well he was involved with iaxis right back at the beginning. His town house suddenly went on fire when all this shit was going down after the deal fell apart. The fire brigade said it was an electrical fault on a domestic appliance that caused it...'

'Sure it was. "Accidents" happen all the time,' I say, *naturally* looking for a reaction. He's not bothered at all and quickly changes the subject as he tries to bring me up to speed on Internet peering and connectivity and talks me through the very basics.

(...Internet backbone connectivity is really the connection of two companies' Internet networks. Once this connection is established both Internet backbones then exchange Internet traffic across each other's networks. This is called Internet peering. And the connections take place at Neutral Internet Exchanges, or NIXs. However, as far as iaxis is concerned, it is essential that we get as many Internet peering contracts in place as soon as possible. This will improve our Internet backbone's efficiency and this is paramount when we're trying to sell space on it to potential customers. iaxis is building one of the most advanced Internet backbones in Europe. The first thing our sales and marketing people will be asked when they try and sell capacity on it, is which other Internet backbones we are connected to. Not what technology we have...)

'So you understand Steve, nothing is more important to the iaxis Internet backbone than who our backbone is connected to at these NIXs. And this now falls down to you, mate.'

The passing cars are now flashing at me telling me to dip my eyes!

'Fucking hell, Nathan! This sounds as difficult as rocket science!'

He laughs. 'It's not that difficult to understand. Just ask Merlin and me loads of questions and read the basics a few times. It will sink in naturally,' he says, as I notice a dark coffee stain on my new *Church* shoes.

'Look, do you have anything on Internet peering and connectivity which I can read?' I ask, as my heart is beating a few beats faster than when we walked into the coffee shop several minutes ago.

'Sure, I've got loads of stuff. And there's a fantastic web site called "whatis.com". Nearly everyone in iaxis is plugged into it all day long, trying to learn the techie definitions,' he says, as I laugh at the thought of everyone winging it.

'It's true, it's how everyone at iaxis understands things, but we learn quickly. Anyway, thank fuck it's a Friday!' he adds, as he launches off in to a major yawn that rings his eardrums so much he has to prod the left one with his little finger like he's scratching his brain. This sets me off on a yawning spree as well.

'Do we have a peering contract already made up which I can send out after I call them?' I ask, trying to cover up my yawn as my eyes water.

'Well, most companies have their own Internet peering contract and are not too fussy about which one is used. Some will even peer on a gentleman's agreement. What iaxis has done is this: we got hold of Level 3's peering agreement and chopped it up. We got it down from seven pages of American lawyer-speak crap talk to two pages and called it, the "iaxis Peering Agreement".'

'Didn't they mind?' I ask, seeing the funny side.

He shrugs his shoulders, unconcerned. 'I don't know, nobody's said anything. And besides the document has now got iaxis written all over it, so technically it's fucking ours!'

'How many of these Internet peering contracts do I have to do?'

He pulls out a list of all the members of the other Internet backbones that I've got to establish a connection with. There are over one hundred and ninety Internet and telecom companies.

'How long is it likely to take?' I ask, as I dip my eyes.

Nathan shrugs his shoulders. 'Maybe six months if we're lucky. But how long is a piece of string?' he says, as he laughs quietly.

I don't laugh at all.

'Well good luck, Steve, just brass it out as much as you can.'

I start to gently bite my bottom lip at the K2 climb facing me as I prepare to leave base camp. I stare out of the coffee shop window and it is still pissing it down.

'So you like Leftfield then?' I ask, as 'A Final Hit' is still in my head.

'Yeah, big time,' he says, as we nod in agreement on the brilliance of their music.

'They're fantastic. I can listen to their music any time of the day,' I say, taking a sip of my hot cappuccino.

Nathan completes his jigsaw of me in under a second and totally agrees. (I don't tell him that if the band were standing in front of me in the queue at Marks and Spencer's food counter on Putney High Street on a Sunday afternoon, I wouldn't recognise any of them.)

'Their music reminds me of the time I went travelling when I was still an undergrad at Cambridge,' he says, relaxing and subconsciously drifting back to this idyllic memory of the not too distant past.

'Oh really, where did you go travelling?' I ask, keen to expand on this increasing area of common ground.

'Two mates and I drove an old 1974 Land Rover 101 from London to Kathmandu. We travelled through North Africa, Egypt, the Middle East and right down to the southern tip of India and up to Nepal.'

'That's outstanding. So what was the best place?'

'Iran. The people are so friendly and helpful.'

'Yes, I like the Iranians as well. When I was in shipbroking, they used to send us a fax at Christmas time sincerely wishing us a "Happy Christmas". You'd never get the Saudis or Kuwaitis doing that.'

(He tries to remember the last time he saw a fax, which was probably in 1995 or something!)

'So did you have any dodgy moments? That sounds like a few hairy places to be travelling in,' I ask out of interest.

He takes another big draw and slowly exhales. 'Yeah, we got shot at by the Syrian Secret Police just outside Damascus.'

My eyes focus on his as my ears sharply register this sudden and unexpected statement. My face doesn't give away any surprise.

'Shit, that's different! Why did they shoot at you, were you in a military area?' I ask, as I put down my cappuccino without taking a sip.

'Well, sort of, it was just off the main road into Damascus, forty miles east of the city. We were asleep in the vehicle when their motorbike lights woke us up. We started the motor and tried to bolt, thinking these guys were bandits out to turn us over. Then they opened fire on us! Three rounds came through the side door, one missing the gas canisters by about two fucking inches and another missing my mate's head by less than a foot. He was lucky. They pulled up alongside us and aimed their AK-47s at us while I was driving away. And they held their aim at my head.'

'So what happened then?'

(He takes another big drag on his fag.)

'We stopped and we were all dragged out at gunpoint, forced to the floor and were spreadeagled face down on the dirt track with a barrel touching the back of our heads. After they frisked us, we were bundled into an unmarked car and they took all three of us, plus our vehicle to the Secret Police's central headquarters in Damascus where everyone was in plainclothes apart from the boss. Back there they had a quick look inside at all our gear and realised we weren't terrorists, but were tourists. And British tourists. And that this was a big balls-up on their part. Their superintendent then went fucking ape-shit with his paramilitary squad and afterwards they gave up their rooms for us so we could get some sleep!'

'And the next morning they looked the other way?'

'Basically, yes. A smartly dressed middle-aged Arab appeared at the headquarters and he spoke perfect English. After a few minutes he got this tricky situation all cleaned up. Our Land Rover was taken away and our bullet-damaged door was expertly repaired. It was a very professional job, almost like it never happened.'

(Nathan's fag is now finished and he lights up another one.)

'So were you looked after okay?'

'Yes, we were really well fed, with them all joining in laughing away asking little discreet political questions. Then all of a sudden, this smartly dressed Arab who sorted out the situation, just pulled out a little Minox and took our pictures eating breakfast, relaxing, having a laugh, and then got up and left.'

Nathan takes a sip of his hot black coffee as his mind races back in time. 'That was fucking terrifying,' he says, as his eyes stare wildly out into the street.

'Shit! That sounds a bit hardcore, mate,' I say, as my mind races back, thinking about the headlines in the *Daily Telegraph* if they'd all been wasted in Syria.

"THREE BRITISH CAMBRIDGE STUDENTS SHOT DEAD BY SYRIAN SECRET POLICE. FCO OUTRAGED."

A few of the chaps around the desk would have gone absolutely bonkers at that!

Trying not to laugh to myself, I rub my eyes and tell him nothing's ever gone wrong on my travels so far, as I touch the wooden table. I take a deep breath and inhale most of Nathan's Marlboro Light.

'You go travelling as well?' he asks, looking surprised.

'Yes, I've done loads of travelling and photography in the Third World.

That's how I met Wacko, we were on the same backpacking trek in Peru going to Machu Picchu nearly five years ago.'

'Really? I'd never have guessed. So where else have you been then?' he asks sounding totally surprised that this person from 'suitland' knows what a backpack is.

'Well, I've also trekked in Argentina, Bolivia, Sri Lanka, Nepal, Kenya, Tanzania, Zanzibar, Botswana, Namibia, Zimbabwe, Zambia, South Africa, China, Thailand, Malaysia and Singapore. Last year I was in Cambodia and Vietnam, and took thirty-seven rolls of Fuji Velvia film with me.'

'That's excellent. So what's your favourite place so far?'

'Peru. The Inca Trail to Machu Picchu is simply stunning. I've never felt so at peace. Namibia is a close second. The orange sand dunes in the Sossusvlei are the highest in the world and were totally amazing. It took the group over an hour to climb to the top of the biggest dune. I got in some good photography as well.'

'Outstanding. So are you with a photographic stock agency or anything?'

'No, I've never really bothered to do anything with my travel portfolio, but I might do in future,' I say, as I think it will now be a while before I see the old Hilton Hotel in *Islamabad*.

'What gear do you use?' he asks, looking serious.

'Well, for 35mm I use a Leica R8. But for medium format I've started using a Mamiya 7 II.'

He takes a draw on his fag and exhales before speaking. 'My stepmum's current boyfriend was a top photographer during the Vietnam War.'

'Really? What's his name?' I ask as my mind races through all the Magnum photo agency greats and other world-class photographers whose work I am familiar with from that era.

'Have you heard of Tim Page?' he asks shyly.

My chin just misses my cappuccino, and my eyes light up the whole street.

'Tim Page!' I say, totally gobsmacked and now in sudden awe of Nathan's presence. 'Yes, of course I have heard of him! I've read all his books and been to see some of his work on display. He's even got one of his award-winning shots hanging up in the Foreign Correspondents' Club in Phnom Penh.'

'He's a really good guy and he's also lucky to still be alive,' says Nathan, who now looks a bit serious.

'Yes!' I say knowingly, having read about him getting shot to pieces by US 'friendly fire' during the "American War" in Vietnam.

'So what is he up to now?' I ask, as I could do with going away on a photography trek.

'He's doing a photographic assignment for Bloomberg's,' says Nathan, as if Mr Tim Page has just gone down to the newsagents to buy his morning newspaper.

'That's interesting,' I say, not wanting to tell him that I was round at Bloomberg's office yesterday having an interview to work on their corporate production line! 'I hope he's not taking photos of their charts, mapping out the price differentials of dollar derivative, forex future bond swaps in New York!' I say, as we both laugh. His new jigsaw is quickly completed. As is mine of him. The common bond is now clearly established.

'So you know Wacko pretty well then?' he asks, as he looks around the coffee shop.

'Yes,' I say, as I keep eye contact and nod my head.

'He's a good guy and a great boss. Everyone likes working for him. But iaxis is hitting a bit of turbulence right now. Wacko knows, but don't let on I've told you. It's being kept very quiet. There's a bit of shit going down at senior shareholder and board level and it's turning very ugly.'

'What's that?' I ask, as I mentally begin to empty my massive iaxis big picture jigsaw on the floor and slowly begin to put it all together, *without creating a single ripple.*

'Well towards the end of last year the chairman announced, to the world's media, the iaxis plans to build a sub-sea fibre optic ring around the Med at a cost of nine hundred million dollars. The first the board heard about this project was when they read it in the morning papers!'

'So what's happened to him?'

'Well the iaxis shareholder board demanded that he brought a new CEO on board to look after day-to-day company matters while he looked at the overall corporate strategy and future direction of the company. And all of a sudden this new CEO was then running the shop taking us to flotation on the NASDAQ and the chairman was canned almost overnight. He's now known as the ex-chairman.'

(...The ex-chairman and some shareholders have already asked Rothschild's to look at selling iaxis. This took place in November and December 1999. Some shareholders want to sell now, while others want to float on the NASDAQ. The battle lines are drawn and change on a daily basis. The new CEO pitched up and saw all this was going on and was not happy (well and truly pissed off). He was under the impression he was taking iaxis to IPO on the NASDAQ and nothing else. He basically accused the board of lying to him. Nothing in iaxis is as clear-cut as the glass boardroom

table. The horizon is made even less clear by all the smoke and mirrors which iaxis is very good at putting up.)

'But I'm sure everything's going to be okay. The telecoms and Internet market on the NASDAQ is out of control,' I say, as we pack up and leave.

'I hope so!' he says, as we walk out of the shop and onto Gray's Inn Road. 'Pity you didn't start yesterday. There was a good party at the company flat last night.'

'Where's that located?'

'It's in Bloomsbury, just off Gower Street. It's very smart and chic, with lots of space.'

'So it was a good one then?'

'Fucking right, it was great! There were birds, booze and "goodies" everywhere. Some of the rooms had a couple of bodies in and were locked and Claire in Personnel left with Nick. They were spotted going back into the office by Swampy who should've been monitoring the NOC, but was leaving to go to the pub instead! But my birthday will be a large one, so I hope to see you there. It'll be good, with the usual crew on top form,' he says, yawning tiredly.

'I'll be there,' I say, as my brain cell slows down for a tyre change.

'Good. And if you ever want any "goodies", ie dope, pills, coke, whatever, just give "Mr Nice" a shout and he'll get you sorted.'

'Cheers.'

I've never been into drugs apart from sometimes smoking ganja. After this week my head feels like it could do with a Wal-Mart sized trolley full of goodies! But I don't think I'll be having any. I need all the clarity I can get.

'Oh, and I'll give you all that Internet backbone connection crap to read, now I don't have to do it any more!' he says, relieved and laughing as if a heavy Bergen has been removed from his back after a long walk around Glencoe.

As we approach the large swivel doors at the entrance to the ITN building, Merlin walks out. He's wearing a trench coat and is carrying a brolly and a medium-sized Samsonite suitcase... Thinking about Merlin's previous career, I have trouble peeling my eyes off this thing!

He walks up to us both.

'Well good luck Steve. With Nathan showing you the ropes you'll do well here.'

'Thanks,' I say, looking at that 'suitcase', as he smiles and tries to put my mind at ease.

'I've decided to take my wife to New York for a long weekend. Lastminute.com got us a good deal.'

An anonymous black taxi is waiting for him and I'm still looking at that suitcase, with a big fuck-off 'Merlin' device in it!

'See you Tuesday morning, all being well...' he says, as he climbs in the back of the taxi, which pulls away slowly.

This suddenly reminds me... Why does the USA need a "Son of Star Wars" missile defence shield, costing billions of dollars, when these so-called "rogue nations" and terrorist groups can slip a suitcase nuclear bomb into America via their diplomatic bags? ["...Just like the Russians did."]. *Or smuggle nuclear material into America covertly across the Mexican border* ["...with material acquired before 'Project Sapphire' in Kazakhstan"]*? Perhaps it has been too hot in Texas and Pocantico Hills and they haven't thought about this. Maybe someone should go and tell them...*

Back at our quad I need to have a paracetamol, which I sponge off Nathan. I sit down in my very comfortable reclining chair and log on. Nathan drops a load of peering documents on my desk and before I get a chance to open them, everyone is up and about putting their jackets and scarves on.

It's nearly twelve noon, and Wacko walks up to my desk.

'Sorted?'

'Getting there!'

'Good, get your jacket on. We're going over to the pub. It's lunchtime.'

The Blue Lion is practically opposite the ITN building, so we don't have far to walk to quench our thirst.

Wacko, Nathan and myself all walk in, and the warm smoky air is a welcome relief from the piss storm currently washing the road outside. There are plenty of other people from iaxis in here, all keeping the bar warm, and they look like they've been here for a while.

Wacko gets in three drinks. Nobody's drinking pints of bitter. It's all bottles of "fizzy piss", vodka and Red Bulls; a few have pints of lager and a couple even have bottles of Hooch. One bloke has his back against the wall eyeballing people and is drinking a pint of Guinness.

Nobody's heard of Sovereign's Parade here. An RSM from the Scots Guards would end up pulling his teeth out if he tried to get these fine people fit for Sovereign's Parade. He'd probably pull their teeth out as well.

I am introduced and made to feel very welcome. Most seem to work for Wacko in Biz Dev, or in Marketing.

McGowan is built like a block of flats. He is in his early forties and comes from Govan. He supports "Glasgae Rangers". He also has a smallish scar on his right cheekbone. He is one very hard bastard. I've often wondered if that scar was from a fight or an industrial accident (bullet wound). If it was from a fight then McGowan must've been asleep. If he was awake, then there must be one truly frightening hardman walking the mean streets of Govan. (Unless he is now banged up in Barlinnie.) He works in network implementation and enjoys a drink and a good laugh.

Merlock also works in network implementation and is standing next to his mate McGowan. He is also eyeballing me up and down and looks just as hard. He's in his late thirties. Over the years they have both worked on many dark fibre optic projects for Cable and Wireless. Today they are wearing their trademark desert boots, blue jeans and black leather jackets.

Nick is about my age and is tall and good looking, with dark hair and bright blue eyes and a big wolf-like grin. He's always looking out for "Miss Little Red Riding Hood". His eyes are constantly scanning the bar for chicks. He works overseas in Biz Dev.

Howard is a mate of Wacko's and is a director of commercial activities. Or rather he makes up prices and these can go up or down, depending on what mood he's in… He's in his late thirties and likes sailing and taking the piss.

The Guinness drinker is Seamus and I'm told he's from some dark corner of Ireland. He's in his mid-thirties and is now organising something *big* on his mobile and leaves the group to go outside. He works in "marketing blag" and I'm told he likes a good laugh when he's not eyeballing people suspiciously. He's been eyeballing me a couple of times and we've had an eyelock and he now thinks that I recognise him from somewhere. He sits opposite Howard.

Stalker is about thirty years old and has a striking similarity to the comedy actor who says, *'Ohh! Suits you sir!'* I think this line has been said to him 3,287 times and it's starting to piss him off. However, in the last few minutes I've only heard it being said fourteen times, so he's got nothing to complain about. He seems honest enough and works for Wacko in Biz Dev doing outfitting for co-location buildings.

Everyone is speaking about their fortunes and my head is buzzing with this entire Internet peering role that is now my new career in this strange, but very welcome, new life. I like learning new concepts and I've been locked away in shipbroking for five years, but this learning curve looks as steep as a sheer ice wall. And it was only this morning that I set off from base camp.

Nick clicks my drink with his vodka and Red Bull. His blue eyes are looking right through me at some chicks that have just walked into the bar.

'Welcome aboard, Steve,' he says, as he sips his drink.

'Cheers Nick.'

'Did you manage to buy shares in iaxis?' he asks, in a slight West London accent.

'No, I've joined too late, which is a shame,' I say, as I shake my head looking sorry.

'Too right it's a fucking shame! Hey Wacko!' Wacko looks up at Nick.

'What kind of mate are you, bringing Steve into a company in which everyone's going to be millionaires, and he gets fuck all?'

'Fuck off back to Marseilles, Nick!' says Wacko, having a laugh. 'Besides, Steve will be well looked after. I'll be needing a crew for my yacht and Steve's worked in shipping, so his name's already at the top of the list!'

'Cheers mate!' I say, raising my bottle of Bacardi Breezer to him.

'So are you living in Marseilles now Nick?' I ask him, just as he is looking at Claire from Personnel and a whole posse of beautiful girls whom I've seen walking around the office. They are now standing at the bar waiting to be served.

'Yeah, I got moved over to Marseilles towards the end of last year and it's fantastic.'

Then it hits me. This must've been the Nick that Nathan mentioned to me when he was speaking about Claire and last night's party. I'm usually a bit sharper than this, but I've recently had a lot to absorb.

Nick takes a big draw on his Silk Cut. 'This place was starting to do my head in, so Wacko and his senior VP decided to move me down there and look after the Southern France and Spanish Projects.'

'What's wrong with this place?' I ask, feeling slightly unsure as Wacko's assessment this morning of iaxis being better than Euro Disney is not really that wide of the mark.

Nick takes another sip of his drink as his eyes scan the posse girls now being served. He's hungry and it's his feeding time.

'I wasn't getting any work done,' he says, as his eyes zero in on a target.

'Why?' I ask, thinking everyone looks pretty busy.

'Well, everyone is working flat out, but I was spending too much time and money on partying and enjoying the girls and the goodies. There's loads of young girlies in here and they were distracting me all the time. It got that bad I was thinking about checking into therapy!'

'What for, Nick, alcohol and drugs?' asks McGowan, who's just downed his large whisky and is getting the crew another round in.

'No, for sex addiction!' he says, as we all have a good laugh.

I didn't know it, but they knew he was being serious and was not taking the piss.

'Nick, if you went to a mixed group therapy session and met a woman there who was also getting help for being addicted to sex, you'd never get in to work before 11:30 a.m!' adds Howard, laughing away.

We all see the penny drop in his eyes. He never considered this pick-up angle before and he suddenly looks flushed. Nick loses interest in drinking and asks a passing barman if he has a copy of the Yellow Pages.

'Nick, it is "T" for Therapy, not "S" for Sex Addiction!' shouts Nathan, as we all have a good laugh. The Breezer is going down very quickly.

Nick gets hold of the Yellow Pages, and after a short while takes out a pen and starts taking down some numbers on a scrap of paper.

'What does Nick do in Marseilles?' I ask Wacko, who's just about finished his drink.

'Good fucking question! Sometimes we don't hear from him for a few days, he just disappears. If Nick's not getting seduced by some French bird, he'll be out on the pull. He spends the rest of his time lying on the beach, smoking spliffs, downing beer and catching sunrays and doing work from a laptop. He's a top bloke and knows the fibre optic and co-location business back to front. He was one of the first people to join, but we keep him down there now. He distracts the girls too much.'

I look at his body language and it is good. Very good. For such a professional charmer there is not an arrogant or conceited bone in his body. He is chilled out and makes people laugh very easily. Women do not feel threatened by him in the slightest. And they warm to him immediately with his black hair and deep-blue eyes. I guess they just find him hard to resist. And he finds it even harder to resist them. He has it made, I think to myself, as he rejoins the group, now smiling away with his new numbers.

'So what are we doing in Southern France and Spain?' I ask Wacko.

'Nothing really just yet. The iaxis office is run out of a large four-bedroomed villa with a pool which iaxis has bought. Nick lives in it and works from there. He is responsible for getting us fibre optic networks and co-location buildings across the whole area. We've got the contracts sorted out, even paid some money as little deposits. To be fair to Nick he does work really hard. Because of him, iaxis is totally ahead of the game in this part of Europe.'

Another Breezer appears from outer space and is thrust into my hand, just as Claire walks up to us with a girl called Suzie. I can't help noticing after a couple of drinks that Suzie's breasts look very attractive. She sees Nathan looking at them and the poor lad gets lost. She then cups them in both hands and juggles them at him! We all crack up as she retrieves her drink from Claire. And she loves it. I'm told that she's nineteen years old and works as a secretary in the legal ("illegal") department.

Nick and Claire have eyelock and the chemistry spilling over from last night is making their drinks fizz. Claire introduces me to Suzie who's mouthing off about what a shit day she's having.

'Steve's a mate of Wacko's. He joined this morning and is going to be doing our Internet peering connections, so you'll liaise with him for all the "illegal" paperwork.'

She smiles and nods at me.

I just hear those words 'Internet peering connections' and it makes me shiver.

'So why are you dressed so smartly, Steve?' Suzie asks in a North London accent, as she proceeds to open my suit jacket to see which tailor designed it. 'Alexandre's of Savile Row!'

Now everyone's eyes are suddenly on me as if I have suddenly been lit up like Oxford Street on Christmas Eve. And I hate being the centre of attention.

'How much did that set you back?' she asks as she feels the quality of the fabric.

'Far too much, considering I'll never wear it again,' I say, as I take a massive gulp on my Breezer.

'You should try and sell it back to one of the old boys in shipping!' says Wacko, having a laugh.

'No, they only buy their cuts from "Thieves and Hawkes" down at no1,' I say, quickly remembering what he calls them. He laughs, but Suzie is yet to finish.

'So Steve, what did you do before iaxis?' she asks, as I see her dark brown eyes mentally scan me up and down.

'I used to work as an oil tanker broker chartering ships to oil companies.'

She smiles and raises two finely plucked eyebrows and slowly nods her head, working her tongue inside her cheek. Then she delivers the results of her scan.

'So you're a City wanker then!' she says with a dirty grin.

I don't flinch. I just nod my head in agreement and laugh with everyone else. 'Suzie, I'll give some names and numbers of plenty more if you want?'

She beams out in a lovely warm smile.

'No, you're okay there, mate! Glad to see you've got a sense of humour though. You'll need it at iaxis.'

Claire and Nick have disappeared. Wacko is also showing signs of being impatient; he downs his drink in one go and tells me to do the same. 'Right Steve, it's time to get some food in from the greasy spoon down Gray's Inn Road.'

Just as we are walking out of the Blue Lion, two absolutely stunning girls walk in. Both say 'Hi' to Wacko and he just grunts back. They see I'm with Wacko and both smile warmly at me and say 'Hi'.

I have eyelock with the blonde who smiles at me. My heart suddenly races up into my mouth and my ears explode on impact as the door closes behind them.

'Steve! You look like you've just witnessed the *Second Coming!*' he says, laughing.

'Who were they?' I ask, as my throat now feels dry and my heart beats frantically.

'Jemma is the foreign-looking one and works in international marketing. Sasha is the blonde and works in market research. I think they're both twenty-four. They share a flat together in Notting Hill.'

Sasha's hair was like silk and it is all I can now see as I nearly get wasted by a passing taxi as I try to follow Wacko crossing Gray's Inn Road, thinking about that chick from Venus!

'As well as doing the Internet connections I might get you involved in looking for co-location buildings,' he says, as he tries to bring me back to reality. My brain cell is telling me three seconds to *meltdown*.

'Wacko, this Internet peering stuff is frightening as hell. In fact it looks fucking terrifying!'

'Don't worry about all the techie shit. Just concentrate on getting as many Internet backbones connected to ours as possible. You already know more about this peering crap than most people do in here,' he says, laughing as I chew my bottom lip!

It is almost 3:30 p.m. when we get back to work and I am now reading up on all the Internet peering material and manuals Nathan has kindly given to me. I have even got a few emails from Suzie. I open these and see that I have been included on Suzie's 'Guys and Dolls' office circulation list of hardcore pornography distribution. (Fantastic!) Copied in on this little batch must be over one hundred people including the very senior iaxis management. And currently going around the office are about half a dozen images that are apparently depicting Posh Spice's head superimposed on hardcore porn poses. Her face and upper body are covered in sperm and she is surrounded by several large erections close to her mouth and breasts. (Everyone is now raving at this lot!)

My mobile rings and it is Natasha. I can hardly hear her as the "animals" on her floor are still fighting over food and feeding time has long since been and gone.

'Hi Steve, how's the first day going?'

'Excellent thanks; it'll be even better when I understand what I'm doing! How's your day after yesterday?' I ask, still concerned for her. I know the work she puts in pisses off some of the chaps on the floor. But she gives as good as she gets. And fortunately for her, her very senior management has seen to it that her own glass ceiling has been removed.

No amount of clout can remove the glass ceiling at the ITN building. And iaxis on the Seventh floor is closer to the *'signs in the sky'* than anybody else in the building.

'It's much better, thanks. I've recovered all the losses. But fucking Chile had better watch it!' she says, with a laugh, feeling much more upbeat (which is of course far better than feeling beaten up).

'Are you coming round tonight?' I ask, as I haven't got a clue where I'll be later.

'No, I'm going back to my flat straight after work. I'm off to Paris for a weekend shopping trip with the girls,' she says, as the noise picks up again.

'Well have fun then! And thanks for the note this morning.'

'You're welcome...' Lots of sudden shouting in the background and then her line goes dead.

I read and re-read Nathan's techie manuals, *Training Methods (ED-101)* and *Essentials of Windows NT (CT-111)*, and all the various papers he has also kindly given me, and after about six reads it does start to come together. But only just. That website, "whatis.com" is a huge help. I think to myself that I should sign off the dole as it looks like I'll be staying here after all. Later on I also phone my Israeli chartering friend and tell him I've managed to find a new career in the world of telecoms. He wishes me all the very best.

'Steve, get your jacket on, we're going to the pub, it's the weekend,' says Wacko looking at his watch. It is finally 6:30 p.m. and as we walk out of the ITN building, my senses feel shot to hell. Thankfully there are about four taxis waiting to take us to a pub down at *Temple.*

Much later, when I am over the legal limit to even walk home, I manage to flag down a cab, which takes me back to Fulham. My day one of year one is over and I have survived it.

And I sleep a very deep and blissful sleep and dream again about this log cabin in the middle of a forest that I have found.

CHAPTER 5

'Merlin, I've had an idea how to get as many Internet backbone connections as possible without them asking too many questions about our lack of customers.'

Both Nathan and Wacko look up as well. Merlin puts down his latest miniaturised IP *(nuclear)* circuit map and, totally out of character, Nathan turns down the Leftfield vibes on his mini-speakers as well. It is the track '21st Century Poem' and I tell him there's no need for that, so the volume soon goes back up.

'It's just a thought, but if we phone up all the Internet backbones, it will take forever. What I propose doing is sending them our peering/connection agreement by email with a covering letter attached.'

Two nods of agreement. Wacko nods and nearly nods off to sleep as he yawns.

'So how do you propose to get them to sign the contract quickly?' asks Wacko, as he sets his alarm for two minutes, time just in case he falls asleep at a potential techie overload.

'Send out the iaxis peering agreement by email. Put another page onto it with our techie details. And then on the fourth page we can leave it blank so they can fill out their techie details. At the end of the fourth page have a line that informs them that completing their techie details on here and emailing it back to iaxis will constitute an agreement to our terms and conditions.'

'Sorted,' says Nathan.

Wacko advises me to run it past one of our lawyers to make sure they're happy with not getting a signature. Nathan phones one of them who sits in a cage at the far side of the office near Swampy's space-age Network Operations Centre ["...or a "Pandora's Box" as we'd call it if it were an Overall Command Centre out in country GCHQ..."].

The lawyer says they can't come round right now, because they're in a meeting with a creditor and they've all just received a standing ovation, so he will send young Suzie round instead.

As Suzie comes up to the quad, she sees Nathan looking sheepishly away at his screen. 'Hey Nathan!' she shouts to him. As he looks up she proceeds to juggle her breasts at him once again! He blushes red, as do I, when she turns and does the same to me. She giggles away, loving it.

'Hey, Suzie, thanks for the emails,' I say, as the rest of the quad rapidly agrees.

'No problem boys, shall I send over some more?' she says, burning with enthusiasm.

I try to say no, but my head moves up and down fighting the forces of gravity.

'So what would you boys like? More of Posh, or the "Pam and Tommie home video"?' she asks, as if she's got a whole data bank of the stuff.

'Whatever you can get your hands on, love,' Nathan and I say simultaneously.

'Yes, send it round to us first for vetting!' says Wacko, laughing.

Young, fit Suzie just takes it all in her stride and leans over to look at my screen, deliberately giving me a massive eyeful of her cleavage, so much, that my contact lens prescription will have to be renewed this afternoon.

'Yes, that's okay Steve, just print their replies off when they come in and keep them in folders on your desk where I can get my hands on them,' she says, as she playfully grabs my neck.

'Well, let's see how many Internet backbones out there actually want to connect with iaxis,' says Wacko, who is now out of his seat walking around the quads trying to avoid Hannah who is walking about.

As the days pass I realise that no two are the same. I still find it hard to adjust at times. Nobody speaks about anything remotely political and wanting to have people shot. Nor is anyone shouting and screaming at colleagues. I have not heard a single phone being slammed down followed by the words 'That fucking cocksucker!' But my mind still flashes back to the tanker desk from time to time and there is nothing I can do to stop it. The sight of George snarling and screaming as he proceeds to savage Justin's ears to pieces for another missed opportunity is still very vivid. Here, there is no Mr Burns stalking somebody's desk and then having a screaming frenzy.

The worst flashback by far is the sound of a phone being allowed to ring and ring, and then ringing off unanswered at an unoccupied desk. Sometimes when this happens my heart starts beating and my palms sweat. I then look up from behind my flat screen, looking and waiting for a change of expression on a face, waiting to see someone go absolutely berserk at the surrounding desks, because nobody answered it. Here it never happens. When my phone rings, I pick it up in under a second. Sometimes they haven't even heard it ring in their earpiece. *Old habits tend to die hard.*

I once asked Nathan about this phone business and why they are sometimes just left to ring. He just shrugged his shoulders and said, 'If it is important they will leave a message, contact the person's mobile or send an email. And if we think it is important we'll get back to them! Most of the time it's a supplier phoning about not being paid, a customer phoning about their order or a contractor out in the field doing some techie shit,' he said, sounding not really too concerned.

But in general I am very happy to be out of tanker chartering and the old boy atmosphere of Seamart. This is despite my eyes being constantly wide open and staring away trying to take in as much as possible. However, on this particular Thursday morning I'm looking a bit rough after the session in Centro's last night.

'Steve how's your head?' asks Wacko.

'Grunt.'

'Come on, I'll buy you a cappuccino down at Manhattan's,' says Wacko, as I get up on hangover autopilot and leave the office with him. I like sitting in Manhattan's chatting away and watching the world go by. (And sometimes seeing the lovely Carol Vorderman on her way into the ITN building.)

'So how's it all coming together?' asks Wacko, as he takes his watch off and starts playing with it.

'So far everything's going great. I've spent ages just reading Internet peering and backbone connectivity material and familiarising myself with terms and techie concepts. These techie manuals are a big help.'

'But you're still enjoying it, yeah?'

'Totally. I can't believe how friendly and helpful everyone is, not just towards me, but with everyone else as well. It's real teamwork. I'm used to someone screaming 'fuck off!' if you ask a question at the wrong time. And if you are asked a question you should know the answer to, being publicly made to feel and look like a twat in front of everyone!' I say, as he laughs at his own memories of life in a City suit. 'But thanks a lot for bringing me in. I can't believe I'm getting paid to work here and learn something new.'

'I know, it's great isn't it?' he says, as he gulps a mouthful of coffee, which is way too hot for his mouth and tongue to cope with.

'You're not wrong,' I say, as I shy away from taking a sip on my drink.

'Don't worry Steve, everything's going to work out... so far so good,' he says, trying to compose himself, after wiping the tears from his eyes.

After his mouth recovers, I tell him that one of my very well-connected friends who works in UK Equities has recommended that I buy some shares. I went for Fayrewood, Robotic Technology and the fruit company Fyffes who have a good B2B trading product due to be launched soon, and I have invested most of my redundancy money in them.

'Just remember to invest what you can afford to lose,' he advises, now sounding like a City fund manager.

'Can you afford to lose the ninety thousand pounds you've borrowed against your salary to buy shares in iaxis?' I ask him, out of interest.

'No, of course I can't! But iaxis is a dead cert. In fact I'm binning the idea of getting that wannabe Warrior 40 yacht.'

I look surprised. 'Are you going to buy a Ferrari or something else expensive?'

'No, I'm going to buy an Oyster 55 sailing yacht. If you're serious about sailing, then that's really the only one to have. If I turn up in Lymington with a Warrior 40, the local yachting sect will think I'm a *Big Issue* seller!' He says, as he goes for another sip.

'How much is an Oyster 55?' I ask, thinking that a Warrior 40 must be crap.

'It's about six hundred thousand pounds depending on what kit you have on it. I'm also going to sell my two-bed flat in Islington. I should get a packet for that as well. You know Suzie, the foxy illegal secretary who juggles her boobs about the office?'

'Yes, of course I know her, how could I forget her? I get about sixteen hardcore emails a day from her!' (Along with all the other members of iaxis staff.)

'Well, she's a star and she stands to make around half a million dollars with all her shares. Others have taken out loans from banks and families to buy additional shares and to spend on goods knowing the money is going to be coming in. And some people have even got their friends to lend them money and invest in iaxis. If it hits, they get a good share of riches. A few of the board have done this. The ex-chairman has even privately sold some of his shares off to members of staff. Several paid upwards of a hundred thousand pounds for an extra wad of shares!'

'So what it is that is so great about our pan-European fibre optic backbone?'

'Well, at the moment, iaxis has the most technologically advanced fibre optic backbone in Europe,' says Wacko, very confidently.

'So the price of bandwidth must be going through the roof?' I ask, as I can picture our glass ceiling struggling to contain the telecoms and Internet market frenzy... no matter how far iaxis can see up in to the sky.

'No, not at all. In fact it's very much the opposite. At the moment prices are falling like skimpy underwear. People have caught on to the iaxis idea and everyone's building their own fibre optic networks for telecoms traffic.'

'So why is the NASDAQ in such a frenzy about telecoms and Internet stocks?' I ask, as Wacko looks out of the window and up at the sky *above* Gray's Inn Road. The sky is clear today, but it is still very cold on the ground *below*.

'Well, I guess it's like a gold rush mentality. But there's no denying it, telecoms and the Internet are the future. Last summer our ex-chairman was quoted as saying, "If you can't make money in telecoms then you should be in a mental institution." That statement inspired a lot of people to look at the European telecoms market and invest billions of dollars in it. But now he reckons he's seen the future and the pan-European market is *doomed*. But he's in a minority and all he wants is money to fund his fibre optic network around the southern Med, *Egypt* and North Africa. This is a huge nine hundred million dollar, fucking *"Pi in the sky"* project, even in this market!' says Wacko, rubbing his eyes.

'Why?' I ask, looking blank as the plant behind me is catching the water now dripping from behind my ears.

He looks at me like I've still got shit loads to learn about this vast and complex industry.

'It's obvious mate,' he says, with a smile, as he downs the remainder of his cappuccino.

'To you it might be, but I don't understand it,' I say, feeling a bit thick.

'Steve, *Mummies don't use fucking telephones!'* he says, laughing. 'Come on, I've got to meet my senior VP in five minutes. The shareholders have all fallen out yet again and our new CEO is going ballistic. Anything is possible right now.'

A few days later I arrive into work and one email stands out from the rest in my inbox. With nineteen yet to be opened from Suzie, some more peering info from Nathan and a IP *(nuclear)* circuit design from Merlin, the words 'Level 3' and subject 'Internet Connectivity/Peering' have my full attention. I have been waiting for their reply for a while and I am not disappointed. They have said they will connect with the iaxis backbone and they have sent us the Level 3 Peering Agreement. In techie Internet terms, this is very good news. I look at their contract and where we have used it in ours and it is a classic cut and paste job!

Nathan is chilling out listening to *'Feat'* by Chicane and the sun is shining through the glass ceiling, which feels good.

'Merlin, Nathan, Level 3 have said they'll connect their Internet

backbone with ours in London, Amsterdam, Paris and Brussels. All we have
to do is sign their contract and return it!'

Merlin looks up from his circuit and puts down his book on *'EA-041
Waveforms'*. He's obviously cracked the latest version of *'nuclear'* weaponry,
which he's been *covertly* designing to fit inside his lunch box, as he's smiling
away.

Merlin stands up and comes round to see my screen.

'Well done!' he says, with genuine enthusasim.

'Yes, they think we're going to be massive!' I say, feeling well pleased.

'Yes, but we are going to be massive. We could be the next UUNet when
iaxis floats and we get the cash for further development,' says Nathan, full
of optimism.

'Merlin, who should I get to sign this Level 3 contract?'

(A leading American Internet corporation like Level 3 will always
require a signature. Their big cat corporate lawyers are so savage they should
be kept in London Zoo. Our big cats should be kept at *"The Circus"* for all
the stunts they can perform! And their secretary, Suzie, should be kept on the
top shelf in a newsagent shop and her mind should be kept well hidden under
the counter!)

'Get Wacko to sign it, he's the boss. He's over in marketing in a meeting
with Howard and Psycho, so collar him when he gets back.'

'Nathan, is everything okay with Level 3's contract?'

'Yes, it's fine, but it's a very thorough peering contract, written by
someone who really knows their stuff. But it's very American and way too
long,' he says, as I try and move my mouse, but the PC's having none of it.
The screen seems to be frozen. After slamming the mouse down hard on to
the desk a couple of times I tell Merlin.

'It's probably the sight of that Level 3 email saying they'll peer with us!
Computers are *sensitive* things and the shock of seeing it has probably taken
out your system. You'd better call TTT; he'll have to sort it out this time. I'm
just putting some finishing touches to this new network design,' says Merlin,
as he has a mouthful of black coffee from his new TMinix freebie mug.

I pick up the phone list and look up TTT's phone number on the internal
name sheet. I'm not looking forward to this, as I haven't yet had a crash
course on techie speak. As I hit his number it rings for ages before it is
answered.

'Hello, is that TTT?'

'Grunt.' (Some techie sounding noise in the background.)

'My PC seems to have stopped working. Could you come and fix it
please?'

'Grunt... (some techie speak)... Intel 486... grunt.' And the phone line goes dead.

I put the phone down and think to myself that Claire in Personnel was right to be firm with him. But then I see him leaving Techieland and walking over. I mentally revise my scan of him. It's really good of him to come over so quickly.

As he comes much closer in to eyeball view I see he's carrying a folder and is still wearing his worn-out WRANGLER jeans he bought when I was probably still watching 'The Man from Atlantis.' But now I've seen it all. He's proudly wearing a MAGIS/Sun SPARC-20 T-shirt from some techie function and he's got a mobile phone on the right side of his belt with a Maglite torch on the left. And to top it all he's wearing a *'Radiant Mercury'* baseball cap.

'Thanks for coming over so quickly, TTT.'

'Grunt.' No eye contact whatsoever. And he hasn't shaved for a couple of days. He sits at my desk and places a red folder with the techie words 'SunOS MP-109' on the floor and goes to work on my PC. After a couple of minutes it's done.

'Grunt... Windows 98.... grunt... crap... (techie speak)... grunt.'

'Thanks a lot, TTT,' I say, as I test the water at my first chance to make small talk with him. But my mind goes blank and the words just escape out of my mouth.

'So have you found a new place to live yet, mate?' I ask, as he picks up his folder.

That broke the ice.

He is shocked that I know his personal business. He just stands there, eyeballing me, staring wildly and looking horrified, twitching and staring away. The whites of his eyes light up my face so much that it'll now be Easter before I'll need to use a sunbed again. Then without warning, the sound of Nathan laughing breaks his trauma and he bolts it off back to the *Office of Technical Support* in darkest Techieland.

While Nathan tries to calm down and stop laughing, he manages to blurt out the fact that I'd just survived a 'near techie meltdown,' just as Howard from marketing blag walks over to our quad.

Howard's looking a bit white after being in a meeting with Psycho, who runs marketing.

'What's up, Howard? You didn't get caught in Psycho's shower curtain leaving his office, did you?' Nathan asks, jokingly.

He laughs ever so slightly. 'Psycho has gone and hit the bathroom ceiling this time!' he says, as he paces around our quad, shaking his head away.

(We all know how mad Psycho is. He's not even bothering to wait for his shares to come through as he's just gone and splashed out on a very fast purple BMW M3. This is despite the fact he gets freaked out at driving above forty mph and his psychiatrist has banned him from driving on motorways!)

'Why?' three open mouths ask all at once, as the slightest little thing can trigger Psycho off.

'Well, you'll never guess what that stuntmaster Porn Star has gone and done?' he says, eyeballing us all.

Blank looks all round.

(I have heard this name being bandied about the office. He is a well-built six-foot bloke with an eighties-style shoulder-length haircut. He's also head of international sales. This guy is the stuntmaster of blag and is capable of pulling any stunt in the ring.)

'Well it's more the case of what the fuck he hasn't done!' says Howard, still on his feet.

We're all hanging on to his every word, like dogs waiting for scraps of food, as Howard takes a deep breath to get the words out.

'I don't know where to start... Last week he went to a sales and marketing trade show in Amsterdam and actually took a Polaroid picture of Psycho's sexy PA giving him a blowjob in his hotel room! It's true. It's even been discussed at senior VP level!'

We'd heard the rumour, but it's now confirmed as correct and we fall about laughing.

'So what is Psycho saying about this?' asks young Nathan, practically lifting his jaw off his keyboard.

'Psycho wants to kill him!' says Howard, who has just seen the whites of Psycho's eyes and is still shivering.

This has us on the floor in stitches!

'But it gets worse. Porn Star has also gone and lied to us on his CV.'

'What did he say?' asks Merlin, sounding very serious.

'He said that he had an MBA from INSEAD in Paris. Fucking INSEAD! So Psycho went and checked him out. All Porn Star had from INSEAD was a certificate saying he had completed a six week sales training course! And get this, his "former boss" at Global Crossing has never heard of him!' There are tears in all our eyes now as Howard continues without stopping for an interval. '...and instead of selling bandwidth which is his fucking job, he has been trading his own private ventures, wheeling and dealing away on the side all from his desk,' says Howard, looking at us all for signs of our moral indignation.

'So what's he been selling then?' asks Nathan, who is struggling to get the words out as we're all laughing away at his golden-coated brass-neck.

'He's been buying and selling Porsche sports cars and trading Rolex watches. He's hardly sold any fucking bandwidth at all!' says Howard, looking shocked.

'Shit, I bet Psycho is well pissed off,' I say, laughing.

'Steve, Psycho has just eaten a full box of Prozac! He is going to have to go home to calm down,' says Howard, as he sits down in Wacko's chair with a hot flush. We all crack up laughing, as this is just too much.

'How much salary was he on?' I ask. My stomach is starting to hurt from laughing and some tears are escaping from my eyes.

'About one hundred thousand pounds a year, plus his bonus.'

'Fuck!' say three open mouths.

'Is he getting sacked?' asks Nathan, now wiping away his tears.

'*Sacked!* He's been fucking promoted! He's now head of international co-location sales! According to the board, if he was sacked it would send the wrong signals out to the market. And when we're gearing up for the high-yield bond and then listing on the NASDAQ, it is just not on,' says Howard, as he leans back in Wacko's chair and puts his feet up on his desk. 'Market perception is everything just now. But after the NASDAQ closed yesterday, Psycho is convinced that iaxis is going to be worth well over four and a half billion dollars after flotation!' he says, shaking his head and laughing.

This sets us all off again. Then the email from the CEO hits our screens: (Names changed, but retyped as sent.)

I am pleased to announce that Porn Star has been promoted to managing director for iaxis Net Centres/Co-location facilities. This is a new post with the key focus to build the profile and revenue of iaxis Co-location as a business unit and establish iaxis as a key player within the International Web/Applications Hosting and Net Center Market. Porn Star is one of the few people in our industry having several years of experience in this specific and specialised field. He has extensive experience in the strategic, financial, commercial and technical side of the Co-location business.

Porn Star will be reporting to me and be responsible for the creation of a team with clear vision, responsibility to establish the goals and develop the new business plan for the Co-location Centers. The Co-lo team, which will include Paul and Peter, will be recruited from inside and outside iaxis. The existing teams in Business Development and Customer Service will be used for implementation and design of the Co-location Facilities. Porn Star, *Paul* and *Peter* will also develop a strong direct and indirect distribution, launch marketing campaigns and lead and motivate the team to increase revenue and market value to iaxis.

Please join me in congratulating Porn Star on his new role at iaxis.'

CEO

This email from the *'chief entertainment officer'* keeps us all entertained for a good thirty minutes.

'So what's been going on around here?' asks Wacko, now back from Psycho's office and evicting Howard from his chair. Wacko is also struggling to stay calm, while he looks at his TAG 2000 watch, probably wondering if Porn Star could get him a good deal on a Rolex.

'Level 3 have said they'll peer with iaxis.'

'That's great! Are you shagging some bird over there?'

I laugh and tell him that I haven't even spoken to anyone over there. I just sent them our standard email telling them that we would like to connect or peer with them, and they think iaxis is going to be massive. I hand him the contract to sign.

'It's free, yeah?'

'Yes,' I say as he puts his Bic pen to it and a perfect squiggle is then produced.

I fill out his name with my Cross fountain pen.

'Ask Charlotte on reception to book a taxi to deliver the document. It should be round there within the hour,' he says, as I pick up the phone and get a taxi sorted out. 'Nice one. Let's go over to the Blue Lion and sink a couple of drinks to celebrate our first peering contract! I could do with a drink after spending nineteen minutes with Psycho.'

Both Nathan and Merlin leave to go to their meeting with Hannah, who smiles at Wacko as she walks past our quad. Wacko looks down at his Timberlands and avoids her intense gaze.

At reception I drop the contract on Charlotte's desk and see that she's away chatting to Swampy in the NOC. We carry on walking towards the reception glass doors to leave the office and the stunning Sasha approaches us from the opposite direction.

'Hi Steve!' she says warmly, as she raises an eyebrow at me, and I feel my heart suddenly miss a whole load of beats and my vision goes into a strange light.

She knows my name and we've never even spoken!

I try to gain control over my eyes, not from dilating, but from popping out altogether. My mouth is wide open and I must look like I've just opened my gas bill and I've been unwittingly billed for the whole of the Fulham Road. I somehow manage to regain the lost energy and say 'Hi'.

"Sad bastard" is written across my forehead. And in Sasha's own subconscious league table of sad bastards I have just won the premiership. (And Easter is still a long way off.)

'Leave him alone,' says Wacko, suddenly concerned for my welfare.

A lovely warm smile radiates from her mouth as her eyes lock on mine. She carries on walking through the doors. I look back at her as she flicks her long blonde hair; her legs are the longest I've ever seen. Even Swampy would have trouble climbing those.

'Steve, you look like a fucking puppy dog. Get a grip and don't be such a twat!' says Wacko reassuringly, as we get into the lift.

'She is a real honey. Her blonde hair is like silk. And that body!' I say, as my vision is all hazy. There is nothing I can do to break free.

Wacko takes a deep breath and, showing restraint, says, 'Steve, here's a few words of advice, mate. Forget her. She's *untouchable*. Even for you. She's a *goddess* and a right ball-breaker of a flirt!' My head feels light from the experience and from the lift descending at speed to the ground floor.

Outside my eyes are struggling to refocus on reality... I can make out Wacko and he is now eyeballing me.

'Look Steve, she's driven a guy called Damon insane. He works in operations support and now he's possessed, and it's all because of her! He used to be a top bloke, great live-wire personality, bright and funny. Then she joined and smiled at him, and his brain fucking melted! Now she just wiggles her little finger at him every time she wants something. She's got him *brain washed,* he just goes running up to her desk like a fucking lapdog. She feeds on attention. It's like a drug for her, so forget it. You've got more chance pulling Jennifer Lopez!' he says, as we both cross Gray's Inn Road.

Suddenly we're in the Blue Lion and a couple of drinks arrive.

'Anyway, well done on getting the first Internet connectivity/peering partner.'

'Cheers,' I say, as we click bottles.

'So what else is going on upstairs?' I ask, as my head starts to calm down after a massive gulp.

'It's starting to look pretty grim in the glass boardroom. All the shareholders have fallen out and are fighting amongst themselves and the ex-chairman has been told that the board has no confidence in him at all. So he's flown first class to Australia, on iaxis, for a little break. When he returns, he'll have no operational role in the running of iaxis whatsoever.'

Chapter 5

'That's a bit steep. Didn't the bloke start up iaxis in the first place?' I ask, feeling totally sorry for him.

'Well, yes he did, but the trouble is you need to have the heart of a beast to control it right now. And he's not the person. He's got great vision and ideas, apart from the Med fibre ring, but the people who've ploughed in millions want to try a new manager. A bit like "The Boro" fans with Robson just now!'

I sheepishly finish my drink. It slides down faster than "The Boro's" position in the premiership as I consider this United Fruit Inc ["...Operation Fortune"] style South American coup.

(...Towards the end of last year, the new CEO was trying to take us onto the NASDAQ, after the high yield bond iaxis is trying to raise. However, the CEO has also been working flat out with the board trying to sell iaxis. But iaxis will only be sold if we can get the one billion dollar receipt. However, the ex-chairman actually brought in the new CEO to run the place while he concentrated on the big picture. From day one the CEO was under no illusion, acting on instructions from the shareholders, that he would now be the number one and top dog in iaxis. It was a classic boardroom coup. The ex-chairman was on some business golfing jolly in Florida when he got the phone call from his loyal PA telling him that his office had been cleared by 'his' new CEO, who was actually clearing it himself. Once he was at his desk, in the ex-chairman's chair, he drank some tea and announced that he was the boss. And this is life in a suit further up the food chain.)

'So who are the main shareholders then?'

'Well you've got the ex-chairman who owns twenty-five percent and is the single largest shareholder. Then you've got investment houses like Chiltern, Wynchurch, Gilbert's and Hunter Capital.'

'So is there any chance of more investors coming in, or is everything too late in the light of the high-yield?'

'No! Right now we're trying to get Bain Capital to invest about thirty million dollars. If they do this then one of the original investors will put in an extra thirty million dollars as a top-up. But we need hard cash and very fast. You see, although we've built this fantastic network, nothing is paid for apart from a few little deposits. There is no money to fund the iaxis telecoms networks whatsoever.'

'Really?' I gasp.

'Yes, that's why we need to raise the three hundred million dollars through a high-yield debt issue. And it looks good on the balance sheet before we float on the NASDAQ. '

'So is everyone still going to make their millions, then?'

'Without a doubt! The Internet market is going supersonic. The City banks and VCs have invested tens of billions of dollars in the telecoms and Internet industry. And when the next generation of 3G mobile phone licences comes out, they lend *even more* tens of billions to the players. It's all going fucking mental! And iaxis is a major European telecoms company, right in the middle of this booming market. And we're on the verge of floating on the NASDAQ and walking away with a cool one billion dollars!'

We click drinks, but I bite my bottom lip as I feel "The Boro" are sliding down the table and are nearly at the bottom of the premiership (again).

'But if bandwidth prices are falling then the market will fall sooner or later.'

'*Steve!* Don't be such a *"prophet of doom"* and stop worrying. Fucking hell, you'll be going on holiday to Megiddo next!' he says, laughing.

'Okay, well, look at it from this perspective. In the past, when Brent Crude was ten dollars a barrel and sometimes less, nearly all the future oil developments and exploration activities in the North Sea were cancelled almost overnight. The offshore shipping market that supported these rigs and platforms was suddenly on its knees. Charter rates for oil rig towage vessels fell from the sunshine days of fifty thousand pounds per day to less than four thousand pounds. Owners that had extended themselves in the good times building new ships to support the "endless summer" suddenly got burned when their new ships were delivered and there was no work for them to do. Suddenly there were more ships than *fish!* The charter rates went to the bottom of the sea and companies folded.'

'Steve! Have another fucking drink! I'm going to get you out looking for potential co-location sites, that'll stop you topping yourself with all this doom,' he says, trying not to laugh too much.

'What's this co-location building stuff I keep hearing about?' I ask. His drink is almost finished and it's time to get some food.

'A co-location facility is a building where the Internet lives,' he says, as he notices that my face looks as dumbfounded as George W. Bush's must have done when members of the "High Cabal" informed him at Kennebunkport, Maine, that he would be "their" next presidential candidate.

["Don't worry young 'Temporary', just do as 'Magog' says and everything will be fine, boy…"]

'Don't worry, me, McGowan and maybe even Nick will all bring you up to speed on co-location.'

'Sounds good. So when is Nick next back over from Marseilles?'

'Fuck knows. We've lost all contact again.'

CHAPTER 6

My brain cell is charging round one of Merlin's circuits and is struggling to absorb all the information. In fact it is close to a "Merlin sized meltdown". I feel cold and my temples are tired from all the Internet connectivity information. The iaxis Internet backbone will be live in the coming weeks and all of our Internet connection/peering agreements will be on the agenda. I cuddle up to Natasha and feel her heart beating against my ribcage, and I wonder what stresses this big one had to cope with today (much more than mine). And I am the one now awake. Natasha leaves for New York this weekend and she has kindly spoken to some people with clout about the eighteen-month future of the telecoms/Internet market. The NASDAQ is going to get brutal and *"Crucifixions"* are in the air. The future is not "Orange". It is in fact a very dark chocolate orange that is close to melting. *And this is as clear as glass.*

I drift back off to sleep with the lovely smell of Natasha's skin calming my mind, while the gentle sound of a *St Clair* crystal glass slowly being tapped in an old boardroom is still ringing in my ears.

'Nathan, look at this. We're getting replies from loads of Internet backbones wanting to peer and connect with iaxis!' I say, as my inbox has now got more positive replies in it than hardcore porn from Suzie and I've only just turned the PC on.

He looks up and turns down the music (that classic Faithless track *'Reverence'*) and walks round to my screen.

'What a blag! These Internet backbones are actually signing up to peer with us on the iaxis peering agreement!'

'Fantastic,' says Merlin, looking very happy about this and at the even smaller-looking *(nuclear)* circuit now on his screen.

Nathan picks up his fags indicating he wants to go down to Level 2 for a smoke.

'Nathan, listen to another track, I'm just going across to marketing blag, to let them know we're now getting peering connections set up for when the Internet backbone goes live. I'll be a couple of minutes then we can go downstairs and I'll buy you a coffee.'

'Okay,' he says, as he then selects another track from one of his 30,000 Napster downloads.

I could easily have sent Seamus and Howard an email, but then I wouldn't have been able to walk past and see the lovely Sasha. Not to speak to her, of course. Lesser mortals like myself are not on her agenda. But a glimpse of her is simply good enough.

As I walk into marketing I see that Sasha is not there. And the enthusiasm now to be in 'blag central' disappears like zeros on a burning piece of paper. I wander up to Seamus and Howard's quad. The four bloggers who sit here sit closer to the SFO building than any other quad. Howard has his back to the building, but Seamus sits facing it and just eyeballs it back all day long, and I'm surprised it's still standing.

I have a good laugh with Seamus and he's always having a laugh within his quad. He doesn't drink much. Which, for an Irishman, I think is suspicious.

'Stieve boy, wat's de fookin craic den?' he says, as he clicks off his "ROCKETEER" screensaver and starts to look busy.

'Seamus, we're starting to get Internet peering connections on the iaxis Internet backbone,' I say, full of enthusiasm.

'Dat's great. But wit de fook dis it mean?'

'It means we might get some customers on it.'

'Foor fook saek, sounds like wirk t'me, ye wee fooker, so ye ire!'

Judging by his dialect, he's definitely from the border area, on the southern side. I also see that he's got a little badge of Glasgow Celtic FC lying next to his keyboard. His clothes are casual and nondescript. He wears a black diving watch on his left wrist with the face turned around so it's on his inner arm. His blue eyes are always cold and suspicious and he's a short and hard-looking fella. I wouldn't mess with him. But he enjoys a laugh.

'So where are you from "across the water" Seamus?' (That *pinged* him!)

A big ray of light escaped from these two diamonds and then his eyes focus sharply on me.

'Crossmaglen,' he says suspiciously, before smiling.

'Nice countryside, but I prefer Killarney. The locals are more friendly.'

'Wil dats coz ye'ir a fookin Brit!' he says, as we both have a laugh.

'So how long have you been on the "mainland" then?' I ask, trying like hell to blow his cover. And to test his sense of humour.

'Ovier fourtien fookin yiers.'

'That's a long time, mate. Do you not miss it back home?'

'Na, ah goes back te see de' family en dat's it.'

'So who do you report to over here then?'

'... Fookin Psy-kho, de mad fooker ovier der,' he says, as I see he's working on the iaxis 'Voice over IP (TD-2H9)' network product. I take one of his business cards when he's looking at the grey SFO building. He doesn't see me, as there's no reflection in our glass wall in today's low light. It says 'Marketing Director of Network Products', which sounds impressive and means he's responsible for marketing our fibre optic telecommunications backbone.

I look over at Psycho, who's in his glass cage (which is not locked). However, today he looks calm. Or rather at this particular moment in time after a whole sugar mountain-sized dose of Prozac, he looks calm. Now he's just sitting at his desk, staring out the window (probably trying to pick up yet another signal from outer space that will tell him how much iaxis is going to be worth today!)

Just as Psycho appears to get a signal from *Sirius*, Howard gets off the phone to a yachting company and asks, 'So who have we got to er... connect and peer with us?' This term peering and the Internet in general confuse him. He's now leaning back on his chair with his Rockport boating shoes on his desk. When he's not scheming up a major blag, he's quite often sitting back like this, already on board his future yacht which, in his mind, is moored just off the coast outside St Tropez.

'Well Howard, so far we've got Level 3, UPC, Chello, Belgacom, Easynet, *Exodus*, Nacamar, RedNet and World Online.'

'Sounds good, Steve. I'll look at it just before the Internet backbone goes live. Remember to tell Hannah, as she has project responsibility for this, er... IP thing,' he says, as he puts down his pricing book and picks up the latest *Yachting Monthly* magazine and starts to flick through the pages.

(I have a look on Seamus's desk, just to see if he has a copy of *Guns and Ammo* lying around, but unfortunately he doesn't. He must've left it at home. Right now he's on the phone to another Irish person and I cannot decipher a word of the conversation. But it's probably about roadblocks, American money and stress fractures in tall buildings.)

I look at Howard and ask him if he's getting a Warrior 40 like Wacko's.

'*A Warrior 40!* That'll be right. I recently told Wacko that if he bought one of those tarts paddle boats, the gentry in Lymington would think he's mooring up to sell them the *Big Issue!*'

Then déjà vu from a few weeks ago hits me.

'You know, I think Wacko did mention it, come to think about it. He said something about him getting an Oyster 55 instead?'

Howard suddenly hits a coral reef.

'*The fucker!* That's the one I'm getting!' yells Howard, a bit too loudly, as he springs up from his hammock.

'Hey Howard, please don't say that I said anything.'

'No probs, thanks for that Steve!' says Howard, as he launches himself towards Wacko's desk, through all the quads, moving like a cruise missile through the streets of Baghdad.

The other two marketing blaggers on this quad have been on the phone for ages. I'm not sure if it is business related as both are in mid-Southern Hemisphere twang speaking about rugby, cricket, beer and the odd Sheila. Judging by the respective flags on top of their screens, one's an Aussie called Gibbsy, and the others a Kiwi called Tommo. Gibbsy has a screen saver that is now on and it's flashing the word "GRANDSLAM". Tommo's screensaver is a picture of the old Coliseum, but it's not on a flat screen... He's a contractor on seven hundred pounds per day. And he's also got a red goatee beard and wild starey eyes, which suddenly land on me as I'm hovering about.

I walk over to the drinks machine and top up with a cold glass of water and totally forget why I made this *pilgrimage* in to marketing blag...

'Hi Steve! How's it going mate?'

It is Sasha. She's now back at her desk *and she's shouting over to me!*

...I am about twenty-five feet away from her and I can see her eyes flashing fondly. It is like spring has now arrived. My heart starts to race and the feeling inside is fantastic. The hook is in my mouth and an expert is slowly landing me as she is winding me in towards her desk while I kick away. And she loves it... Only I'm not a Canadian salt-water salmon fighting for my life. I am in fact more of a goldfish with an attention span of two seconds. It is therefore no great surprise to her that she lands me with supreme ease. In fact I barely put up a struggle in the half-a-second it takes me to move from the water machine over to her desk!

'How are you settling in, sweetie?' She asks with tenderness, as she rubs her neck and leans back in her chair waiting for my answer.

Never mind Merlin splitting the atom. She has just split my fucking brain cell.

'So far so good,' I manage to say, but how I get the words out is a mystery as I'm now chewing my heart.

'That's brilliant,' she says warmly, as she moistens her lips with her tongue, and I suddenly become haunted by Wacko's voice screaming at me as if I'm a character in his version of the movie "*A Bug's Life.*"

'Don't go near the light!!! She's a flirt you fucking twat!!!'

But it is too late. I go into the light and I am in *The Zone* and only hypnosis from Cornell can bring back any recollection of what is going on...

Sasha then starts to flick her long silky blonde hair and smiles at me. Her whole face lights up and I am the only other person in the world. And in Sasha's famous league table of sad bastards, I have just won the fucking treble two seasons running.

We start speaking. Or rather she starts speaking and I just nod away at whatever she is saying. I can feel stares from some geezer who sits not too far away from her. His eyes are drilling holes into the back of my head. I turn around and we have eyelock where I once had eyes. My ESP tells me that this chap is just sitting there, eyeballing me like fuck. Sasha telepathically tells me to turn my head back round to look at her and I do this immediately.

Who's he?' I ask her in a trance-like drone that she must've found terrifying.

'Oh, that's Damon, don't worry about him, Steve, he's just in one of his sulks,' she says, as if he's a disobedient little schoolboy.

Sasha's mobile rings and I break free from *The Zone*. Feeling tired, I pick up my eyes and notice that she reads *Hello!* and has a photo of the *Great Sphinx* as a screensaver. Her little silver Nokia is in a Mulberry leather case and I think her star sign is *Gemini*.

'I'll bring some network marketing brochures over to you once they arrive and just give me a call if you need to know anything, Steve,' she says, with one of the sweetest voices I've ever heard.

'Will do,' I say, as I pull the ripcord motor for my heart. It starts first time and I get ready to float back to my desk.

Feeling on top form I scan across to this Damon chap's desk and eyeball him back hard, telepathically telling him that if he fancies his chances taking me on, then I'll take him outside and bitch slap the motherfucker about the ITN carpark!

Then suddenly he gets up and glowers back at me. As he leaves his desk, I can clearly see that he is a lot bigger than I am. In fact, he's a fucking monster, almost the size of King Kong! For starters he could knock me into next week. As for the main course, I'd get that fed to me on a drip...

I land safely back at my desk yawning and feeling knackered. I see that Nathan is sweating away. His eyes have gone all starey like he's in the Egyptian Desert and he thinks he can see water seventy metres away in the distance. His speech is also fucked. He looks like he'll spontaneously combust on the office floor if he doesn't have a Marlboro Light within the next thirty-three seconds. (But I'm sure his fags will be saved.) His Faithless CD has also finished. Then the words eventually come out.

'Fucking hell! That's the longest two minutes I've ever seen!'

And within four seconds we're practically running down to the smoking area on Level 2.

'Nathan, what do you think of Sasha?' I ask, out of breath.

He struggles to get the words out. 'I might have guessed that's what fucking kept you!' he says, as he's struggling to take in oxygen, and he twitches away focusing on his new packet of fags, which he's clutching in his left hand.

We could have gone outside to Manhattan's, but that would have been an extra thirty-one seconds, which in Nathan's current state is far too long.

'But Nathan, she seemed interested though.'

'Steve, she's a flirt!' he shouts loudly, as he rips the arse out of his cigarette packet to get a fag.

Over the next few seconds there is no communication as the nicotine begins its journey to hit the spot. His fag is nearly finished and his body starts to stabilise once again.

'Get that in to your head mate,' he says, as he takes another big gasping draw. 'Sasha doesn't even let smooth-talking Nick get through her door...' (He takes another huge draw) 'And even he gave up trying after three hundred days. She bled him dry of all his energy,' says Nathan, whose fag is now finished just as his eyes start to refocus.

'So is Sasha seeing anyone?' I ask curiously, but gagging for an answer. I can still see her sweet smile radiating from her mouth between her perfectly sculptured cheekbones.

His second fag comes out of the packet.

'Fucking hell, Steve! She's like that with every bloke in here. She loves it when guys like you pay her attention. She feeds on it. It gives her energy!' he says, as I somehow feel I will no longer be getting my no-claims bonus on my self-respect policy this year.

He takes a deep breath to help the magic words come out just a little bit easier.

'Her boyfriend ditched her a few months ago.'

'Ditched her! I gasp. 'Who was he, George Clooney or someone?' I ask, thinking that I should start reading *Hello!* instead of *The Economist* every week.

'He was just a normal geezer who couldn't keep up with her. I heard he got tired too quickly and decided to move on. So now she lives it up big-time, partying and clubbing away at the weekends after bleeding sorry bastards like you dry of all their energy during the week.'

'Cheers mate!'

He laughs as I'm now mentally blowing out the flames on my wings from flying far too close to Sasha.

'But anyway, well done on the Internet peering connections, it has surprised everyone. Word of that success has gone to VP level, as they were all flapping about this issue and it's given them peace of mind. So it's good to see you can wing it.'

'Yes, well, I lost sleep thinking about it.'

Nathan laughs and tells me he's lost sleep over all the money he's borrowed to buy shares in iaxis...

'So are you not worried that things will not work out and the market could turn?'

'Um... we'll see. But when we float on the NASDAQ and I cash in my shares, I'll make a fucking mint. I've even borrowed money from my bank and family to pay an initial ten-thousand-pound lump sum up front. So as soon as the dosh come in, I'm going to buy a Porsche Boxster.'

'Yes, that sounds good. Just remember me when the dollars start to come in! But what about old Merlin? That tight Scotsman must have a fair bit stashed away? He doesn't seem to be a big spender and never talks about his cash or anything else, apart from circuits and *encryption*.'

'Yes, you're right. In fact you're more likely to get him to open up on the visitors CERN had from the Near East during the Eighties than you are about him spilling the beans on his dosh. But anyway, let's get back to the quad, we've got plenty of work to be winging it on with,' he says, as he stubs out the last bit of his fourth fag and we both stand up. He looks a lot steadier on his feet now than he did a few minutes ago.

After last night in Centro's I wake up with a raging thirst and there's one thing on the news and it's starting to piss me right off and it's been going on for days. The *Today* programme can't get enough of it and if I weren't so tired I might give them a call. My grievance is about the reporting of the black squatters invading white-owned tobacco farms in Zimbabwe. The reason I'm ranting on about this is down to lack of sleep, but it is dominating the British press and the cream of news media such as BBC Radio 4.

Take a look at the hours and hours of airtime that are being given to comment and analysis on these developments of black squatters. And I'm certainly not forgetting or overlooking the very sad fact that a handful of white farmers have been lynched in the process. But let us put this into perspective. So far there have been about five white farmers tragically butchered to death. But how much airtime is currently being given to the *millions* of blacks now dead and dying of starvation this week across the rest of Africa? Or of the *millions* of blacks dead or dying a very slow death through AIDS on the continent? Yes, I'm sure you've guessed it. Jack shit.

(I take a deep yawn here because I'm knackered.)

You see, it is just not newsworthy for the time being. Even when it is "mentioned in dispatches" it rarely dominates the headlines for days on end. We in the West have moved on from Ethiopia and the mid-eighties. Ethiopia is now in a major civil/border war with Eritrea and the country is in a worse mess than ever. It is a tragic and sickening fact of modern western life that we have come to view mass starvation as a way of life in Africa. Any visitor to Africa will know that civil unrest is also a major fact of life here. A machete has settled many arguments. *And has started many more.* But in the twenty-first century, civil unrest against a few white farmers is far more newsworthy than the "old news" of millions of blacks starving to death, getting slaughtered in a civil war or dying of AIDS. In the first year of the new century that coverage takes place close to the end of the news summary, just before the sports and cricket news.

And what am I going to do about it?

I'm going to get a cappuccino and a croissant in Starbucks on the Fulham Road, read about Posh and Becks in *Hello!* and think about where I am going to go backpacking next. That is after I've fully woken up from last night's bender in Centro's. Most of us ended up there after we were working in the office until well after nine. We tend to work this late nearly every evening.

Going past Knightsbridge on the Piccadilly Line, I think to myself about the global warfare that would be raging around the desk over this tragedy in Zimbabwe. I can just picture Henry getting scraped of the office ceiling, Horace looking up in the atlas where Africa is and old Rupert bouncing around and opening his battered old Filofax, screaming away to Executive Outcomes, DSL, Sandline and a few other international "Jim'll fix it" set-ups. No doubt he'll be demanding to know 'what the blaady hell *"The Circuit"* is going to be doing down there...' Those are the days I do not miss walking in to.

After spending more time than I should have reading about Posh and Becks, I arrive a bit late at the ITN building. As I get out of the lift on the seventh floor, I can see that there are quite a few suits in the glass boardroom. If I didn't know that it was expensively designed and hand-crafted glass sculptures on the glass walls, I would have thought it was steam and condensation. This is because in that room the shareholder board very recently turned down an offer of five hundred and seventy-five million pounds to buy iaxis. They would've walked away with thirty percent or more returns on their investments. The staff would've made several hundred thousand pounds. The ex-chairman would've walked away with twenty-five percent of the value of iaxis.

However, greed has taken over and this has shortened their sights and widened their vision ('we could be massive...'), and this one billion dollar ticket is the drug surging around the big shareholders' veins. And it is a high like no other. The iaxis management board, with their finger on the market pulse, and who are running iaxis, all wanted to sell for five hundred and seventy-five million pounds. Their requests were ignored.

With all eyes focused on the NASDAQ it is almost a one billion dollar or bust scenario. The ex-chairman has seen the bust coming. The price of European bandwidth is falling and the rising number of entrants into the market is not helping to keep the sun shining through this "endless summer". But now he has been ousted in a "bloodless coup" so clean that even "Her Majesty's BOX 8-50" would've been proud of the mechanisms at work in iaxis during November 1999. But in March 2000, being the single largest shareholder in a company he founded, the ex-chairman is still at the table as a shareholder. He also has his say in the present post-"coup" climate like all the other big shareholders.

When he was top dog, the ex-chairman told all the staff who had invested in iaxis that they would be millionaires if they put their money in and bought into the share scheme. If iaxis had been sold, like he wanted, then this assumption would now be true for those who put their money where his heart was. 'Build fast and sell quick' was always the game plan for iaxis.

Sadly, the offer of five hundred and seventy-five million pounds has just been rejected by the big shareholders around him and we have already pulled out of one attempt to raise a high-yield bond in October 1999. Now the money is getting very tight. We have built two huge new networks in Germany and Central Europe and iaxis has no money to fund them whatsoever and we are completely *winging it*. Our big suppliers are providing us with vendor finance with the written guarantee that they will get an equity stake in iaxis when we float on the NASDAQ. However, we need to raise a three hundred million dollar high-yield bond just to keep us going.

We have a lot of customer orders for capacity on the telecommunications network, but with the pitiful remains of the money pile on fire these cannot be serviced properly. And the system slowly but surely starts to malfunction. iaxis has a ferocious appetite for hard cash and can burn money fast, *very fast indeed*. It is therefore high yield in April 2000, or death.

The iaxis staff all had to write their cheques by mid-January, including the vice president and chief financial officer who put in over one million dollars of their own savings. But looking back at what the iaxis personnel now know, all was not well during the cold month of January 2000. And with a new "father figure" at the "iaxis throne", something is definitely "rotten in the State of Denmark" as far as the telecoms boom is going. And in the boardroom the air is now very frosty.

...And from within the old wooden cabin, the wolves are out in the distant, dark forest, and they're not too far away. And all who sit around that glass table can now hear them...

'Afternoon Steve!' says Wacko, as I dump the Starbucks' copy of *Hello!* in to my bin.

'Tequila maniac...it's your fault!' I say to Wacko, as I sit in my chair and log on.

Wacko laughs.

'Hey Wacko, how much did the whole boardroom cost?' I ask, looking at my Omega watch. It's only 9:19 a.m.

He puts down the 'LAN Management Overview MP-214' network map of the Frankfurt fibre optic local loop and thinks for a moment. 'Well the glass table itself was over a hundred and fifty thousand dollars. But overall I think it is in the region of half a million dollars or more,' says Wacko, as he gets up and goes for an office walk; Hannah is looking like she might just wander over to him.

'Shit, I wouldn't have liked to have copped the bill for that one,' I say to Nathan, as he mentally adds up the decimal points to get to the final figure.

'Neither did iaxis!' he says, having a laugh. 'The ex-chairman just went ahead and had it designed and then ordered it! It's not paid for, like most things around here.'

'Really! So what about the CEO, what did he say about it all?'

'Well he came in and blew a gasket at the extravagance of it all. But really there are no checks and balances in here. We have set up a massive fibre optic network around Germany connecting twelve cities and we have no orders for it. And we're well under way in setting the next phase, which links Frankfurt, Zurich, Paris, Milan and Geneva. We've sold loads of capacity already here, but neither network plan is fully funded, so we're just blagging it out and winging it like fuck until we float on the NASDAQ.'

'Isn't anyone concerned?'

'No, everything will get sorted with the high-yield and NASDAQ flotation. After that we'll all fuck off when a big fish comes and writes a big cheque and takes us over.'

'So what about budgets and cost savings?'

Nathan laughs as if these are concepts he's not totally familiar with. After all, iaxis is his first job after graduating from Cambridge.

'Well, the best laugh was when the new CEO told everyone they were now going to fly easyjet around Europe. The ex-chairman informed the travel booker, with a few "f" and "c" words, that he wasn't flying 'effing, c-ing easy effing jet, c-ing anywhere'! So he went and booked a holiday, flying first class to Australia for a month on iaxis!' says Nathan, leaning back in his chair.

'That's right,' says Wacko, who's now back at the quad scanning the other desks and holding one of the bottles of tequila I bought him for pulling me in.

'Wacko, there's loads more Internet backbone connections now.'

'Excellent. Just keep blagging it out and get in as many as possible. It's all free, right?'

Nathan nods his head, feeling tired after last night's tequila session as well.

'Steve, could you go and make sure Hannah knows? She's putting together a presentation for a merchant bank for the high-yield.'

'Okay,' I say, as Wacko sits back and relaxes, both at the number of Internet backbone connections iaxis is now getting and, more importantly, at the fact that he doesn't have to go up to Hannah's desk.

Wacko begins to read *Yachting Monthly* as he now has to choose a different yacht after Howard said he would pay someone (Seamus) to sink his yacht when it was moored up in Lymington! (He'd get a warning of course.)

'When I speak to Hannah, shall I put in a good word for you at the same time, mate?'

Wacko looks terrified. 'No you fucking won't!' he says, laughing after seeing I was joking.

Hannah is in her fortieth year and comes from a *'Murders and Assassinations'* (Mergers and Acquisitions) City background. She is still wired up to the City with City talk. However, she is also one of life's thirty-nine-year-old Cosmopolitan readers, who is actively hunting for a toy boy. Hannah has an intense stare, *The Force*, which frightens the hell out of every single male in iaxis. She is also totally and completely infatuated with Wacko. She loves to sit on blokes' desks and this is a terrifying experience. It is known to all in iaxis as *'The desk treatment'* and is a truly frightening encounter.

But Hannah is a very sweet person. However, according to Wacko, if you had a brief fling with her and then said 'I think we should just be good friends, etc,' then your family's pet rabbit would get cooked and your kids might enjoy a day trip to Alton Towers! But Wacko has not "been there with her" and she craves him. I think this, more than anything iaxis can throw at him, is what wakes him up in a cold sweat during the night.

I approach Hannah's desk very carefully, scanning the walkway for tripwires that she has quite possibly rigged up, earnestly hoping some young guy walking past will trip and land on her lap. No amount of hand-to-hand combat training could get you out of her passionate grip.

'Hannah, we've got loads more Internet peering connections,' I say, as I arrive safely at her desk having skillfully avoided triggering any of her booby traps.

'*Steve, that's super!*' she gasps, as she jumps up from her seat with a huge smile on her face. Her eyes are only a few inches from mine as she proceeds to mentally rip my clothes off. I smile back politely and a thin bead of sweat breaks out on my temples as *The Force* moves closer. I nervously bite my bottom lip and scan the room for the fire exits. I know exactly where they are, but I look at them for reassurance.

'Are you charming all these people, or what?' she asks, gazing very affectionately into my eyes.

Her nose is now almost touching mine and I take the bait.

'Yes, I must be!'

'*Brilliant!* You look like a charmer, so you can charm me. Come on, let's go outside to Manhattan's. You can buy me a coffee.'

I manage to keep my straight poker face, while inside my head all I can think is how the fuck did I allow this happen?

She picks up her Benson and Hedges and puts them in her Louis Vuitton handbag. (Hannah made a fortune in the City and now lives in a very plush pad just off the King's Road, alone, *for the time being...*)

We walk past Wacko's desk and he turns away laughing his head off. (Bastard!)

Hannah and I hit the ground floor and the lift doors open. As we prepare to walk out, Carol Vorderman walks in to go up and my chin smacks off the lift floor. Hannah hears it, turns around and quickly sees the puppy-dog look on my face as I come very close to dribbling at the unexpected delight of seeing the lovely Carol. (We all love Carol on our quad.)

However, Carol doesn't notice me at all. This is of course no great surprise, as Hannah practically drags me out of the lift while I try to tell her I've left my wallet upstairs.

'I'll pay, sweetie,' she says firmly, as if dissent were no option whatsoever.

The word 'bollocks' runs silently out of my lips as we walk the short distance out of the ITN building down to Manhattan's. It is quite noisy in the street outside as COLT are digging up the road, drilling away in order to lay a fibre optic cable.

While Hannah gets the cappuccinos in, I grab a couple of seats next to the window and watch the world go by. I also text Wacko's mobile to tell him I've just seen Carol Vorderman downstairs in reception. *And she looks fantastic!*

Hannah eventually arrives with a couple of drinks. 'So how are you settling in sweetie?' she asks with interest, as she sits down.

'Very well thanks, but it's a massive learning curve,' I say, trying to avoid her intense gaze.

'Yeah, you're right honey. I found it the same after I left the City,' she says, as she breaks eye contact and lights up.

'Yes, I bet you did, but the teamwork in iaxis is great and our quad is fantastic,' I say, as I breathe in and sample some of her B&H fumes.

'Yes, I've never seen teamwork like it in any other place,' she says, as Mr Nice walks past the window, and she suddenly looks away in order to avoid him. Mr Nice is the only bloke she doesn't terrify.

…His starey eyes have her on edge and it is fantastic when he turns it around and sits on her desk. She just sits there gripping the arms on her chair, like he's some Texas governor away to hit the fry switch. And all he's doing is telling her about his next 'shipment', which is probably from Arthur M. Brown's employer in Burma.

'So isn't there any helpful teamwork in the City?' I ask, already knowing the answer.

'What! Those wankers wouldn't help you even if you slipped on the office floor and broke a leg!'

'Well, that's your own fault for wearing high heels!' I say jokingly, as my eyes check out her *Hermès* silk neckscarf.

Then the world seems to stand still.

…It is as if they were all beamed from 'Deep Space 9' straight onto Gray's Inn Road: Wacko, Nathan, McGowan, Merlock, Stalker, Porn Star, Howard, Seamus and Gibbsy suddenly appear in front of Manhattan's, banging slowly on the window. All are staring away, with their eyes lighting up the whole coffee shop like Wembley Stadium. And they have a crazed, possessed look on their faces, which frightens everyone inside!

'Where's Carol??!!!' I hear Wacko yell in a demented drone over the sound of the roadworks outside.

I shrug my shoulders and motion with my head, 'back up to the office'. To which they all turn slowly around and start walking up the street like extras in a Romero zombie film, with their arms slowly waving about as if they are feeling their way back up the road, all possessed and looking for Carol!

Past the awful sounds of people screaming and taxis crashing, I see that Hannah's face does not hide the fact that she is now heartbroken. I'll text Wacko later and tell him in order to save his own life he should now go for a long meeting this afternoon and maybe even an overland trucking holiday from *Cairo* to Cape Town.

She summons some inner strength and continues.

'When I saw you on your first day wearing that pinstriped suit, I thought you were a City wanker coming back to haunt me. I thought you were an old boy, Steve!' she says, eyeballing me again.

'No, not at all!' I say, as I take a sip of my cappuccino and attempt to wrestle the Romero images out of my mind. I can just picture the crowd of "zombies" all walking blindly possessed with their arms waving about scouring the ITN building as they bring terror to the other floors. All droning away, *'Where's Carol?!!!'*

Hannah quickly brings me back from *Zombies Dawn of the Dead*, just as Carol, Jon Snow and Trevor MacDonald are escaping through the hatch on the roof of the ITN building!

'Yes, but I was wrong Steve!' she says, as she suddenly and without any warning whatsoever, firmly places one of her hands on top of mine to thrust home the point she's making.

I suddenly jolt backwards as I get an electric shock. All her repressed sexual energy has turned into live static and surged through my body on her connection!

'Wow, there's a spark between us!' she says, with a beaming smile. 'I'm just kidding sweetie, you've done really well to fit in,' she says humorously, as she notices that I'm now starting to look completely fucking terrified.

Somehow, I start to control my fear. I don't know what Wacko's been through. He just starts to shake and shudder when I broach the subject of Hannah with him. I'll now be getting that counselling number from him later on. Hopefully before he departs for *Egypt*.

'So how long have you been here?' I ask, as I think hear a helicopter taking off from the ITN roof.

'Quite a while now… pretty much from the start really,' she says, sounding like a bearer of *ancient knowledge*.

'So how did iaxis take shape and develop?'

She takes a glance at the time on her elegant ladies' gold Omega wristwatch.

'You've heard of Kevin Maxwell, the son of Robert Maxwell?'

'Yes, of course I have.'

'Well his old company was involved in the creation of iaxis,' she says, as she flicks some dead ash into the ashtray.

'Really! So does he have anything to do with iaxis now?' I ask, as I realise there are loads of pieces missing in my iaxis puzzle.

'No, he doesn't have anything to do with us now, but iaxis was born out of a Maxwell company called Telemonde, which Kevin Maxwell set up a few years ago. Nearly all of the senior directors in iaxis worked with Kevin at Telemonde, but he was always in the background then.'

'So who are Telemonde?'

'Telemonde are a company selling bandwidth and voice traffic (minutes). They're very successful in selling minutes to Russia and the Middle East. Our ex-chairman even went to Russia with Kevin and helped him to get set up. Kevin's a very sharp and intelligent cookie. He's also very charming and could sell you an ice cube in winter!'

'Yes, I've heard that.'

'We even saw Jonathan Aitken round at our office on Grosvenor Street. He never came in to see us of course, just Kevin Maxwell. Political connections are very handy in the telecoms world, young Steve. But nobody really knows why Aitken was there.'

'He could've been getting some change for the parking meter,' I say, with a knowing smile.

'Yeah, right, sweetheart!' says Hannah, as she smiles and continues my morning briefing…

(…The senior persons of iaxis all worked for the Maxwell/Telemonde set up and helped to revolutionise transatlantic (TA) bandwidth sales on the sub-sea fibre optic cables. Our ex-chairman saw an opportunity to move away from the old boy PTT /Telco cartel which basically set the prices for the massive TA bandwidth contracts. A company called Gemini, which is a joint venture between Metropolitan Fibre Services (MFS) and Cable and Wireless, built their own sub-sea fibre optic cable across the North Atlantic and began selling capacity independent of the cartel. Gemini lit the fibre in early 1998. Our ex-chairman and vice presidents at Maxwell/Telemonde had

the idea to buy a huge wedge of capacity from Gemini and resell it quickly at a profit.)

'So roughly how much did this Maxwell set-up buy?'

'Loads of capacity. I think it was approximately one hundred and eighteen million dollars worth of telecoms capacity making up an STM-16. We then sold it all in sixteen separate blocks,' she says, following another deep drag on her fag.

'So whom did the Maxwell/Telemonde group sell it on to?' I ask, as I feel my throat going dry at the amount of fag fumes drifting my way.

'Just for a single block of capacity on this new fibre, Carrier 1 paid ten and a half million dollars in June 1998 for a trans-Atlantic STM-1. Carrier 1 was their first customer. But it was a success, so the ex-chairman just went out and bought another STM-16 from Gemini's rivals Global Grossing. It was all done through front companies and trustees around the Caribbean. The other board members at Telemonde found out about this second STM-16 a few days after it was done.'

'So what did the chief financial officer say about that?' I ask, feeling stunned.

'Well, he used to have black hair, but it turned grey overnight!' she says, laughing at the memory.

'That's a huge amount of cash for transatlantic capacity. Aren't bandwidth prices falling right now?'

She laughs.

'Yes, they're falling like an elephant that's just walked off a mountain. Right now you can buy the same capacity for approximately two million dollars and it will fall a great deal more in the future.'

'So how exactly was iaxis born out of the Maxwell/Telemonde set-up?' I ask, as I share her fag fumes and think about my out of court settlement with the tobacco companies.

'Well, the ex-chairman had this idea of building a pan-European fibre optic backbone in September 1998, but the Maxwells were not interested, so there was a split. We went to court to try and keep using the Telemonde name, but the judge said we could use it for just a short period of time.'

'And then the company split in two very separate ways?'

'Exactly. The people who shared the ex-chairman's vision of building a pan-European telecoms network all left with him in early 1999. A couple of them were former senior bods at WorldCom in London.'

'So what about the name iaxis, where did that spring from?'

'We contacted a firm called Enterprise IG to come up with a sharp-sounding name. And iaxis was born. It's short for "*Information axis*". We hit the ground running in April 1999. The name itself cost us a quarter of a million dollars.

'And that was it?'

'Well that's just the beginning. After this, we all got to work. A great saying from the very top in here is "Just do it, we'll worry about the money later". You see iaxis has never really had a fully funded business plan, but we put together a pan-European backbone in little over one hundred and twenty days and lit the fibre. And this had never been done before.'

'Right, so you got credibility.' I say, as I try and grasp this *pyramid*-type puzzle.

'Absolutely. In the telecoms world we got instant credibility for this huge achievement. We then sold a lot of the capacity on this first network within a couple of months and I think Carrier 1 was our first customer here as well. After that we've never looked back.'

'So the iaxis network, it's not paid for, is it?'

'Don't be silly! We've paid a few deposits here and there and winged it the rest of the way. There's lots of money coming in, but where that goes is anyone's guess. iaxis has a huge appetite for cash, and shelves out a fortune in salaries every month. I don't even think some of our licences are paid for!' she says, laughing.

'So who were the first investors in iaxis?'

'Have you heard of a boutique investment bank called Chiltern?'

'No.'

'Well, they are described by many in here as our "Guardian Angels". They have strong Iranian connections, which goes back to the old days when very wealthy and well-connected mullahs deposited money with them. Then the Union Bank of Switzerland bought them. But in the mid-Nineties when UBS and Swiss Bank Corporation merged, the Chiltern team bought themselves back out and started trading as Chiltern again. They are very well respected and connected in the City. They were involved with us at the Telemonde set-up. But even they were totally unaware that Kevin Maxwell was involved as well. They only found out afterwards. Kevin was always kept well hidden in the background.'

'So how come this Chiltern investment house became involved?'

'Well, a chap called *"Mr Luciani"* brought them in. He has been with us from the start and is well connected in Italy and other places. He is always coming and going from the office. But just for this introduction, he got paid a nice wedge of a consultancy fee. Anyway, Chiltern's lent us ten million dollars to get started. And if it weren't for that money at the time it came, we wouldn't have turned the idea to build this network from an idea on a scrap of paper drawn up in the pub... into reality.'

"Luciani". Didn't his house have a big fire when iaxis was working on the "Italian Job" with the *Mafia*?' I ask, as my usual discretion is having a morning coffee break.

She looks around the coffee shop and is amazed at my indiscretion. Thankfully the place is relatively empty.

'Never mention that, even in jest, sweetie,' she says, looking deadly serious, as I suddenly feel a chill around the back of my neck as my heart misses a couple of beats. She continues, 'Chiltern also provided us with our chief financial officer. He's Iranian and used to work for them. He made a fortune in the film industry. He was the managing director of Soverign Pictures and was involved in the financing of films like *My Left Foot, Hamlet, The Commitments, Reversal of Fortune* and *Cinema Paradiso* and has even been to the Oscars ceremony in LA.'

'Now that is impressive. So he's joined the right company if he's got a background in entertainments!' I say, laughing *naturally*.

'Have you met him yet, sweetie?' she asks, not really seeing the funny side to my humour.

'No, but I've seen him walking around. He's very quiet and keeps a low profile. Seems nice enough though.'

'He is probably one of the most honourable people you could meet, very honest and sincere,' she says, with utter candour.

'And he's invested his money in iaxis as well?'

'Yes, he's put just over one million dollars of his own money into iaxis. He wrote his cheque out with everyone else in mid-January when iaxis was already running on empty.'

'So what about the high-yield bond and the IPO/flotation on the NASDAQ that you're working on?'

'Two things: firstly we have no money whatsoever to fund our current network developments. Secondly, if we're going to float on the NASDAQ, the City likes to see high-yield debt on the books. But basically we need it to survive. Getting a large amount of debt shouldn't be a problem, the banks are fighting to take us on to the NASDAQ. We just have to choose which one. The telecoms market on Wall Street is out of control right now, but it won't last. *Time is very short and anything can happen.*'

'So how much are we trying to raise to cover everything?'

'It's close to about three hundred million dollars. Which means I've got to love you and leave you, as I'm presenting the Internet backbone angle on iaxis to some City wankers,' she says, as she stubs out her fag and we both stand up to leave.

As we walk back through the ground floor reception I nod to the security guards who are looking relieved that the ITN building is secure once again. (But I feel gutted when I see that there is no Carol Vorderman waiting to go up in the lift.)

Upstairs, Wacko's trance has now worn off. He sees us both walking back towards him, and runs into an office to avoid Hannah. He starts chatting away to Eryl the chief technical officer, probably about the weather, as both of them are looking out of the glass wall window at the storm clouds in the distance heading towards the City of London.

I get back to my desk and check my emails for more Internet backbone connection responses from other big players, and there are quite a few.

Wacko walks back to our quad and is eyeballing all the surrounding desks making sure it's safe. But Hannah has already left with her iaxis laptop, the latest and most expensive high-tech piece of gizmo kit on the market.

'Was Carol Vorderman really downstairs?' he asks, almost out of breath with anticipation.

'Yes, she looked at me and smiled. It was wonderful, she was about to start speaking, and then Hannah dragged me out of the lift. Carol looked at us and thought we were an item!'

'Shit, you don't need that at all!'

I shake my head and look severely disappointed.

'So what happened with Hannah? She didn't try and drag you in to the toilets or anything did she? You were gone for fucking ages.'

I look at my watch. 'It was just over thirty-three minutes.'

'All that time with her!' he says, as he shudders at the thought.

'Yes, she's very knowledgeable. And she does like you.'

As soon as I say this, horror begins to engulf him and he suddenly looks like a man beaten around the head, struggling to find the will to go on, while trying to find an exit out...

'What did she say?' he gasps in terror, *hanging* on to my every word.

'Well it was the way she smiled fondly and gazed out of the window when I mentioned your name. She spoke very warmly of you, saying how she loves having a younger man like you as her boss. It's well obvious she likes you.'

'Too right it is,' says Nathan, who's only just returned to the land of the living and hasn't got a clue about where he's been for the last *thirty-three* minutes.

'And Wacko, she asked if you were seeing anyone,' I say, trying not to laugh, as he puts his bald head in his hands and shakes it in despair.

'*Oh christ*, can't she find someone who's older than her? Someone who's about to peg it?' he says, as fear sets in.

'Hey, she also said Kevin Maxwell was involved in giving birth to iaxis when we were part of the Telemonde set-up.'

He rubs his eyes, which are now looking traumatised.

'Yes, that's right. But it's *ancient history*. Everyone in the industry knows that. But how's the Internet peering connections coming on?' he asks, composing himself.

'Great. I've got a good few more in. Along with Suzie's hardcore porn distributions.'

'*Jesus!* I forgot to say, she flashed her boobs at the window cleaners who were working outside on their ledge this morning! The poor lads nearly fell off it!' says Wacko as we all fall about laughing.

'Come on, let's go over to the Blue Lion. It'll be open. It's nearly lunchtime.'

Wacko and I walk past the Network Operations Centre, heading for the exit doors in reception. As we walk past the NOC, the glass doors open and some hard house tunes are thumping out of their sound system. It's *'Church of RA'* by Digger and it's beating loudly as Sasha walks out.

'Hi Steve!'

Sasha's voice nearly trips me up as I was looking at the glass ceiling feeling the beat of the dance floor. I have an eyelock with Sasha and my posture starts to melt. She does have an amazing figure and looks stunning in that short YSL black skirt with a black poloneck Versace cashmere jumper, worn with a smile that is priceless.

(Wacko clearly sees this mad case of puppy love and wants to smack me in the face!)

'Hi Sasha!'

Seeing her just now has made my day. Wacko just grunts at her and looks ahead at the glass reception doors. Sasha and I just keep smiling at each other as we walk closer.

...But young Nathan is right. She is soaking up and feeding off my stares more than ever. I can feel all the energy I had forty seconds ago being slowly drained from my soul as I enter the light as she passes me and it is as if my body is giving away pints of blood. I just gaze at that face on a body with those legs. She flicks her silky long blonde hair and carries on walking more sexily than ever before...

I hear Wacko shouting at me, just as the swivel doors on the ground floor of the ITN building are suddenly two inches from the tip of my nose. That was a close one, as the doors come very close to taking my pecker off. As we hit the street I feel weaker. The effects of *The Zone* are yet to wear off and and I slowly begin to recover from this almost *"Jacobs Ladder"* type experience. We get outside and I suddenly realise I have lost all sense of coolness as my mouth feels like it has been open for fucking ages.

'She's lovely,' I say, as I become aware that Wacko is standing over me eyeballing me, pointing and shouting away telling me I've now been *brainwashed* by her. I'm not really sure what he's saying as this killer trance is far from wearing off. Jon Snow walks past us both and thinks this could be a news item - *'Murder on the front doorstep.'*

We both cross Gray's Inn Road to go to the Blue Lion.

...In a parallel universe, I cross the same road using ESP and somehow manage to avoid all the taxis, as my brain cells adjust from that almost nine-megahertz ELF transmission from Sasha!

'Steve, if you mention her name over this drink I'll fucking sack you! Two vodka and Red Bulls please,' asks Wacko, laughing and shaking his head as the barman approaches us.

'Right, co-location, pay attention, this is your training. I'll bring you up to speed on where iaxis is on this and that should take your mind off Sasha.'

I am still staring wildly while he's talking. I take a gulp of the drink, which attacks the sudden dryness in my mouth and throat.

'Have you heard of a company called Digiplex?'

'Yes, I've heard the name bandied about the office.'

'Good. Well Digiplex are a massive co-location outfit which was born out of iaxis. It is a joint venture between iaxis, Carrier 1, Providence and the Carlyle Group. Have you heard of the Carlyle Group before?'

'No,' I say, as my face looks blank and I try to get Sasha's telepathic messages out of my mind.

Wacko has a good mouthful of his drink before bringing me up to speed and handing me a few major pieces to the *overall jigsaw puzzle.*

'The Carlyle Group is a hugely powerful and very low-profile US investment house. They have over twelve billion dollars in assets and average around thirty-five percent returns on their global investments every year in oil, defence, consumer goods, real estate, health care, IT and telecoms all over the world. The former US Secretary of State during the Gulf War, James Baker, is currently their senior councillor and they are also very close to the Bush family. In fact, the former US President George Bush Sr is one of their leading advisors right at the top.'

'So they're a major player then?'

'That firm can pick up the phone *and make a call.* Basically, they are the top investment bankers for the American "High Cabal". They have got the elite of Washington and Texan Republican politics behind them and they are also helping to fund George W. Bush for the election later this year. They also have lots of people with "grey" backgrounds on their staff. There is no other private investment bank more powerful than they are anywhere in the world. And their ability to pull in big banks like Chase Manhattan for joint investments is second to none. The old U.S. Defense Secretary Frank Carlucci is their chairman and is still very close with George Bush Sr,' he says, gulping down his drink.

'Never heard of the Carlyle Group before, but *Frank Carlucci* and *George Bush Sr*, I know all about them,' I say, as the Beta wave signals in my brain suddenly become scrambled once again as I notice a picture of *John Lennon* on the pub wall...

'I'm impressed Steve. So you'll know that George Bush Sr was once the Director of Central Intelligence at the CIA and Frank Carlucci was also a senior CIA officer for years, and in 1978-*80* he was their deputy head. He was briefed on the "Covert Programs" during *that* time and was awarded the National Intelligence Distinguished Service Medal in 1981. And you didn't get that for sitting on your backside in an office doing fuck all during the "Cold War" in the Seventies and *1980.*'

'Yes and after the "arms to Iran" thing ["with the CIA's St Lucia Airways..."] blew up the Reagan administration, Carlucci was made Secretary of State for Defense,' I say, while thinking about the White House arms to Iran scandal with Oliver North, ["...SETCO and Bank Cantrade, Switzerland. Deals which humiliated America's ally at the time, good old Saddam Hussein of Iraq, something which one knows all about, dear boy..."] and the various CIA deals which went back to 1981.

'That's right. After the Contra affair ["...Involving Otto Reich,General John Singlaub, John Negroponte and the CIA trained Battalion 3-16..."], Carlucci was the new low profile Defense Secretary with all the clout,' says Wacko, stirring his drink.

'Yes, and he still has clout...' I add, as I have a sip on mine.

'Too fucking right he has. Now Carlucci's the chairman of the Carlyle Group and has billions and billions of dollars to invest all over the world. They have massive connections globally, especially in Washington and Saudi Arabia. In the early Nineties, in the years after the Gulf War, the Carlyle Group received more funds, and their investments were extended from real estate.'

'So what are their connections like in Saudi Arabia?' I ask, as I know quite a bit about the Kingdom.

'Absolutely brilliant. In 1994 they were appointed as the official advisor for the Saudi Government's "Economic Offset Programme". But from a City angle, the Carlyle Group has cherry picked the best fund managers and economists in the world to be on their staff. Even our ex-Prime Minister John Major works as an advisor for the Carlyle Group. He's currently on their European Advisory Board, advising them on their European investment strategy. They want him full time for a leading role in the group, as he really knows his stuff.'

'Too right he does. So is the Carlyle Group strategically aligned with anyone else?'

'Well they're very private, but the Carlyle Group has a close relationship with George Soros and a strictly unofficial relationship with Henry Kissinger of Kissinger Associates. Also a good few ex-world leaders seem to be involved with them in some way or another, all big friends of the old Bush administration at the end of the "Cold War".'

'I'll check them out later. It sounds like they're a force to be reckoned with.'

'Oh yes. And they are in bed with iaxis for this Digiplex set-up. Look at their website, it's really quite informative if you want to see who works for them and where they invest some of their money. You'd be surprised at their spirit of "Glasnost" here.'

'So why did they get involved with iaxis?'

'Well, after iaxis was formed in April 1999, we were looking for co-location buildings around Europe and the USA, with the help of some Iranians. We were going to buy the buildings and iaxis would lease the buildings from the Iranian front companies. They'd get an income stream through property rentals and we'd have a building for twenty-five years.'

'So what happened?'

'Fuck knows. The money never came, probably because they had to go and fight a war or something! But the ex-chairman still had his connections. One of whom was a very senior figure in the Carlyle Group, someone at the top. The Carlyle Group looked at the business plan, liked it and put money in.'

'So has Carlyle made a big investment here?'

'This Digiplex set-up is their single biggest investment in Europe. Co-location is going to be huge in the future. They've also invested hundreds of millions in co-location facilities in the USA and elsewhere. The potential to make serious money is there.'

'Really? So how much is being invested in Digiplex?'

'It will be a total investment of over two hundred and fifty million dollars before all the buildings are finished. But Digiplex is going to be worth well over ten billion dollars after they float. And Carlyle are the main shareholders. iaxis, along with Carrier1 and Providence, are only fifteen per cent partners and we're well under way building and kitting out our own. We stand to make a fortune.'

'So are Carlyle good at making money?'

'They sure are, and making a shit load of it that will be sustained over many years. And they are very, very good at doing this. But on a lighter note, bear in mind the clout that the Carlyle Group carries in US politics, so don't ever fuck with them!' he says, laughing, as I decide I won't be going for a walk over Blackfriars Bridge in case I lose my balance and fall off it.

["...Or worse, 'commit suicide' under it, Steve!"]

'So this was the start of the iaxis involvement in co-location?' I ask, as two more drinks arrive.

'Basically, yeah,' he says, yawning before taking a swig on his Red Bull mix. 'But separate to our joint venture with Carlyle/Digiplex we are also sourcing our own smaller sites around three thousand square metres.'

'Really. So how big are these Carlyle/Digiplex sites then?' I ask, as I drink the remaining Red Bull from the can.

'Their sites are massive. They're about ten thousand square meters plus and are all over Europe, but their co-location building in in Frankfurt is a monster of a thing at fifty-five thousand square meters!'

'So what is a co-location site like these ones iaxis and Carlyle/Digiplex are sprouting up?' I ask, as 'Imagine' by *John Lennon* starts to play on the pub jukebox.

'It's a building where the Internet lives.'

I look blank again.

'Okay, it's basically a massive high-security warehouse that stores the gear that powers and runs telecom and Internet networks. You've heard of telecom DWDM gear, Juniper and Cisco routers and ATM switches for voice minutes, yeah? Well these pieces of techie kit are all housed in these co-location buildings that power the fibre optic networks.'

A big flashing beam of light suddenly bolts out from my eyes and hits the pub wall!

'I've heard these ATMs being mentioned around the office and I didn't want to say anything, but I thought we were getting involved with installing cash machines!' I say, as he nearly falls off his barstool laughing away.

'We might have to drive a JCB into a building society to get our hands on one! These developments won't be fully paid for until we float on the NASDAQ. Until then it's small deposits where necessary.'

'So I take it that none of these developments are paid for, right?'

'Well, not yet, but the money will come. But if you know anyone who can drive a JCB, just let me know!'

'So how does it all get tied together?'

'Well, a co-location building is kitted with all this techie gear which is then stored in rack space, connected to fibre optic telecoms cables. Then Internet servers can be housed in the rack space and this is where the Internet Service Providers (ISPs) technologically operate from. It's where a website basically lives.'

'I don't get it,' I say, as I down another gulp.

'Basically everything that's online in the world such as Yahoo, Hotmail, AOL and thousands of others are housed in and technically run from these co-location facilities. The amount of telecoms and Internet traffic that flows through these buildings is really frightening.'

'I never knew that. I thought the Internet was housed in offices.'

'So did I, but the websites are managed from offices. But these buildings are where the Internet lives. You know people think the Internet is clean and environmentally friendly, but that is a load of crap. Do you know how much electricity it takes to power just one of these co-location buildings?' asks Wacko, as my mind is being brought up to speed in seconds.

'No idea,' I say, as my stomach tells me it is time we had some food.

'About a minimum of six megawatts of power. And six megs is enough electricity to power a small city in the UK.'

'Six megawatts! That's outrageous! How many buildings eat up this much power in the UK?'

'There's about thirty, mostly in the London area, with Docklands the main hub of activity. But there's hundreds going to be springing up all around Europe, and some co-location centres can ramp up the power to fifty megawatts. There are also some massive ones in *Chicago* and *New York* and there's more on the way. Buy shares in electricity companies if you want to make money. That is the future, but when the planet starts to cook from the inside we'll be sorry!' he says, as he finishes his drink and asks the barmaid for two more as the place is starting to fill up with Granada Media staff.

With our alcohol supply secured, he continues. 'iaxis is looking for these facilities all over Europe. Right now we are looking for buildings to convert in Holland, Germany, Italy, Denmark, France, Sweden, Norway, Belgium, Switzerland and New York. This co-location roll-out is a major part of our strategic network development strategy, which I am responsible for, as I buy all the fibre, buildings, implementation kit and this adds up to a shit load of money!'

'So where are the buildings in these cities?'

'Good question after three drinks! They are located near the main fibre networks and a shit load of electricity. *Just before Christmas*, we signed a twenty-five year lease for a fantastic building in Amsterdam. Only afterwards did we realise it was too far away from the main power lines and it barely had enough juice to power a Sinclair ZX Spectrum!'

'So what did iaxis do?' I ask, as I'm hoping that I don't make a mistake like this.

He has a nice big gulp of his drink. 'We just tore up the contract and posted it back to the landlord! We said in the covering letter that the building wasn't suitable for our needs.'

'So what did he do?' I ask, amazed that iaxis would brass this out on a written agreement.

'Don't know. Nobody takes his calls. I think he flogged it to somebody else,' he says, totally unfazed.

'What happened to the person who made the decision to go with the building, was he sacked?

'Oh no, he's still here. In iaxis, nobody gets sacked for making mistakes. It's how we all learn. You always get a *"Third Chance"*!'

'So how come the big balls-up?'

'Well, basically I think this was his first visit to Amsterdam and he just fucking went for it. After living in this small hamlet in Wales, spending all his life staring at sheep, hills and valleys, Amsterdam must've seemed like Seventh Heaven to him! I reckon he saw the first big building after a heavy night out on the town and just signed it up. He's just a young lad.'

I rub my tired eyes, which are now feeling very heavy from these lunchtime drinks.

'So what happens after we find a building close to these main fibre optic cables and power supplies?

He has another gulp.

'We kit it out with other essentials such as biometric security, you know, palm print and eyeball scanning stuff, CCTV, bomb-proof walls, fibre optic connection points, cooling systems, air conditioning, fire prevention, unlimited power supply systems. The security of these buildings is essential. In fact a good few of these co-location companies all have ex-senior US military personnel sitting on the boards as directors. To even get into some of these buildings is like entering a NATO facility.'

'So how do we make our money here?' I ask, as I hear yells that say someone has just won a lot of money on the pool table.

'Once the building is kitted out, iaxis will then sell floor space and racks to the telecom and Internet companies and make lots of dollars in the process. Well, that's what it says in the business plan.'

'Does Swampy in the NOC know about this massive demand for electricity behind the Internet?' I ask, as more money changes hands on the pool table.

'No he fucking doesn't! If he did know he'd probably trash the NOC and chain himself up in there in protest, so don't go and tell him whatever you do! I don't want to spoil his hippy fantasy that the Internet is snow white and eco-friendly and all that fairytale bollocks. But don't ever forget it. Never in the history of the planet has something chomped away at so much electricity as the Internet and telecoms networks.'

'Right, and these co-location facilities power the whole system?'

'Correct. And there are hundreds of these buildings powering the Internet backbones and telecoms networks all over the world. In fact I'm surprised the planet isn't being cooked. And as mobile phones take off we'll all get fucking microwaved as well!'

My head starts to spin, as I think to myself that this sounds as terrifying as a few nights at the YMCA in *Beirut* in the mid-Seventies!

'Well, that's your co-location training over with, come on, drink up, we'll go and get a pizza for lunch at Roberto's. Put it down as training on expenses.'

I down the rest of my drink and my eyes water, as there was more vodka than Red Bull in it. I just wish I'd got up earlier and had some breakfast.

'Also, as part of your *"training programme"*, you'll be going overseas on a site visit soon,' he says, as my eyes try to focus on the door of the Blue Lion as we leave the pub.

'Won't people get pissed off with us taking a lunch on the company?' I ask, with a slight slur in my voice.

'No, it's training, and besides, Psycho has three-course lunches every other day on iaxis! Also we fly first class, no matter what the new CEO wants with this "easyjet" policy, and we stay in expensive hotels when we travel as well.'

'Sounds good,' I say. I zip up my jacket, as it looks very dull outside and on the verge of a little *Hawaiian* storm.

The afternoon is one long blur as I try and read an article about John McMahon.

CHAPTER 7

My tanker chartering days seem a distant memory. Since I started at iaxis, the massive widescreen TV has hardly been used. Natasha has settled in very well in New York and we send each other emails every week. I keep hearing sweet words of advice from her: 'Just keep looking forward and never look back.' I only look back in amazement that I stayed with Seamart for so long. But now, I am just very happy that the chaps binned me and gave me the chance to move on.

'Nathan, happy birthday mate!' I say, as I sit down and hand him his presents, a Japanese import of the twelve-inch CD single of 'Insomnia' by Faithless and a bottle of tequila.

'Cheers Steve,' he says, totally surprised as he puts on that classic track.

Merlin walks in as Nathan looks up the tracks on the CD. He hands him a card and a present: a couple of frightening-looking manuals on naval cryptography called *NTC-21: Understanding the Public Telephone Network* and *NTC-22: Business Communication Systems*. Merlin taps the side of his nose and assures us all that it's bloody hard getting your hands on copies of these.

'Cheers Merlin,' he says, genuinely pleased at these gifts, as the "*Classic Wizard*" looks around the room and quietly tells him to put them away.

Wacko, who was in first, has already given him his present: two hundred Marlboro Lights, and there's no competition here as this, according to Nathan, is 'the best present in the fucking world!'

Later on in the day I can see Mr Nice getting everyone sorted with various goodies for Nathan's party tonight. (Whatever you want can be made available on the office floor. Everything is here at some time or another. If you want goodies, the following can be yours relatively quickly: skunk, weed, ecstasy, speed, cocaine, LSD and even poppers.)

Then, like an Exocet missile ready to cause devastation, Hannah walks up to our quad and sits on Wacko's desk. He's not long back from the toilet and barely contains his horror at the sight of Hannah now giving him '*The desk treatment*'! She's gazing into Wacko's eyes and he's flinching in terror as *The Force* hits him. Her back is to me and she can't see me raising my eyebrows at Wacko, intimating to him that she's in love with him. He starts to sweat and rubs his forehead as he tries to concentrate on what she's blabbing on about. It sounds like it's something to do with the high-yield bond issue.

I've been waiting a long time for this. Well, as a matter of fact, it's not even seventy-two hours since I bought the thing. I just knew I'd be able to use it quite soon for the occasion it was bought for... I open my drawer and pull out a small white fluffy bunny rabbit, which I show him (behind her back). I am smiling away at the look of sheer terror on his face as I mimic ripping its head off! It's only a toy, but he just gets up and swallows in despair. He tells Hannah that he has forgotten about a meeting and fucks off, leaving her sitting there.

Merlin is oblivious to our shenanigans and is quietly listening to Mozart on his headphones while playing with a set of Keymat and Skipjack encryption cards.

Hannah slides off Wacko's desk and walks around the quad and then proceeds to sit on my desk-top.

Fucking mine!

Now I physically shiver. 'How did this happen?' I ask myself yet again. And to make matters worse, I'm still holding the white bunny rabbit in my right hand.

(*'Do 'h!!'*)

'That's so cute, Steve!' she says, as she lifts it out of my hand. My brain cell is thinking about what to say in order to blag my way out of this one. My heart has suddenly turned into a sledgehammer and it wants to be out of the fucking building, let alone my body!

'Er...yes, I was just showing it to Nathan. I bought it for a friend who's just given birth to a baby girl. I'm not into fluffy toys, but it'll do as a present.'

Bunny rabbits and children are what she yearns for...

Her hungry, intense eyes are now on me and *The Force* feels deadlier than ever. Hannah's eyes now look like she wants to jump me so much that in her frenzied psychosexual state my back would snap.

'Oh that's so sweet, Steve! How thoughtful of you,' she says, as she crosses her legs and hands it back to me. I am still locked in eyelock as I start to shudder, but she bought the blag with ease.

Nathan is grinning at me and raising his eyebrows as well!

'We've got loads more Internet peering partners,' I say, as I sit very vulnerably in my comfortable chair while trying to get her mind off bunny rabbits and children.

'So who's the latest, sweetie?' she asks, as she affectionately rubs her neck in anticipation of my answer.

I pick up some notes and quickly scan the page as her eyes start to glaze over into a sex-hungry frenzied look. My throat suddenly feels dry and my heart is beating rather fast. Nathan is now laughing away as he sees my pulse struggle to get below one hundred beats per minute and the fact that normal colouring has left my face.

'Er... well we've got some pretty big names joining their Internet backbones with ours: TeleDenmark, Telenor, Versatel, COLT, EuroNet, GLOBIX, Mediaways, Sonera, Demon Internet, Energis, Gigabell, IPCenta, Madge, NTL, NTT Europe, SingTel, BBC, VIANET and loads more...'

'You must come and tell me how you've pulled it off...' she drones on in a sex-starved trance.

I am so busy focusing on anything Hannah might do that I completely miss Sasha approaching me as she walks past our quad. She smiles and says 'Hi'. She is now walking back to her desk in marketing blag and working that sexy body as each foot hits the ground. Hannah's mobile suddenly rings and she slides her bottom off my desk to answer it. It is a little silver Nokia.

'Speak later, Stevie boy,' she says, as she playfully messes with my hair. (Thankfully her feet have earthed her this time. I could very easily have been blown skywards through the glass ceiling. I would've been found some time later sitting in my chair somewhere on Gray's Inn Road just smouldering away.)

Hannah hits the answer button on her mobile.

'Yes, Hannah speaking. Oh, it's you... *What the fuck do you want?*' she asks aggressively, to some chap whom she may have opened her doors to recently. But it sounds like this fella has just lost his pet rabbit and is now left wondering why his kids have suddenly developed a taste for big dippers!

'There must be laws to stop this sort of thing happening,' I say, muttering away to Nathan, almost twitching.

Now it is time for "operational measures" to counter '*The desk treatment*'...

All of the Internet peering contracts are stored in several *red* folders that are filed ND-150 to ND-170 and are stored vertically on my desk. They are in a big pile and measure over one foot high. I tend to keep the OP-301 or the larger IS-180 network peering file wide open beside my keyboard, and a few paper files hanging out. I also leave my Cross fountain pen resting on them so it looks like it has been recently used...

...However, to the naked eye it looks like one big pile of insurance policies. And because it looks so untidy, this large pile of *red* folders should almost certainly be locked away in a filing cabinet. However, in office PSYOPS it looks like I have been busy as hell. I then dismantle the one big pile and make it into four smaller ones, which are then strategically placed around my desktop.

'There is no chance of her sitting on this desk any more,' I say to Nathan, feeling very proud at my advanced level of ingenuity to counter her advances.

'Steve, why don't you just mine your desk with fucking Claymores. That'll teach her. I'll rig one up for you if you want? I made a rocket with a bomb on it when I was eleven years old! It's piss easy to put some stuff together,' says Nathan, who is now looking at some manual he recently downloaded and printed off from the Internet.

'Yes, I'll design you a cobalt bomb if you want, Steve?' adds Merlin, who has now put down the 'Basic Traffic Analysis (TA-103)' network monitoring report and is going through his even bigger pile of desk folders.

'Ah, found the folder,' he says, rubbing his hands together as one of his Fortezza cards drops on the floor.

'If she does it again, it might just come to that, but thanks for the offers, chaps.'

A short while later Wacko returns to the quad. I smile over at him and raise my eyebrows, motioning my head over towards Hannah's desk.

'Fuck off or you'll be sacked!' he says, laughing and shuddering at the same time. He's still not able to wind down, or to generally be with it.

'So where was this meeting then, New York?' asks Nathan, just to take the piss and to make Wacko feel even more uncomfortable.

'It was with the chemist across the road. I needed a box of paracetamols.'

'Yes, I could do with a couple as my head hurts as well now.'

He hands me a couple as Nathan informs him what I've just gone though, which cheers him up. 'Serves you fucking right!' he says, as he goes to put his box of paracetamols in to his desk and then jumps backwards in shock.

(Nathan and I have put the 'dead' fluffy pet rabbit in his desk drawer!)

'You two are evil bastards,' he says, as we both crack up as he dumps the poor thing in to his waste paper basket. I very quickly bury it with some paper, just in case Hannah spots it. (Once his trauma begins to wear off, he'll start to laugh about it.)

Then the office seems to come alive as shrieks and screams of girls in delight penetrate the office floor. I peel my wide eyes off my flat screen and look up thinking Brad Pitt has entered the room. The girls are not disappointed as Nick runs around the office like a hungry dog lapping up all their affection for him. As he goes around the familiar desks, loads of hugs and kisses are then dished out for the boy, as all the girls' faces light up like Manhattan.

(Nick has just flown in from Marseilles specially for Nathan's party.)

As Nick approaches Hannah's desk he asks charmingly, 'Hi sweetheart, you sounded a bit tense on the phone, are you okay?'

'I'm fine thanks, Nick,' she says, in a manner to show him that she is not fine at all. In fact if a person's stare could do damage, I think Nick's testicles would be on the office floor in two or three pieces.

Nick is totally unfazed and just carries on doing the rounds. He has a good long chat with Mr Nice and now seems to be sorted with some goodies.

I decide it's time I trekked over to marketing via Sasha's desk... Moby is singing 'Why does my heart feel so bad?' and it is mellowly beating out of a set of speakers on Gabriela's desk in Network Operations. I look back and see Nick hasn't put Suzie down yet. And by the look of it, she doesn't want him to either.

...Another major rule in office PSYOPS is when you go for an office walk, always carry a piece of paper in your hand. It makes you look busy. You are walking from A to B, and the reason you are doing so is down to the piece of paper in your hand...

I've now got a piece of paper in my hand with our list of Internet backbone connections on it and therefore I look busy when I bump into Claire from Personnel. (She has recently spent yet another weekend in Marseilles with Nick. But I don't think she ever sees much of the city...)

'Hi Steve.'

'Hi Claire.'

'I bet you're glad you are not still chartering oil tankers?' she says, with a knowing smile.

'Sure, I miss it like a hole in my head!'

(I've had a good few little chats with Claire and she has totally fallen in love with Nick.)

'Are you going over to Centro's for Nathan's party?' she asks, out of interest.

'Yes, I wouldn't dream of missing it. Are you going, Claire?'

'No, I can't. I've got a few things to sort out, you know, paperwork and contracts. I'm settling the mortgage with my ex-boyfriend and selling the flat. Things are very hectic just now,' she says, looking overworked.

Nick walks up to her and gives her a kiss and her face lights up.

'Hi, Steve mate!' We shake hands.

'Claire, let's go down to Level 2 for a coffee and a fag. I'm gasping for one after that flight,' says Nick, looking hungry.

As I walk into marketing blag, I can see Kong is at Sasha's desk (again) and as per usual, she's flashing her eyes at him while he gives her "close protection" from any passing spawny chancers like me! If I were to walk up to her desk right now and start smiling and flirting away with her, she would love it. Her sweet face and blue eyes would start radiating with desire and her luscious body would ooze with raw, hungry sexual energy.

And Kong would go fucking mental!

He would very probably pick me up with one hand and throw me out of the iaxis glass wall right into the Serious Fraud Office.

I skilfully slope away from his angle of vision and walk up to see Seamus, Howard, Gibbsy and Tommo's quad.

'Stevie, *b'Jesus* how's it goin, ye wee fooker!' asks Seamus.

'I'm still a bit rough after getting pissed with Howard a couple of nights ago. Did you get the email I sent you with an update on all our Internet peering partners?'

'Ah did jist dat, en ah sees all of der peerin foldirs en yer fookin desk... yuv bein a bizzy wee fooker hivn't ye?'

'Certainly have mate, I'm flat out. In fact we all are in Biz Dev.'

He caught the bait.

'Fook aff!' he says laughing, clearly having none of it.

Howard looks up from his sail.

'Hi Steve, so what brings you over here?'

(Oh no! This is a tough question. There is no real reason for me to be in marketing blag. I'm just hovering around, waiting for Sasha's desk to become clear. I can't say I'm getting my daily fix of seeing Sasha.)

'Er... I just came round to get some er...Internet marketing strategy feedback on our new Internet backbone,' I say, so convincingly that even I am surprised.

Seamus looks perplexed. 'Mirkedin fookin fied baeck! Wat de fook's dat?'

My crash course in Irish speak suddenly comes in handy. 'It's where you can give me a bit of knowledge on how we are marketing the iaxis Internet backbone and what we are getting in the form of feedback from potential customers.'

Both Howard and Seamus fall about laughing at my naivety. Seamus wipes the tears from his eyes and proceeds to memorise this in his mental logbook of events for his next cell meeting in Hammersmith or Cricklewood.

'Steve, iaxis has spent eighteen million dollars in building this Internet backbone, well, I say we've spent it, but we don't actually have any money to pay for it. Those nice people at Telindus/K-Net are giving us it all on vendor finance! But do you know how much iaxis is spending on advertising and marketing the Internet backbone?' asks Howard, speaking in an almost schoolteacher-like tone.

I shrug my shoulders. 'No idea Howard, but hit me with the figure, I'm sure it's huge,' I say, as they both look at each other slowly grinning.

'*Fuck all.*'

'*Fook all.*'

I clearly see that they are not joking. '*No way!*' I say, feeling totally stunned as I start to beam out bright sunlight from my eyeballs which lights them both up. My mouth opens very wide and I forget about maybe catching some flies in it. I'm more concerned about catching a passing buzzard flying high overhead! 'So how are we getting interested ISPs to buy capacity from the iaxis Internet backbone after we've got all of these Internet peering connections in place?' I ask, my eyes now caught between two excellent suntans. Howard suddenly looks like he's been sailing around the Virgin Islands and Seamus looks like he's just got back from Libya!

'Ah fook, wur doin ah fiew traide shows wih Juniper routers.'

'Is that it?' I ask, incredulously.

'Aye.'

'Why?'

'Well apart from not having much money, nobody in iaxis really knows anything about the Internet backbone,' says Howard, who places a TQM guide on top of a few yachting magazines.

'Well, dat is apirt frim a fiew smirt fookers lieke Nae-tan, en fookin Merlin, dat's aboot fookin it,' adds Seamus.

'But if we're launching an Internet backbone on top of our fibre optic network, surely we must inform the Internet world?'

'Well said Steve! Now you go and speak to the shareholder board and also try and get those Dodgers in the '*Fire Department*' (finance) to release some pennies for us to go and spend on a big fucking blag campaign,' says Howard, who's looking at the screensaver of his future yacht, which he's going to name *Tipster*.

'Um...'

'You's in Biz Dev ir spending all de King's fookin silver so ye ire. En der's fook all left fir mierketin!' says Seamus, as I feel like having a couple more paracetamols.

'Oh Steve, wait until next week before you ask the Dodgers to release some money; we must make sure everyone's expenses have been cleared first,' says Howard, who is now wiping some aftersun on his face.

'Hey, I see Wacko is looking at a different yacht now,' I say, pointing to Howard's screen.

'Yeah, well tell him to get a set of armbands as well, just in case he's out of his depth and can't swim!' he says, playing with his compass.

'No I'll let you do that Howard,' I say, as I look at the view of the SFO building. At this time of day it looks a dark shade of grey and the rainclouds seem to be brewing up a tropical storm overhead.

Gibbsy hangs up the phone after a long-distance call to one of his buddies travelling in Guatemala.

'Steve, we're also working on a deal with Hewlett Packard. They've asked for a current list of our Internet backbone peering partners. Would you be able to put one together?' asks Gibbsy, who I see is looking on whatis.com finding out what Internet backbone connectivity or peering actually means.

'Okay, I'll wing something over to you in a few minutes mate.'

…I am not going to give him the list in my hand. I'd have to walk back to my desk paperless and in office PSYOPS this is just not advised…

'Cheers mate. Oh, Steve, if you speak to the Dodgers, make sure they've cleared my phone bill would you, mate?' says Gibbsy, looking down the room towards the *'Fire Department'*.

'Why don't you do it yourself, Gibbsy? They're only sixty feet away.'

'No chance! They scare the *hell* out of me and it's way too hot down there.'

I look at them and he is not wrong.

Fire is an occupational hazard with any company. But in iaxis, our Dodgers and the financial (out of) controllers live with flames every single day. All have fire extinguishers close to hand, wear protective clothing and have thousand yard stares after all the creditor backdraught type blazes they have to tackle. But the iaxis Dodgers are the best in the business and they have swallowed so many big numbers that they can all eat Fire. And most 'blazes' in the iaxis 'Fire Department' are with the big creditors threatening to take us to court and pull the plug. This would certainly finish off the network. And when a two hundred and fifty million dollar telecommunications and internet network is built with no money to pay for it, these brave Dodgers are left to make sure the network is kept live at all costs. Which in iaxis means with no costs whatsoever.

The 'Fire Department' is the only part of the room where the smoke detectors have been removed. They were going off all the time and iaxis has a huge demand for fire prevention systems. It is no great surprise to learn that the only firm to give us a relatively positive credit rating manufactures fire extinguishers in Birmingham.

Most of these brave Dodgers are in fact young backpackers from Australia, South Africa and New Zealand travelling over here for a few years and then back to the lands of sunshine. They'll certainly go back with some tall stories from taxis that nobody will believe back home...

I leave the 'Mierkedin' quad and walk up to Sasha's desk, now Kong is safely back at his. My back is to him, but I'll know exactly the moment he looks up as my ESP will feel his eyes giving me open head surgery.

'Hiya mate!' she says, as her eyes light up.

'Hi Sasha. How's your day so far?' I say, under control and all systems still functioning.

'Oh it's fine Steve, but I'm looking forward to the party,' she says, as her eyes are fixed on mine, dilating away. I don't know how she does it, but I can now clearly see the warm bright light. I'm not in it, but it's almost touching my nose and it looks so bright and feels warm and beautiful... *'Deep fucking breath Steve!'* I hear a voice say and I take a step back. That was a close one. (Words of advice, which Wacko and Nathan kindly shared with me in the pub. And it works!) She looks great, but I'm still in control of myself as I stand back from *The Zone*.

'Are you going to the party as well, Steve?' she asks, with that smile and a look in her eyes that says *'come closer to me sweetie'*, only now I know what happens if I do that: I'll be fucked in the head for the next two hours!

'Too right. Of course I'm going! I wouldn't dream of missing it,' I say, as I suddenly hear big pounding footsteps and I look around and see 'King fucking Kong' stomping towards me. And he's not looking happy. The hairs on the back of my neck have now all bolted and are taking cover, shivering away somewhere down the centre of my spine. This is time for me to exit her desk.

'I'll see you tonight, Steve,' she says so very sweetly.

Kong just stomps right past us both. I think he lost me in the bright lights that bolted out of my eyes when I saw him pounding over. She senses the tension in the air and soaks up all of Kong's energy. As for me, I'm just grateful not to be flying first class towards the SFO building.

And then, without warning, Psycho walks up to her desk and hands her a folder with *'G1 and G1a'* written on it. He has just finished looking out for his usual *'signs in the sky'* and he eyeballs me coldly, which is far worse than Kong's footsteps. His eyes are like those of a shark and he's only gone and missed his daily shovelful of Prozac by *seven* minutes. I say goodbye to the lovely Sasha and quickly slope off before Psycho tries to lynch me as well.

Back at my desk I am still grinning after successfully surviving Kong and Psycho one after the other, while Nathan casually looks up from his PC and hands me a bottle of Becks. He reads the confusion on my face as I wonder where the beer came from.

'Wacko went out and bought a couple of six-packs for the quad.'

'Fantastic. Cheers mate!' I say, as I see quite a few others necking back drinks as well. 'Is it true there's no marketing campaign for the iaxis Internet backbone?'

'I haven't got a clue, Steve. There's some trade shows with Juniper that are organised, but apart from that, I don't know. It's a subject not too many people know about, but it looks good for iaxis to have an Internet backbone on its fibre optic network. So I guess that speaks volumes about the Internet interest from up top in here,' says Nathan, as he takes a swig on his bottle of Becks.

My attention is now on Mr Nice who is walking over towards our quad. He is wearing his hooded sweatshirt with the word "JEWELER" splashed across the front of it and the diamond geezer seems 'sorted'. He also looks a lot more hyper than usual, probably because he's read about himself in *The Narcotics Monitor.* His eyes look like Bez's from the Happy Mondays and he is grinning at what he's about to share with us.

'Hey boys, you've never guessed what's just happened to me,' he says, in a strong "Sarf Landan" accent.

Now, this could be any one of a thousand and two things. And that's just while he's on the office premises. Nathan, Merlin, Wacko and myself are all looking at him, bracing ourselves for 'sam-fin mass-ive'. This could be good. His eyes are beaming wildly and he's far more excitable than usual.

'About five minutes ago, I was in the far end gents' cubicle on Level 2 doing a couple of lines before the party, and guess who walks into the next cubicle?' He says it in a hushed voice, just so we hang on to his every word.

We all look blank. It's a big glass building with lots of famous people in it.

Mr Nice looks around the office floor. 'Nick and Claire! They walk in giggling away, clearly on something, and lock the door of the middle cubicle and start going at it like there was no tomorrow! I thought the wall of the cubicle was going to come down, because fucking hell is she a screamer! I had to do another line after listening to that.'

We all have a good laugh after this one.

'I wonder if Nick's checked into therapy yet?' says Nathan, trying to keep his laugh down.

Mr Nice floats off to another quad to give them some speed (and to bring them all well up to speed).

'It's nothing new. Before he went into exile in Marseilles, the middle cubicle on Level 2 was practically Nick's second office! Pub toilets are another favourite, as was his desktop!' says Wacko, laughing and shaking his head.

Centro's, opposite the ITN building gets very busy on a Thursday night. With tonight being Nathan's party most of iaxis is in here, the drinks are coming in round after round and I'm trying my best to keep up. With plenty of comings and goings it seems everyone who's been sorted for gear has got tucked into their goodies. The wide-eyed, starey-eyed and crazy-eyed are all bopping away unable to keep standing still, all shouting *'down, down, down...Yeah!!!'* as the main iaxis drinking game is in full swing. It's hugely simple, that's why it's used a lot.

It's not just the under-thirties that are here. Management at all levels are enjoying the fun, necking the drinks and buying the rounds. The ex-chairman wholeheartedly created this fantastic atmosphere in iaxis, and this is fundamentally what has enabled iaxis to build one of the most technologically advanced European fibre optic networks in just over one hundred days. This will never be beaten by another start-up and the iaxis office culture is one of the reasons why iaxis is unique.

There is no structured hierarchy like you'd find in a blue-chip corporation. You can walk in and speak to any member of senior management as a friend and vice-versa and there are no layers of management to go through, no committee meetings on policy *('Just fucking do it!')*. If you have an idea or want something to be sorted, you can speak to the ex-chairman or a senior VP, either in their office or down the pub. This will not piss off a whole wedding cake of internal layers of management between you and the ex-chairman for doing it. The only pub rules in this place are: get to the bar for opening time, stay there till closing, drink as much as possible, buy a few rounds and have fun. *This is iaxis.*

It would be wrong to say this is the cause of the iaxis problems. BT's problems are far, far bigger than the ones at iaxis. They have rules, procedures, committees and a very structured management hierarchy and this is just to buy the office telephones. (And BT has dialled up a staggering forty-four billion dollars' worth of debts in what is the biggest phone bill in British corporate history.)

I can see Nathan is out of his tree dancing on some tables. Wacko is waving Nathan's bottle of tequila around and a few more bottles have been bought. Seamus has got his back to the wall (as usual) and is drinking a pint of orange juice. Only this evening he's listening intently to whatever Merlin is telling him and eyeballing anyone (Stalker) who shows the remotest interest in the conversation.

Sasha has about six blokes standing around her. Kong is also by her side providing her with his usual "close protection", making sure none of them do a "Paul Keating" and put an arm around her. If any of them dare try such a thing, he'd rip it out of its socket and probably eat it! Sasha and Kong are not even an item. Sasha has just melted his brain and he can't break free. I try and catch Sasha's eye, but she doesn't see me. Kong sees me and is now watching my every move. Sasha looks gorgeous, full of raw energy that she has been soaking up for this weekend's partying.

Claire is away sorting out her paperwork and contracts and Nick is looking hungry. He's chatting up the lovely Jemma from international marketing who shares a flat with Sasha in Notting Hill. Nick's been here a short while and already he's looking flushed. The body language between the two of them is very good. Nick could score here. He's got an Owen-style run and the Argentine defence is uncharacteristically slacking with complacency. Hannah looks over at him from time to time, but she's 'networking' with a couple of senior VPs between giving Nick the evil eye. And Wacko is avoiding Hannah like a trip to the vets.

Later I am having a laugh with Gibbsy from the 'Mierkedin' quad. Tommo, the other chancer on the quad, is in the centre of "Buffalo," the iaxis drinking game. He has just been Buffalo'd or, rather, he got caught taking a swig of his drink with his right hand and about forty people screamed *'Buffalo!'* at him. He then has to down his drink, a pint of Bitburger, in one go and this is not an easy feat, even for a Kiwi. As it goes down, the drink escapes through his nose, eyes and ears!

I am on my fourth bottle of San Miguel and a shot of tequila is beamed into my hand from Wacko and it is quickly downed in my left hand. Wacko is already back at the bar, grinning away wildly, getting more rounds in. I refocus on Gibbsy who was moaning about the lack of Aussie fizzy piss to drink.

'So where were you before iaxis, Gibbsy?' I ask, as that last shot of tequila starts to make my body shiver.

'I was backpacking around Europe for a year and I signed up with this agency, who got me into WorldCom doing some marketing stuff. I did all right and ended up meeting a Sheila and stayed for a couple of years,' he says, takes a massive swig of his Bitburger with his left hand, and then farts loudly just as Howard is passing.

'*Strewth!*' he yells out. 'Hey Gibbsy! You're not in the Northern Territories now Skippy!' he says, taking the piss.

'Yah rippa!' he shouts, grinning away.

Howard skippers his way to the bar shaking his head.

'So how come you left WorldCom for iaxis, Gibbsy?'

'Well I just wanted a change. WorldCom is just so big, it was time to move on.'

'Sure. And was it easy to get in here then?'

'Yeah, I just asked my agency if there were any other jobs they could put me up for. After a day, they came back with marketing products manager with iaxis. Psycho and Howard interviewed me in the Blue Lion in the middle of a session. They were both fucking slaughtered and I joined them and stayed for a further two hours. After this we had an Italian meal in Roberto's, but I was far too pissed to even taste it! They offered me the job as they were getting the bill in. All I had to do was see if I agreed with the package that the agency was going to come up with.'

'So did you get a good pay deal from iaxis after you left WorldCom?' I ask, as my tequila starts to hit the spot.

He starts laughing away and looks around to see if anyone's earwigging who shouldn't be. Everyone's out of their heads. Nick is now in the fast lane and is going for it, as he's gazing into Jemma's eyes and playfully rubbing his nose against hers. I can see that Merlin, who's speaking to Seamus, is suddenly waving his arms up in the air and it looks like they're talking about something big going off… And in the background, I hear that two of the Dodgers have just been Buffallo'd!

'Between you and me, Steve,' he says, as he only just starts to calm down, 'I was on thirty-eight thousand pounds at WorldCom and I told the agency I wanted forty-five grand, maybe a little more, if I joined a start-up like iaxis and guess what they offered?.'

'No idea mate,' I say, as another tequila appears from nowhere and finds a home going down my throat.

'They offered me fifty-five thousand pounds!' he says, grinning away, like he was the kid who'd got a toyshop for Christmas.

'Why did they do that?' I ask, looking amazed.

'It was the agency! They misheard me with my Aussie accent, they thought I was asking for fifty-five thousand pounds from the start! I didn't say fuck all of course when I took it.'

'No, of course not!'

'But when I got the iaxis letter I was shaking. I had to go down to the pub. I phoned Psycho from there and accepted it. Then I started work one week later and that was one year ago. I've also bought a ton of shares and will buy a speedboat with the money from here when we float,' he says, still laughing at his ten thousand pound windfall (as one does).

'Well good luck mate! Cheers!' I say, as I look around the room and quicky see that Nick is nowhere to be seen. Jemma takes a look around the place and sees that nobody is paying her any attention. Good, that is exactly what she wanted to see. She takes a discreet sip on her sangria and puts it down. She then leaves to walk through the wooden doors, to go downstairs to the toilets...

The music seems very loud and it's mostly iaxis people left. Everyone else has been frightened off. Unfortunately the iaxis company flat is out of bounds for further partying on this particular evening. One of the senior management who sits at the glass boardroom table is now back at the flat with a girl half his age from the office. No doubt she'll be telling all her friends about the illicit private entertainment she dished up for him tomorrow morning. Like she did last time. And every other time come to think of it...

Suzie and a couple of others have stripped off their bras and, just for a laugh, are flashing their breasts at passing motorists. At Henley last year, about six of the girls all stripped off their tops and started flashing at the rowers. Mostly after the champagne had been finished and the customers had long since left, but the drink was there to be drunk and what happened afterwards isn't written here...

Both girls are now safely back inside Centro's as Faithless's *'God is a DJ'* is beating out from the sound system. Gabriela, who is a sexy, fun-loving Latin girl from Panama, is lying back on a table and is now supporting some fella's head as he licks out the salt she's kindly sprinkled into her lovely belly button for him... The room starts to spin even more as those solid, classic vibes beat away and I see a few hot bodies bouncing away as well. I've lost count of the number of tequilas that have passed my lips tonight.

Gabriela then gently takes the lemon back out of the geezer's mouth with her tongue and places it in Suzie's mouth. A few seconds later, Wacko pushes Gabriela back down on the table and pours a small capful of tequila into her belly button. Nathan is standing closest to her and she tugs his shirt, pulling him slightly closer and he doesn't need any instructions as he licks it off her naked, flat stomach... Just a little birthday treat for the lad!

Mr Nice has left to go back across the road to the office. Not to catch up on some work, but to do a couple of lines of "Charlie" on the glass boardroom table, with a girl called "x." And no doubt after the lines are finished they'll use the boardroom table for something more natural in human behaviour, like a meeting of minds. *And bodies.*

Later on, most of the hardcore crew heads down to Covent Garden to go to the Roadhouse to party until 4 a.m., and then back to the office ready for work the following morning.

Gabriela lives in Putney, so we share a taxi home together.

This is just a typical iaxis Thursday night session. The next day, though bleary as hell, is just a normal Friday in the iaxis office. Whatever normal means in the dizzy heights of a pre-flotation telecoms/Internet company in the first quarter of the year 2000 A.D., when everyone in the office is going to be a *'fucking millionaire!'*

CHAPTER 8

Today is a work morning. It might be a Tuesday, but I'm not sure. I've been awake, well, sort of awake, for about four minutes. I know it's a work morning because those good people on the *Today* programme suddenly started speaking as my alarm went off. If it weren't for them I wouldn't be awake and I'd still be enjoying a very deep sleep.

Yesterday was a busy day and last night was tequila wild. I got Buffalo'd twice before we even got started on the tequilas. Today feels like it should be a Saturday, but it isn't. I don't know what day it is, because I've turned the radio off. I'm still lying in bed at 7:33 a.m. And I haven't been in bed for very long.

I hear my mobile ringing. It is lying somewhere on the floor and is buried under some clothes. I must have forgotten to turn it off and the thing seems to have been ringing for a while. I see Wacko's name is on the LCD as I answer it.

'Steve, you must have been in front of the mirror, I've been trying to reach you for fucking ages!'

'Grunt.' My throat is very dry this morning.

'Bring your passport and an overnight bag with a change of clothes for looking at a couple of co-location buildings, okay?'

'Um, grunt.'

'Sorted, see you in an hour. We fly first thing.'

'Um?'

The line goes dead.

I wasn't feeling sharp enough to ask any questions. It was the 'see you in an hour' and 'fly first thing' that got me out of the bed, in the shower, packed and out of the front door and across the street in about twelve minutes. I am also carrying a two-litre bottle of Evian to kill my thirst as my head is thumping and the street still seems to be spinning.

Before I walk into the ITN building, I visit Manhattan's for a cappuccino and two sausage bagels to soak up all the alcohol from last night.

As I get to the quad I see that Wacko's black leather bag is on his desk. He's walking about signing bits of paper authorising various things for Stalker to go and do.

While I am eating my breakfast, my stomach feels like it is reaching up in to my throat to impatiently pull the food down. I am so hungry, I don't think I ate any dinner last night. I've already checked my wallet and there are no receipts in it.

'Steve, I just got a call from my VP first thing; we're off to Copenhagen to look at a building we want to take over and turn into a co-location facility. Then we're flying to Amsterdam to see the iaxis co-location facility there. McGowan is also coming with us and we're meeting Nick in Amsterdam. He knows the power supply person we're meeting tomorrow, so he'll be useful to have around.'

Big McGowan is an expert in fibre optic telecommunications and has an "interesting" background.

'We'll be leaving in a few minutes. There's a taxi taking us to Stansted Airport.'

'What time are we seeing the site in Copenhagen?' I ask, thinking I'll be feeling much better when I eventually get this food inside me.

'As soon as we land I'll telephone the local property agent and he'll meet us at the building. Then we'll get some grub and fly to Amsterdam.'

'Sounds good mate,' I say, as my head feels slow.

Wacko sees Hannah walking over and promptly walks off to the far side of the office to see the Dodgers. Hannah walks up to our quad and she's eyeing up my leather Mulberry weekend bag which is on my desk.

'I've got that exact same bag as well sweetie,' she says, as her eyes light up at the thought of us going away for the weekend together. 'Where are you off to?' she asks, lightly touching her eyebrow.

'Copenhagen and Amsterdam.'

'Really!'

Oh shit! All my five senses and ESP are now triggered. Her mind and her eyes are now working away in that fantasy and it is barely 9:30 a.m. It's just as well there's no room for her to sit anywhere on my desk. But then I notice a small swelling and a slight colouring of purple just above her left eye in the centre of her forehead.

'Is that a bruise just above your eye, Hannah?' I ask, as I notice that her make-up isn't doing a very good job of covering it up.

Her face gives away the shock of me seeing it as she leans against my desk.

'Oh no! Can you see it, Steve?' she asks, as she gently touches the wound and tries to cover it up with her left hand.

'Ever so slightly. What happened?' I ask in a very soft and caring tone, which I genuinely mean.

She takes a deep breath as her right hand comes up to her mouth, almost forcing the words back in. She knows she can't blag her way out of this one as she doesn't have a partner, so it's impossible for her to walk into doors.

Her posture starts to relax.

'A couple of teenagers tried to mug me on my way home last night,' she says calmly, as if this is one of those things that sometimes happen to one when walking home from South Kensington tube station.

'Mugged you!' I say, as I jump out of my seat to see her forehead.

Her heart melts.

'Yes, these two kids, they only looked about fifteen, tried to grab my Vuitton handbag when I was walking home.'

'Are you okay? Is there anything I can do?' I ask, with sincere concern for her welfare.

In her eyes I can see there's plenty she wants me to do.

'Oh, it was really no problem, Steve. I managed to keep a firm hold of my bag and head-butted one of the little bastards. They were so shocked they turned and ran. I walked the last few hundred metres still shaking.'

'Shit, did you contact the police?'

'No, I got home and just poured a large Scotch and cried. It took a while before I stopped shaking.'

I swallow and almost feel like crying myself after what she's gone through. But then Hannah would have gone home, packed *her* Mulberry bag and met us all in Amsterdam this evening. Wacko would then have head-butted me and sacked me on the spot for allowing this to happen. And he and I are best mates!

'Look, you must phone the police and let them know. It's really important that they have a log of the incident. It's a piece in their big picture and they'll help you with victim support and stuff. You never know, those two kids might have been nicked two hours later for something else and blabbed they were in the area when they attacked you. The police will not turn you away. That's serious.'

'I'll call them later, sweetheart,' she says, with passion in her voice as she walks back to her desk, looking over her shoulder at me.

Wacko walks up to the quad and grabs his anonymous black leather bag off his desk. Big McGowan is beside him and is scanning the room. Wearing his black shades he looks meaner than ever.

'Right Steve, let's fuck off. The taxi's meant to be outside,' says Wacko, and we then march out of the office.

Wacko, big McGowan and myself all look impatient and serious as we walk out of the ITN building and on to Gray's Inn Road. All three of us are wearing black leather jackets, shades, blue jeans and Timberland desert boots. Each of us is carrying a holdall-type bag filled with some clothes and iaxis blag material. The security guards clock us and immediately stand out of our way, all of them thinking we're tooled up and are away to take part in a big fuck-off bullion robbery in South London!

Outside we are all walking about, scanning up and down the street, talking away on our mobiles and looking on edge. It looks like we're trying to see if there's any heat on us before we do the job. But we are actually looking for our taxi as it is late. And so are we.

Big McGowan looks at one of the Italian shopkeepers who suddenly looks like he wants to board up his shop. He starts to pull his kids inside just as the taxi driver pulls up from nowhere and slams his brakes on. Half the street look over their shoulders as we all pile inside in less than two seconds. It's a nice big juice-hungry black BMW. We are running late and the apologetic East End cockney driver then drives the motor like it is a getaway car all the way to the airport. Both McGowan and I are braking with our feet, and we're sitting in the back. Wacko is in the front with his eyes closed and is getting ready for the impact of another car.

After a beer at the airport we get ready to board and although we aren't stripped, we get well searched before they allow us on board the plane. (McGowan looked at a police dog and it went berserk.)

I manage to get some sleep on the plane.

The building in Copenhagen is very good. The fibre optic cables have recently been laid in the street. We also check the manhole covers on the road to see which fibre suppliers also have cable here. I use the digital camera to take photos of the Telia fibre supplier's manhole covers and everything else in and around the building. This information is useful for our database.

The building itself is about two thousand square metres and was once an empty warehouse. Some of the spare space has been rigged up as a temporary photography studio for a sex shoot. (The couch, sex toys and underwear give it away.) The building is also next to a power substation, which means this place isn't going to run short of juice in a hurry.

McGowan looks through his 'Frame Relay TD-04V' document, ticks a few boxes and says 'Yes'. Wacko gets on his mobile and calls Merlock and Stalker and a contract is now being rigged up. It will be sent over very soon, as the building is perfect for iaxis.

'We'll be making an offer for it right away,' says Wacko to the property broker, who is now smiling wildly.

I just hope the landlord doesn't go on a lavish spending spree after we've signed a twenty-five-year lease. We'll pay for it sometime in the future (maybe).

We get a taxi to the Hard Rock Café in central Copenhagen for lunch and then back to the airport. We did the job and only the property agent would recognise us again. (But we know where he works.)

We arrive in Amsterdam shortly before 6 p.m. The hotel is four star, very central and expensive. They even have someone playing a harp at breakfast, or so they say in their marketing blag on the wall in the lift. Nick has already checked in and as usual his mobile is turned off.

We open the doors to our respective luxury suites and throw our bags in, lock the doors again, and head out. We're all mates and we don't need to do much talking. Our minds just seem to be connected on this unique occasion as our bodies are propelled against all our will to the nearest "coffee shop", which is about forty metres from the hotel.

And as we walk inside, the dope fumes hit us hard.

Nick is already inside. And like a kid in a sweet shop he's smiling away. He's been here for a while and has already smoked a few joints. It is like candy to him. He is now chatting up the attractive Dutch girl who's working behind the counter and she is lapping it all up. But her colleague doesn't look too happy and he's eyeballing Nick furiously. This stops when he sees the three of us are with Nick.

'Hello boys!' says Nick, sounding pleased as hell to see us all as he introduces us to *"Naomi"*.

Four big reefers filled with finest Afghan skunk appear in her left hand and she hands them over to us.

'How long have you been here then?' asks McGowan, with a big smile on his face.

'Not long enough!' says Nick, as we notice the three butts already in his ashtray.

We get ready to light up. The three of us are not regular skunk smokers, especially not of this quality. The dope hits the spot after only a few draws and we get up from the counter and kick back on a sofa. Nick takes a big toke on his king-sized reefer as I do the same on mine. My head feels like it's one of those balloons at a funfair that has somehow broken free and is floating up into the sky. I think I can see two other balloons up here as well.

After letting go of his balloons, Nick is still on the ground eating his candyfloss. He's also grinning away like he's just about to get on the big dipper, and it is just as well that Hannah hasn't taken him to the funfair...

'So, how are your hash plants coming on, Nick?' asks Wacko.

Nick's little weed farm on the iaxis villa's balcony is legendary in the office back home. All for personal use and iaxis staff visits, of course. He would rather give it away for free than sell it.

'Pretty good. In fact some should be ready very soon, so I'll be smoking this crop when Claire and Jemma next fly out to see me. Claire's coming out a week on Friday.'

(Girls from the office are always getting cheap flights over to see him for a rampant weekend of drugs, drink and *lots of sex.*)

'Claire says she's fallen in love with me,' says Nick, with a look of contemplation on his face. Coming from Nick, this sounds like she's just offered to make him a cup of tea.

'Has she said that?' asks McGowan, who suddenly looks very mellow.

'Yes, she's been sending me some heavy emails. Not the usual email sex I get from her and a good few others, but emotional, heavy stuff. She wants us to be an item!'

'So what do you want?' I ask Nick, as both Wacko and McGowan start to laugh. It's not really too hard to guess what he wants...

'I want to see Jemma and the others as well!' laughs Nick, as he coughs out some dope fumes, grinning away. 'Jemma is going to be in *Gibraltar* for a marketing jaunt early next week. She's calling in to see me this Sunday, and she'll be staying at the pad for the night,' he says, as he relights his spliff.

'So what are you going to say to Claire?' asks McGowan, as we are all well on our way skywards.

'Nothing. She thinks we're both just friends and nothing will happen!' he says, toking away as we all crack up.

...The chances of nothing happening when Jemma stays the night are about as remote as 'Tin Knickers' walking into Sinn Fein's West Belfast constituency office and then having a 'tea and sympathy' session with Gerry Adams and the local West Belfast Brigade!

'Yeah right!' says McGowan, laughing, as everything is moving well slow and mellow.

I cannot get this big grin off my face and McGowan is still smiling at some memory, Wacko is on his yacht and Nick is on the big-dipper as it is slowly being pulled upwards, waiting for the ride to start. Just as Nick gets to the top he has a very big toke on his joint and starts to look a bit serious at the three of us.

'A good few months ago was when it all started kicking off with Claire. It was the post-Y2K piss-up at the company flat. We started flirting at the party and decided we both wanted it. The bedrooms were locked so we sloped off and came back to the office for the boardroom table, but someone was already on it, so we went for it in reception on the sofas.'

I take another big toke and my head feels like it has just broken through the ozone layer and buzzed a couple of Adv Orion spy satellites.

'I had bruises on my wrists after that session! But then the next day she ditched her boyfriend and started to focus on me. This did spook me, but after she came over to stay a few times, I got used to it,' he says calmly, like it's an everyday occupational hazard in his work.

I take another toke.

'But she's a damn good ride!' he says, as he stubs out his roach, with his eyes glazing over at his many fond memories.

I'm still in outer space and I've just seen Wacko flying past me as he heads towards a couple of Magnum and Mentro satellites as well.

After a good hazy half an hour or so, Nick suddenly remembers which city he is in and I start my descent back down to Earth.

'Come on, let's go to a sex club and see a show. I was given these tickets,' he says, as he hands them to Wacko, who is also making his way down through a *White Cloud*.

'Shit, I've heard of this place. It's classy and very expensive,' he says, staring away.

'I know it fucking is, that's why I blagged them from a Dutch fibre supplier,' says Nick, who is nearly at the top of the ride and waiting to be let free with a big grin on his face.

As we stand up to leave our legs feel like rubber, and the geezer behind the counter gives Nick a free joint for smoking so much dope.

'Cheers mate!' says Nick, as if he's just been given a free bar of Dairy Milk. As we get outside he hands the spliff to me and the street seems very surreal.

'Here you go tiger, you can have this.'

'Thanks Nick!' I say, as I carefully put the joint in the inside pocket of my leather jacket for later on.

McGowan says goodbye as he's arranged to meet some of his old mates who are over here on a job, and he staggers off.

A few minutes later, after an amazing amount of debate, discussion and persuasion with Nick, we decide to first go and get some food in the hotel restaurant before we head off.

The meal arrives and Nick shovels down his food. It is almost like he's a demented Doberman that hasn't been fed for two days and there's suddenly a bitch on heat outside his back gate barking away for him.

After the meal, it feels like we are slowly being pulled towards the red-light district and when we walk through the doors of the sex club, Nick is practically running down the dark stairs and banging away on the doors to be let in. Wacko taps my shoulder and informs me that no matter how stoned we are and how pissed we get, we are not here to pull. This is one of the most exclusive sex clubs in Amsterdam and if you left with a girl from here you wouldn't get much change out of fifteen hundred dollars. As we walk in, the sweet smelling perfume hits us all even harder than the dope fumes in the last place. On the stage about ten metres from the bar there is a live lesbian sex show in full swing. The three stunning girls are all using large toys for maximum stimulation.

Nick's at the bar getting in a couple of magnums of champagne and he flinches big-time when he sees his bill. No doubts it'll be winged through on expenses as an office consumable. (A new photocopier or something.)

There aren't too many people in here tonight and before we know it we are all sitting on big sofas with champagne and each of us now has two stunning semi-naked continental girls all over us. And these very sexy girls are trying their best to get us (with our credit cards) to leave with them.

I look up in between gulps of champagne, and the other two are buried in semi-naked flesh as well. All seem to be blonde apart from a girl covering Wacko. My brain cell feels like it's going through a pinball machine as the Danish girl on my left is whispering unspeakable things into my ear about what her and her friend would like to get up to with me back in my hotel room! The other blonde is working slowly away all over my body with her hands as I take a mouthful of champagne and pour the girls some. After the dope and the champagne, my Visa card is fighting the awful temptation to leave with them. The card would need a new set of shock absorbers if it took a hit in here tonight. And the cash machine would definitely spit it back out on to the high street.

On the stage there are now two blokes and a very fit sexy blonde woman. All are hammering away like it's an Olympic race to the finish, and the finishing line is miles away.

After what seems like ages, I look up from the Dutch girl's breasts that she's casually placed in my face and remove some of her blonde hair from my mouth. The Danish girl has been expertly nibbling my ears while her hands wander all over my body. I look up to where Nick is and my heart suddenly hits a crash barrier and starts thumping away. The pinball lights are flashing *Game Over!* when I see that Nick has left with his two very sexy girls.

Wacko's ESP must have felt my brainblast as he looks up to where Nick was sitting. He shakes his head, telepathically telling me that Nick is one mad bastard.

After a while the girls see that we aren't going to leave with them, so they chill out with us over a few drinks while the shows are in full swing. And I do mean in full swing. The Olympic race on the stage is still going full on as they get ready for their "*Midnight Climax*" which I am sure is going to happen very soon.

Later on we get a taxi back to the hotel, and whilst we are in the taxi the driver is sniffing away furiously at us. (It is highly likely that he will have to go and get the inside of his car fumigated now.) Wacko tells me that if that were a casting couch we were on, then he'd give them all leading roles. I don't disagree with him, as we've both been sandwiched by very beautiful naked flesh for the last couple of hours.

It is about 1:00 a.m. and I'm just back inside my room and I need a shower. This intoxicating smell of what seems like very cheap perfume has to be washed off me before I sleep tonight. This set of clothes will go straight in the wash when I get home. In fact it might take two washes with super-industrial strength Daz Ultra to remove this particular toxic brand of sex-enhanced perfume spray.

My head is still buzzing from that den of sexual debauchery as I switch on the TV and suddenly remember that there is still a joint inside my jacket pocket. I get off the bed and pull it out, and for a brief moment think about flushing it away. I do have a meeting first thing tomorrow. However, it would be a shame to waste it and besides, I'll drift off to sleep until my wake-up call at 7:30 a.m. I look around my room in contemplation and see that the hotel even has a box of matches for me.

Sorted.

I light up the spliff and flick through the channels on the TV. I skip the porn channel as I've seen enough live sex already this evening.

While I am smoking the joint I notice that it doesn't taste as smooth as the one I had earlier on in the coffee shop. This one is far rougher, but I still manage to smoke it all. And as I do, I can feel myself getting stoned very fast. Then without any warning, as I get ready to stub out the roach, my heart starts beating faster and I suddenly do not feel well. Very quickly the illicit mix hits me. And then all hell breaks loose as my heart beat suddenly screams up to what feels like one hundred and thirty beats a minute…

I am warm and then the shakes come. A few hit me mildly and then they get stronger, much, much stronger and my body starts to tremble uncontrollably and I have to lie down on the bed. Within a couple of minutes my body is out of control and I cannot feel my feet as I begin to crawl to the toilet, convulsing away… I barely manage to climb up on to the lavatory seat and I have to sit down to urinate and vomit. In the bathroom, the room starts to come alive, as I become aware that the walls are starting to move. I really

don't want the hotel lobby to see me like this and I somehow manage to crawl
back into my room feeling much worse. My room is now in a new dimension
that I have never seen before and I am trembling and trembling.

The TV is now alive and it is showing CNN. They are having a studio
interview in my hotel suite and they are all jabbering away. They are asking
questions to some geezer in a suit and I haven't got a fucking clue what they
are saying. On the wall of my room is a picture of a white horse. It is also
alive and as I go to try and touch it, it runs out of my grasp. Then the vivid
colours and flashing lights start to fill up the room. I curl up in the corner
shaking and trembling as the wires for the TV turn into snakes and two big
black hairy spiders suddenly start running all over the walls of my room. I
have the remote control in my hand and try to change the TV channel, but a
bolt of light blasts out and   drop it. Three skeletons come out of the TV and
are running about in my room. I close my eyes and curl up into a foetal
position. My mind is telling me I am dying. My body is telling me it is dying.
I am still shaking and trembling as my mind goes screaming skywards and
out into very dark space.

And then blank.

The phone is ringing and ringing as I get up from the floor to answer *my*
wake-up call. The time is 07:30 a.m.

In the bathroom my guts feel torched as I vomit in to the toilet and my
brain is still burning away. At least the room is not moving into the hallway
any more. Slight aftershocks of the shakes are still running through my body
at random as I vomit again and enjoy a good dose of the shits.

I look in the mirror and I look like dog shit. My eyes are still on full
volume, drug crazed, and trip level max. There is no way I can turn them
down and my head feels like it's been hit by a massive earthquake as I climb
into the hot shower and lie under it for about forty minutes.

The TV is still on and it's showing the CNN morning news. I turn it off
and steadily put some clean smelling clothes on and dump the toxic
perfume-smelling ones inside my weekend bag. If a sniffer dog sticks its
nose in it this afternoon, the poor thing would drop dead on the spot.

I feel melted as I walk out of my room and down to the hotel reception.
Here I see Wacko and McGowan are already checking out; both are looking
rough as well. McGowan takes his black shades off.

'Steve, what the fuck happened mate?'

Wacko looks up.

'Shit, you look wankered! We've got a meeting in twenty minutes' time.'

I put down my bag and use the counter to lean back on.

'Remember the free joint Nick got from the geezer at the coffee shop? I ask, as I put my hands in my pocket to stop them from suddenly shaking.

Both remember, albeit hazily. McGowan looks really rough as well, come to think of it.

'Well the fucker must have spiked it with speed and LSD. I spent most of the night tripping, trembling and shaking to the darker side of *Hell*. I didn't think I'd see morning. There were snakes and demons in my room,' I say, as my eyes are still vividly flashing back the trip.

They don't laugh.

'Bastard,' says Wacko.

Wacko pays my bill on his AmEx card as McGowan looks outside at the taxi which has just pulled up. We pick up our bags as Wacko informs us that Nick never made it back to the hotel. Room service have checked and his baggage is still there...

'Daft git!' says McGowan, as we leave the hotel lobby and head for the taxi, which will take us to the iaxis co-location building.

In the car I keep on closing my eyes as the world is blurry and all the cars seem to be travelling far too fast. Even big McGowan jumps when I react to seeing, in my drug-fuelled mind's eye, the taxi getting buzzed by a large unmarked black helicopter.

'There's no fucking helicopters, Steve! Look, don't say fuck all in the meeting. We'll blag it out for you!' says McGowan, as they both laugh. My hands are still shaking, despite being inside my pockets.

The electricity power rep is already in the car park and is getting out of her car just as we arrive at our co-location centre. She shakes hands with Wacko and McGowan and sees from their eyes exactly what caused them to be so bloodshot. She has seen it all before from visiting telecoms people that she meets the day after they've flown in.

She goes to shake my hand and suddenly looks terrified. I shake her hand and can't even force a polite smile. I'm sure I haven't blinked for about seven minutes and I seem to drift back into deep space every so often.

'Steve's got food poisoning,' says McGowan, very convincingly and even looking concerned. But she knows better. And I know fuck all and I'm meant to be here to learn.

We sit down in a meeting room, drink some strong black coffee and start speaking about the shortage of electrical power in Amsterdam. I take in nothing whatsoever as I look at her and wonder what planet I am now on. Then all of a sudden, the meeting room door flies open and Nick appears, not carrying any baggage. He's also looking starey-eyed and he's grinning wildly.

'Sorry I'm late, but I stink like fuck. So just excuse me while I go and sit in the corner!' he says, as he just wanders in as if he's taking a morning stroll across the beach.

The lady just smiles at him, as she knows Nick from way back. And Nick knows her as well…

Wacko and McGowan now both look like they too have just seen that black helicopter as well.

After what seems like the longest meeting I've ever endured, we get up and go for a walk around the co-location facility. McGowan shows us all around the site, pointing out things here and there. I still feel weak as he shows us the rack space that will house the Internet servers for the world's leading Internet companies. Assuming we can sell the space to them.

Shortly afterwards the meeting winds up, as our contact has another meeting to go to. After she says goodbye, Nick has a brief chat with her outside in the car park.

I ask Wacko and McGowan if Nick really did walk into the meeting and say what he said. They both assure me he did and I wasn't tripping out of my head.

Nick walks back in from the car park. 'We'll be okay for power,' he says, confidently.

'So where did you end up last night, Nick?' asks McGowan.

Nick just shakes his head and looks completely knackered as he starts yawning.

He then looks at me.

'Are you all right, Steve? You look like you've seen a ghost!' he says, looking well shagged out as he gives out another massive yawn.

I shake my head and proceed to tell him about *his* joint that was spiked.

'Yeah well, you've got to be careful about that, Steve mate, there's loads of bad shit in "The Dam",' he says as he pulls out his mobile from his jeans and switches it on. He makes three calls. One call to Jemma, then one to Claire and finally one to the young French maid who cleans the iaxis villa. He says he'll be back home for about sixish. He laughs and giggles with her and tells her to wear black, like she did the last time! He then orders a taxi back to the hotel for his gear. (And to have a shower.)

At the airport, our plane is delayed for four hours, which is fine by me as I curl up on three chairs in the departure lounge while my own descent begins. I sleep with total confidence that I will be woken up when we are about to board. Then in what seems like no time at all, I get several nudges to wake me up just as we are called for boarding. I still feel like shit as

McGowan picks me up by the collar as if I'm a straying cat that has wandered off too far.

I see Wacko is on his mobile listening away intently, slightly nodding his head then suddenly his mouth is wide open.

'*Fuck!!!*' he says loudly, as other passengers start to move even further away from the three of us. We've all got our shades on and nobody is looking at us.

Wacko's face looks as if some of his life has flashed across it as he clicks his phone off. I've never seen him so nervous, even when we rafted the rapids on the Urubamba River in Peru. And that was terrifying.

'We're in big trouble,' he says, taking a massive deep breath.

I can't breathe and my legs are refusing to go forward. 'Why? Who grassed about last night?' I ask him, as I swallow my career with iaxis down my throat.

'Eh? It's not that! iaxis *expects* you to have fun when you visit "The Dam", he says, as if last night was one of the more tame experiences iaxis staff have when they come here on business.

'So what's up?' asks McGowan, as I feel so relieved it's nothing to do with me.

Wacko chews the horrible words out of his dry mouth.

'The NASDAQ is *crashing*. And iaxis is looking *fucked*. All the banks and VCs that were looking at taking us to high yield and flotation on the NASDAQ are now running for cover,' he says, as I take my shades off and look at some youngster who immediately starts to bawl his eyes out.

We board the plane in silence and I sleep all the way home. And as soon as I get home I sleep again.

...And during one of the coldest and darkest nights the forest has ever seen, a couple of hungry wolves run past the cabin. And stop.

CHAPTER 9

On the office floor it is just business as usual. 'It'll soon pick up again...' is a phrase that sums up the mood.

'Nathan, what time is this Internet presentation?'

'2:30 p.m. and it'd better not go on for too long, I've got a shit load to do for this Hewlett Packard project,' he says, looking at his rather large HP UX 9.0.7 *red* file.

'But you are going?' I ask, as it is a no-smoking event and could take up sixty minutes of our time.

Nathan looks stunned. 'Too fucking right I'm going, they've laid on free beer!' he says very enthusiastically.

In a cunning ploy by 'mierkedin' to get everyone to attend the presentation, a good few crates of Becks have been brought in for us to get stuck into during the talk and discussion afterwards.

Eventually everyone turns up, clutching three or four bottles of Becks and the talk on the iaxis Internet backbone, which has just gone live, begins. A great deal of time is spent speaking about peering and Internet backbone connectivity. The outline of the backbone's design looks very impressive and it is the first in the world to have all Juniper M40 routers. However, the best bit of the presentation is the graphs outlining our potential sales growth from the Internet capacity we hope to sell to the world's ISPs...

Success is almost '*written in the stars*', according to Psycho (who seems to have picked up another marketing signal from the stars of *Orion's Belt*). The projected revenue graph that Psycho has drawn up now looks so steep that 'Eddie the Eagle' would be sweating with fear if he thought he had to ski down it. There is no doubt whatsoever that this anticipated revenue stream is going to be huge. In a matter of *seven* months iaxis could be the new Tier 1 Internet company, like UUNet, PSINet or Genuity.

The gathering splits up with not too many people any the wiser about Internet concepts. iaxis is after all a telecoms company that is trying to get into the Internet market. And it looks like we just might struggle. However, the bottles of Becks all found their way safely back to everyone's desks.

'At least the Internet backbone peering is sorted, so let's see how much we can sell to all the potential websites,' says Wacko, who has wandered back to the quad with a crate of Becks for us all and wanders off again.

Later I hang up the phone to my pal Kathryn in the USA and, with perfect timing, Sasha walks up to my desk, moves the anti-desk treatment devices and sits her bottom down. I make a very conscious effort to close my mouth and remain cool. Today she's wearing a cream coloured Burberry short skirt and spring has definitely arrived.

Wacko and Nathan are just sitting staring at me, with their mouths wide open. This is advanced flirting.

'Here's all the new network marketing maps after the deal with FLAG and Qwest,' she says, with a sexy smile, as her eyelashes flash so much she could be communicating in code, secretly telling me she wants me this weekend.

'So how was your trip to "The Dam", Steve?' she asks tenderly, as I look at Wacko and he kindly opens his mouth and closes it with his forefinger.

I then quickly close my mouth.

'Well, it was pretty good until some tosser gave me a poisoned spliff. I spent the rest of my night tripping out of control,' I say, with a real feel-sorry-for-me look on my face as she crosses her legs, leans forward to see my screen and playfully rubs my hair... just as Kong walks past my desk.

'Oh you poor thing, Steve,' she says, as she touches my hand in sympathy and my heartbeat races skywards.

(Wacko starts yawning away showing no sympathy at all!)

'I had some bad drugs in Manchester a few weekends ago. I was up there with Claire from Personnel and I thought I was really dying,' she informs me.

'Really, so what happened to you?' I ask, looking very concerned, as her eyes are dilating fondly at mine.

'There was a little blast of a party at a friend's flat and I did a few lines, an "E" and a spliff. Then I just went off my head and totally lost it. My friends were all really concerned, and were trying to calm me down. It wasn't a good night, Steve. I spent all of Sunday in bed feeling ill. And the party was still going on and I missed most of the action.'

'Sounds like a shit night. I wish I could've stayed in bed the next day. I had a meeting at 9:00 a.m. and spent thirty-three minutes staring wildly at this poor Dutch woman. I never blinked once!'

'So what were you doing before iaxis?' I ask, as she balances a shoe on her big toe with her right leg outstretched.

Sasha thinks carefully about how to phrase her past career, but it comes out rather well.

'I was with an advertising agency and got out. There was too much white stuff mixed with office politics, affairs and things. Telecoms seemed like a good thing and the pay here was good, so why not? And I haven't regretted it for a day,' she says, feeling very pleased at her career path.

'So what degree did you do to get into advertising?' I ask Sasha, while thinking to myself that if I never went into shipbroking, advertising would be my ideal career, as it is just an example of *"mass psychological warfare"*.

["One of the leading CIA PSYOPS experts of the 'Cold War', Lt General Edward Lansdale, started his civilian career in advertising. He went on to take over the CIA aftermath of Operation Zapata (*Mongoose*), which ended in Dallas... Rockefeller's Allen Dulles and John J. McCloy then coordinated the 'commission'. And this is something which the old President of Zapata Offshore knows a great deal about..."]

'I did an MSc in psychology,' she says smiling, as her eyes flash away at me.

...This vital piece has just been placed into the "overall jigsaw puzzle" which is far from complete.

'An MSc in psychology! I'm impressed. I studied psychology in first year at Uni, but hated all the statistics so I just ditched it and focused on politics and international relations.' I say, thinking back to recent memories and *"challenging career opportunities"*.

'Oh that's so cool, I wish I did that! I like current affairs,' she says sweetly, as her little silver Nokia starts to vibrate inside its Mulberry case. She answers quickly.

'Oh hiya *Jonah* mate! How are you doing sweetie?' she asks, very warmly.

(Silence.)

'Yes, I'd love to see you next Saturday night, send me an email,' she says, as she laughs and giggles a few times and then clicks free as she smiles fondly.

Whoever the fuck this '*Jonah*' is, I can honestly say that I don't like him.

'Anyway Steve, I've got to shoot, we're doing a trade show to launch the iaxis Internet backbone,' she says, as she begins to fit her black leather Bally shoe back onto her right foot as she slides herself back off my desk.

'That's okay. Thanks for the material,' I say, thinking about her weekend ahead with this *Jonah* character.

'No probs mate. See you later!' she says, as she turns around to walk back to marketing blag central. My eyes follow her, as her body walks that sexy walk back to her desk.

Nathan clicks his fingers at me. 'See Steve, psychology degree. That's what we've been saying for months. She plays with your fucking head!' he says, laughing.

'A postgrad MSc in psychology! I didn't even know that,' says Wacko, who's looking at me as if I've just been a silly tosser and gone out and bought a Betamax video recorder.

I look a bit down and they try and cheer me up.

'Steve, she may have been sitting on your desk, but she won't be sitting on you next weekend by the sounds of it!' laughs Wacko.

Nathan in his young, perceptive worldly *wisdom* kindly informs me that she'll be sitting on someone called *Jonah* instead and I am now firmly back in the land of the living.

'Give us another Becks, please!' I ask Wacko, as he kindly lobs one over to me with an 'I told you so' look on his face. We drink up and go over to Centro's to finish off the day.

While my breakfast goes down, I can see the morning sunshine penetrating the office through the glass ceiling and glass walls of 200 Gray's Inn Road. I am also trying to arrange a quick coffee with Kathryn next time she's in London. This lady is our account manager from one of the biggest and most respected Internet companies in the world. iaxis is buying Internet services from this company and she has been looking after me for weeks. She's been in our office once before, but this was only for a very quick passing visit so she could put 'a face to my voice'. In a couple of weeks time she will be flying over to the UK again and I can't wait to see her.

Just as I hit send for my email to Kathryn, Hannah walks up to our quad and Wacko's senses all start to go haywire. I see the hazard lights in the whites of his eyes as Hannah tries to have eyelock with him. She's like a lorry heading straight towards him, and stopping is not an option.

However, today she's with a well-groomed, big chap who is over six feet tall. It looks like he's just started this morning, as I've never seen him around before. In under two seconds, I scan him in to my sophisticated profiling system. He's an old boy. But he is clearly not just any old boy. This big chap looks like he is from the very top of the *Establishment*, as he's wearing a Gieves and Hawkes dark grey, hand-cut double-breasted suit with some old boy school tie. The chap also wears solid gold cufflinks and has a huge gold signet ring on his little finger, proudly bearing his star sign. I think this chap is a *Scorpio* and he looks like he means business.

Hannah introduces Old Boy to us and says that he'll be sitting at her quad and he'll be trying to sell capacity on our Internet backbone to all the dotcoms and websites.

'Good luck, mate!' says Wacko, sitting back, scanning the big fella up and down as well.

'Wacko, I think it would be a good idea if Steve moved desks and sat over on my quad as well, so we can coordinate the Internet strategy, sales working in synergy with Internet peering and connectivity,' says Hannah, smiling fondly at Old Boy and myself.

Shit!! I slam the fucking brakes on. I look at Wacko's face. The surrounding area is just made up of shapes, dark shadows and noise. There is nobody else in the world right now. We have eyelock as he actually considers it for approximately *5.62 seconds.*

'What do you think, Steve?' he asks, just in case he is misreading my body language, with a frantic expression of horror on my face.

'No danger! I'm staying here. Old Boy can join us on our quad and he can work in double synergy with Nathan and me. Internet backbone connectivity, products and sales all working as a "Unit" on the same quad. He'll learn shit loads more sitting here with us three.'

Merlin has gone over to help out customer support and bring them up to lightning speed on Internet *(nuclear)* concepts. So there's now a spare seat on our quad.

'Steve, why don't you want to sit with us on our quad?' asks Hannah, who now looks very pissed off. (I have just gone and foiled her masterplan to surround herself with guys all under the age of thirty!)

'We've got a good team here and Nathan knows more about the Internet than anyone else in the whole company,' I say, as I am very close to spitting out my dummy and trashing the toy room.

Wacko then jumps in and pulls rank, stamping his authority on the situation.

'Right Old Boy, sorted, you can move over here and sit with us on our quad. Nathan and Steve will bring you up to speed on any Internet matters you want answering, yes?'

Both Hannah and Old Boy nod their heads in acceptance. He looks very thankful indeed, but she looks upset. She's just lost the potential to have two more fellas sit with her at her quad. Now she looks like she's going to start boiling her pan, but Wacko promptly advises her that Mr Nice is looking to move desks and he might place him over there with her. That shuts her up and she walks off around the office... on another office manhunt.

Old Boy practically runs back to Hannah's quad and brings his gear over to ours, and it takes a few minutes to get the circulation going down to my legs again.

'Thanks Wacko,' I say, as he's grinning away.

'You owe me a shit load of drinks now, Steve!'

'Hey, no problem whatsoever mate. In fact, I'll get you drunk!'

Wacko just laughs and informs me that he did consider it, but the "karma blowback" would've been far too severe to handle. Old Boy arrives at our quad, shakes all our hands and wipes some sweat off his brow.

'Blaady hell! She's off her rocker, that one!'

'Don't worry Old Boy, you'll get used to it,' I say, as his eyes are having a flashback as they continue to scan the office.

'She was gazing into my eyes, asking me if I'd like to go out for lunch and then some drinks after work tonight!' he says, as he takes a seat at his new desk, still shaking his head as he straightens up his tie.

We all have a good laugh as Old Boy recounts his first experience with *The Force.* He is very pukka, strongly built and over six feet tall. But even with Hannah's slim frame, in her current psychosexual state she would break his back. The fact that he joins in the craic and is laughing makes me revise my scan. I was obviously given the wrong test results.

'Old Boy, there's just one little thing, before we go over to Centro's for some training. I know it's going to be hard, but it's the policy of the quad that you're not allowed to utter the words, "blaady hell", "bugger" or say the word "really". And if any of your chums call in you're not allowed to call them "old boy" either!'

'Yes. And each breach means you get fined a drink,' says Wacko, as Nathan agrees, nodding his head in anticipation of all the free drink that could soon be coming his way!

'Really? Blaady hell!' he says, taking the piss out of himself already.

'Do you have any experience of the Internet?' asks Wacko, laughing.

Old Boy looks blank. 'Bugger all really. I got the job after meeting the iaxis senior vice president while on my honeymoon in Botswana.'

Kathryn's email comes through from the USA; the time and date of our next meeting is confirmed. This short and hopefully friendly meeting will be held in our office.

'Ok, I'm sure you'll fit in and do well in iaxis. If you're unsure just ask lots of questions, but make a few mistakes and you'll learn. But really, just blag it out, wing it like fuck as much as you can and try and cut some deals,' says Wacko, as we all simultaneously look at our synchronized watches and get up from our chairs to go over to Centro's.

Old Boy's training has to start some time.

Four bottles of San Miguel land on the table, and Old Boy is told that we've got one of the most sophisticated Internet backbones in Europe. It is fully protected and ringed with Juniper M40 routers. His job will be to target all the dotcoms and get them to buy transit (space on our backbone) from us, rather than go to PSINet, GTS, UUNet or Level 3. We all know that selling Internet capacity to companies who've never heard of us is a tough nut to crack. We also tell him he's banned from drinking pints of bitter. This is why his eyes keep looking out onto Gray's Inn Road, just to see if any of his old boy chums are passing and clock him drinking bottles of fizzy piss.

'So, does iaxis have a dedicated sales force selling this Internet capacity?' he asks, as all three of us hold in our laughs and eyeball each other.

He doesn't spot it, but we are grinning like hungry wolves before a feed.

'Well, sort of,' says Wacko.

'So how big is the iaxis sales force selling the Internet capacity?' asks Old Boy, as it is now his turn for some water to start dripping from behind his ears.

We all look at each other and wonder how to break the news to him, but Wacko pulls rank yet again and hits him with reality.

'Old Boy, it's just you, old son, and you've got eighteen million dollars of capacity to sell!'

'Blaady hell!' he bellows loudly.

For a good few seconds he holds his stare of disbelief at Wacko, just to see if he was being perfectly serious. His shoulders might be broad, but he's now got nine million dollars worth of Internet capacity resting on each of them. And it's going to be his job to shift it in a market that is going down, and nobody in the Internet world has heard of iaxis.

'That's an on the spot fine, Old Boy, it's your round!' says Nathan, rubbing his paws together.

'Yes, breach of quad protocol,' adds Wacko.

'Oh bugger off!' he says, catching on and laughing as the barman brings four more drinks over to us.

Wacko takes a call on his mobile. It is the finance raiser and the Dodgers on the line. He has to help them come up with some new daring payment delaying tactics and some refinancing stunts *(fire-eating)* in order to keep iaxis in business...

'So what does the sales force do?' asks Old Boy with real concern.

Nathan and I look blank and shrug our shoulders. We haven't really got much of a clue as the sales force is a bit of an enigma.

'They sell bandwidth on our fibre optic network between cities around Europe and get paid a fortune,' I say, sounding like I know what I'm talking about.

'Yes, and there are some classic stories there as well,' adds Nathan, taking a mouthful of beer.

'Like what?' asks Old Boy.

'Well for starters, last year we sold a fourteen million dollar telecom circuit to VIANET and iaxis botched up on the contract and sold the same capacity for four million dollars! A stroke of a pen and ten million dollars of potential revenue gone straight down the pan. Nobody knows what went wrong over that one and nobody is saying a word!'

Old Boy's mouth is now wide open as he shakes his head in shock. (He's only been in the office for a few hours as well!)

(iaxis also did a deal with Deutsche Telekom for some European capacity which we sold to them. The senior executive at Deutsche Telekom whom we were dealing with insisted that iaxis sponsored his son's rally car. This was a 'thank you' for him doing the deal with us. This shameful act of apparent 'corporate bribery' is why a rally car is going round Germany with the name iaxis plastered all over it...)

'But what about the capacity on the Internet backbone, doesn't the iaxis sales team get involved in selling it as well?' he asks, picking up the jargon very fast and seeming to understand it.

'No, they haven't got a clue about the Internet. They all come from a telecoms background and this Internet stuff goes straight over their heads,' says Nathan, who's now on to his third fag. (Old Boy smokes Marlboro Lights as well, so they're now best buddies.)

'You see, they all make huge amounts of commission on big-ticket bandwidth deals. Internet capacity is small fry to them and none of them have any commission structure in their pay for selling this Internet stuff, so they just haven't really been bothering,' I say, as I look very closely at Old Boy, watching his reactions.

'Yes, but Psycho, who's the nutter running marketing, did come up with the idea of giving away free holidays to any member of the sales team who flogged any Internet capacity!' says Nathan, clicking my bottle as we all laugh at one of Psycho's mad schemes.

'*Blaady hell!*' says Old Boy, shaking his head wildly at what he's gone and got himself into.

'That's another round!' says Wacko, who's still barking orders to the *'Fire Department'* on his mobile.

'*Bugger!* I'll get the hang of this!' he says as he gets out a large leather wallet, which looks pretty full. In fact it looks so full, this chap could finance an iaxis bender in this place on a Thursday night all by himself!

I decide to give Old Boy's wallet a rest and get the round in.

'So Old Boy, what were you doing before you landed on iaxis?' asks Wacko, whose mobile phone is now switched off and is smoking silently away on the pub table.

'Well, for about four and a half years I was a freelance news editor in Hong Kong, starting with Reuters.'

'Really!' I say, sounding and looking very surprised.

'Yes.' he replies, still sounding in shock at this new challenge facing him.

'Look Old Boy, I was totally wrong mate, I had you down as a member of *The Ditchley Foundation* or an ex-City banker from Rothschild's or Schroders. Are you sure you're not from that sort of background?'

He just laughs at the results of my scan. 'I think that's what my family would've wanted, but it's the last thing in the blaady world that I would consider doing.'

'So how did you get in to Reuters?' I ask; I'll definitely be getting a new "profiling system" fitted into my head at the weekend.

'About five years ago I was travelling around South East Asia and Hong Kong, and I shot some footage in Burma and the Opium Triangle. I blagged my way into Reuters and flogged it to them. Once they'd bought it, I asked if they'd give me a job and train me up... And they blaady well did!'

'Excellent! So how long were you with Reuters for?' asks Nathan.

'I was only with them for the summer months, because I hadn't finished my degree. Not that I told Reuters Hong Kong that! But I was with a Mr (name withheld) being trained up in their Avid news editing system and then I left after four months to come back to Brunel to finish the degree. As soon as I graduated I went back out to Hong Kong, but Reuters wouldn't look at me, so I went freelance and learned to use the Media 100 news editing system with some other company. I stayed there for over four years and even won some international awards for blaady news editing!'

'Nice one.'

'So then what happened?'

'Simple really, I got married, moved back to London and wanted to get into the Internet, that's the future. And iaxis is where I landed!' he says, as he takes a good swig on his drink.

'Blaady good, Old Boy! So, which school tie is that back in the office?' I ask him, as we made him take it off before we came down here. (I think Upingham, but then again he's got far too much class to go there.)

'Harrow,' he says with pride, whilst taking a good mouthful of fizzy piss from the bottle.

'Blaady hell!' escapes from three beer-filled mouths.

'So what about the family, Old Boy. Do they all work in the City, if that's what they wanted you to do?' asks Nathan, really putting his grasp of human perception to the test.

'No, my family was in the hotel business until they sold their stakeholding a few years ago.'

Old Boy suddenly looks concerned at the information he's just shared with people he barely knows.

'Which hotels were those? asks Nathan, who is now lighting up again.

Old Boy is looking really concerned now as he looks around the bar for any iaxis ear-wiggers. There are none. Everyone else is at the Blue Lion, but we are in here for training and general team building. He looks at all three of us and the words come out much easier than he could've imagined.

The Savoy Group.

'Fuck!' says Nathan, as his fag practically disintegrates.

'Your family *owned* the Savoy Hotel?' I ask, as all of our eyes and mouths are wide open.

'They didn't own it, but they were the major shareholders and a "controlling influence" in the running of the chain. We used to run that hotel and the others. My grandfather established the group and he was the Lord Mayor of London.'

We are all speechless.

Old Boy sits forward like he's reading the six o' clock news and is now looking very serious indeed. 'Look, please do not say anything in the office would you? I would like to keep the old family business out of the office. I like being anonymous.'

Everyone totally agrees. We will not let him down. That is sorted.

We drink up and get ready to go back to the office. As we leave Centro's, I look over to Manhattan's. Sitting in the coffee shop is Claire and she is crying her eyes out and looks totally devastated. Her friend Jemma has her arm round her and is giving her some moral support in her time of need. You don't need to be Freud to work out that Claire's relationship with Nick has suddenly ended.

This morning I'm playing 'Saltwater' by Chicane as Wacko walks back from a top-level *'fire-eating'* discussion with the Dodgers. He sits down and puts his head in his hands.

'The shit is starting to hit the fan about iaxis,' he says, chewing the edges of his 'widescreen' calculator.

'What's up?'

'Well, you've got the NASDAQ, the creditors and the debts and it's all looking like purgatory after the crash. But anyway, I'm off to another meeting and you are going to Sweden tomorrow. It's just for the day, as I need you to look at an IBM building and assess whether it's any good to be turned into a co-location facility. The rest of the market thinks it is fantastic. Sort yourself out for a taxi; you'll need to be at Heathrow for 6 a.m. Your flight is booked, so you'll get your tickets when you get there. But you'll be flying economy class this time, okay?'

'That's okay. So what's happening with iaxis after the NASDAQ going down?'

'As I said, it's looking like purgatory. Until the word is no to a high-yield, we keep moving forwards, but the chances of coming up with a bank are now remote.'

'Okay, so what's the deal with FLAG and Qwest that we keep hearing about?'

'It's just an agreement allowing us to sell capacity on their networks, and they can do the same on ours. We can say that we can sell bandwidth from Frankfurt to China and FLAG can do the same. We don't envisage selling much capacity like this, but Psycho reckons it looks great on our marketing blag.'

I look at some of the material Sasha has left for me, and 'OPLAN 34-A' looks very convincing.

'You know, Psycho has got a point. It makes us look global. From having a pan-European backbone linking about twenty cities iaxis now spans the globe!'

'I know, but we can't sign any new bandwidth customers on to the fibre-optic backbone.'

'Eh?'

'Don't worry about it. It's Ciena. We're trying to get it sorted out. We owe them quite a bit of money,' he says, looking under pressure.

'Anyway, to change the subject, can you remember McGowan meeting his mates in Amsterdam?'

'Er…sort of…'

'Well he ended up getting totally pissed in another club and walked out completely wankered on booze and pot! Only this time he hasn't got a clue where our hotel is, so he gets on the phone and jabbers away to Merlock's mobile answer machine telling him about his night out, the fact he's completely pissed and has no fucking idea where he is! He eventually staggered into the hotel at 6 a.m…'

'I remember now, he was looking a bit rough as well.'

'Yes, well you'll never guess what Merlock and Murray have gone and done?'

'What?' I say, as my head is scrambled. They both support fucking Sunderland and are therefore capable of pulling any stunt in the book.

'They've both gone and downloaded the fifteen-minute voice message McGowan left on the mobile and set up a website and put it on there! Everyone in the NOC has been listening to it for the last twenty minutes!'

'Are they still alive?' I ask, half expecting the team from "Taggart" to start interviewing everyone about a double "murrdurr".

'Yeah, the three of them all go back years,' he says, laughing away.

I start looking up the web site and have a good laugh at McGowan's antics, while Old Boy is on the phone to his wife (again). She's shouting at him for some unknown reason...

The next morning the taxi is waiting outside my flat. I do not sleep in, nor am I rushed as I get ready and place the digital camera in my laptop shoulder bag. I am only going to Stockholm for the day to assess what this old IBM building is like for a potential development into a co-location facility. IBM sold it off a few years ago, but there has recently been a lot of interest in this site. At least I don't have to sign anything, but I've brought along my iaxis pencil just in case the need arises.

At Heathrow Airport I buy the book *Strange Places, Questionable People* by John Simpson. I also have a very quick read through some market information on Sweden, which I brought with me from the office.

Right now, in the early part of year 2000, the Swedish economy is booming, and it is all because of the new media, technology and telecoms sector which is currently sustaining Sweden's "endless summer". All of the major telecoms and Internet players are in Stockholm. And therefore on this *"wheel of fortune"* iaxis must be here as well. Major mobile phone companies such as Nokia and Ericsson are from this part of Europe and are world leaders in developing WAP technology for the future of mobile Internet comunications.

WAP translated from ancient Chinese stands for 'a right waste of effing noodles.' (Well it does in my language book.) In years to come the debts that have been built up in the irrational bidding ["...Game Theory..."] for 3G mobile phone licences could collapse some global telecoms players and even the odd bank. However, HM Treasury got very lucky when they stepped forward and cashed in the UK's biggest ever winning rollover lottery ticket and walked away with over twenty-two billion pounds.

So where is the revenue going to come from, Mr Phone Company?

'*...Now if you don't know the answer, you can't phone a friend, as you've got no more lives left and this is your final chance... And twenty-two billion pounds is a lot to gamble. But it's your choice... Please stay quiet, audience...*'

*'No!... Punters surfing the Internet on their mobile phones is the wrong
answer. I'm sorry, but you've just lost twenty-two billion pounds!'*
'But... But... But... what about mobile e-commerce?'
'What about it, Mr Orange?'

And with all this telecoms hype, the demand for potential co-location
facilities in Stockholm has not just taken off, it has blasted off, and there is
no glass ceiling at the old IBM building in Stockholm to contain it. In
Sweden there's just a nice big juicy hole in the ozone layer for the market
greed to aim for, and the prices for co-location buildings are currently going
right through it. And in the meantime, the electricity demand for these co-
location facilities cooks the planet. (Not that I think about this when I use a
mobile or surf the Internet.)

As soon as I leave customs, the local property broker is waiting outside
the airport. His BMW 328 Sport takes us to this massive building, which
IBM closed in the early Nineties after the "Cold War" ["...the world's greatest
gameshow"]. It was the centre of IBM operations in Scandinavia and at its
time of operation it covered sixty thousand square metres. It is located about
twenty kilometres outside Stockholm, near the airport. The building itself is
a very solid structure and was built during the "Cold War", long after
Thomas J. Watson Sr. had passed away. A strong tornado wouldn't leave
much damage to this old "Big Blue" facility and it is very clear that this IBM
building was made to withstand a "Merlin" type blast in the event of
Armageddon.

["...Mr Thomas J. Watson Sr saw that his IBM was the backbone of Nazi
Germany's infrastructure. Hitler was IBM's biggest foreign customer as the IBM
punchcard sorting machine, the Hollerith, 'automated' the Holocaust's killing of six
million Jews. Hole 8 was for Jews. Nothing moved in Nazi Germany without IBM
knowing about it..."]

Digiplex/Carlyle have also been to see Stockholm's former *"Solutions
Company"* building and are very impressed at its potential for being turned
into a co-location facility, and from inside I can see why. The space and
security are perfect. This old IBM building can easily house thousands and
thousands of Internet racks. Yahoo has ninety racks in a London co-location
facility (location withheld) and this is where that Internet player lives...

["...It wasn't just IBM who traded with Hitler and the Nazis. Henry Ford and
GM made Nazi tanks, Du Pont made explosives, Standard Oil supplied fuel,
JPMorgan/Chase money, ITT comms equipment, and Rockefeller's Standard Oil also
semi-owned the IG Farben group which made the gas for Hitler's concentration
camps... And Kykuit made a fortune from the Nazis and the 'Final Solution'."]

...The power supply to this former IBM facility is huge, twenty megawatts, and it can be increased to ninety megawatts, when this future "Internet City" feels like expanding. Local fibre optic cables are in the area, but there has always been "leading edge" fibre optics connected to IBM's old vast *complex...*

["...These American corporations and the Federal Reserve Bank of New York, Chase Bank and Allen Dulles OSS Swiss operation knew all that was happening at the time. Their wartime corporate dealings (along with Rockefeller's America IG) helped to sustain the Holocaust and the Nazi war effort. Allen Dulles and John F. Dulles were related to the Rockefeller family, and their old legal firm, Sullivan and Cromwell, had extensive legal representations between Hitler's J. Henry Schroeder Bank and the Rockefeller family's Standard Oil 'German Interests'... Allen Dulles went on to run the CIA and his brother John Foster Dulles became the US Secretary of State..."]

...Apart from manufacturing IBM products, IBM Stockholm was also the Central Computer Operations Centre for "Big Blue's" corporate operations for the whole of Scandinavia, and underneath the factory floor was one of the largest private networks of nuclear bunkers in the whole of Sweden. There are now at least four that have survived, each is over two hundred square metres in size, and they are *hidden* from view.

[" ...Right, first question; Between 1939 and 1945, did millions of Allied servicemen die while 'America Inc' traded with Adolf Hitler's Third Reich? Now you've got three lives left, but take your time '*Mr Ryan*' as there are some war files in the Federal Reserve Bank of New York, old Chase Bank NYC and Paris and the Bank for International Settlements in Switzerland which will never be released..."]

I switch my laptop on and take out my digital camera. With everything set up I start clicking away and the *evidence* that this old IBM building has great future potential as an "Internet City" is emailed back to London within a few minutes.

["...It's the right answer! The US wartime dealings with the Nazis and Tojo/Kishi's Japan were covered up for decades by the US government and profits ran into billions of dollars. The gold bullion payments went back to America's Wall Street via 'trust companies' and banks in Switzerland, Lisbon, Austria and Stockholm..."]

After we leave IBM's old complex, the real estate broker kindly shows me another building that has just come on to the market. It is the Kodak development and processing facility for Scandinavia. It is almost next door to the old IBM building and has the same power connections. It is also a very good site with a lot of potential to be turned into a co-location facility. However, it won't be vacated until July 2000 and in Internet and telecoms terms this is far too long to wait. Telecoms companies want it last week and ready for next week and *money is no object...*

["...The Federal Reserve Bank of Philadelphia handled most of the gold from these US/Nazi wartime deals... And after the war, ITT and other corporations put in claims to the US government for "business interruption costs" caused by occasional Allied bomb damage to machinery in their Nazi factories during 1941-45... And the US government paid up, *'Mr Ryan'...*"]

At the airport I say goodbye to the broker and thank him for his time. *He looks a bit sad* when he hands me his business card and I tell him that I seem to have 'forgotten' mine. Someone else can hand over theirs when we sign up for a twenty-year lease and put down a few pennies as a deposit. If we're interested, we'll look at the 'small print' and the 'history' of this old IBM facility some time in the future...

["...And when IBM's Thomas J. Watson died, President Eisenhower said *'The nation has lost a truly fine American - an industrialist who was first of all a great citizen and a great humanitarian.'* The American-Nazi business dealings of Thomas J.Watson Sr, Edsel Ford, Paul Warburg, Walter C. Teagle, Herman Metz, Owen Young, Thomas H. McKittrick, *Prescott Bush* (1941), Roland E. Harriman, Irenee du Pont, Southenes Behn, Charles Mitchell, Winthorp Aldrich, J.P. Morgan Jr and the Rockefeller family were never part of the trials for *war criminals* at Nuremberg..."]

I touch down at Heathrow on the Scandinavian Air Services flight. The cabin crew are always so friendly, much better than others I have to use. Walking through passport control I switch on my mobile and find that Wacko has left a voice message on it. The IBM building looks great and the management is keen to run. However, they want to see how many dollars are involved, because right now with the *'trustees'* in the glass boardroom, all is not looking well...

["...Now audience, if you lost a serviceman during World War Two, you could launch a legal claim against the Bank for International Settlements, the Rockefeller family and the owners of Ford Motors, IBM, General Motors, General Electric, Du Pont, ITT, J.P. Morgan-Chase and Standard Oil/Exxon companies. Especially after the Rockefeller oil shipments from Aruba to the Canary Islands/Spain kept Hitler's Ford manufactured tanks for North Africa, Normandy and Russia fully fuelled up..."]

At Heathrow airport a taxi is waiting to take me back to Fulham. I stop in at a newsagent where I buy a National Lottery ticket for the weekend's rollover draw. A short time later I arrive back home and crash on the sofa feeling very tired after this long day-trip to Stockholm. As I turn on my huge Sony TV set, I see that *Family Fortunes* has just ended, but I'm home in time to watch *Who Wants To Be A Millionaire?* During this gameshow, the main punter is not greedy and walks away with a very tidy sum after a few easy questions.

["...And it was business as usual during the 'Cold War', as David Rockefeller and His Chase Manhattan Bank traded with Communist Russia while 58,000 American troops died in Vietnam... And the Council on Foreign Relations ran the world's greatest *gameshow*, with the perfect hosts: Mr John J. McCloy and **Mr David Rockefeller**."]

The next morning Wacko is in another meeting with Emma from vendor management, the finance raiser and all the iaxis Dodgers. Since Wacko buys all the fibre optic Ciena gear, Nortel switches and co-location buildings, his accountancy skills are in demand now. In fact he is the man - *always under orders from above* - who buys all the gear to build the network. The fact that none of it is paid for is the reason for this meeting. He had to go out and buy his special edition widescreen calculator to add up his department's bills.

But Wacko is brilliant when it comes to eating numbers and getting our creditors to agree to extended payment dates, alternative payment schemes and lower interest rates for more share options, etc. Over his last ten years as an accountant he's pulled off a few great feats and has even had to leave a certain Eastern European country in a 'reasonable hurry' during one dark night.

Old Boy still hasn't sold any capacity on the iaxis Internet backbone and he's starting to look concerned. He's been wading through all the latest Internet magazines he bought from WH Smiths near Chancery Lane and for days on end he has been contacting every single 'blaady' Internet company that has got a glossy advert in those pages. But nobody wants to buy space on our Internet backbone. In the last six months, these European dotcoms have already bought capacity from the big players.

'Blaady hell, no bugger's heard of us!' he says, looking knackered and putting down the handset after yet another soul-destroying attempt at flogging our capacity.

By now Old Boy owes the quad a whole off-licence in fines, but we've given up, so Nathan and I decide to bring him a little bit more up to speed on iaxis's Internet backbone.

'Old Boy, do you know how much money iaxis has spent on advertising the Internet backbone?' I ask as I turn off Bloomberg's website page and save the recent changes I have made to my CV.

He is a bright chap when it comes to business, so he starts to mentally calculate all the big dollars involved in promoting such a product.

'Round about four hundred thousand pounds or so?'

Nathan and I look at him seriously.

'Old Boy, we've spent fuck all.'

This freaks him out as his eyes go all wild and stary.

'Stay calm big fella, you've got to get used to shocks and surprises working in iaxis!' says Nathan, itching for a fag.

'Look Old Boy, there's no money left in iaxis. In fact we've survived by spending other people's money and running up lovely big debts. iaxis needs a high-yield bond issue for three hundred million dollars just to carry on. And right now that's hanging by a thread,' I say, trying my best to reassure him.

'Jesus! I wasn't told this in blaady Botswana!'

'Look at it as character building,' I say, grinning as Old Boy clearly sees that I am taking the piss.

'Look here old boy, I went to blaady Harrow for my character building!'

'And what a fine job it did,' I say, laughing in agreement.

'So how are we going to get business on to it?' Old Boy asks with such commitment that we are both very impressed.

Nathan and I both shrug our shoulders and look back at our flat Sony PC screens, while Old Boy gives a deep sigh and looks up at the *'signs in the sky'* that are now becoming apparent through the glass ceiling of 200 Gray's Inn Road. The sun, high *above*, is shining brightly into the ITN building down *below*, and the temperature at seven floors high is now going to *rise...*

CHAPTER 10

'The gulf between books and experience… is a lonely ocean.'
White Teeth by Zadie Smith.

Today is the warmest day of the year so far and Nathan is playing 'Spying Glass' by Massive Attack. Old Boy is on the phone to his wife and I can hear her from my seat. It sounds like she's having another screaming frenzy at him. I catch Old Boy's eye and he looks like he's heard it all before. His eyes are not just glazed over, they look like they've got double-glazing in them.

Charlotte on reception phones to let me know that Kathryn from the USA has arrived and is waiting for me in reception. Usually when some bloke from the industry comes in to see me, they ask beforehand if I can take my time in coming to collect them from reception. They like to look at the two girls and chat away to them. (Only these two fine girls will probably chat them up!)

I wander into reception to meet Kathryn, and quickly see that she is not sitting on the comfortable leather sofa. She is in fact on her feet and is looking into the Network Operations Centre, or the glass goldfish bowl that houses our very own "*Pandora's Box*".

We speak just about every other day and have a great rapport. This lady has turned out to be my key mentor in the Internet world (after she checked me out of course). And it turns out we coincidentally have a mutual "*friend*", which means she's far more open with me than with others.

'Hi Kathryn,' I say warmly, as she turns around.

'Hey Steve! Good to see you again buddy. The traffic from Palmer Street to here was terrible!' she says, smiling warmly as we shake hands.

Kathryn is in her early fifties and would not look out of place buying clothes and furniture from Laura Ashley. She is incredibly intelligent and her personality is warm, *sensitive* and honest. And she's been in the Internet world for quite some time. There's nothing she doesn't know about the Internet industry, and also her previous one. For a number of years she was with the US Navy on 'permanent secondment' to America's National Security Agency ["…No Such Agency"], starting as a systems engineer under their Naval Security Group. She was based at several NSA stations, specialising in communications security (COMSEC) of the NSA's communication systems. Kathryn really knows her stuff when it comes to Electronic Key Management Systems (EKMS) and the development of Unified Cryptologic Architecture (UCA). And the lady still has her buddies in Maryland, Washington D.C. and a few other places.

She now works for one of the top Internet backbones in the USA, which has strong connections with the US government. Due to her own request, her identity and company will not be revealed here, but my management knows her, because iaxis has signed a big contract with this company. We are paying her company for their Internet connection, even though iaxis is not yet live in New York. They delivered their services on the date that we requested, but we have other technical Internet problems to fight in NYC before we can start to use her company's Internet backbone. When we become live we will probably buy her company's network security products as well.

Kathryn thought she'd seen and *heard* it all before. That was until the first time I showed her our boardroom. Like our ex-chairman, she also has a passion for expensive hand-sculptured glass. But today we can't go into the glass boardroom, as it is currently full of suits, so we go to the canteen on the lower ground floor of the glasshouse. The sun is shining into the ITN building and the weather outside looks fantastic. We get a couple of drinks in and find some seats well away from any potential ear-wiggers. (A newsreader from ITN was behind us in the canteen queue.)

'So what's happening with iaxis after the NASDAQ crashing?' she asks, as the warm sun shines down through the glass ceiling and right on to us both.

'I really don't know. Nobody seems to know, it's all being kept quiet. It's like the NASDAQ fall was a dark cloud on the horizon that will come and pass.' I say, as she laughs and shakes her head. Her info comes from way beyond the glass ceiling.

'It will be the end of 2004 at least before the US and the European telecoms market starts to recover, and even then it is unlikely the industry will fully recover at all,' she says, with a lovely warm caring smile to ease my mind as it crashes back to planet Earth.

'Why so long?' I ask, as I realise that I still have a lot to learn.

'There is too little demand for this huge supply of telecoms and Internet capacity that is currently being built and developed in Europe. Hundreds of billions of dollars has been borrowed to build all these networks, and I'd like to see where all the revenue is coming from in the future. Wall Street has created the biggest "paper tiger" ever with this "new economy" and somebody, somewhere is going to have to tell "*the King*" that he's "*not wearing any clothes*" and that the market was never really there in the first place.'

'So what about neutral co-location facilities?'

'Don't even mention neutral co-location facilities over here! After all the developments that are going on, there will be more than four times supply versus demand for European co-location facilities. There needs to be some major consolidation in Europe and lots of companies will go bust during the next eighteen months,' she says, looking deep in thought.

I just nod blindly at her global knowledge. (The cappuccino down here is crap.)

'So why didn't iaxis move quickly enough for the high-yield last year? The market was perfect for you guys. I really do think that you've missed the boat. And Steve, you know what happens to people who *"miss the boat"*?' she says, as she clasps her hands together and brings them up to her chin, watching me like a hawk.

'Yes, I do know what happens, and we've well and truly *"missed the boat"*. And now we're rather short of cash to fund the networks, let alone pay for them,' I say, as I take a sip of the shit cappuccino.

'So what went wrong?' she asks, as I can almost feel the cold metal on the back of my head as I see the boat leaving the harbour.

'iaxis did the roadshows to find an investment house in order to raise the debt for funding the future roll-out plan of the network. We eventually chose the bankers DLJ to look after this for us. Then the market turned in the third quarter last year and high yield was no longer an option. DLJ went and pulled their offering and iaxis *"missed the boat"*. However, we still went ahead and built two further huge fibre optic networks around the rest of Europe with no funding whatsoever! Afterwards, one of the shareholders appointed Rothschilds to sell iaxis on the quiet. But I don't know why iaxis was dragging its feet last year on the high yield bond issue. I haven't got to that part of the puzzle yet.'

'You'll find out why sooner rather than later, I'm sure of that. My company came in and had a look at your business plan with a view to us acquiring iaxis, but because you guys use Juniper routers and we use Cisco it wasn't good. And then there are your debts! In the end we had to decline the opportunity and walk away.'

'Yes, I can understand that.'

'But anyway, when do you think iaxis will be live in New York?'

I shrug my shoulders and my face genuinely gives off the impression that I don't have a clue on the date. 'It could be soon, but we get pissed around by the unions at that co-location facility.'

'Yeah, the unions in New York are not the easiest to deal with!'

'You can say that again. We're already several months behind.'

'I know, but in the mean time, I just hope some big hungry company buys you guys up soon. And if you know anyone called *"Noah"* from your last career, tell him to get his boat ready for you guys!' she says, laughing slightly.

'You can say that again. I'll check my phone numbers later!'

'So are you liking your new career?' she asks with interest, as she knows a great deal about my background.

'Yes, it's fantastic. I enjoy learning new concepts. It's been a real challenge.'

'Good. You've made a good choice coming into this industry. Now just find the right company that stands a chance of surviving.'

'Thanks, but that's easier said than done! So how come you ended up in the Internet?' I ask her now, as she's not always so open on a landline.

'The telecoms company I work for also designs and manufactures encryption systems, for both the NSA and CIA. It was easy for me to join them as they have an office in Fort Meade. I had quite a lot of dealings with them when I was part of the NSA, so when I wanted to get out of the NSA and into the private sector, this company was my first choice. I had my high security clearance and they took me and quite a few others on.'

'So could you have worked for any others?'

'Sure I could! Last year I was approached by Control Data Corp of New York who wanted me to join them and help upgrade their CIA-backed *"Population Identification Number Project Infrastructure System"* and to help sell it to more foreign governments for mass population surveillance and civilian data profiling. Then recently E-Systems of Dallas called me. They were pioneers of modern electronic warfare (EW), which the NSA used during the "Cold War" against the Russians. They are a very well respected company in their field and both the NSA and the CIA are silent partners with them. In fact lots of ex-senior officials currently work for them.'

'Really? I've never heard of them.'

'E-Systems is a highly secretive and very specialised company, with some very powerful friends in Washington and Fort Meade. In 1975 they bought the CIA's *Air Asia* operation in Taiwan and in 1977 they helped develop one of the worlds' most sophisticated digital processing systems ever used in population data profiling. It was for the Argentine secret police and it was called the *"Digicom System"*. The Pentagon approved of its "deployment", as it made Henry Kissinger's covert policy ["during the CIA-backed Operation Condor..."] with General Videla's Argentina so much easier to manage. That system, along with the NSA-developed CONDORTEL, was a "leading edge" at the time.'

["...President Ford's Defense Secretary, Donald Rumsfeld, had responsibility for 'The CONDORTEL Communications System', which his Pentagon trained in, and supplied to, the US-backed regimes like Videla's for Operation Condor. The CONDORTEL linked up the six secret police force comms into one US-developed digital network, with covert access by Langley, Meade and the Pentagon, who heard everything. President Ford awarded Donald Rumsfeld the US Presidential Medal of Freedom in 1977... And what was going on in the women's sections at the Orletti and La Perla torture centres in Argentina, was quietly forgotten by all... *Their screams couldn't be heard from the White House lawn...*"]

'So are E-Systems pretty big then?' I ask, thinking about General Videla's "direct assistance" from Washington ["...directly from 'subversive lists' drawn up by George Bush Sr and Henry Knoche's CIA...where Nobody cried for Argentina in 1976..."].

'Sure, and they're bigger than ever these days! In 1991, after the Gulf War, they were awarded a three billion dollar contract for the installation of an electronic border between Saudi Arabia and Iraq. They are currently looking at doing an electronic border between Turkey and Iraq due to the problem with the Kurds and the PKK. I could easily have joined them after leaving the NSA and gone into EW sales, but I'm an encryption data geek at heart. However, I do get approached quite regularly from some very big players with strong links to the NSA and CIA.'

'Interesting. So which other companies have strong links to the NSA and CIA?' I ask, as I notice her eyes don't miss a thing.

'There's Bill Studeman's TRW, it has strong connections, as does CACI and Computer Sciences Corp, which is a massive one. In fact, following CSC's two and a half billion dollar 'SAMIS II Project' for Saudi Arabia's domestic intelligence service, or the *al Mubaith*, they also wanted me to look at working for them, but I said no to them as well,' says Kathryn, as she gently lifts the lemon and ginger herbal teabag out of her teacup.

'Why was that? Saudi Arabia is the most important country in the world, and they're going to be one of the most technologically developed countries in the entire region.'

'Well there's no alcohol for a start! But seriously, due to the *Wahhabism* state religion, there's more democracy and civil rights in Iran, where even women can vote and drive a car. And right now in Saudi Arabia there is a great deal of anti-Western feeling which is currently at an all-time high. This is due to the American bases on their soil, the origins of the Gulf War and the continued debt repayments to America for the so-called "defending the Kingdom" way back in 1990.'

'Yes, it all goes back to the *origins* of that war with Saddam occupying Kuwait,' I say, with "informed confidence", while thinking about the current sanctions on Iraq and the subsequent deaths of over one million men, women and children since 1991.

'You can say that again, Steve. I was working in Washington at the time of the Gulf War and I know the history here very well. Do you remember April Glaspie, the US Ambassador to Iraq?' she asks, with a cunning look in her eyes.

["...April Glaspie met Saddam just one week before he invaded Kuwait. Saddam was told that America would not get involved in an 'Arab conflict' between Iraq and Kuwait and that his 'Kuwait issue' was of no concern to America. This was following her 'direct instructions' from George Bush Sr and James Baker in Washington..."]

'Yes, of course I do. And I also remember a full-on debate about her at university while I was studying the Gulf War.'

'Steve, you know that diplomacy is "war by other means" and in this grey area *there are always two edges to a sword*. On the twenty-fifth of July 1990, April Glaspie held a meeting with Saddam and passed on the view of the Bush administration regarding his "dispute" with Kuwait. Two days later, President Bush wrote Saddam a personal ["...and friendly"] letter and April went on her annual holiday. Then, I think it was five days later, Saddam invaded his entire old province.'

'Yes, and then all hell broke loose.'

'It sure did! And afterwards, *Bush* started calling Saddam the *"New Hitler"* to the world to get United Nations support, and the rest is history. But in reality the Gulf War was a CIA war and *"The Company"* was running the entire show from the very beginning. It was all about enhancing US national security interests such as oil, money and future arms deals in the region. Take a very close look at George Bush Sr's *National Security Directive 26*,' she says, as she takes a gentle sip of her very hot drink.

'I'm familiar with NSD-26, but what happened to April Glaspie?' I ask, as that name also seems to have disappeared from the pages of history, along with the debt repayments Saudi Arabia is still making to America for fighting the Gulf War ["and Saddam was left in power..."].

'There were a few questions she had to answer to the Senate, but she was fully cleared of course and last I heard she was in Cape Town. However, to my knowledge no details of NSA SIGINT (signals intelligence), EW Ops (electronic warfare) or even Richard Stoltz's ["...the CIA's Deputy Director of Operations or DD/O in August 1990"] files and operational cables ["...to and from Kuwait and Saudi"] were ever made available to Capitol Hill as part of the inquiry.'

'Strange that, isn't it?' I say, whilst trying my best not to sound too surprised.

'You know there are "unofficial" files in CIA Langley and Bill Studeman's ["...and Bob Prestel's"] old NSA offices that hearings in the Senate will never ever see, no matter what. The NSA and CIA can cover themselves very well. And these days Congress can be like a big pussycat with the IC (Intelligence Community) breathing down their necks. "Oversight" is just a little word, you know, and the real power in American foreign policy "agenda setting" rests with David Rockefeller's Council on Foreign Relations in New York. But to be fair to April, back then she was only the Ambassador and did not have access to the overall picture, which Washington did. Never forget what Sun Tzu wrote over *two thousand* years ago, when he said that "all warfare is based on *deception*". That is so very true and "The Art of War" is still used by military planners to this day, but I can't go into that Saudi electronic warfare stuff,' she says, with a hint of *revelation* in her eyes, as she intentionally raises her left eyebrow.

'I know. It's amazing what you can get away with, if you plan it properly. And Saddam was America's "friend" for so long as well!'

'You got that right! ["He was in the 1970's Safari Club..."] During his war with Iran, the NSA and the CIA used to share intelligence and all sorts with him and even helped him with IMINT (imagery intelligence) for gassing Iranian troops. This covert support was especially true after Reagan's NSDDs 114 and 141 ["which George Bush Sr was privy to"]. But in 1990 this relationship had all changed. Iraq was suddenly the "new enemy" of the world and the NSA was listening to Saddam's and the *Mukhabarat's* comms traffic around the clock. This was easy to do since America supplied new comms gear to him the day before he invaded Kuwait; it was termed "advanced data transmission devices" and Iraq paid almost seven hundred thousand dollars for the equipment! The NSA saw and heard the troop build-up outside Kuwait taking place prior to the invasion and Washington knew his plans to take all of Kuwait in advance. The NRO (National Reconnaissance Office) might think it owns the night, but the Naval Security Group at Menwith Hill, Fort Gordon and Fort Meade has the best code-breakers in the world.'

'Knowledge gives Strength to the arm, right?'

'Sure. And SIGINT is critical to US national security on a global basis. The National Signals Analysis Center is always on the ball and the interception of all shortwave communications in the entire Persian Gulf and

Indian Ocean is still done by the Naval Security Group's FLAGHOIST surveillance system at our Diego Garcia base. And just like your Falklands conflict, *it takes a great deal of comms traffic for a government to mobilise an entire army for the invasion of even a small country.* Nothing in the Near East escapes Fort Meade's attention as the National SIGINT Committee and SOTA ["...SIGINT Operations Tasking Authority"] keeps Saddam and the entire region, *especially* the House of Saud, under constant electronic surveillance for the US government's SIGINT product. Saudi Arabia was *never* a target of Saddam's, that's the overall *big picture,'* she says, as she looks down at her drink and stirs a spoon in it.

'I know, but the Saudis did get very spooked at Saddam's so-called *"imminent Iraqi invasion plan".'*

'You can say that again! After Iraq invaded Kuwait, the NSA heard that the House of Saud were *"mooting"* the idea of buying off Saddam, if he thought of quickly invading Saudi Arabia as well. This set off the alarm bells in Washington. After George Bush Sr was briefed on this development, he sent Dick Cheney and others to meet with King Fahd who was then shown some dodgy satellite photos from the Iraq-Saudi border. This meeting was all about getting the Saudi royal family to *"do the right thing"* and approve the deployment of US troops on Saudi soil, in order to *"defend the Kingdom"* from an *"imminent Iraqi invasion plan"*. If the House of Saud had bought off Saddam in August 1990, it would have seriously disrupted our "overall strategic objective" at the time.'

'I don't think I heard CNN report it quite like that!'

'No, you wouldn't! CNN only repeats what it gets fed. After the Gulf War, Chas Freeman the US Ambassador to Saudi, was given the CIA's prestigious "Medallion medal" and Menwith Hill won the "NSA Station of the Year Award" for its "technical achievements" during the campaign.'

'Really?'

'Too right they did! George Bush Sr even visited the NSA HQ and expressed his appreciation for the NSA's SIGINT product from the entire region. He also thanked the heads of the CIA, who later named the *'Centre for Intelligence'* at CIA Langley after him. That's how close he is with the CIA. In fact, once you join *"The Company"*, you never actually leave.'

'It sounds like you miss the good old days,' I say inquisitively, as I think about the origins of the Gulf War, which the higher echelons of the Bush administration ["...including Bill Webster's CIA and Dick Cheney's Pentagon"] had expertly created ["...engineered dear boy, engineered"].

'Sometimes, but I'm really very happy where I am. And my contacts with my old profession stay with me for life.'

'You certainly sound happy with your Internet career when we speak, but how come there are so many ex-military people working in the Internet world? Just about every other person seems to be ex-military, especially in America,' I ask her, as I mentally note that there are also people like me winging it. (And our numbers run in to thousands!)

She smiles and tries to help out. 'It's called "career migration" and there's lots of former NSA staff working for IT companies like Cisco and Unisys. In fact they were both partners in a top-secret NSA cryptology project called "Project BLACKER" for the Pentagon's *Defense Data Network* and people move across just like I did.'

'I've never heard of that project!'

'Not many people have, it was a host-to-host encrytion program going back twenty years. But Cisco and the NSA still work together on data encryption and network routers. The CIA also uses the Cisco Catalyst 7500 router with IOS software for its Intranet and Langley is also big on IBM LAN servers for its other secure networks.'

'I see, but Cisco, aren't they one of the main players in the Internet world?'

'Absolutely. You see Cisco routers handle approximately ninety-eight per cent of the world's total Internet traffic and they've been in bed with the NSA for years! In fact Cisco, IBM and Microsoft all have "representative" offices at Fort Meade for all the classified work they do with the NSA. The Cisco routers are central to the modern Internet, and the National Cryptologic School at the FANX complex in Fort Meade even has a special course on them; it's called the '*NT-252 Cisco Router Configuration*' module. And just out of interest, another popular course is the '*CT-112 Architecture of Windows NT*'. A lot of personnel with the NSA's Service Cryptologic Element attended this module *and it's not run by Microsoft!*' she says, with a glint in her eyes.

'I'm sure it's not! So what other types of NSA staff attend courses at the cryptologic school?'

'In that place, you've got math gurus building classified encryption algorithms for future codes, computer scientists working on microprocessors, massively parallel systems and Critical Infrastructure Protection programs. There are also courses for software engineers developing knowledge-based systems in UNIX/C, JAVA, Perl and C++ and there's many other classified modules on the Internet, which are run by the NSA for "linguistic technicians" that you don't get to read about in the *Washington Post.*'

'Of course not! And I guess the NSA's reach into the Internet is quite extensive?'

'Just a bit! You know the NSA and the Pentagon are actually behind the development of the modern day Internet far more than people actually realise. But having said that, people generally have no idea where the Internet came from. Do you know how and *why* the Internet was originally built?' she asks in a friendly manner.

'Was it something to do with linking the top American universities and the defence establishment, during the "Cold War"?' I say trying to remember what Merlin once told me, as my knowledge here is very patchy.

'Yes, that's right. The Internet was to be used as a vehicle for the transmission of defence data from the top universities and their defence research departments to each other, and to the Pentagon and other places. The aim was to link up this computer network coast to coast and hopefully keep up a redundant line of communication in the event of a nuclear attack on America,' says Kathryn, as she adjusts her Liberty silk neckscarf slightly.

'Yes, I thought so, but when exactly were the roots of the first Internet development?'

'Well, you know the real roots of the Internet development can be traced back to just after the Soviets launched the first Sputnik rocket in 1957,' she says casually.

'Really, as far back as that?'

'Oh yes, you see after the fall out from the Sputnik rockets, the Pentagon set up the DARPA, or Defense Advanced Research Projects Agency (it used to be called ARPA). One of the main functions of DARPA was to focus on research and "technical superiority" in the quest for Command and Control Research (CCR) in computer technology. It was put in the hands of an MIT scientist called Dr Licklider and he was given responsibility by the Pentagon to manage the highly classified DoD Project.'

'So how did he pull it all together?'

'He basically went and pooled together the leading computer geeks in America and set up a department called the Information Processing Techniques Office (IPTO). This had a sole aim which was to develop the dream of linking up whole computers and the geeks behind the screens with other computers at remote locations for the transmission of military data between them.'

'So how long did it take to really develop?' I ask, chewing my lips at my own lack of knowledge about the foundations of the Internet.

'It wasn't until 1967 that defence chiefs from the DARPA and the Stanford Research Institute (SRI) developed this into a fully funded secret program for the Pentagon and termed it "Resource Sharing Computer Networks". The chiefs at DARPA in Washington agreed with the potential of this program and soon the real funding took off. It was given the official title "Project ARPANET" and this was the world's original Internet of the now World Wide Web.'

'And then it just took off?'

'It sure did. A company called BBN, who also specialised in encryption devices for the NSA and the CIA, won the contract to develop the communications technology for this "Project ARPANET." Then, in 1969, BBN and the leading computer geeks from universities such as UCLA and SRI met to work out the mapping for the ARPANET. Later that year they successfully delivered the first data from one computer to another separate computer in UCLA's computer lab. We now call this data "Internet traffic." And then things started to really happen.'

'So the whole thing wouldn't have taken off if it wasn't for the NSA and the Pentagon using computers for the US military to communicate?'

'That's correct. You see, once it was established that computers were going to be the "communication vehicle" within the US military intelligence community, the quest was on to link computers as a communications medium with a view towards establishing modern-day networks like the *Defense Information Systems Network* (DISN). This was not only for military data transmission as the Pentagon originally intended. At the time it was also clear that the flow and *control* of information in the future would be as vital as the flow and control of oil and money. So the Pentagon saw the original development of "Project ARPANET" as the first steps of a strategic communications network for "*information management*" in not only the US military and Federal Government, but also the anticipated global economy as well. And this was going on when ECHELON was under development and the INTELINK-P was just a dream, but that's another story.'

'So all this really started to kick off in the Sixties and Seventies?' I ask, as I feel I've learned more in the last fifteen minutes than in all my years at university, when the Internet didn't exist as far as I knew.

'Yes, and the first transmission with the "@" sign in it was actually developed by Ray Tomlinson at BBN. He first sent this "@" sign in 1973, when BBN was pioneering the development of product switch technology using Honeywell 3-16 processors, and before long it just quietly took off. Computers in several universities' defence research departments now became interconnected with each other. Soon afterwards they also became interconnected with the Pentagon, RAND and various other US government agencies. This extended ARPANET; IP-routed technology was the foundation of DoD networks like the *Defense Message System* and INTELNET, both of which came much later. But back in the Seventies this secret military data could suddenly be communicated computer to computer across America via the US telephone network ["...with Bill Baker's NSA-backed Bell Labs"] using ARPANET-type IP technology. The original ARPANET/BBN backbone is now turned off, but today Genuity's (BBN) AS-1 network grew out of ARPANET, it is the world's leading Internet backbone, and it's used by leading US corporations for their global Internet developments.'

'Wow, you know, it just makes you see how far behind we let ourselves become in this area.'

'Hey, a few years before I was stationed in England, I think it was in 1976, you guys invented one of the best encryption tools ever used by the US Navy. In fact, I think it was even better than IBM's "LUCIFER" encryption algorithm, which the NSA sponsored, so you're really not that far behind!' she says, as she smiles at the memory.

'You were based here in the UK?' I ask, as the light-switch in my mind switched itself right back on.

'Correct, I was stationed here from 1980 to 1983 and I just loved it.'

'Whereabouts were you stationed? Molesworth?' I ask, taking a random guess.

'No, but I've got a couple of CIA buddies who work there.'

'I've only driven past it and it looks impressive.'

'Oh it is. It's a huge Joint Analysis Centre and plays a major role in the Pentagon's ISR (Intelligence, Surveillance and Reconnaissance) program. Lots of sensitive NSA SIGINT covering Russia and the Middle East gets collated there, as does CIA IMINT (imagery intelligence) from their KH-12 series of birds. It's been a long time since I visited that place.'

'But you were never actually stationed there?' I ask, sounding a bit casual.

'No, when I was in England I was stationed at the National Security Agency's London HQ at 7 North Audley Street. It's one of the many anonymous "outpost" buildings the NSA has around the world. Officially, this was always the HQ for the Commander in Chief US Naval Forces, Europe ["CINCUSNAVEUR is now located in Naples, Italy..."], but they shared it with the Naval Security Group (NAVSECGRU) of the NSA. The CO for the unit operates under the covert name of '*Office of the Senior United States Liaison Officer*' and during the "Cold War" it was one of the most important buildings the NSA had in the world. Basically, it is the same building as 20 Grosvenor Square, but *we* used the side entrance. It's just across the road from the American Embassy and in fact there's an underground tunnel that links the two buildings.'

'So when did the NSA take over this location?'

'Well the NSA has been stationed in there since 1952, but the US government has had the building since 1941 after your government kindly leased it to us when it was a hotel. You know, I was told we paid the Duke of Westminster a down payment of just under half a million dollars and annual rent of one hundred pounds for almost a thousand-year lease!'

'Now that sounds like a pretty good deal for that piece of real estate! But out of interest, back in 1982, during the Falklands conflict, were you at 7 North Audley Street?' I ask her this very tentatively, while expecting her forefinger to gently tap the side of her nose. But to my pleasant surprise she shares a little bit of her past with me.

'Yes, I was working there as a systems engineer, managing the NSA's packet switching nodes (PSNs) and interface message processors. The operational commands and SIGINT for your Admiralty's traffic going to the South Atlantic Fleet was routed through the interface message processors in that building. We supplied you guys with intelligence and you also used our global communication network for the war, and we saw it all.'

'Really, including the *General Belgrano* sinking?' I ask, feeling that I am now pushing my luck.

'Yes,' she replies, slowly nodding her head.

'So why do you think she was sunk?' I ask, as my eyes are full of sincerity and don't leave hers for a second.

She thinks very carefully for a moment.

'In reality, the sinking had to happen because the war needed to be kick started; the peace talks at the UN were ["unexpectedly..."] gathering pace. You see, what is often ignored is the fact that war is good for the economy and for mobilising the population behind the government. Back in the very early eighties your economy needed a war, and Margaret Thatcher's government, at the time, sure as hell needed a helping hand. Her sinking had nothing to do with protecting the fleet. Until then, the mood at the UN, and the international community at large, was one of "mediation" and "potential compromise". The sinking was really your government's crossing the *"point of no return"* by *"aggressively developing"* the theatre of operations in the South Atlantic.'

'I see. So could our sub have sunk the *Belgrano* sooner?' I ask Kathryn, as I cover up a little yawn, thinking that wars don't really happen over a few sheep eight thousand miles away from London.

'Well, your sub was shadowing the *Belgrano* for a day and a half, and the

NSA was also monitoring her communications, which were then communicated back to London, so technically she could have been sunk sooner. The US Navy also had one of its subs (name withheld) in the area helping out with EW and intelligence operations during the conflict and that's not widely known about.

'I didn't know that, but why the delay in sinking the *Belgrano*?'

'Well there's any one of a number of reasons, but reading between the lines, so to speak, she was a former US Navy ship, called the USS *Phoenix* which survived Pearl Harbour and won nine battle stars during the Second World War. The attack on the *Belgrano* was run past Washington for final authorisation ["...as was the militarily sound idea for attacking the Argentine mainland military air bases, to which the 'Cousins' said *No*..."] and this probably caused some delay. And you know old seadogs do have long memories. In fact the NSA still hasn't forgotton what Israel did to the USS *Liberty*. But anyway, the thought of the *Phoenix* ending her days in such a horrific manner in the icy South Atlantic was a reality that was hard to swallow.'

'But that's war, I guess?'

'Yes, and the hawks running the show on both sides of the Atlantic didn't want to "give peace a chance". In the end I think she was thirty-six miles outside the "Total Exclusion Zone" when the torpedos were ["eventually..."] fired into her hull. Then her days were over, and so were the lives of three hundred and sixty-eight Argentine sailors. I remember it well.'

["...The USS *Phoenix* was launched on 13th March 1938 and served the US Navy with outstanding meritous distinction. On 4th April 1951, she was sold to the Argentine Navy for $7.8 million and was renamed the *17 De Octobre*. In 1956, she was renamed the *General Belgrano*. She ended her days on 2nd May 1982, while heading home in international waters."]

'And so the sinking of the *Belgrano* sent the clear message to the UN and General Galtieri's junta that the war in the South Atlantic was on?'

["...The 1976 CIA dealings with Gen. Galtieri's 2nd Army Corps at Rosario and also the ESMA (when George Bush Sr was DCI at Langley), are still locked away..."]

'*That's right*. And Britannia ruled the waves until Galtieri sent the first of a few very serious messages back to your government by sinking some of your ships. If the *Belgrano* hadn't been sunk, Exocet missiles wouldn't have been skimming the ocean surface when they did, some forty-eight hours later. Then it became very clear that with the *Belgrano* on the seabed, Exocet now ruled the waves, and the whole fleet was in serious danger. But that's speaking with the benefit of *hindsight*.'

'So then the war took off for real?'

'Sure as shit the conflict took off for real. However, after the Exocet attack on the *Sheffield*, reality hit your government hard. The Exocet missile was the invariable that was never fully taken into account when the "overall gameplan" was being drawn up. And after you started losing ships and men, some people in your War Cabinet wanted to call off the campaign and bring the Task Force home. The war at sea was deemed out of control. *And it was out of control,*' she says, as I clearly remember once singing *Rule Britannia* at junior school (and feeling very proud).

'How did that call go down?'

'It wasn't entertained at all. Ronald Reagan's NSDD (National Security Decision Directive) 34 was signed and I think some people in your War Cabinet forgot that you can never get forty-nine percent pregnant. The "*point of no return*" had been crossed, and besides, turning back was never part of the "*overall gameplan*" for Operation CORPORATE.'

["...In the years following Operation CORPORATE, the Ministry of Defence, under the full authorisation from the Joint Intelligence Committee, turned to Stena Offshore (now called Coflexip Stena Offshore) of Aberdeen, Scotland to undertake *sensitive* diving operations in the South Atlantic. A Stena vessel, called the DSV *Constructor*, was under charter to the MoD to carry out selected diving work. HMS *Sheffield* and HMS *Coventry* both had nuclear warheads on them and these had to be recovered.

However, even more important than the warheads was the recovery of the communications CTS (Cryptic Top Secret) codes and cryptographic devices still on the vessels. Diving operations were carried out on these two ships and also on HMS *Ardent*, HMS *Antelope* and the *Atlantic Conveyor* (all coordinates withheld). The operations were successful and all 'necessary materials' were recovered.

Also, as part of the overall operation, there was a diving operation carried out on the *General Belgrano*. This operation, which included a large detachment of Royal Naval officers and men, on board the DSV *Constructor*, was a complete success. The objective was achieved and *The Firm* 'acquired' the CTS codes and cryptographic equipment from the *General Belgrano*, which rests on the seabed at coordinates 55 degrees 24 minutes DELETED seconds South, 61 degrees 32 minutes DELETED seconds West.

At the time these diving operations took place, it was deemed necessary for the West to have the *General Belgrano's* cryptographic devices. The last thing the US government wanted was for the Soviets or Chinese to get their hands on this fine piece of NSA-developed technology, which Washington had sold to the Argentine Navy during the Seventies."]

'And then you helped to send the comms traffic down to the South Atlantic fleet?' I ask, as I notice that she is looking at the well-manicured nails on her right hand.

'That's correct Steve,' she says with a smile, but more out of my sudden understanding of her background than happiness.

'And if you helped the communications get sent down to the fleet, how did that actually happen?'

'All of your Admiralty traffic, both to and from the South Atlantic, went over the NSA's global secure data network system.'

'And this communications network that went through 7 North Audley Street was all part of the Internet infrastructure back in 1982?'

'Oh yes, you see back in 1982 the NSA's worldwide secure communications structure had grown out of the original ARPANET. Now the NSA had its own global Internet backbone, which was a more secret and advanced version of the *Defense Data Network*. This was primarily because it handled such Secret Compartmentalised Information ["SCI..."]. 7 North Audley Street was always part the NSA's global Internet communication system,' she says, as she looks at the large ring on her left finger.

'I see. So how did that work?' I ask sounding surprised.

'It was basically very simple. After a message left Chequers, or the Admiralty at Northwood, it was routed via the NSA at 7 North Audley Street. From here it went two ways. One packet went to Cheltenham and then onwards by SATCOM systems to your ships and submarines on active service in the South Atlantic. The same information packets were also sent to another message interface processor at Menwith Hill and then back to the NSA's HQ at Fort Meade. Once it left Meade, the product would then be routed over the SCI LAN network to the *White House Communications Agency* (WHCA), where it would be read by my government's officials in the Situation Room. Lt. General Lincoln Faurer was responsible for the NSA during the conflict and if *"The Consumers"* didn't get the product, he had to answer for it.'

'That's really interesting. I think I'll go for a drive down North Audley Street later on, as I don't think I've ever seen that building,' I say, as I try and mentally picture the location, as I know that part of London very well.

'Steve, the NSA is not, *and never has been,* in the business of advertising their presence! But to give you an idea, three floors of the work in 7 North Audley Street and the Situation Room in the basement are all NSA. In fact, when I was there, some of Rickover's submarine spyops were also administered from that building.'

'What were those?' I ask, sounding a bit too interested.

'Well sometimes it is not always as easy as soaking up SIGINT with satellites and surveillance systems on board warships, submarines and aircraft. Most of the time, to get to a foreign government's sensitive and secret comms systems, you've got to get to their fibre optic cables.'

'And then attach bugging devices?'

'That's right. If it's a sub-sea cable, the US Navy's submarines on secondment to the NSA can do this with what we called "Hubble-Bubbles" anywhere in the world. During the "Cold War", this was coordinated through the NSA's Naval Security Group. At the time we called it "Rickover's Navy", and these spy programs are legendary in the NSA. However, to get to a land cable for foreign SIGINT, the NSA's Deputy Director of Operations office will organise the covert digging of a tunnel in any city in the world in order to place bugs on the fibre optic cable. All of these spyops are compartmentalised and the product from these European land and sea operations mostly came through the message interface processors in 7 North Audley Street enroute to the desk of Colonel Harold Vorhies ["...who was then Deputy Director for NSA operations in Europe"]. Harold later went on to work for E-Systems.'

'I see, so are all of these operations fully authorised by the Oval Office and the Director of Central Intelligence?'

Kathryn laughs.

'Hell yes! As you well know, it is the NSA's job to steal foreign comms secrets, and the ANCHORY-type SIGINT databases at Fort Meade are very extensive these days. I'll tell you about ILETS and ECHELON another time, but the President authorises all of these spyops and knows full well that they are going on. He is, after all, the main *"Consumer"* of the NSA's SIGINT product. And when it comes to the recognition for NSA's submarine cable-bugging operations, Presidents Carter, Reagan, Bush and Clinton have all given presidential awards to US subs after successful NSA bugging missions that involved the tapping of foreign sub-sea cables. This stuff's been going on for nearly forty years. *And it still is.*'

'Really?' I ask, sounding surprised, hoping she'll share some more knowledge.

'Sure, you could check it out. In fact I'll get you a USS *Parche* T-shirt if you want!'

'Thanks! And Carter is still promoted as a man of peace, isn't he?'

["Frank Carlucci and John McMahon's covert CIA files will make some 'interesting' reading as Equador joined 'The CONDORTEL System' and Saddam Hussein came to power all when Mr Jimmy Carter was the American President..."]

'A man of peace my ass! Check out his covert policies in Afghanistan which created the Mujahideen ["...with Zbigniew Brzezinski, 6 months before the Soviet invasion"], and El Salvador with the CIA-trained "Argentine death squads" ["...and also his re-arming of Pol Pot in Thailand by Langley"]. He'll get found out one day, but interestingly, Carter even has an electronic "special ops" warfare (spy) submarine named after him. It is called the USS *Jimmy Carter* and the full capabilities of this next generation nuclear sub are leading edge and highly classified. But the USS *Jimmy Carter* will be one of the main NSA submarines that taps into sub-sea fibre optic cables anywhere in the world in order to deploy and recover "Hubble Bubbles". And after nearly one billion dollars ["£666 million..."] which is being spent on refitting the beast with electronic warfare systems, it will be ready for operational service in the year 2004. After that, *"The Jimmy Carter"* will be the most *deadly* spy in the world!'

'Now that's typical! But it's amazing what goes on out of view of the public domain,' I say, with a tone of reflection on a recent memory, as I feel the warm sunshine on the back of my neck as my ears begin to heat up.

'It sure is. The "Cold War" might have been one big *"gameshow"*, but these were highly sensitive missions and right now as we speak, every day of the year, the US SIGINT System (USSS) never stops. A foreign communication cable, land or sea, is up for grabs and when it comes to the National SIGINT Special Activities Office, there are some corridors where even the shadows have *shadows*! But that's reality and the NSA's SIGINT product from all over the world is read on a daily basis by *"The Consumers"*, at the highest levels in the US government. It's known as *The SIGINT Digest* in the Oval Office and the State Department. And this highly classified brief from Meade's NSOC ["...National Security Operations Centre"] covers everything from Brussels to Beijing.'

["...The code-breaking of both Japanese and Chinese governments' *sensitive* communications takes place at the Naval Security Group's Misawa Cryptologic Operations Centre (MCOC) in Japan, and is supported by Marine Company E. The 403rd Military Intelligence Det then collates the product. At the Regional SIGINT Ops Centre at Menwith Hill, the 451st Intelligence Squadron processes the *sensitive* SIGINT of the EC, the Israeli, French and German governments in 'Near Real Time' (NRT) and the 713th Military Intelligence Group then analyses the product. Both of these Regional SIGINT Operations Centres (RSOCs) report directly to the National Security Operations Centre in Fort Meade, 24/7. Here, under the Central Security Service, linguists from the 22nd Intelligence Squadron disseminate the most *sensitive* product via Special Access Programs ready for *The SIGINT Digest* and the President."]

'Really?' I ask, as I hear some noise coming from upstairs.

Kathryn looks at me square on, with an informed and hawkish look in her razor-sharp eyes.

'Yes, but that's the sharp end of international relations that you don't get to see in real time on CNN. And these spying operations all take place when the public is kept focused on gameshows, soap operas and ball games,' says Kathryn, with a deadly serious tone in her usually warm voice.

'You know, the thing I like most about this job, is that you learn something new almost every day,' I say, as my head feels much heavier than it did this morning.

'Well Steve, *"the truth shall set you free"*! But you can check it out, it wouldn't be too hard for you,' she says warmly, as she glances at my watch.

It is almost midday and the sun is hotter than ever in the clear blue sky above 200 Gray's Inn Road.

'Anyway, I must be heading off; there's a gathering at one of your country manors at Taplow, Berkshire to discuss INSCOM's TROJAN *Data Network-2*. There's probably half of Cisco going to be there as well, speaking about its old 4000 Router.'

'Sounds like a fun-packed afternoon!'

'Yeah right! You Brits want to hear all about its encryption devices ["...the KIV-7HS and KIV-19 units"], but I'm just going there to meet somebody from Fort Belvoir that I haven't seen in years. I fly back to my home in Virginia tomorrow morning.'

'Enjoy yourself,' I say, as we both start to get up and leave the cafeteria.

'Are you going over to the RIPE peering conference in Budapest next month?' she asks as we are getting into the lift on the lower ground floor of the ITN building.

'Yes, I just got the okay from my boss a couple of days ago. Just my colleague Nathan and I are going. Are you going to the conference as well?' I ask, sounding surprised.

'I'd love to, but some buddies have got an unofficial reunion at NSA Fort Medina in Texas that week.'

'That sounds fun!' I say, as I nod to the security man in reception.

'Yeah, I'll have lots of fond memories to catch up with. Fort Medina looks after the NSA's South American interests, so it'll be interesting to find out what's been happening in Argentina recently. But in RIPE Budapest, you'll get to meet some of the major technical players in the Internet peering world. Just keep a *low profile* and your ears open.

'I will do. I'm looking forward to it,' I say, as a well-known ITN newsreader walks through the swivel doors of the ITN building and nearly walks into Kathryn, who gets out of his way.

'Tell me, have you heard of the Carlyle Group?' I ask Kathryn, as we walk out into the hot air on Gray's Inn Road.

'Of course I have. Now there's a company with an interesting concentration of wealth and power built up in the years following the Gulf War with Saddam. There are some big hitters from around the world in there.'

'You're telling me!'

'Yeah, not many private investment banks have covered so much ground in ten years as the Carlyle Group has done, but it helps when you see who works there! George Bush Sr, Frank Carlucci and James Baker are major players in Carlyle. But be careful of the Carlyle Group's reach and power, as they're unofficially very close with David Rockefeller's Council on Foreign Relations and also with Henry Kissinger's Kissinger Associates. And just like *"the beast with seven heads"*, they are never to be crossed,' she says, as she takes out a pair of dark sunglasses from her handbag.

'I know and all roads seem to lead to *David Rockefeller* and not Rome!'

'Oh yes indeed, he has been the centre of power behind the White House for decades. The President might be the CEO of "America Inc", but David Rockefeller is the *"chairman of its board"*. And this board of trustees doesn't exist, if you get what I mean. No US President is ever foolish enough to think that they are more powerful than David Rockefeller is. And when it comes to Henry Kissinger, he's just Rockefeller's errand boy. Without the Rockefeller family backing over the years, he'd be nothing.'

'Well that's one way of putting it! But what do you know about the Carlyle Group?'

'It's a bank for the boys! In the early nineties, they got George W. Bush a job with (name withheld), which was one of their investments. Look at their connections with the *Middle East Policy Council* in Washington. And even more interestingly, check out Carlyle's relationship with *"The Company"*, and also *its* relationship with Prince Alwaleed bin Talal of Saudi Arabia. Just remember what I said earlier about George Bush Sr and the CIA ["...there were 'Houston' and 'Barbara' bank accounts in Noriega's Panama involving US Dollar printing plates left over in Iran from 1979"]. There are lots of colours in the world, and one of them, young man, is *grey*. Anyway, you've got enough pieces to the *"overall puzzle"* to get it looking almost like the *box* now!' says Kathryn, as she puts on her dark shades as we walk to a car that has just pulled up.

'Thanks, I'll check out all this stuff later. I've really enjoyed seeing you again!'

'It's been real nice to see you too. Let me know how you get on with the developments in New York, as our Internet services are ready as soon as the iaxis point of presence is live. And say "Hi" for me to our *"friend"* next time you two meet!'

'I certainly will! You have a safe journey home. And watch out for those *"monkeys"* at Monkey Island in Taplow!'

Kathryn laughs a knowing laugh as we shake hands and say goodbye to each other. As she climbs into the back of the black Lexus, her driver casually eyeballs me whilst he cleans his shades. Kathryn hits a quick-dial number on her mobile as the car slowly pulls away avoiding all the taxis. *Anything is just a phone call away for some people.*

As I walk past the *pillars* of the ITN building, I look at the time on my *Omega* watch. It is twelve noon exactly and it feels like summer as I head back inside. When I get out of the lift on the seventh floor and walk back in to the office, I see that Swampy's Network Operations Centre [*"Pandora's Box"*] is now *empty* and the whole office is deserted. The office floor is like the *Mary Celeste* and the place feels well spooky. There are cups of tea and coffee left around and people's work is still open on their desks, just where they left it. Maybe there's an emergency meeting on Level 2 to inform us about the future of iaxis now that the NASDAQ looks so *unstable?*

At our quad, Nathan and Old Boy's fags are nowhere to be seen and their cups of coffee are left right where they put them down. Both have hardly been sipped, and I touch one of them and it is still warmish.

I can't be bothered going down to Level 2, so I'll get an update from Wacko when he gets back from the gathering. I sit down at my desk, open my Microsoft Office Inbox and scroll down all the unopened emails and I can't believe my eyes. The last email I've received is from Sasha and it says '*I Love You*' and it has an attachment to it! My mind is way too scrambled to think about what is really in it. My heart just races around my whole body as I break the land-speed record to open the fucker! This is the best email I've ever seen and she sent it just over half an hour ago. And it is my last one. This is pretty strange, I think to myself as I open the attachment and all hell seems to freeze over on my PC, as I can't move the mouse and read her sexy message.

TTT is on the phone when I dial his number, so I get up and practically run over to the *Office of Technical Support* in order to have some words with him. As I get to the glass door of Techieland (with a 'SYBASE 11' sticker on it), I see that TTT is grunting away in techie speak about some NetViz tool and the 'SIM Database' and he's looking very stressed out. I have no idea what he's jabbering on about and then I realise that this is the first time I have ventured into this truly frightening office. All over the place there are bits of computers, printed circuit boards and weird things like the techfest guides to the Wang XTS-300, Nova Interface, SATAN, 'Essentials of SOLARIS 2.X (CT-126)' and the TAC-4 HP712/100. There are also other techie collections like freebie mugs and T-shirts with VxWorks-CORBA, Exabyte 220, Y-MP EL and DiamondTek on them!

Just as I pick up a serious looking *red* CY-60 manual, TTT's other colleague, 'Tommie The Techie' (TTT2), suddenly hangs up his phone and begins to bark some instructions at me.

'Don't touch your fucking PC, Steve! There's a massive network virus going round the globe and it's crashing all the PCs it enters!' he shouts out, gasping away, as he takes off his '*Ghostwire*' baseball cap and wipes some sweat off his brow.

'Really?' I say, as my head starts to feel numb.

'Yeah! And then it goes for all the email addresses you've got stored in Outlook. It's a big one this. It's travelling by the name '*I Love You*'. Sasha got one and she opened it. Daft dizzy blonde! Her PC has all the iaxis employees' email addresses centrally stored on it, so every sad bastard in iaxis opened it the second it arrived from her. It then went into everyone's Outlook address book, which has now sent the virus to all the emails they had stored in it. It's happening all over the world and now my system has fucking melted as well!' he yells out, as he throws a UNIX SVR4 manual across the room.

'Fuck,' I say, as I really did think she loved me and I am now gutted.

TTT2 takes a call and starts shouting and grunting away in techie speak about 'Firewall-1' and asking for an 'EA 1-0-6 digital signals analysis' something or other?

While I begin my slow walk back to my desk, my heartbeat frequency changes from a puppy-love beat to one of being shit-scared. I suddenly become very concerned and I feel as if the "*Looking Glass*" could soon be on me. I had over seven hundred addresses in my system. All the worlds' telecom companies and various "*others*" were in there as well. No doubt I'll be asked round for "*tea and biscuits*" to explain this one away...

My mobile rings.

'*Steve old boy!* Where the blaady hell are you mate?' asks Old Boy, as a full on bender is going down in the background.

'I'm sitting at my desk. Where are you lot?' I ask, as the room begins to spin.

'We're all at the blaady pub getting completely pissed. Sasha sent round an email saying she loved us, so we all opened it and it crashed the blaady network!!' he yells, laughing away.

'Which pub, Old Boy?' I ask, as a loud scream about "*Oracle 7*" escapes from the "*Office of Technical Collection*"...

'The Duke. We're all getting blasted by the sunrays. Bring your shades mate, it's blaady hot out here and I'm just getting a round in!'

'Cheers Old Boy, I'll see you in a minute.' I say as I switch my PC off and place copies of the latest techie guides to DynaText, HP-VEE, and Virtex EM into my top drawer. (Just in case I ever have future trouble in getting to sleep!)

'*Blaady hell Steve!*' says Old Boy with a big grin on his face as he hands me a cold bottle of beer. I must admit I've got a huge grin on my face as well. We're all getting paid to sit outside in the sunshine, kick back and chill out with a good few drinks.

There are about one hundred and twenty people standing and sitting around outside the pub. And they are all going for it. And they all work for iaxis.

'Cheers mate!' I say, clicking his bottle as Mirwais's 'Definitive Beat' is beating away out of Nathan's latest "MUSIC SYSTEM" (his laptop) as I start to down my drink.

The drink goes down even better as these vibes beat away outside in the hot sunshine. I look around me and see that there are bottles of everything, anything that the bar can serve. The lovely barmaids inside the Duke of York are so worried that supplies might run out for us that they've got someone down in the cellar passing up boxes of booze as the session develops. If supplies ran out here just now, all hell would break loose.

Word has just come through from TTT2 that the network is 'fucked' and the PCs are down for a minimum of forty-eight hours. This is like Christmas for everyone out here. Only nobody is opening up any presents, just loads more bottles of beer and anything else one can neck down.

Some forward-thinking people have also been down to the chemist to buy some suncream and it's being passed around. A few other things are being passed around that you can't buy in a chemist.

Mr Nice is wearing his 'UFO-9' t-shirt and Oakley shades and is sorting out another 'shipment' on his mobile.... 'Sorted, yeah?' he says, smiling as he clicks off his call and starts looking over his shoulder and up and down the street, walking down to the 'fackin land line' phone boxes outside the ITN building.

I look over towards Sasha. On this hot afternoon, she is surrounded by blokes and is soaking up a lot more than sunrays. Kong is right next to her (as always). His eyes don't leave her and he hasn't blinked once since she's been outside. His ESP tells him I'm now on the scene and his eyes are on me in seconds. He looks well pissed off as he glowers at me telepathically telling me to keep my fucking distance. (He got the email from her as well and I think he practically ate his flat screen when he realised it was only a little virus!)

Old Boy sees me looking at her. 'Don't worry, mate. Half the blaady office thought they had a chance!'

I just laugh at the sight of the attention she's getting as Old Boy takes a call from his wife. She's always phoning him...

While Old Boy takes his call, Nathan hangs up his mobile. He's just been getting an update from another Cambridge University Internet wizzkid.

'So Nathan, where did this world-class virus come from and how come it's spreading so fast?'

'Well it's piss-easy to rig one up.'

'How's that then?'

'Well you see, most email applications will not allow any kind of program to run automatically when an email is opened. This email carried the virus as an attachment, which was an innocent looking visual basic script. So you are basically running the program or script when you open the attachment. But Microsoft Outlook is full of security holes and it's not like iaxis uses *Firestarter* network protection,' he says, as he takes a swig of his beer and has a big draw on his fag. 'And one glaring security hole is that Outlook will allow you to run a visual basic script from an email. This script holding the virus was a simple list of instructions to Outlook for a virus to install itself on your computer. The virus in this visual basic script then looked up everyones' address book for emails and then forwarded the virus to them. It looks like the script has installed a virus that is now trashing any image files on our hard drives. But the net effect of this fucker in your PC is like a *nuclear fission reaction* and when opened everyone in your entire address book gets it.'

I'll understand the meaning of what he has just said one day.

I nod my head to look intelligent and have a good mouthful of my cold beer. (I just hope the virus doesn't take out the shopping tills where Nathan buys his fags. He'll be stressed out then!)

Old Boy is still sitting by the fence getting a briefing from his lovely wife and Wacko has just kicked back with a beer in his hand. The meeting in the boardroom broke up when the state-of-the-art system linking New York suddenly went down. He's now on the mobile to TTT2 and he just shakes his head a couple of times and then hangs up when the call is over.

'That was TTT2, he said something about JavaXML and I haven't got a fucking clue what he was on about! But our PCs have just forwarded this bug to everyone in the industry phone book!'

As far as everyone's concerned, I've done nothing wrong, so I just keep a low profile. But everyone's on their backs laughing away anyway at this rampant destruction that is going around the globe!

Wacko is looking concerned, as 'Adelante' by Sash is now beating out of Nathan's laptop.

'What's up mate?'

He looks around to see if it's safe to talk. 'The cash is getting really grim. Everyone's dreams of being a millionaire are over. We can kiss high-yield and floating on the NASDAQ goodbye now.'

'So the market is slowing down from supersonic.'

'It's not just slowing down, it is accelerating fucking downwards! The only way you're going to be a millionaire now is if you buy a "National Robbery Ticket" for Saturday's draw and hope all your numbers come up!'

'Haven't we just got some dosh in the bank?'

(In the middle of last month iaxis received thirty million dollars in cash from Bain Capital to plough in to iaxis. But this will be used for our survival until we get bought out. All the Eastern Europe and Scandinavian developments have been cancelled.)

'Yes we have, but Greenspan... Shit, we were far too slow.'

'What's the chairman of the Federal Reserve got to do with iaxis?' I ask, almost taking the piss.

Old Boy has had his briefing from his wife and thrusts two bottles of beer into our hands. He then wanders over to McGowan and Stalker to speak about shooting.

'Everything was well until he went and opened his mouth and raised interest rates last year.'

'How come?' I ask with a face that says 'I look a bit lost here, help me out!'

'Back in *August 1999*, iaxis tried to raise three hundred million dollars in a high-yield debt issue. We eventually used DLJ as the lead manager, but the very day before we were going to announce the price of the stock, Greenspan put interest rates up and we couldn't high-yield, because from iaxis's point of view, this fucked up the debt markets for our plans.'

'So what happened?'

'DLJ pulled their offering the following day.'

'That really was *missing the boat*,' I say. I'm now drinking this beer rather fast.

'Too right, it was,' he says, looking around. Everyone is now going for it. The barmaids have never been so busy.

Wacko starts pulling the label off his bottle. 'There's more to it than that. You see, the management in iaxis had originally wanted to use Bear Sterns to be our high-yield lead manager. But because of shareholder politics, one of them wanted Bears to be dropped. And this held up the high-yield for about seven weeks. We eventually had to bin Bears and appoint DLJ instead. But the shareholders messed around and we missed the chance and the market beat us. We'd be laughing if we went with Bears.'

'So what did Bear Sterns have to say about this?'

'They invoiced us for two and a half million dollars worth of fees.'

'Shit! Have we paid them?' I ask, thinking about this *October Surprise*.

'Have we fuck! We've just put their invoice to the bottom of the pile, after the paper-clip bill. But it is starting to look very grim. iaxis has to be sold. Flotation on the NASDAQ is no longer an option.'

'Really? So what happens to the CEO who was specifically brought in to take us to flotation?' I ask, as the weather feels as hot as downtown *Tehran*.

Wacko suddenly rips the label off his bottle of beer and looks around.

'The shareholders have decided to pay him just over one million dollars to stay on, keep quiet and to help sell iaxis. The payment has, as far as I know, already gone through.'

'*He was paid one million dollars just to stay on!*'

'Steve, keep your voice down!' he says, while rubbing some factor thirty-three suncream on his face, as the sunrays are turned up to full volume and are blasting us all to hell.

Wacko suddenly ducks down like there is an incoming missile and tells me not to look around as he stares at the ground and adjusts his *Gigster* sunhat, using me as cover. I hear Hannah being called away from us by someone at the far side of the gathering.

'That was a close one,' he says, as he takes his shades off and wipes away the sweat from his forehead. His eyes are locked on to her moving away towards Chris Harper.

'So what happened in the glass boardroom after DLJ pulled the high-yield?'

'Well they all walked out with thousand yard stares after that meeting! But GE Capital are trying to help finance this debt and if they give us the money, we will then guarantee to pay the likes of Ciena with it. This saga has been going on since before Christmas,' says Wacko, as he blags a fag from Nathan, who staggers past us to turn up the music. Wacko doesn't usually smoke, so this is a clear sign that the "State of Denmark" is heading for sheer turmoil.

'You should have sold the company last year,' I say, with *hindsight* as he agrees.

'Only last month we had an offer from Fibrenet, for about five hundred and seventy-five million pounds. But the market was still supersonic and our mates in Carrier 1 had just floated and were worth over two and a half billion dollars on the NASDAQ. The shareholders rejected it outright. They wanted one billion dollars or nothing. And now we are completely winging it just to stay alive. But from here on, iaxis is now in a downward spiral and the only positive news is that we should get bought quite soon.'

A couple of glasses of alcohol-enhanced sangria appear in our hands from thin air. We both take a good swig and soon feel the effects.

'So who's been in so far then?' I ask. I'm sure I tasted a lot of tequila in that *Madrid* type sangria special.

'Just about everyone in the phonebook! We've given detailed presentations to Tyco, Williams, Enron, Carrier 1 and Pangea. Some have even taken it further and seen the business plan.'

'So you've binned the idea of buying that nice big yacht?' I ask tentatively.

'Steve, after this I'll be lucky if I can afford to buy a fucking airbed!' he spurts out, as his dream is now *eclipsed* by a big howling nightmare.

'So are we okay for cash?' I ask, hoping that my expenses will clear this month.

'We're okay for about three, maybe four months. iaxis has a burn rate of about six million dollars every month and most of that is on salaries and the rent for the ITN building. But channel cards from Ciena are not cheap. They cost around one million dollars per set. And we've had loads of sets from them over the last twelve months!' says Wacko, looking up at the sky where the "signs" high *above* are now becoming very obvious to everyone down *below*.

Nathan and Old Boy pitch up, and both of them look totally hammered. Old Boy has got a nice big jug of sangria and Nathan's holding four glasses. There has been a lot of sangria, plus vodka and Red Bulls, going down in the last couple of hours. Someone else has also kindly brought down their laptop as Nathan's battery ran out. You just can't sit outside in temperatures of what feels like the high eighties, drinking sangria, and not have a sound system beating away a mellow vibe.

Old Boy tops up my sangria glass as we start to down the jug.

'So which hotels were in the family chain, Old Boy?' asks Wacko, not too loudly in case an ear-wigger close by picks it up.

'Well we ran the Savoy, the Berkeley, Claridge's, the Connaught, the Lygon Arms, the Savoy Theatre, Simpson's Restaurant and that blaady florist.... The er... Edward Goodyear,' says Old Boy, looking well on the road to being trashed. (He reels them off like I'd list a few Third World countries that I've travelled in!)

Just as we start to take the piss, Old Boy's mobile rings and it is his wife giving him some more sound rage. I don't know what he's done wrong, but she's not happy. I can hear her way past the din everyone's making.

After about a minute, Old Boy hangs up the phone. 'Blaady hell, we're supposed to be going to a dinner party tonight, but I've said I'm way too pissed to go and she's not happy!' he says, slurring his words.

'She's a bit demanding isn't she, Old Boy?' I ask, feeling a bit sorry for the big man.

'Demanding! I'm almost deaf in my right ear with all her shouting. And it's always over the slightest blaady thing.'

'So what was her outburst over this morning?' asks Nathan, topping up his drink.

Old Boy struggles to remember. He's had about three 'soundblasts' since then.

'Oh yes, I remember now, I forgot to put the butter in the fridge and some breadcrumbs and jam were still in the tub! I also left the blaady knife out as well!'

We all lie back and crack up. He is totally in love with her. And he tells us so all the time.

Old Boy's lovely wife is the daughter of a leading estate agent. I have of course met her and she is a very beautiful, warm and caring lady. But if your name's 'Old Boy' and you're married to her, just do as she says or else. There is no denying it; she rules the roost. She might be a little over five and a half feet tall, but she can shout very loudly and can kick his backside around SW1 any day of the week.

We all find it hilarious that she calls him six or seven times a day with a whole shopping list of demands. His eyes just go into double-glazing mode and his mind then switches over to autopilot and he starts daydreaming. He then says "yes" at the end of a few key moments and after the receiver is replaced, he just shakes his head and says 'blaady hell' and doesn't care too much. He'll send a few emails and make a few calls and within fifteen minutes he's forgotten all of her demands. And she of course she phones him again and goes totally ape-shit with him. This keeps the quad entertained for hours and therefore we all love her to bits as well.

'What does your wife do?' asks Nathan, who's starting to slur his words.

'She works as an interior designer with her mum and sister. They've only got a small office and yours truly is the main topic of conversation all day long. Sometimes my ears get so blaady hot I have to buy a can of Coke from the drinks machine just to hold it to them. Those buggers seem to be melting these days!'

'Don't worry Old Boy, it shows that she loves you,' I say reassuringly, with nods of agreement from Wacko and Nathan.

Old Boy looks a bit sheepish now and takes a deep breath. 'We're putting the house up for sale and moving to a bigger one.'

'Why?' asks Wacko, stirring his potent sangria mix.

'She's mentioned having kids,' says Old Boy, as his face gives away a flashback he's reliving.

'*Fucking hell!!!*' say three wide-open drunken mouths as they hit the pavement aghast and united in total horror.

'So what are you going to do mate?' asks Nathan, who's now pissed along with the rest of the one hundred and twenty iaxis people lying back outside the the Duke.

'I'm going to buy her a puppy dog instead,' he says seriously, as he takes a sip of the world's strongest sangria mix.

Bags of laughter all around. This is too much!

It gets worse as he tells us that his wife has already booked a visit with a top doggie breeder next week. He is utterly serious and our drunken eyes are watering with laughter. I seem to have drunk so much I can't control the facial muscles around my mouth.

A few minutes later I have to get up and leave them to it. They're all on the pavement lying back in the sunshine, still laughing away. I manage to stagger down onto Gray's Inn Road to buy a large sandwich, which I shovel down my throat in record time. Nobody out here seems to have eaten lunch.

Waiting to cross the road, I see Porn Star quickly walking into Centro's looking casually over his shoulder up and down the street before he walks through the door. Following right behind him is a sexy piece of work from customer support. She also looks over her shoulder. If Porn Star is carrying his Polaroid camera, I can't see it. However, this particular temptress could well be carrying it for him in her bag.

The whole street is spinning as I get back to the crew. Another jug of sangria is waiting. Everyone round me seems to have collapsed on to the pavement. But sadly Claire from Personnel is looking upset. The amount of alcohol going down doesn't help her at all. She's now in tears as her 'friend' Jemma brings her another drink and puts her arm around her, giving her moral support and words of comfort in her heartbroken time of need.

In the same parallel universe, I lie down on the pavement and the whole street is spinning wildly. Gabriela pulls my head on to her very comfortable shoulder for support as she plays with my hair...

'Wacko, what's happening with Nick these days?' I ask, as he's now leaning against the pub wall looking completely spannered.

'Fuck knows, we can't get a hold of him, he says, now slurring his words and staring wildy up and down the street just in case Hannah is on a mission. He looks over at Jemma. 'Jemma's going out to Marseilles tomorrow to meet up with "a friend from University",' he says raising an eyebrow, as nobody else has a clue, or remotely cares what we're talking about. But we both know why she's going to Marseilles...

I can see Jemma just slightly by lifting up my head. I look over at her attractiveness and very obvious intelligence. She also did an MSc in Psychology. Her brass neck is completely solid. She's incredibly attractive and discreet. And she seems to have no conscience whatsoever as she takes a call on her mobile and her face lights up...

Lots of eyes are on Sasha, who is now sitting on McGowan's knee, smiling away in her Gucci sunglasses, wearing a sexy little white T-shirt with the word 'Fastlane' spread across it. Kong is just standing there looking completely stunned. He might be a big fella, but even he knows McGowan could smack him into next spring with one punch. Sasha senses the tension from Kong and leans back on McGowan soaking up all of Kong's energy. The sunrays are beating down on her as she takes a sip on her sangria through a straw. McGowan places his arm around her flat stomach to give the girl a warm and reassuring cuddle.

On seeing this, Kong's brain cell suddenly explodes and he stomps off in a silent rage. I can hear the sound of all the carnage Kong creates as he crosses John Street to get down to Gray's Inn Road.

Sasha's face now looks as bright as Chernobyl and, feeling satisfied, she gets up and goes over to speak to Jemma and Claire. She's already soaked up enough raw energy this afternoon to last a whole romper of a hardcore summer in the hot Med.

McGowan seems totally unfazed. He's older and far wiser than any chancers winging it here. He looks over to Merlock and they both start to laugh. Both he and Merlock were the field engineers responsible for getting the network built so quickly. We sent both of them over to the continent to frighten the French and Germans into working at breakneck speed and

putting in eighteen-hour days. This is really why the iaxis fibre optic network
was built and lit so quickly.

Old Boy's mobile rings yet again.

'Hiya love…'

'!!'

'*Blaady hell!*'

'!!!!!!!!!!!!!!!!!!!!!!!!!!!!!!!!'

'Bye love!'

Old Boy has to leave right now or else. The dinner party is still on, and
he is expected to be there. He gets up slowly, using a lamp post for support,
and says goodbye. He is staggering over the entire place, stepping over
bodies that are on the pavement, propped up against the pub wall and on the
road. The world's strongest sangria has detached his mind from his body in
a blissful sense as he staggers towards Gray's Inn Road to flag down a taxi
to drive him back to SW1.

I can just see it when he walks into their kitchen feeling totally and
blissfully pissed. 'Soundblast' is dressed up and looking totally stunning,
ready to go out. And he has drunk so much he wonders what day it is!

'Blaady hell! What's the matter girl?…stop shouting!!…' Then smack…
'***@*^^"!!'…

Old Boy wakes up on the kitchen floor several hours later, with a raging
headache, and wonders why a Dyson vacuum cleaner is lying on its side
close to his head. No doubt he'll be feeling a bit numb, wondering how it got
there.

I drift back down from planet daydream into the side street beside the
Duke. I am now worried about getting up. My face feels numb as I bite my
bottom lip to test my alertness. The street is spinning and my legs feel
wobbly. My heart might be London, but my *head* feels like it's in Scotland.
I look up in to the evening sky and I receive a signal from the stars of *Orion's
Belt* (where Psycho gets his latest marketing info from). It tells me to go
home now! It's almost *seven* o'clock and I can hardly walk. I somehow make
it down to Gray's Inn Road and flag a taxi to take me back to Fulham. I
eventually get home and crash out.

At 3:12 a.m. I wake up in my bed and I'm still wasted from yesterday
afternoon. I also realise that my throat feels as dry as a bush in the Sinai
Desert and I desperately need a pee.

A short while later a large bottle of Evian is emptied and I go straight
back to sleep with my head spinning and pounding away. I roll over, not
awake but also not asleep, and after what seems only a short while I notice
that the alarm clock now says the time is 10:07 a.m. But to guess what day

it is is a complete struggle. I totally forgot to set my alarm and therefore the *Today* programme wasn't able to wake me up and tell me what day today is. But my pounding head tells me I need a hot shower, lots of water and a greasy fry-up. *And fast.*

Sitting in a greasy café at the foot of the Fulham Road I switch on my mobile. I've got a text message from Wacko: 'pcstilldown.cu@duke.'

Another bender looms and the sunshine looks good.

I catch the morning press when I walk in to the newsagent on the Fulham Road. I decide to leave *Hello!* on the shelf and look for a copy of the *Economic Intelligence Weekly*, but it doesn't seem to be in, so the *Economist* will have to do instead.

Today the morning papers are ramping up this 'Love Bug' virus. According to Nathan, who was going on about it yesterday afternoon, the 'Love Bug' was kids stuff. It won't be the biggest and it certainly will not be the last. The media might think it is space age in this morning's papers. But take it from me (Nathan), it was nothing. It was "Blue Peter" stuff. And there will be bigger ones.

However, although this little charmer was nothing, it took out every computer that opened it. Yet governments and corporations have spent billions of dollars in preventing this type of "cyber warfare attack" ["Project Firestarter was a joint DARPA/NSA project at the Rome Laboratory in this area…"] and their investments proved to be totally useless. The UK economy lost millions yesterday and no "CyberKnights" with "RoboHelp" came to the rescue.

["…The Pentagon/NSA has also spent millions on developing 'cyber warfare' as a first-strike electronic warfare capability by units under the global command of the 67th Intelligence Wing at the National Security Agency HQ at Fort Meade."]

After drinking a can of Red Bull on the tube, I get off at Russell Square and walk back to the the Duke. Here I see that I'm quite late to start work today, as there are loads of iaxis people outside the pub already. Wacko and Gibbsy are carrying a large round of drinks and both are looking rough.

'Steve! You must've slept in. Here's a drink.'

It's a vodka and Red Bull.

'Cheers!'

It turns out that after I left yesterday evening some of the remaining iaxis people went down to Covent Garden for an Indian on *Great Queen Street*. The hardcore crew carried on to the Roadhouse. (It was the only place that would let them in.) They left at 3 a.m.-ish. And now they are all here at the Duke again. They were banging on the pub door at 11 a.m. to be served.

Porn Star looks completely knackered, as does the girl from customer support. He looks at one of his Rolex watches he has been trying to sell and makes a call on his mobile.

Nathan is yawning and looks like he hasn't had much sleep. He's also on vodka and Red Bull, just to tempt his taste buds as he lights up again.

Then round the corner walks Old Boy. He looks really rough and we all laugh at him. We feel rough, but he still looks pissed! If I asked him if he knew what day it is he wouldn't be sure. He spots us all laughing at him as he walks up.

'How was the dinner party, Old Boy?' I ask, as I slowly remember why he left so promptly.

'I never went. My wife went on her own.'

'Why?' I ask, as my head feels very numb.

'When I left here for the dinner party, I was so pissed and starving I walked into our house eating a large McDonald's Big Mac and fries. My wife saw this and went blaady mental. I woke up during the night on the landing outside our bedroom with no idea how I ended up there!'

(I think I've got a good idea of how he ended up there!)

Seamus, having just arrived, walks up to us all looking as rough as dog shit, and proceeds to eyeball every single one of us. Come to think of it he looks totally unhinged. This is weird. He was only around for a short time yesterday and left looking sober. He probably left to go for a cell meeting in some upstairs room in a pub in Kilburn and got lifted.

'Seamus, what's up with you?' asks Wacko, who's actually as concerned as the rest of us for his well-being.

Seamus looks at us all with his hardened ice cold blue eyes, waiting for the first person to flinch. His sense of humour has also crashed as he starts to speak.

'Some fooker spiked ma drink wie LSD, yestirdae fookin evenin.'

Loads of laughter!

'Wir de fook is *Mr fookin Nice?* Coz he'll soon be 'Mr fookin dead' wen de fookin nuttin squad shows up,' he says, as he gets out his mobile.

'It couldn't have been him, he left before you showed up, Seamus!' says Wacko, trying to help Seamus narrow down his long list of suspects.

'What happened?' asks Nathan, who shows remarkable signs of bravery as he wipes the tears of laughter off his face.

Seamus takes a deep breath and steadies himself against the pub wall. His eyes are still not blinking and both are still staring wildly up and down the street. 'Ah got en de train at Liverpool Street, feelin sobir as a fookin judge. Ah wiz reading de paper en aftir de train pulled away, all fookin hell went off inside ma head. Colours, flashin fookin lights, en den ah started breakdancing on de floor o'de fookin train! A couple of big fellas pulled us aff at de next stop and ah landed en de platform. Ah woke up in some doorway wee de Salvation Army askin if ah wuld like some fookin soup. Ah got home at t-ree tirty dis fookin mornin!' he says, as everyone laughs wildly. (In fact there are tears on the pavement as Swampy practises his breakdancing technique with about five others!)

'Fook aff ye mad fookers!' he says, as he steadies his back to the wall and is looking even more suspiciously at everyone. His eyes also look wild and scary, like he's just survived a night-time walk across the Serengeti. He knows about my recent trip so I'm off his "SOCRATES" network-type databank list of suspects. He is mentally processing this list as a pint of black stuff is placed in his hands.

Seamus is feeling a bit vulnerable, so I decide to go up and have some fun with him. What he doesn't know is that I've found out some "*interesting*" information about his background...

'Seamus.'

He looks up at me, walking towards him.

'It wiz fookin you wisn't it! A fookin knew it!'

'*No!*' I yell, laughing away seeing that he wasn't being serious. (If he were being serious, I'd now be "Mr fookin dead!")

He looks around at everyone. 'Fookin bastards!' he says, still eyeballing anyone out of character, or glancing over at him. But the trouble is everyone's out of character and everyone's looking over at him, laughing away!

He takes a good mouthful of his black stuff and it looks like his mind is still in a drugged-out frenzy. I discreetly look around as I decide to make a little move...

'Seamus, you worked in Iraq, in the three years leading up to the Gulf War in 1990, didn't you?' I ask *very* quietly, as I stand a bit closer to him.

Seamus's white face suddenly turns even whiter and his eyes look like they have just seen the *Fourth Horseman of the Apocalypse* gallop up the street!

He is barely able to get the words out. 'How de fook did ye know dat?' he asks, totally startled, swallowing hard and eyeballing me intensely.

I take a deep breath and hold eye contact. His brain is now completely scrambled and his chin is practically resting on the pavement. I look around in a hugely deliberate conspiratorial manner, just to make sure that he sees I don't want anybody to listen.

'It's a long story, Seamus, but I'll go and get a couple of drinks in,' I say quietly, as his wide open eyes haven't left mine just yet and he starts to sweat, while he supports himself against the pub wall.

I leave him for quite a while as I go to the gents and then to the bar. While I'm at the bar, I am in no hurry to be served and allow plenty of thirsty people to jump in front of me.

Fifteen minutes later I walk out with a large round and after handing the drinks around, I walk back up to Seamus and I see his mouth is still open and his eyes are yet to blink. I remove the empty pint glass from his hand and replace it with a full one.

'So how de fook did ye know dat?' he asks, quietly as his mind has a flashback to South Armagh.

I remain calm and look serious as I continue to look around the street, still piling on all the mental pressure I can muster, I summon huge reserves of strength and inner character to look hard in to his eyes, while trying not to laugh.

'Seamus, I got your CV off the printer, mate!' I say, smiling away and breaking out in to a laugh.

His mouth hits the ground!

'Fookin bastard!!' he yells out, as he collapses with laughter. This sets me off again as I tell him that I've waited for about four weeks for the right moment to spring this one on him.

His laughs keep coming and coming every time he looks at me. 'Fir fook sake, ye daft fooker!' he says, as he wipes away some tears.

Now I'm leaning against the wall for support!

'Ah, wit ah fookin wind up, ye had me, so ye did!'

People are looking at us and don't have a clue what's so funny. It was only a few minutes ago Seamus was ready to call in the 'fookin nuttin squad'.

He gets some air back in to his lungs. 'Dat's de best wind-up ave had en fookin yiers!' says Seamus, taking a mouthful of black stuff.

'You're welcome! But the "industrial project management" work you did in Iraq for that multinational sounded interesting,' I say, as I manage to get some words out as my cheeks and stomach are starting to ache from the recent laughter attack.

'Come on ye wee fooker, let's go en sit en de wall ovir der en get some sun, en a'll tell ye all aboot it,' he says, as we both stagger across the street. 'It's fookin yeirs since a've bein wound up like dat!'

We get to the wall and sit down.

'So Iraq... What's the story there then?' I ask, as I notice we are well away from potential ear-wiggers.

'Well, ah wiz wirkin for dis company called (name withheld) dat wiz buildin dez huge industrial plants all ovir Iraq, Iran en de fookin Middle East, ye know, chemical plants, power stations en oil refineries. But ah wiz de senior fookin project manager for Iraq, responsible for all de software en de hardware dat make up de distributed control systems dat keep des industrial plants goin. Well dat was until de fookin war wie de Yanks.'

I deliberately raise my suspicious eyes wide open. He still hasn't blinked yet. He's heard all our gags and just laughs.

'Ah know wit yer t-inkin coz ah've been t-oroughly checked out bi you fookin Brits. It all happened just before de Gulf War. En ah know all o'yez en yer mad fookin quad luv te take de piss callin us a "sleeper", en alwiz goin on fookin "bomber alert" checkin under yer chairs every time ah walks past yer fookin "Unit"! he says, laughing and shaking his head at our childish and immature sense of fun. (Seamus has provided our "unit" with hours of quality entertainment!)

'But look Seamus, an Irish man, from the Catholic community in darkest South Armagh doing engineering and project work and travelling all over the Middle East and then back to a quiet semi in suburban England... It sounds and looks well suspicious, mate!'

'Suspicious! De fookin Peelers wiz fallowin us for months!'

'I bet they were. So how did you get *pinged*?'

'It was ma fookin bank in Stevenage. Dey wir gettin suspicious cause dis company wir payin us out o'der Swiss bank accounts, all fir der domestic tax reasons like. En ah wiz livin aff expenses, buying foreign currencies, airline tickets, hotels, clothes and havin payments of fifteen grand or more, goin in te ma bank account te cover ma wages en travlin every month. Ma fookin bank informed de Peelers en den MI5 bought de fookin house across de street!'

This sets me off laughing once again.

'So they kept you under "close observation" then?'

'Ah fook! Fir weeks der wiz BT vans, British fookin Gas vans all piark'd up in de street, ma telefones wiz always hummin, en de TV wiz alwiz goin en de fookin blink. En der wiz loads of fellas alwiz wantin te read de fookin gas meter. Even de neighbours' dog wiz trained to watch us!'

'That's funny mate, you know they don't do that "across the water". In Armagh County, the whole estate is sealed off and about thirty soldiers will storm a house to search it. Then afterwards they'll leave a couple of 14 Int or E4A people behind in the loft for a few days, till the next raid and they'll listen to your phone calls from Island Hill,' I say, as a matter of fact.

'Yeah, ah fookin know!'

·

'So what was it like with your bank? They have a very special relationship with the authorities in this country.'

'Yer right der! Whin ma wife went in to de bank te pay a bill o'somthin, all o'de fookers in der wiuld just stare en not say a word to her. She spotted dis right away, she's a biochemist from Cambridge University, en is shirp as fook. Once win ah just got back from Egypt en Israel, she wiz tellin us about our fookin bank en der treatment of her. She wiz really upset. So ah goes down de high street en walks in te make a withdrawal te buy a car. At de counter ah hands ma caird te de cashier en de wee fooker was smiling till he swiped de caird troough de machine. All ma details came up en he den starts te shiet it,' he says, only just forcing a smile out.

'Brilliant! So how much did you take out?'

'Twelve fookin grand.'

'Well that would've triggered the alarms all the way back to *Castlereagh*! So what did the fella in the bank do?' I ask, smiling at the crazed look in his eyes.

'His jaw hit de fookin desk! He must've pressed a switch cause de manager came through en helped him. De young fella stirted shakin like Shakin fookin Stevens countin all de cash out. He looked up at us en ah just stared so hard at dis wee fooker; he's probably still gettin terapy for it now! Ah walked out and dey both wir probably tinking ah wiz going te level der fookin buildin, daft Brit fookers!'

'Well, withdrawing that sort of amount tends to set of alarms well away from the high street branch, Seamus mate.'

'Fookin right! De next day aftir dis, der wiz a wee springer spaniel runnin round de back girden sniffin like fook fir guns' 'n fertilizer mixes. Ah went out de back door en dis big fella just appeard behind us as if from outa space, sayin he'd lost his wee dog!' he says, as he takes a good mouthful of black stuff, still laughing at the memories.

'So did they make a move on you?'

'O' yea, me en de missus. We wiz in de home and dey knocked en de door. But de Peelers knew fookin every-ting! By dis time, dey had been through de family history tree all de way back te yer days of Oliver fookin Cromwell! It wiz just "routine" questions, but dey even knew ah had a mole on my left fookin airse check!' he says, as I start laughing.

'Seamus, I hope you got rid of that TV, mate. It was probably watching you!'

'Whit...? ...*Fookin hell!*'

'So they didn't try and pin anything on you then?'

'No, te be fair, de Peelers wir fookin good. Very t-orough, en askin loads o' questions o'which dey had all de fookin answers for! But every time ah wiz at Heathrow dey got freaked out ye know…a fookin Irish man carrying six grand in dollars en den flying to fookin Damascus en places!'

'Yeah, I can see why, you know mate.'

'Well at de fookin end, aftir all de fookin questions and checks dey wir satisfied ah wiznae a fookin bomber, a sniper, a lily-white fookin sleeper or any other fooker.'

Two more drinks appear in our hands from Old Boy. He's looking a bit pissed again. I was away to tell him to watch out for Dyson vacuum cleaners, but he was running back to have some words with Stalker.

'So what did your company say, as they'd have been contacted on the quiet?'

'Well dat's de ting, dey sais fook all te us like. En den a few months later, Saddam went en took Kuwait. Ah wiz in de UK office when ah gets dis call from de big boss o' de UK division. He wiz sayin ah had te go up te his office right away cause der wiz some fooking military people in, en dey wanted te see fookin me! Ah tell ye, aftir all ad bein troough wid de Peelers ah wiz shittin it.'

'Why? You were clean.'

'Ah know dat, but where ah come from ye dinnae jump fir joy whin yer told dat de fookin army wants te have a fookin "word" wie ya!' he says, as he has a sip of his drink. 'It wiz a long walk te de boss's office. But wen ah walks in dey were four officers all smiling and relaxed, shakin ma hand and bein all polite en fook.'

'So who were they?' I ask, pretending to be casually listening to his story whilst looking up and down the street.

'Dey wir tou Yanks, one Brit en a French officer, all senior air force fellas from de Allied Strategic Air Command. Dey was all from der Strategic Planning Wing. Ma boss said des people were going te need ma help to bomb de plants dat we'd built for fookin Saddam in Iraq!'

'That's quality mate!'

'Yeah! En it's all fookin true. Ah wiz told ah hid bein toroughly vetted en wiz "invited" te spend a week workin width dem in a "neutral office" in de Home Counties. All fookin hush hush, like.'

'So you went from being bomber suspect number one, to helping them to plan their bombing in Iraq all within a few weeks!' I say, smiling at the turn of events.

'Yeah, it wiz fookin great,' he says, laughing.

'So what exactly did they want you to do?'

'Well at dis neutral office, dey went over all de designs fir des industrial plants dat we'd designed en built for Saddam. Ye see between eighty-six and nineteen ninety, ah wiz personally responsible fir building all de nodes in de industrial plants' command and control centres. Take out des fookers an den de plant is fooked fir yiers. En all ah wiz doin wiz showing dees officers where all de nodes were located in de plants en also pointing out all de air vents and shafts. Ye see der missiles had to destroy de overall distributed control system. Take out dis fooker, an all der redundant software systems dat are run from dis ting are fooked as well.'

'Excellent mate. How many industrial plants did you help bomb?'

'Just de six dat we built. One wiz evin dat "baby-milk plant" where all o' dose poor fookers got killed.'

'Yes, I remember that one. So was it a baby milk production facility?'

'Of course it wasn't! De fookers en Iraq had changed all der software an wir making chemicals fir der weapons. Der Revolutionary Guird wir goin te be putting dis stuff in der fookin warheads. It wiz a shame dat dem poor fookers got killed, but Saddam put dem en der en didn't give a fook whedther it wiz bombed or not. But ah wiz responsible fir pinpointin out de nodes in dat facility, coz we fookin built it. Ah also had te tell de officers de tickness o' de concrete in various pairts o' de plant so dey wirked oot de size o'der smirt bombs. Der were evin fellas from de navy der as well, all listening away to us en askin lots o' fookin questions.'

'Well, the Cruise missiles were fired from ships and subs in the Red Sea and the Persian Gulf,' I say, as I clearly remember watching the CNN footage from the comfort of my living room sofa.

'Yeah, fookin right dey were!'

'So how many bombs would it take to destroy these facilities if they were strategically targeting them?'

'Well, de operational capability o' der plant could be wiped out width t-ree missiles. De strategic planners didn't want te level de ting with ten-tousand fookin warheads! De emphasis wiz on destroying de operational capability o' der place wid de least collateral damage as possible. And dis ment takin oot des nodes dat made up de redundant command and control distribution system.'

'So after all these nodes and command and control facilities are destroyed, how long will it take for Saddam to get the thing working again?'

'Oh, fookin yiers, four to five minimum. De software wir talkin about here is all bespoke fir dat particular plant. It's all designed, coded, tested and integrated with de central command system in de fookin plant. No two systems are de same any wir en de fookin world. And dis is state o' de airt stuff. Ye can't jist walk en te PC World en a Saturday mornin en buy dis stuff aff de fookin shelf ye know!'

'I know! So was the military okay with you?' I ask, as I notice his hands are still randomly twitching.

'Ah yeah, dey wir fookin brilliant, ah wiz well looked aftir en had a great time. En since den ave never had any trouble from de Peelers an ave changed ma fookin bank.'

'Well done old boy,' I say, as we click drinks. 'There's no nodes near our quad are there?'

'Fook aff!'

'Just kidding! But did you ever think it was strange why George Bush Sr left Saddam in power, and the CIA support of the Kurds ["...and Marsh Arabs"] just stopped?'

'Well it wiz strange ah guess.'

'Strange! Seamus, *"think out of the box"* mate, the US Central Command had just established a "strategic presence" in Saudi Arabia and Saddam was just left in power."

'Fook, a'd never really t-ought about it.'

'Well I'll tell you a bit more. Take a look at which family has a massive share ownership of ExxonMobil, Gulf Oil, Texaco and Chevron ["...and Saudi ARAMCO"]. The Gulf War was all about oil control and future arms deals to Saudi Arabia. The Bush administration left Saddam in power because they wanted to make Saudi Arabia feel vulnerable in order to sell the Saudis loads of expensive modern weapons. The UN was just used as a "smoke screen" to start the war ["... and to end it"]. After the war with Saddam was "completed", the House of Saud bought more tanks and fighter planes than they had drivers and pilots for!'

'Well fookin Saudi's got more money dan dey know what te do with. En dey love big expensive toys, even if dey don't have de electrical fookin sockets fir de stuff!'

'I know that! But wars are all about winners and losers *and the transfer of assets*. Do you know why Saddam invaded Kuwait and he thought he'd get away with it?'

'Yeah, it's coz he's a mad fooker! En 'd greedy bastard wanted all o' der oil.'

'Well that's sort of true, but he thought the Americans wouldn't mind, because that's what they'd just told him the week before the invasion of Kuwait. And Saddam also took delivery of US-made communication devices *the day before* he invaded Kuwait and George Bush's White House ["...and Bill Webster's CIA and Bill Studeman's NSA"] knew about it.'

'Really?' he says, as he gulps down some black stuff.

'Yes. It's not well known about, of course.'

'Ah wiz'nie told dis stuff at de fookin plannin wing!'

'Probably not! Don't forget that the Iraqi Ba'ath Party was connected to America all the way back to the Fifties with the CIA's Allen Dulles and Rockefeller family oil interests in both Iraq and Mossadegh's Iran ["all coordinated by the CIA's Middle East Chief, Mr Kermit Roosevelt"]. And during the 1980's Iran-Iraq War ["when Donald Rumsfeld was President Reagan's 'Middle East Special Envoy'..."], Saddam and his army were trained and armed by the US government. This was done with direct help from the Pentagon, Kissinger Associates ["...Alan Stoga, Lawrence Eagleburger, Brent Scowcroft and Dr Henry Kissinger who later represented Christopher Drogoul's BNL'] and the US-Iraq Business Forum when Saddam was the State Department's close friend in the region.'

'Sounds a bit like swings en fookin roundabouts!'

'Absolutely! And in 1989 and after George Bush's NSD-26 freed up one billion dollars to go to Iraq, Saddam used the money to buy even more US arms and chemicals ["...with kind assistance from the CIA, Ex-Im Bank, Bechtel and BNL'] to build up his own war machine again. Bush Sr approved this "agricultural" loan to him even after Saddam had gassed the Kurds! And the amount of chemical and germ warfare agents ["including tons of Sarin and Anthrax..."] which America supplied to Saddam throughout the Eighties, is frightening ["...Donald Rumsfeld, George Bush Sr and Dr Henry Kissinger will remember this well..."]. But crucially, following Saddam's 'Holy War' with Iran, Iraq had no money as Saddam ran up billions of dollars in debts and this is why he was in such a tight corner.'

'Yeah, en fookin wars iren't cheap.'

'Of course they're not! And added to this is the forgotten fact that Kuwait, with "direct" help from America ["...Thomas Twetten's old legendry Near East Ops Division at CIA Langley and Technical Support from CIA Reston"], was actually waging "economic warfare" on Saddam and slowly driving him to war.'

'How de fook wiz dis done den?' he asks, as his eyes start to switch on.

'Well firstly, they stopped their loans to him, and then got the Kuwaitis to deliberately demand loan repayments pronto, and thirdly by *"encouraging"* Kuwait to break their OPEC oil export quotas. This was primarily through their drilling operations, which were American planned ["...the CIA's Bill Webster and his DD/O Richard Stoltz will remember how"] and managed in Kuwait by KPC's Santa Fe Drilling ["...where President Bush's National Security Adviser, General Brent Scowcroft, had extensive 'senior contacts'..."]. This "economic warfare" on Iraq was "ramped up" soon after NSD-26 was signed in late 1989. But central to all of this stuff is the fact that the Kuwaiti Petroleum Company was stealing Saddam's oil with America's full knowledge and help!'

'Really!'

'Yes! You see the Kuwaiti drilling operations in Saddam's Rumeillah oilfield were done by "horizontal drilling" from inside Kuwait itself. And this "economic warfare" hurt Saddam's ability to service his debts with the Paris Club and several international banks including ["...David Rockefeller's Chase Manhattan Bank ..."] BNL and the old BCCI.'

["...Which was used by Germany's CIA COREA units as part of the CIA's Near East MC-10 Operation. Webster and The White House knew all about this CIA Black Op. BCCI's 'black network' was also a CIA 'back channel' to Saddam over the years..."]

'*Right*, so, er, wit de fook is dis "horizontal drillin"?'

'It's where an Iraqi oil well deep inside Iraq's territorial borders can be sucked dry by a drilling operation from inside Kuwait's borders. There are also UN Resolutions against Kuwait for doing this and the Kuwaitis were stealing his oil for ages ["...with direct help from Near East Ops in CIA Langley and Dick Cheney and Colin Powell's Department of Defense"]. Saddam kept on warning the Kuwaitis to stop the drilling as it was destabilising his economy.'

'Shit, so wit did de fookin Kuwaities do den?'

'They did as they were told! Santa Fe and KPC didn't just stop the drilling; they increased it! And this is what lit Saddam's fuse ["...just as George Bush Sr, Dick Cheney, James Baker III and General Brent Scowcroft knew it would"]. Then the week before he invaded Kuwait, when Saddam's patience was "on the brink", he had a meeting with the US Ambassador to Iraq.'

'Dat wid've bein a fookin good meetin!'

'It was, *I've got the transcripts*. In this meeting, Saddam was explicitly told by the American Ambassador that the US government would not get involved in "Arab conflicts" between Saddam and Kuwait. The Ambassador was only repeating what she was fed by Washington. *And Saddam bought it.* But in reality the *Bush* administration *lied* to Saddam, by painting a pretty picture for him to look at. And this picture was very different to the one Bush, Cheney, Baker and Scowcroft were looking at in the White House Situation Room in Washington. Saddam was unaware of George Bush's NSD-26 of 1989 ["...which set in motion the covert mechanics of what led to the Iraqi invasion of Kuwait in August 1990 and the Gulf War..."] and so was the rest of the world.'

["...*National Security Directive 26* signed by President George Bush Sr on the

2nd October 1989 states the following... 'Access to Persian Gulf oil and the security of key friendly states in the area are vital to US National Security. The United States remains committed to defend its vital interests in the region, if necessary and appropriate through the use of US military force against the Soviet Union or any other regional power with interests inimical to our own... The Secretaries of State (James Baker III) and Defense (Dick Cheney) *should develop a strategy for a long term program of arms sales to Saudi Arabia and other GCC States that serves our national interest...* Normal relations between the United States and Iraq would serve our long term interests and promote stability... We should pursue, and seek to facilitate, opportunities for US firms to participate in the reconstruction of the Iraqi economy... Also as a means of developing access to and influence with the Iraqi defence establishment...'. End quote."]

'This was the *"big picture"* George Bush Sr was looking at when he was dealing with Saddam, Kuwait and Saudi Arabia in the months leading up to the Gulf War. The United Nations and King Fahd knew absolutely nothing about this "policy mandate" in August 1990,' I say, slightly raising my eyebrow to make the point clear.

["...Did you know about National Security Directive -26 two days before Saddam invaded Kuwait, when John Kelly briefed you, Congressmen?"]

'Fook, ah didn't know any o' dis stuff.' says Seamus, rubbing his eyes again.

'Not many people do. CNN didn't even know where Iraq was when this shit was going down! After Kuwait was invaded, George Bush Sr convinced the House of Saud that they were next and that they should allow US troops into Saudi, to help them "defend" themselves from "further aggression", and it was going to cost them billions! ["And then Bush Sr just left Saddam in power."]'

'Yer fookin well informed,' says Seamus, as his eyes are shooting up and down the street.

'Like I said earlier, the Gulf War was all about oil control and future US arms deals with Saudi Arabia and the Gulf States. And it was **"deliberately engineered"** by the Bush administration ["...and the former President of Zapata Offshore, with its old legal councillor, Mr James Baker, deliberately left Saddam in power..."] to protect America's national interests in the Persian Gulf.'

["...And it was all 'quietly approved' by David Rockefeller's Council on Foreign Relations in total secrecy... as the CFR never takes an official position on anything."]

'Fook, d'ey don't tell ye all dis shit en de pages o' *TIME* and fookin *Newsweek*.' He says, as in the distance someones laptop starts beating out 'Naïve Song' by Mirwais.

["...And so the pieces to the 'overall jigsaw puzzle' slowly come together to look like the picture on the box. The Gulf War 1990/91was a *fraud* and one wonders why 'The Great Satan' has His problems with the Arabs today."]

'Of course they don't! And Britain's hands are far from clean in the region as well. Until a few decades ago, Kuwait was actually part of Iraq until we Brits carved it out of the desert and called it Kuwait. But it was probably some "Rupert" holding a map when he was lost!'

'See, der yous Brits go agein, alwiz causin fookin trouble!' says Seamus, laughing as we both click glasses.

["...National Security Review 10 - 'US Policy - Persian Gulf,' signed by President George Bush Sr on 22nd Feb 1989, will make some 'interesting' reading, Mr Senators and Mr Secretary General of the United Nations."]

'So do you know which company the two main players went to work for after the Bush administration lost the election?'

'No idea,' says Seamus, shaking his head away looking concerned.

'The Carlyle Group.'

'De company dats involved width iaxis fir dis fookin Digiplex set-up?'

'The very one. I'd never actually heard of them until I joined here, that's how quiet they are. But their political clout and connections in Saudi Arabia and Wall Street are second only to the Chase Manhattan Bank.'

'Fookin hell!'

'Check out their website, it's pretty good if you want to see where they invest their money.'

'Right, ah will fookin check it out!'

'So why were you printing off your CV, Seamus? Are you looking for another job?' I ask, as he looks around to see who could be listening. There's nobody as everyone is currently getting smashed.

'Ah fookin knew you'd ask dat question. It wiz coz o' fookin Psy-kho, he said he wanted all de senior directors' CVs on his desk. Dey aier goin flat out te sell iaxis. Dees CVs ire ta show buyers all our professional backgrounds. Dat's how fookin Porn Star got found out fir fookin lying en his CV, en he's anoder mad fooker as well!'

'You can say that again mate! But just make sure that there's a couple of chairs for us both to sit on when the music stops playing.'

'If any fooker sits on ma chair de'll be fookin dead...!'

Seamus still feels, and looks, rough as shit. He struggles to get up and decides to call it a day. As he gets up ready to leave, he carefully looks up and down the street just in case there are any transit vans away to pull up. A precaution he learned back home, "across the water".

["...A familiar transit van, with an unfamiliar driver, driving around XMG in the very early hours of the morning is not generally the start of a good day. In fact, if 'Stores And Supplies' are involved, it is usually the end of someone's day."]

Seamus slips away unnoticed, while I join Stalker and Old Boy (who will be fucking dead if he misses tonight's dinner party as well!).

CHAPTER 11

Back at the cabin, the two hungry wolves who stopped have been howling to all the other wolves in the forest telling them that they've found a cabin with a good feed inside...

Wacko and the finance raiser ('*hellraiser*') both walk up to the quad. Wacko looks around for inspiration and '*hellraiser*' just carries on walking back to the '*Fire Department*' with a thousand yard stare. They have just got back from doing a numbers stunt *(fire-eating display)* in the boardroom and they don't look very happy.

'I think we're going to have to buy a shit load more fire extinguishers. It is all going to get very "hectic", as they'd say at Hercules House,' says Wacko, looking "under pressure" and feeling "challenged".

'Yes, I see that the Dodgers are starting to look pretty nervous,' I say, looking at my *Skull and Bones* screensaver and thinking that it's going to be a "particularly hot summer" as well.

'Too right they are. All the suppliers now want payments in full delivered to them yesterday. Our competitors are putting the word out that we're about to go under.'

'So what does that mean?' I ask, as I save even more changes that I have just made to my CV.

'Well for starters we've got some pretty gruesome meetings ahead over the next month or so with all of our main creditors.'

'Well good luck mate, but don't drag me into any 'cause you know I'm afraid of heights!' I say looking over my shoulder at the steep drop below.

'You'll do as you're told! And also, your briefing for the RIPE 36 in Budapest; just listen in on the techie conference talks and collect as many business cards as possible.'

'Yes, sure.'

'Oh, and importantly, you must email back news of any deals you can earwig. But basically wing it, network like fuck and brass it out, yeah?'

'Yes, it should be good.'

'Sorted then. Oh and if you and Nathan go to any strip clubs it's not on expenses any more. Cash is going to get very tight in here now.'

'Yes, no probs.'

'Good.'

Old Boy is on the phone to *Soundblast* as I can see the double-glazed look in his eyes, while Nathan is just back from a meeting over at Hewlett Packard. It was a non-smoking building, which meant he lost a great deal of sleep during the night worrying about this aspect.

'Nathan, I've had an idea about doing an Internet network capacity swap.'

'What's that then?' he asks, knowing that we still haven't yet made a sale. It's not Old Boy's fault, he's been working like a dog.

'Okay, in order to get some Internet traffic on the backbone why don't we do a swap with a leading US backbone who has a limited network in Europe, but an extensive network with lots of Internet peering partners across the USA? A straightforward Internet traffic swap; they put their Internet traffic on our backbone and we do the same with theirs. This could be used in a marketing blag as we could then say that our Internet reach in the USA will be fantastic. I've done some checking and USAT2 (real name withheld) is the best one to go for as they are still rolling out in Europe. But they are huge in the USA and they are also in the same co-location facility as us in London's Docklands, so connectivity is not a problem.'

'That's a good idea,' says Nathan, looking at Wacko.

'Is it free?' asks Wacko, whose face gives away the fact that he never understood a word of what I'd just said!

'Yes, sure it's free. It's a swap.'

'Sound, just let us know what it means when you translate it into fucking English!' he says, as he gets up and goes to see how the Big Cats in the "illegal" Department are doing.

Old Boy hangs up the phone following his briefing from *Soundblast*. 'Blaady hell! I've got to go and buy that puppy dog tonight.'

(Old Boy and *Soundblast* finally went to see a breeder last night and she fell in love with one of the little puppies. She wanted to take it home there and then, but Old Boy wanted to wait another day just to really think it through, which is an amazingly responsible attitude for the big chap to have. Well she's thought it through and Old Boy's got his orders: '*Buy that blaady puppy tonight!*')

'What kind of dog is it, Old Boy?' I ask, as I see him touching his red ears.

'I haven't got a fucking clue mate!' he says laughing... That is until his phone starts to ring again.

My concentration on my Internet peering swap with USAT2 for North

America is shattered when I see Sasha walking towards our quad. I casually remove one of the peering folders and place it on the floor. There is now enough room for Sasha to sit down if she chooses to stop by.

Sasha stops at my desk. 'Hiya mate!' she says, as she casually climbs onto my desk, gets her bottom comfortable and then crosses her legs. 'I'm really sorry about opening that email virus,' she says, with total innocence, which of course I immediately buy.

'Hey there's no need to worry about that, Sasha. It was fantastic. We spent two days outside a pub and the office PCs were down for the whole weekend!'

...TTT and TTT2 are still traumatised and they are getting some 'techie therapy'. The only therapy I need is a long weekend in *New York* with Sasha... I look at her *Omega* ladies' watch: it is close to twelve noon.

'It's nearly lunchtime; would you like to go out for some lunch?'

'Yes! That would be lovely, Steve,' she says, as she slides back off my desk.

'Lets go down to Roberto's. They do some very good food,' I say, as I place my well-used Mulberry leather wallet into my pocket.

'Excellent, I'll go and get my bag.'

Old Boy is on the phone to *Soundblast*. This is his fourth briefing of the day. This one is for their summer plans. Nathan looks at me and shakes his head while he turns his right hand into a pistol and points his forefinger and index finger to his temple... *And then fires a single shot.*

I walk with Sasha over to marketing blag and look at Kong as we pass his desk. He looks pissed off. In fact he looks mad as fuck. I can feel the aggression hit me as his eyes are now giving me open heart surgery and a head transplant. Sasha picks up her bag and announces to the whole department that we're off out to Roberto's to have some lunch and she can be reached on her mobile... Kong hears this and I feel the shockwave as his head has a brainblast. His face now closely resembles the 'Incredible Hulk' who has just gone and eaten a large beehive!

As we walk past Kong's desk, I look out of the glass window towards the Serious Fraud Office. Half of me is expecting to go hurtling towards it, while the other half is now mentally racing Steve Cram down Gray's Inn Road. Strangely Sasha doesn't acknowledge Kong's presence at all and I feel a little chill in the air as she makes a point of looking away.

We also walk past Wacko and he telepathically tells me that I am one sad bastard and that I'm going to crash and burn on this occasion.

When Sasha and I walk through the reception area there are even more cold stares. In fact the ground here has suddenly developed a thin layer of frost and I can feel Charlotte's eyes on us both, which is out of the norm. And is therefore suspicious...

'Sometimes I really hate this place,' Sasha says, with true emotion as we wait for the lift.

'Why's that?' I ask, thinking it's a great place. Ever since I've started to work here I haven't looked at a single *Exodus* holiday brochure.

'It doesn't matter, Steve,' she says, looking downbeat.

On the ground floor, Trevor McDonald walks past us. Usually when we see him in the building he looks his usual happy and charming old self. Today for some reason he looks madder than Kong upstairs. I wouldn't like to be working for ITN today as he looks like he's going to let rip as soon as he walks into the office.

Outside the weather is beautiful. Sasha takes two calls on her mobile and then we arrive at Roberto's on Gray's Inn Road, which is one of the best Italian restaurants in the area. But today I haven't booked a table, as I clearly didn't have time. However, I know that the waiters in Roberto's will always make a table available for a beautiful lady with long blonde hair.

We get a seat by the window. The reserved sign that was on our table is now placed at a far less prominent table well away from the window. Sasha switches the power off on her Nokia, which I think is incredibly well mannered. She leaves it on the table as I order a bottle of Chianti.

About ten seconds later the wine turns up. She moistens her lips with her tongue as she prepares to take a sip. She says that the wine is perfect and we both order our food. We go for the seafood pasta, which is one of the specials of the day.

'You don't look very happy. Are you sure everything's okay?' I ask, easily sounding concerned as she slowly flashes her eyes at me.

'No, not really Steve, I feel like I've just lost a friend.'

'Why?' I ask, with a voice so full of compassion I have no real idea where it came from.

'It's Damon (Kong); he's just started going out with Charlotte on reception, and it is just to make me jealous. They even went to see a show at the weekend and then went back to her place. They're seeing each other now.'

A shade of green covers her face as she realises Kong has deserted her and is now giving "close protection" to another blonde in the office. (What a bastard, eh?)

'So were you seeing him?' I ask, pretending that I'm not really interested in her answer.

'*No!* He wants to (of course). But I just want to be good friends with him. And we are good friends. But all this will change if Charlotte is on the scene. I will hardly ever see him now.'

'So what does your flatmate Jemma think you should do?'

'Jemma's not really bothered. She's sleeping with Nick, playing her own little game. She reckons he'll come running back though,' says Sasha, as she takes a deep sigh and shakes her head at the love triangle Jemma is involved in…with her 'friend' Claire and Nick.

'I think he'll be back as well.'

She shrugs her shoulders. 'Oh, I'm not sure Steve. He gets pissed off very easily.'

(Yes, sweetheart, I can tell!)

The food turns up and it is very good.

'But anyway, I'm going to go to Egypt for a couple of months when my shares can be cashed in,' she says, taking another sip of her Chianti.

'Do you really think you'll have shares to cash in?' I ask, as nobody in iaxis is speaking about their potential wealth any more.

'I think so. I've invested twenty thousand pounds of my savings and have huge payments to make every month to pay off the fifty thousand pounds I've borrowed from the investor.'

'But the NASDAQ has crashed and iaxis is winging it just to survive.'

'Yes, I know Steve, but somebody will buy us and then I'll get the money. A few weeks ago Fibrenet nearly went for us, but the shareholders said no because it wasn't one billion dollars!'

Her eyes are flashing at mine as we both share a little laugh at the madness going on at the top.

'But we need a solid offer with lots of money very fast, or else it could turn messy,' I say, as I nearly finish my drink.

'Really? Haven't we just had an injection of thirty million dollars from Bain Capital, just before the NASDAQ crashed?'

'Yes, but it's being drip-fed to us and it won't last long here. Spending money, whether we've got it or not, is a favourite hobby of iaxis!' I say, as a huge sexy smile beams across her face at the fun of it all. 'Look Sasha, the cash front is so bad that at one stage last year we owed Ciena almost fifty million dollars. Their board is yet to have a good night's sleep since they started doing business with iaxis. Also, we cannot afford to provision new customers wanting to sign up and buy capacity on our fibre optic network. And right now we can't sell anything at all on the Internet backbone. That cash from Bain Capital is really for survival,' I say, as I start to refill our two glasses and my mind starts to wander.

'Well I still think everything will be all right, Steve. The ex-chairman will come in with some super company and buy us all out with big money. The market will turn again for us.'

...I just smile and hide the fact that what I'm really thinking is that it is far more likely Jon Snow of Channel 4 News will be on location doing a live broadcast from inside the NSOC at Fort Meade. And being told the Truth by Dick Cheney ["...and the NRO's Jimmie D. Hill and ex-CIA men, Bill Webster and Robert W. Gates"] *about the faked NRO/CIA KH-11 'imagery intelligence' (IMINT) which was presented to the House of Saud in August 1990. Not to mention the Pentagon's electronic warfare (EW) operations displaying on Saudi radar screens an entire Iraqi army along the Saudi border;* ["complete with Iraqi troops' voice traffic in their headsets..."] *no wonder the Saudis were so 'spooked' at Saddam's so called "imminent threat" to the Kingdom. In fact Ant and Dec have got more chance of presenting the Today Programme than CH4 News being allowed access to the OPS-1 facility at Fort Meade to do this 'Special Report' on the Bush administration's desire to create a Middle East war and then get their Saudi 'friends' to fund it; all to enhance 'America Inc's' oil and defence interests in the region...*

'Sasha, the odds are pretty slim of our ex-chairman coming up with a big-ticket buyer the way the market is heading,' I say, as I think about the *Today* programme's '*Thought for the Day*'.

["...The Truth might set you free 'Magog'...but it also has dirty hands."]

'We'll see. Have you ever met the ex-chairman?' she asks, looking fondly out of the window.

'No, I haven't, I've seen him around, but he wouldn't know me from *Adam*. I joined well after he'd been removed. I think he was in Australia at the time.'

'Well he's a lovely man, a real charmer. He took eleven of us girls from the office over to his pad in Brussels for the weekend,' she says with a radiant smile on her face.

'Yes, I remember that. It was a few weeks ago wasn't it?'

'Yes, but I'm just getting my photos developed now,' she says, looking at the wine label with appreciation.

'I've seen other photos from the trip and they look good! So how many did the ex-chairman end up having for himself?' I ask, with a very cheeky smile and a knowing look in my eyes.

She picks up on it right away.

'Oh that would be telling, Steve! What happened in Brussels stays in Brussels,' she says, as she smiles and flicks her silky hair in her carefree manner.

'So do you reckon this Med fibre optic project the ex-chairman is planning will take off?' I ask, to get the conversation away from Brussels.

She considers this for a few seconds. 'Yes, well we hear Tyco are planning one, so there must be a market and therefore we should be doing it as well.'

'But it's going to cost nine hundred million dollars to build! There might be over three hundred million people in the region, but how many of them have telephones in their tents and shacks in North Africa? Israel is a bit more advanced, but they're always too busy throwing stones! You've got to look at the business plan and see where the revenue stream is coming from,' I say, as she laughs at this one.

'*A business plan!* What's a business plan in this industry? The City bankers know nothing about the Internet and telecoms. But they have the belief that it is the future. So we just invite them in and dazzle them with science and numbers and let them ride the hype. They ramp it all up amongst themselves. Who does the biggest deal is king. If an Internet company like, for example, Lastminute.com is really only worth fifty million dollars maximum, City bankers will stick a zero on this figure to keep it up there with the hype and they all want to be seen to be doing big deals. And don't forget leading global investment banks like Merrill Lynch, Salomon's and Morgan Stanley Dean Witter will take off a huge fee if the value of the company is half a billion dollars when they float it. But what fuels it all is investors; they all want millions back in minutes these days!'

'Sure. That's spot on. Investor confidence is what really fuels a market, and it's been sky high,' I say, as I see the sharpness and very obvious intelligence in her blue eyes.

'Back in January, if you had "dotcom" after the company name, these bankers would throw millions of dollars at you and your value would go up by at least thirty per cent overnight.'

'Yes, I remember all the articles in the FT at the time.'

'Of course, you see in this industry it is all about *perception*. We are very good at providing glossy blag material that shows we are global. Have this backed up with a few revenue graphs drawn up by the likes of Psycho, make up all the numbers in the spreadsheet and then wing it like fuck doing the presentation. And if they ask any questions then just blag these out as well. Then sit back and wait for the money to roll in. That's basically how the telecoms industry worked in 1999 and this is how iaxis got the money last year. And it only came through after we'd finished building the first fibre network. The money always comes in for iaxis,' she says, smiling at the fun everyone had in running up more than two hundred and fifty million dollars' worth of bills with peanuts in our offshore bank accounts.

I look concerned, and she picks up on this.

'So what's the solution, Steve? she asks, as she leans forward, tempting me to come closer.

'Well, the market has been turned on its head and these City banks can pull investments in a heartbeat in a bear market. And the future is looking very grim for the whole of the telecoms and Internet industry,' I say, in a hushed voice, as there are some suits sitting not too far away.

Sasha's sexy smile is brutally cut short when we see Kong stomping past the window. He's looking straight ahead and doesn't see us. But everyone on the pavement sees him and gets out of his way.

'I just hope he's happy with Charlotte,' she says, as if this liaison Kong has struck up has really got to her.

'He'll be back, but look, iaxis has to be sold to the first company who comes along and offers a decent and fair price. You won't get five hundred million dollars now. But this company, whoever they are, will need to have pockets as deep as the North Atlantic, filled with hard cash and a willingness to spend it,' I say, feeling very impressed with her intelligence. She might be blonde, but this girl is razor sharp.

'Yes, that'll do. I'm sure we can spend plenty of their money for them!' she says, as the bill arrives.

'I'm sure you're right!' I add, as I pull out my AmEx card and pay for the meal.

'We'll be all right. The ex-chairman will pull something off,' she says confidently.

'We shall see,' I say, remaining unconvinced.

But if we see Jon Snow leaving the ITN building with NSA men in black suits, earpieces and dark shades, climbing into a blacked-out Ford people carrier, then I will be very impressed!

'Thanks for lunch, Steve. It was lovely,' she says, as she slips her arm through her leather handbag.

'That's okay. It was a pleasure.'

Walking back up Gray's Inn Road, I ask Sasha if she would like to meet up next weekend or a Friday night after work.

She smiles discreetly to herself.

'I'm sorry Steve, but I don't do Fridays and weekends are for partying! Send me an email and we can go out for a drink in the Blue Lion one evening after work.'

I cover up my disappointment very well. This is helped by the mental images of Nathan blowing his brains out and Kong going fucking berserk and throwing his desk (and me) out of the seventh floor office window.

'I can't do next week. I'm in Budapest for an Internet conference,' I say, as I am now slowly kicking my heart back up the street.

'Lucky you! I need another holiday clubbing somewhere in the Med. I'm getting a bit bored with London,' she says, smiling away as I start to speak about the weather.

As we approach the ITN building, there are no blacked-out Ford people carriers with men in black suits and dark shades. Today, as always, there are just the usual friendly security guards on the ground floor reception. However, these fellas are now under new orders to see everyone's passes, which we pull out as we walk into the lift area. Their usually highly sophisticated facial recognition system, complete with its nod and wink clearance device, has been withdrawn from use!

I get back to the quad and I am not looking happy.

'Blaady hell! Lunch with Sasha, eh Steve...' says Old Boy, looking impressed.

'Did you ask her out then?' asks Wacko.

I look up and see that they've all frozen in their postures anticipating my answer. 'I did, but she said "No" because she doesn't do "Fridays".'

They all have a laughing attack.

'Don't worry Steve mate, but blaady good effort!' says Old Boy, reading an article about *George Bush Sr* and grinning away with not a care in the world.

'Steve, join the club. If you work here, she's *untouchable*', says Nathan.

'At least you asked her, Steve, and she's just let you know where you stand,' says Old Boy.

'Yeah, right in the middle of some dog shit by the sounds of it!' laughs Wacko, doing his best to reassure me.

I nod my head in agreement as a huge yawn escapes from my whole body and forces its way out of my mouth.

'How's the quest to get some customers on our Internet backbone coming on, Old Boy?' I ask, as I switch my PC monitor back on.

He looks up at me and puts his *Manhattan Institute* paper in the bin.

'Nobody is blaady interested in iaxis, they're only interested in buying capacity from the big names. It's a complete bugger,' says Old Boy, looking at his "NEWSDEALER" screensaver as it flashes away.

'Just keep banging away, someone will crack and sign up with us,' says Wacko, full of optimism.

Old Boy picks up the phone and gets another briefing from *Soundblast*.

This time it is a nine-second soundburst telling him that their summer holiday will be in Tuscany.

After surfing the Internet for ages and checking my Hotmail, I decide to make the call to USAT2 to see if they are interested in my idea about an Internet capacity swap. I've got the lady's number to call as we've already signed an Internet connectivity agreement with them for a peering connection at a European co-location facility, which both our companies are located at. There's no answer from her office landline, so I call her mobile and it rings. After a good few rings she answers it and sounds tired. And then I realise my mistake. She's in California, it is not even sunrise yet, and her pet dog is barking wildy away at this unexpected phone call. I introduce myself as the Internet peering manager from iaxis. She remembers the name 'iaxis'.

Lucia is a director for 'Global Internet Development Strategy' for USAT2, so I don't think she lives in a trailer park. In fact it sounds like quite a big house that she lives in, as I can still hear her dog howling away in the background. It is a weird howl as if it's trying to tell her something urgent…

'I'm really sorry Lucia, I didn't check the time. I'll call you back at your office and let you get some sleep.'

'No, no, that's okay,' she says, with a lovely warm voice as she calms her dog down. She tells me she is just walking back to her bedroom and is climbing back into bed. Her phone was in the kitchen where it woke up her dog. And then by the sounds of it, her dog has gone and woken up the whole neigbourhood.

'So Steve, tell me why I'm lying in bed talking to one of my Internet peers in London?' she asks, in friendly tone.

'Now I really do feel bad,' I say, feeling awful.

'I'm just kidding. Anyway what have you got for me?'

'Well it's just an idea that's come up in the iaxis Global Internet Strategy meeting we had earlier.'

(The rest of the quad have kicked back to watch this blag go down and to see me winging it here. This 'meeting' has set them off.)

'So what's the plan then?' she asks, sounding intrigued.

'Well iaxis would be very interested in doing an Internet capacity peering swap on our respective backbones. This would give your customers access to all our European Internet connection partners. And our customers (when we got some) will get access to all your Internet backbone connections in the USA through your backbone.'

Wacko looks lost. But he's still listening, which is a world record.

'Yes, that should be workable, just send me your peering/connectivity spreadsheet showing which Internet backbones you are currently connected with and at which exchanges. We've done this kind of swap with other companies over here, so lets take a look at what peering connections iaxis has got.'

'That would be great,' I say, giving the thumbs-up to Wacko and Nathan. 'Thanks, now I'll let you get back to sleep,' I say, with a warm tone in my voice.

'No, it's okay Steve, sunrise has now broken and it's time for my four-mile run along the beach with my dog.'

'Four miles running in sand! I'm impressed.'

'Yes, well my dog is only young and he loves the exercise.'

'What kind of dog have you got?' I ask, as there are wide-open stares from the rest of the quad.

'He's a two-year-old German Shepherd and he's my baby.'

'A German Shepherd, that's cute, what's his name?'

(Fits of laughter now!)

'He's called Bosco and he's real cute.'

'Well tell Bosco that I'm sorry for waking him up as well!' I say, surfin' my way through this international business call between London and LA.

'Will do Steve!' she says laughing, as we say goodbye with the sound of young Bosco going completely fucking wild in the kitchen!

'Nice one!' I say to the quad after I hang up.

'Was that you chatting up her fucking dog as well?' shouts Wacko, who is now out of his chair laughing with the rest of the quad.

'Excellent!' says Nathan, as all of the Dodgers start running for cover.

Then the fire alarm starts to ring. And it rings... and rings...

Normally when a fire alarm goes off in here, each company has its own meeting point outside and round the back of the ITN building. Here the staff can safely meet and be counted. iaxis also has it's own designated area. It's called Centro's, the Blue Lion or, as a last contingency plan, the Duke. (That is if the fire is ever severe enough and the pubs across the road have to close.)

'Right, lets go over to Centro's and get some beers in,' says Nathan, who feels he is due a fag break.

We get up and leave everything where it is. We are the first ones out of the office, as we want to get a seat in the pub. Approximately thirty seconds later we're outside on the street, and our day in the office is over.

I get in eight bottles of San Miguel for the four of us. (You won't be able to move in here in the next couple of minutes when iaxis moves in.)

We finish the first bottle just as the fire engines eventually show up. One fireman is even eating a large McDonald's.

Seamus and Howard walk in. Reality has hit Howard hard. His yachting magazines have gone in the bin and his Oyster 55 screensaver has been removed. He now has a screensaver proudly showing off his young baby son, which Wacko reckons he and his missus bought on the Internet! (Well, the kid just appeared on his screen one day, what else were we to think?)

The bottles of San Miguel start to go down.

'I'm thinking of selling my Sony widescreen TV if anyone's interested in buying it?'

'How much for?' asks Wacko, showing huge interest.

'About one thousand five hundred pounds. And that's a bargain; it's hardly been used.'

'Fuck off!!' he yells out, laughing away.

The other two aren't interested. Nathan has now got the biggest student debt in the UK to pay off, and I think Old Boy's family own a cinema chain.

'Right then, I'll put an ad online in "LOOT". That's a good place to start. And it's free.'

'Yeah, it's the best way to get rid of stolen gear in London,' says Nathan.

'It's not hot, in fact it comes with the receipt!'

'I'm just pulling your leg!'

A short while later when the place is packed, Old Boy shows signs of looking thirsty as he makes a 'four more drinks' signal, via a sequence of hand movements, to Merlock who's at the bar getting served. The deal is done and the four drinks will be delivered at a given price within the next five minutes.

'Blaady good chap, Merlock!'

'How's the Hewlett Packard deal looking Nathan?' I ask, as a cloud of fag fumes engulf me.

'So far it's going really good, but we're at a crucial stage.'

'What is the deal exactly?' asks Old Boy, sounding like he wants to know something new.

'Well basically HP are going to roll out web-hosting facilities across six of our co-location facilities throughout Europe. This is for dedicated server hosting, virtual private networks, content distribution, networks and operational support. We chose HP because they were the best. They're way ahead of the likes of Intel, Dell and Compaq. They've also agreed to set aside those lovely two words for us.'

'Which two are those?' asks Old Boy, trying to wisen himself up very quickly on the iaxis method of financing.

'*Vendor Finance,*' says Nathan, rubbing his hands together.

'How much is that going to be?' I ask, as Old Boy collects the drinks from Merlock and squares up the debt with a 'cash on delivery' payment.

'It's around one hundred million dollars,' says Nathan, with his mouth full of San Miguel.

'Blaady hell! That's good of them!' says Old Boy, just as the drinks are placed on the table.

This is going to be a long night...

'Now tell them the bad news,' says Wacko.

Old Boy looks a bit perplexed, as what could the bad news be if one of the most respected multinational corporations in the world has agreed, in principle, to set aside one hundred million dollars for iaxis?

'They've asked to see the books and want to go through the balance sheet with a forensic fucking microscope!' he says, looking concerned.

'Well that's what I'd want to do if I was them,' says Old Boy, quite confidently.

'Well there's a slight problem. The finances are in a shit state and if HP saw the books they'd all run out the building, screaming hysterically,' says Nathan, lighting up another fag as he hands one over to Old Boy.

Wacko makes some more hand signals to a new market maker (Howard) at the bar and he prepares to get us all some more drinks in. This place is packed out.

'Blaady hell! Are you sure about this?' he asks Nathan.

'Very sure! When we first approached HP we were on course to have a high-yield bond issue and IPO flotation. Then the NASDAQ crashed and it all got messed up. The dollars are running out and now the shareholders and management are trying to sell iaxis fast. We've got to keep HP away from the books as long as possible. But HP has got a whole team working on this project. In iaxis there's me, Gibbsy and Matt. We'll let them see the books after a takeover,' adds Nathan, scratching his chin as Wacko brings Old Boy up to speed in fifth gear.

'Seeing the full set of books is not on. If word got out how big our debts are it would be game over. And right now all developments have stopped and we're in survival mode. The CEO threatened to resign a couple of weeks ago, so the shareholders paid him over one million dollars just to stay on and help sell iaxis.'

Old Boy looks at Wacko as if he's having a laugh and pulling his leg with what he's just told him. But he quickly sees that we are all deadly serious.

'*That's fucking mental!*' he shouts, so loudly we are all sure some of the suits heard him at the bar.

Old Boy still looks to be in a state of disbelief as shock is beginning to take hold and he realises just how close to the abyss we really are.

'Do you not miss news editing in Hong Kong?' asks Wacko, as he takes delivery of the drinks Howard has just got in for us all.

'Sometimes, but I wanted a change and that's the reason why I'm working in the Internet,' says Old Boy, still looking stunned.

'Well, here's to the future chaps!' says Wacko, as we all knock back a shot of tequila.

Next morning in the office, we are all too hung over to see straight. I am sitting at my desk and my mouth feels as dry as Bob Marley's *old boot*. I begin shovelling down a sausage bagel with brown sauce and a large hot cappuccino to kill the alcohol still in my *blood*. My head is pounding away and I'm sure one of my drinks was *spiked*, as I've not felt this rough for ages. I forward the Internet peering spreadsheet to Lucia of USAT2. I also put my TV in to LOOT online pages and look over at Wacko and Nathan who are also eating their breakfasts as they groan away and think 'never again'.

A short while later Old Boy walks in and disturbs the peace with his total silence. His eyes are crazed with fear and he has a terrorised look on his face as if he's spent the night fighting in the tunnels of Cu Chi just outside Saigon. He also looks like he's still pissed and hasn't had much sleep.

'What's up?' asks Nathan. (I was going to ask, but I had a mouthful of the best sausage bagel in the world.)

For some strange reason Old Boy is unable to speak.

'What's up mate?' I manage to ask after my bagel goes down.

'Grunt.'

His phone rings and his eyes close. He can see the red light on the STU III display and he is twitching away as he lifts up his handset and slowly puts it to his ear.

'How!!!!!!!!!!!!!!!!!!!!
Could!!!!!!!!!!!!!!!!!!
You!!!!!!!!!!!!!!!!!!!!!'

We all hear *Soundblast's* massive sound explosion as her sound bomb rips through his headset, travels through his head and out of the glass ceiling causing chaos with all the satellite receivers on the ITN roof...

The full *blowback* of the sonic boom hits us when her travelling noise-matter goes supersonic towards the clear blue sky!

Old Boy's phone line goes dead and he puts the handset down with a haunted and frightened look on his face.

'Blaady hell,' he says, as he twitches away in trauma.

'What's up Old Boy, you haven't left the butter and knife out again have you?' asks Wacko, who's now got a headache from *Soundblasts* phone call. Half the office is looking over at us. They heard her as well.

Old Boy looks over at me as if he's in a trance. He can't even force a smile. He puts his right palm over his ear and it almost burns his hand. I can clearly see that his ears are a shade redder than hell's door handles.

I look up through the glass ceiling and see some engineers running all over the SKYLINK satellite dishes. All of them are frantically shouting away in to two-way radios trying to reposition them, as *Soundblasts* voice explosion seems to have taken out the *"Global Broadcast System"* as well.

Old Boy puts his head in his hands and is slowly shaking it away, not speaking. The three of us all look at each other and thank our lucky stars that we're not married if this is what happens when one gets settled down.

Old Boy starts to speak.

'Because I got so blaady pissed with you lot last night, I completely forgot I was meant to go out and buy that blaady puppy she fell in love with.'

'Well pick it up tonight mate.' I say quickly.

'You can pick it up just now if it'll make things better,' says Wacko, rubbing his head.

Old Boy takes a deep breath. This is all too much for him.

'She got in around 11:30 p.m. last night expecting puppy and me to be home. But we weren't and she tries phoning me on my mobile, which is still on my desk after that fire alarm. And there was no answer...' Old Boy rubs his very tired eyes.

'So then she phones that blaady breeder to see if we were both okay and the breeder proceeds to tell her that she couldn't reach me on my mobile and she thought we'd lost interest.'

'Well tell her you still want it,' I say, rubbing my left ear.

Old Boy takes another deep breath to stabilise his head.

'She went and sold it to another couple just after 9 p.m. last night.'

'No!!' shout three concerned mates.

'She blaady well did. When I got home at 1:45 a.m. this morning, barely able to walk, I had no idea my wife could shout and scream so loudly, and for so blaady long,' says Old Boy, looking like he's punch drunk.

'How long did it go on for?' asks Nathan, feeling a bit sorry for him.

'Well at three-thirty this morning I told her that there were plenty more blaady puppies in the world!'

'So what happened then?' I manage to ask in between laughs.

'A dinner plate nearly took my fucking head off!' he says, as he gets up and leaves for his morning feed down in Manhattan's.

We have trouble containing our laughter as Nathan throws a softball and tempts Old Boy to fetch it back to us!

Shortly afterwards our laughter is brutally cut short when Old Boy's phone rings. We all recognise the number flashing away, but we're far too scared to answer it!

The phone rings off after six rings.

Wacko starts to open his emails while trying to refocus following this morning's 'sound attack'.

'Check this, the money from GE Capital is available if we want it,' says Wacko, rubbing his ears.

'How much is that then?' asks Nathan, as if he's in a hurry to start spending it on repaying his student debts.

'About fifty-three million dollars.'

'Let's have it!' he says, thinking that that amount will just about clear his overdraft.

(I'm not so sure it's a runner. If it were good news, Wacko would be out of his seat punching the air. And we'd be getting ready to go out to celebrate in about ten seconds' time.)

'I don't think we're going to run with it,' he says despondently.

'Why not?' Nathan and I ask on cue.

'The money will just be used to pay off the old Ciena kit which we've already got. It will not leave any room to buy any new gear or to provision new customers. And this large debt will look crap on the balance sheet. But the fact that we'll have to pay three million dollars in Big Cat lawyer fees will kill it outright.'

'So what's going to happen now?' asks Nathan, who's just waiting to be told by his bank that they no longer like to say 'Yes'. (Well 'Yes' to him that is!)

'Fuck knows. I'm off to a financial management meeting with the CFO *('chief fire officer')*, but I'm sure it's going to get binned. The only hope is for a takeover. But it would be good if you both could blag some business in Budapest. So good luck if I don't see you before you head off. I'm going to see our German fibre supplier, Gas Line in Dusseldorf. I'm heading out with a couple of Big Cats, the CFO and one of the Dodgers, we're all flying out at 3 p.m. today,' says Wacko, as he gets up with a huge calculator in one hand and some charts and spreadsheets in the other.

'When did you find that out?' I ask, trying to remember if he'd already told me.

'About thirty seconds ago when I opened the email from our CFO.'

'Have fun then.'

Wacko looks at me like he's suddenly feeling sick.

(... iaxis was the first company Gas Line leased its fibre optic cables to. McGowan and Merlock flew over to Germany in their black leather jackets and 'had a word with the top'. The 'top man' said 'yes'. Now we owe Gas Line, according to Wacko's calculator, well over twenty million dollars. The CFO wants Wacko and the rest to go over to Germany to come up with some brilliant financial stunt and reason with Gas Line before they try and shut down the network through the courts. They have to come up with something pretty damn good in this meeting, or else it is game over...)

Old Boy gets off the phone to his wife, having successfully removed the micro-processors from that world-leading BAE Systems sound bomb in her voice box, before it goes off again. He is going to be taking her to see another top breeder's doggie collection tonight. And this breeder is 'blaady good'!

After Wacko leaves for the airport, Nathan and I try and persuade Old Boy to come over to Centro's after work, but post-traumatic stress disorder hits him and he has to sit-down.

'Look chaps, if I go out for a beer after work tonight, I will be fucking dead.'

'Well it's up to you mate, but we're only going over the road for one.'

CHAPTER 12

Through the dark trees at the old wooden cabin more wolves are now being seen and heard, and hunger is driving their survival instinct. In order to counter the threat, the iaxis management team is getting prepared for some 'meetings' that might just keep the old wooden door bolted tightly shut.

The sun is shining and Nathan and I are demob happy, as we get ready to leave the country on a business jolly. Old Boy is also looking happy as he and *Soundblast* got their lovely puppy dog. But sadly our mate Wacko could very well be tied to a chair in the Gas Line boardroom (the Cooler) and is probably on the receiving end of the 'flamethrower treatment' (lots of shouting)...

The weather in London is scorching hot and the forecast in Budapest also looks very good. I decided against taking an iaxis polo shirt to wear while I am wandering around the conference. I would much rather be anonymous. (But I have brought a couple of iaxis pencils, just for when I sign the hotel bill.)

Nathan and I leave to get a taxi to Heathrow Airport and of course we manage to get the flight times wrong. We arrive two hours before check-in, which gives us enough time to relax in one of the airport bars.

The only downer on the horizon is the fact we have to fly British Airways. I detest flying with them, but unfortunately I have to from time to time. And each time I do, it just reminds me once again why I loathe the experience. Whether or not it is just me, I don't know. Maybe I'm the only traveller who has noticed that British Airways cabin crew all seem to think they are direct descendants from the aristocracy?

Now I know the BA cabin crews have a serious and important job to do. For example keeping Nathan and I stocked up on drinks, feeding us some average food and hopefully rescuing our backsides if the plane decides it doesn't want to fly today, sixteen seconds after it takes off. But it is their superiority complex, authoritarian posture and above all the way they look down their long snooty noses at one when sitting in economy class. This is what really pisses me off. And I fly economy class all over the world on my backpacking adventures. And with all the other world's airlines, the cabin crews are warm, friendly and genuinely cheerful when they serve you in economy class.

And so far, for my long-haul travels I have used Air China, Aeroflot, British Airways, Bangladeshi Airlines, lots of Middle Eastern airlines, Air France, Malaysian Airlines, Argentinian and Peru's airline (scary). So I know what I'm talking about when I compare economy class cabin crews and their service attitudes. And in my humble opinion as a passenger, BA are truly awful. They are the worst in the world.

When I am at some tin-shack airport in the Third World, I love watching the British Airways cabin crew marching through the dusty terminal as though they were all VIPs, carrying the *"Family Jewels"*, or senior government officials coming out to visit the former colony. I am sure these people were once normal. That was until they walked into BA's superior 'trolley dolly' school. From day one, I am positive it was drummed in to them that all economy passengers are scum.

Over the years I have just accepted their snobby and arrogant behaviour as normal. Normal, that was, until the first time I flew business class with BA, and saw the difference in their attitude, facial expressions and postures. I was geared up for their appalling behaviour and I was shocked. The cabin crew in business class were the sweetest, most charming and helpful people imaginable. If one wanted a shoe cleaned they would have gladly licked it clean for you.

Whilst on board this flight I grew nervous that my BA 'dog shit treatment' theory was in danger of being proved wrong. And for two hours into the flight I was sure all previous BA flight attendants had been binned and this was the new crop. In the end I couldn't take the strain any longer, so I had to find out for myself. I slipped quietly and un-noticed into 'scum class' and had a wander about...

And guess what?

(Yes.)

You've guessed correctly.... *My theory was still intact!*

Rigid firm postures, upright backs, long snooty noses, scowling fuck-off glares on their faces and all displayed through painfully forced smiles. I went up and asked for a drink of water and one was thrust in my hand without a word, let alone a polite smile. I then wandered back down into business class feeling very happy. But the 'trolly dolly' who was designated to spoil me rotten on this flight had spotted me returning.

'Why did you go down there sir?'

Perfect! The mask had slipped and she couldn't cover it up. The 'down there' bit was said with a voice and facial expression as if I'd just gone for a walk across the council rubbish tip!

I said to the 'trolly dolly' that I just needed to stretch my legs. She then went and stretched her legs and brought me the champagne that I asked for. This was so I could quietly celebrate the fact that my British Airways 'dog shit treatment' theory was still firmly intact.

However, my worst flight was not a British Airways experience. It was with Kuwaiti Airlines, who are actually very good. I was on a backpacking trip to Sri Lanka, where I was going to meet up with a girlfriend who was doing a two-year VSO placement, giving physiotherapy to torture victims north of Trincomalee. And before I got there I had to travel real economy class on the second leg from Kuwait to Sri Lanka.

This 2 a.m. plane was full of piss-poor Sri Lankan workers from 'slave jobs' in Kuwait. (Some had not been home for three years.) And they had been sitting on the aircraft for over an hour while my London flight got in late. At forty-seven degrees Celsius, the temperature outside on the tarmac was a Hercules House, *"crisis morning"* type heat.

You do not want to know how hot it was inside the plane.

After the desert night-time heat had chased me on to the plane, the furnace hit me full on. The aircon system was malfunctioning and the whole plane stank without mercy. I seemed to be the only Westerner on this flight as this acrid smell savagely pulled me towards my seat at the back end of the plane. The passengers did not smell because they were unclean. They were very clean. It smelled because they were being cooked. For a Westerner, this particular body smell leaking out of their bodies while they were being slowly cooked was sheer hell. Even though they were really uncomfortable after sitting in this blasting hot tin box waiting for their flight for over an hour, not one of these decent people was complaining.

While I was beginning to support myself as I got to my oven-hot seat, I nearly collapsed when I saw who I had to sit next to: a seventy-year-old woman who must've been causing sixty per cent of the overall stink as she cooked in her seat. I collapsed on my seat and felt like I was choking as the plane's intense smell and heat attacked me.

Within a few minutes I was rescued by a flight attendant who clearly saw that I was being a complete pussy and asked if I would like to be seated up in first class. For a moment I thought I was hallucinating. I had trouble focusing as sweat dripped off my head and into my eyes. I soon realised that I was not, and the memory of her lovely smiling face has stayed with me ever since. And after dozens of flights since then and even more shocking bus and train journeys in the Third World, I can take anything. Anything that is, except a snotty nosed arrogant 'trolly dolly' from British Airways.

I share my BA theory with Nathan in the bar in the airport terminal. He says he's never really thought about it as he's only ever flown BA and thought the 'dog shit treatment' was normal with all airlines. So after we walk out of the bar he is fully trained up to spot their superior postures as they walk around the terminal feeling like VIPs. We then contrast this with the happy smiling faces of other airlines' cabin crews.

He learns very fast.

After Nathan buys the duty-free shop, we head off to the departure gate and we are the last ones to board the plane, which is full. I eyeball all the cabin crew and they seem their usual snooty selves. Nathan's got the window seat and looks pleased and I've got the aisle seat, which is where I prefer to sit anyway. At our seats, the guy in the middle gets up to let us in and the cabin crew takes Nathan's duty-free bag and squeezes it in somewhere up front (cargo hold).

Then we all sit down and it doesn't take long before the smell hits us both. The guy in a suit sitting between us stinks of raw, untreated BO. And just to make matters worse, he's just taken his jacket off, put it on his lap and extended his arms to read the *Daily Mail* which allows his smell to escape freely.

The sweaty stench of this overweight middle-aged British businessman makes me feel sick. (Young Nathan is already holding his sick bag.) This chap is also wearing a wedding ring and I hope his wife doesn't smell the same as him. I never would have thought that a middle-class *Daily Mail* reader would have BO, and seem unconcerned about it.

…But what is the right thing to do here? Have a word with the chap? What can I say? It is just not British to approach a fellow countryman or woman or someone from Cameroon or even Wales, and say, 'Excuse me old chap, but…er, there's no easy way to say this but, you, er… well you smell like fuck, old boy. Now please use some soap.'

(It is just not in our upbringing to be so rude and direct.)

During the flight I can't eat any of the food. (Nathan hasn't even had anything to drink from the free bar on the flight.) I look past the smell to see if Nathan's okay. He's got a night-time eye mask tied around his face, which is covering his nose and mouth. His eyes look tranced out from BO stink (and all the fags he's smoked today). But really there is no other option left open to me, so I decide to go and speak to the BA 'trolly dollies' and see if there's anything they can do.

I walk up to the back end of the plane where a couple of them are tidying up the catering trolleys. My scanners tell me that the initial reaction is good. I get a warm smile, not a matron-style glare down a snooty nose. I then tell them about the sweaty bastard sitting next to me who is reading every line in the *Daily Mail* letting the smell escape.

...And to my shock these two are very friendly. They offer their apologies, but say every other seat is full. Even in first class. But if I wanted I could keep them company and have a chat. Never on a BA flight has this happened before. Any other BA flight I've been on, the 'chief dolly' from 'scum class' would have got out her electronic cattle prod and prodded me all the way back down the aisle to my seat!

So over the next thirty minutes we have a good laugh as they confide in me that they'd smelt the BO smell as well when they were serving the food and drinks. However, they thought the smell was actually coming from me!

We have a really good chat and they agree with my perceptions regarding the pompus attitude of the BA cabin crews. They also tell me that other airlines' cabin crews spot this as well. It is also drummed into them during their training that from day one they are British Airways and are therefore a cut above all other airlines.

However, to ease my suffering, they pull out a large carrier bag and fill it with small bottles of wine, champagne, miniatures and a good few cans of beer. I am taken back by their humour and kindness. They say that they look forward to seeing me again and I just hope these two British Airways flight attendants will be on the return flight. We say goodbye as I head back down to 'stink alley'. I get back to my seat and see that the smelly bastard has fallen asleep and poor Nathan has fainted.

Both of them wake up as the plane's wheels hit the tarmac. The plane comes to a standstill and everyone gets their bags from the overhead lockers. Other passangers are looking discreetly around, painfully aware that there is one awful smell on the loose and it is coming from somewhere. Everyone is unsure whom it really belongs to. I just avoid eye contact and keep my head up, looking straight ahead.

Outside the terminal after several nose and lung fulls of fresh air, Nathan lights up and slowly begins to speak. The smell has left him traumatised and only a few drinks and a packet of Marlboro Lights will cure him.

'Well done on blagging that booze,' he says, slowly shaking away as a taxi driver comes forward and grabs us.

'Cheers, we'll split it both ways and bring it back to the UK. Why start to down it when we've got a free hotel mini-bar?' I say, as I lift the bag up with both hands and place it in the boot of the taxi.

'Sorted! That was the worst flight I've ever fucking had, it was unreal having to sit next to that smelly git,' says Nathan, looking out of the window at the city.

'What pissed me off was the fact he was reading the *Daily Mail* and had his arms outstretched, allowing the smell of his armpits to escape with ease.'

'Yeah, maybe we should email the editor and get the paper to give out free bars of soap.'

'It's an idea, but that bloke would probably eat the bar of soap!'

After driving through this beautiful city, with its magnificent architecture (Madonna's *Evita* was filmed here), we arrive at our hotel. It is the same hotel where the conference is, which is good for a lie-in. Registration is at 9 a.m. and a talk on Internet backbone connectivity/peering is at 10 a.m.. This is one of two things I am really meant to see on this visit, as it's one of the only seminars I'll remotely understand at RIPE 36.

This RIPE (Reseaux IP Europeans of Amsterdam) Internet conference has a simple charter, the essence of which is to promote continuity and standards among European Internet networks. The RIPE conference takes place twice yearly at different European locations and is a venue to discuss IP technical issues, develop contacts and maintain relationships.

My room looks large and comfortable. Nathan's room is a bit further down the corridor. He lobs his gear in and we both head down to the hotel restaurant and bar for a much-needed drink.

The next morning when I awake from a very deep and blissful sleep, morning has well and truly broken. In fact it has almost been and gone. The hotel radio clock says it's 10:49 a.m. *Shit!* What a great start. I heard a kick on the door and that's what woke me. A few minutes later I stumble out of bed and into the power shower. The tiredness is soon water-blasted out of me.

As I head straight for the restaurant to get some breakfast, I see that it is closed. Nathan is already down here and is trying to blag some food and they're having none of it, so there's only one option left for us both as we grab a taxi and go to the nearest McDonald's in downtown Budapest.

The Big Macs arrive and we take them outside in to the hot sun and kick back, having a laugh at what useless tossers we are for sleeping in and missing the first talk. However, registration goes on all day and thankfully the next conference talk is not until 2 p.m.

We get back and register and I see the list and one name stands out. Or rather it holds my attention while I stare at it a few times just to be sure I'm not mistaken. But the name is also on Nathan's sheet. It is Lucia from USAT2. I check my Palm Pilot and thankfully I've got her mobile number stored in it. I programme her mobile number in to my phone and go to reception to find out if she's checked in, and what her room number is. It turns out she is only two floors above mine and she's not checked in yet. Then I momentarily shudder as I also notice some techie seminars that Nathan might have to attend...

'Windows NT/2000 Architecture (DP-770)', 'Introduction to Digital Communications (EA-190)', 'MP-119 Introduction to UNIX', 'MP-219 UNIX Text Processing', 'Datalink Protocols (TD-10V)', 'Modulation (EA-046)' and 'Information Formatting (EA-042)' classes. I shake my head and wonder if this is what techie heaven is really like!

I look around to see where he is in order to offer him some sympathy, and I see that he's gone outside the hotel on a blagging spree with a few of the other delegates. I put the class sheet in my pocket, go out and start to 'network' as well.

In no time at all I meet the people I was hoping to meet. The peering lady from Level 3 kindly takes me under her wing and introduces me around. Very quickly I learn that the top people from the Internet world are here. Not the CEO's and boardroom suits, but the people who actually designed and built it to what it is today. These people are the ones who keep the traffic flowing over the Internet and connect their Internet backbones with other backbones. This helps to make the networks carrying our Internet traffic much more efficient.

We learn that there is a hierarchy among the world's leading Internet technical gurus. They are all American and they all work for America's top Internet and telecoms companies. At the very top of this hierarchy is an elite group. They were present in the Internet when I was buying the first album by *The Stone Roses* (and some have been in it long before that). They are still at the top and exert a major influence in this small community and they command respect and loyalty from all other players.

This group meets up privately in Denver and they are the highest tier of the Internet technical wizards that run and manage the Internet traffic for the big US commercial Internet backbones. And nearly all of them have a high-level security clearance with the US Department of Defense and are familiar with the secret TCP/IP architecture and future KG-175 and KG-75 encryption devices for the Pentagon/CIA's highly classified *Secret Internet Protocol Router Network* or SIPRNET.

["...SIPRNET also enables the White House, the NSA, CIA, FBI and FEMA to access the Pentagon's highly sensitive Global Command and Control System 24/7."]

The downside of this visit is that nobody has really heard of iaxis. It would be different if this were a bandwidth/telecoms conference. We'd be the talk of the show, as we are very well known in the telecoms world. But in the Internet world we are still very much an unknown quantity. This is not that surprising since Psycho and Seamus ran the iaxis Internet marketing blag campaign on a 'need-to-know basis'! (In total fairness to them, the iaxis Dodgers wouldn't give them any 'fookin' money, because they didn't have any to give.)

After this social gathering it is time to go to the afternoon seminars on 'Computer-to-Computer Communications (NE-149)' and 'Communications Security (ND-112)' to see for myself what this techie stuff is all about. This is why Nathan is here. He just absorbs it all and can understand the many complex techie issues with ease. I have seen his maths and physics awards from Cambridge University and they are seriously impressive. Almost as good as some of the '*Z Group Peer*' and '*Star Awards*' that some delegates here have got from their past careers.

As soon as this talk kicks off, I quickly see that it is far too technical, and it goes way over my head. However, Nathan is very interested and sits nodding away and taking notes. Both of us are sitting towards the back, very close to the exit door, and I last fifteen minutes into the two-hour talk. I am able to slope off without drawing any attention to myself. I could learn and understand nuclear rocket science faster than I can absorb this techie fest!

I go up to my room and change into something more appropriate: my polo beach shorts, *MaxSix* sunhat and freebie *SuperNet 2000* T-shirt (so I can blend in). I also grab a towel and some factor four suncream, my Armani shades and mobile phone. Now I'm ready to go to work, by the hotel pool for the rest of the afternoon.

Outside the heat must be in the ninties. I get an ice-cold beer, which I put on my room tab, and wander over to the sun terrace. A sunchair seems to have my name on it and I sit down on it and start punching in the quick dial numbers on my mobile. After several tries I get through to Old Boy.

'It's hot out here, Old Boy, almost like your ears!' I say, as I'm taking a sip on my beer.

'Good! It's Pimm's on the blaady lawn time over here as well mate!'

'I bet it is! So how's the puppy?'

'It's good. My wife loves it.'

'Excellent! Has she stopped shouting at you?'

'No she blaady well hasn't… *She wants me to leave iaxis!*'

'*No!!* You can't leave Old Boy. *Don't do it!*'

'Don't worry Steve, I've told her that there is no fucking chance I'm leaving this place!'

'Good to hear that mate,' I say, as the cold beer is quenching my thirst after that awful fright.

'She reckons you lot are a bad influence on me.'

'Well she's not wrong there then is she!'

'Too blaady right she's not!'

Old Boy was trying to remember something to say to me, but his right ear has a high-pitched ringing sound in it! (Poor bugger.)

I make a few more calls, but all the phone lines seem busy. I am just about to give up and then I finally get through to Howard.

'Howard! How's life with the new 'Internet baby'?'

'*Steve!* You are being talked about here, boy!' he says, laughing away trying his very best to make me feel concerned.

'Yes, well I've just been talking about you too and the need-to-know iaxis Internet marketing campaign. Nobody has heard of us in the Internet world and we've got the "Who's Who" out here. It also looks like we're going to have to re-look at the prices we are trying to flog the capacity for. Could you have a word with Hannah about this?'

'Piss off Steve! She might come and sit on my desk! I'll send her an email from Seamus's PC later on when he's out,' he says, as he's laughing at someone in the background. There is a lot of noise.

'So Howard, what's the goss? Who's going to buy us?'

...Being a senior director, Howard is well informed, but even he has trouble finding his way through all the smoke and mirrors that are now in place around the glass walls. They've always been in place. But now there's loads more smoke and even more mirrors...

'Well Teleglobe, Equant and Computel are all in the frame,' he says, trying to hold his laugh in. He's laughing at something or someone else again.

'Howard, what's going on in there?' I ask, as Howard laughs out loud.

'Steve, Sasha just loved the large bouquet of flowers you sent her!'

I feel my heart stop dead.

'What fucking flowers from me?' I shout out in shock.

(I have just been eyeballed by all the other sun worshippers for breaking the peace.)

'The ones that arrived on her desk this morning, you dickhead!'

'Howard, they're not from me. I didn't send her any flowers,' I say, as I swallow hard.

'Well Steve, everyone thinks they're from you. After all, you took her out for lunch and asked her out!' says Howard, laughing.

'But Howard...'

'Steve, she loves them! She's gone and placed them in a huge bowl on top of her desk and they are so big they engulf her. Not even Kong can see her from his desk. All he can see when he looks over at her is a flower shop that you've sent her!'

'Oh no! What's he saying?'

'He's in shock. He was just walking about looking stunned and he now thinks you're having a laugh at him. He had to leave the office just to calm down and was gone for two hours!'

'No!'

'Oh yes. And also, when Kong is in people's earshot, everyone suddenly starts speaking about you and Sasha and the fact you are now seeing each other!'

'We're not seeing each other. We're just good friends.'

'Steve, look mate, if that hotel's got a gym in it get down there fast and start doing some weights and push-ups. Also if there's a crash course in Jujitsu, then go and do that a few times as well, coz fucking hell is he pissed off with you!'

'I didn't send her them! I thought he was seeing Charlotte now,' I say, as fear starts to take a grip.

'Don't be silly, Steve. Sasha whispered into his ear and he just dropped Charlotte. But now it all fits. You think his eyes are off the ball with Charlotte, so you steam in and take Sasha out for an Italian lunch. You try and get her tipsy with a bottle of Chianti and then ask her out. She plays hard to get, so you send her a fucking flower shop!'

'*No!* It wasn't like that and I didn't send her flowers. *I've been framed!*' I say, as a cold bottle of beer arrives.

'Steve, save your energy boy; Gibbsy's running a book and it's not looking pleasant for you. But I've got some good money on you at 75 to 1. So get down to that gym right now!'

'Shit! 75 to 1 on what? Me smacking him and him going down?' I ask, feeling nervous.

'No you dickhead! 75 to 1 on you still having a fucking heartbeat this time next week!'

Howard clicks off in mid-laugh.

'Shit.'

After a few minutes of trying I finally get through to Wacko.

'Wacko! What's this about some flowers on Sasha's desk?'

'What, the ones you sent her?'

'Wacko, I didn't send her any flowers,' I gasp. (Shit. I was secretly hoping Howard was just winding me up.)

'Yeah, well the whole office thinks it's you.'

'Shave off! What's Kong saying?' I ask, as I now feel light-headed as the sunrays continue to give me a good blast.

'Well he's pissed off with you. I saw him down the gym at lunchtime looking well angry as he attacked the weights. I've never seen him lift so much! But anyway, I've got to go because I'm seeing the CEO (*'chief entertainment officer'*). It didn't go well at Gas Line, but Teleglobe want to buy us and there are loads of meetings next week,' says Wacko, as he hangs up and bolts.

This is all I need. Sasha would love a big drama if Kong chinned me. The only trouble is I might not get up again! I pack up my gear and go to my laptop. I log on and send Sasha an email, kindly telling her that the flowers, despite popular opinion, are not from me. My sense of humour starts to come back, when I think that I really would've paid money to see Kong's face when they were delivered to her desk!

I walk back to the sun terrace and Nathan is there. I tell him about Sasha's flowers, Kong and my slim odds for survival next week. He of course can't stop laughing as he picks up the phone to place his bet.

'Steve, let's go and see a sex show tonight, eh? There's loads of sex clubs downtown,' says Nathan, reading the glossy hotel guide on Budapest.

'Okay. We'll go to an expensive restaurant first for a meal and then we'll take a look.'

'Sorted.'

After our evening feast, we set off to one of the addresses in the glossy rag (which Nathan ripped the page out of). He's briefed that we are just there to watch and not to pull. He's got a long-term girlfriend, so I know he won't be looking at catching a rash in a place like this.

We go to the club with the best women in the advert. Right away I don't like the place; there are too many heavies in black leather jackets working on the door. As soon as we walk in, we see that the girls are beautiful. But the local 'nuttin squad' is standing about keeping a very close eye on things. You wouldn't want to cause trouble in here.

I tell Nathan to grab a couple of seats while I go to the bar and get the drinks in. After buying what seems to be two of the most expensive bottles of beer in Europe, I head back towards the comfy-looking sofas trying to find Nathan. But I can't see him anywhere. I look around to the 'romper stage' and I see that he's sitting on his own right at the front, close as possible to where all the action will shortly be taking place. He's just sitting there waiting for the lesbian strap-on lesson to start. I pull him away from the front of the class and we sit on the sofas. The local girls soon sit down and join us and try and tempt our Visa cards.

The action starts to heat up on the stage, but the girls sitting with us are not as cool and easy going as the ones in "The Dam". Here, if you say no a couple of times, they just get up and leave. Which is no fun at all really.

After Nathan buys a round we leave to get some cheaper booze.

There are a few other normal bars further down the road, which we walk towards, and the bar we land in is only ten minutes' walk from the hotel, which is good if we get tanked up in here. As soon as we walk in, Nathan recognises two girls from the conference talk he attended this afternoon. After we get served, we wander up and introduce ourselves. They both work for a small Dutch Internet company. The dark-haired one is beautiful and looks expensive. Her name is Anna and she's also got an engagement ring on her finger with a large stone from Namibia right in the centre of it. She casually rubs her eye with her left hand, giving me a closer look, telling me all I need to know as I feel my fin sinking slowly back down into the centre of my head.

(Nathan and I keep quiet about the sex club we've just visited. We wouldn't want them both to get the wrong impression and think we were a couple of perverts.)

It turns out Anna is an account manager and, like me, has only been in the Internet industry for a few months and finds the techie stuff hard going. Her job must pay well as I recognise her Hermès silk neckscarf. It is very expensive and so is her watch.

Before long a good few other delegates arrive and a drinking session begins. I go quite easy, as tomorrow morning there's a lecture from one of the world's leading Internet peering gurus. This is one conference talk I must attend. The peering manager from Level 3 has just bought a large jug of beer and a glass appears in my hand as I feel my phone vibrating in my shirt pocket.

(Never put a mobile phone in your trouser pocket. The microwaves from the antenna are still in the thing even when it's switched off. And these don't do one's testicles any good at all. Not that a mobile phone company will ever tell you this.)

I look at the LCD and my face smiles as I see Lucia's name. She's just checked in and seen my name on the registration papers. I have to ask the barman the name of the pub and what street we're on. I tell her I'm with Nathan and that she'll find us standing next to the fag machine. She says she'll be along very shortly and clicks off.

Right now the two Dutch girls are drinking the beer as the jugs are being passed around and a little drinking session begins. Although I say it is a drinking session, it is very tame compared to an iaxis bender: there are no girls having tequila licked off their bodies, nor is anyone flashing their boobs about. There's no hardcore crew to disappear down to the toilets to get topped up on Mr Nice's latest 'shipment'. And that's just after work on any day of the week!

I am standing at the fag machine with Nathan. Or rather, he is kicking the thing because this time it has decided to keep his money and is refusing to give him any more fags. A few moments later, Lucia walks up to me just as Nathan runs to the bar to demand some fags. He nearly knocks her over as he bolts past her! I just knew who she was as soon as I saw her walking up to me. With her shoulder-length blonde hair and tanned healthy face, she certainly looks like she's from California.

She is beautiful.

'Hi Steve,' she says, as she smiles at me warmly.

'Hi Lucia,' I say, as we shake hands.

Lucia looks about thirty-three years old and is an older version of Sasha. I've never been to California, but I suddenly have an urge to go there. In these few moments after we meet, her eyes don't leave mine for a second.

'I thought you were Steve; you looked like you were looking around for someone. I was watching you while your friend wasn't happy with the smoke machine.' she says, as she looks over towards the bar.

I never spotted her until she was five feet away and walking towards me. (Nathan was busy trying to lift up the fag machine and drop it down again. And I was too busy looking out for the 'fookin nuttin squad' coming over to 'nut' him!)

'It's good to see you as well, Lucia. I hope Bosco is being well looked after while you're away,' I say, as I notice that all the jogging she does with Bosco along that Californian beach has kept her looking incredibly fit.

Her eyes and face break out into a warm radiant smile. 'I can't believe you remembered Bosco's name! He's staying with my next-door neighbours,' she says, now looking very pleased at my retained memory skills. (It's not hard to remember her dog's name as I have it taunted at me every day by the other 'mad fookers' I sit with.)

'Well, I have visions that your dog is chasing me through a forest!' I say, as I can just picture young Bosco staying with her neighbours and terrifying the fucking life out of them.

She laughs at my English humour, completely convinced that her dog would never do such a thing. But she has sharp and very intelligent eyes and I try and visualise what she'd have looked like when she was twenty-one years old.

I see that Lucia is also mentally scanning me up and down, so I try like hell to act cooler than Beckham as he takes a dead ball free kick at thirty-five yards.

The vibe is very good as we have a little eyelock. Her scan results are analysed and I've passed. I don't exactly know what I've passed, but she takes my arm as we go to the bar.

Beckham scores against Sunderland!

Lucia has just flown in from Prague and could do with a glass of wine. I order a vodka and Red Bull. She then changes her mind from the wine and orders a vodka and Red Bull as well. At the bar I can clearly see for the first time that there is no wedding ring on Lucia's finger. But like a true American corporate, Lucia gets stuck right in to business. She has seen the list of telecoms and Internet companies that the iaxis Internet backbone is now connected up to, and the company she works for is very keen to proceed. This is a straightforward swap, so no money will change hands. However, we will at least show traffic on our backbone. We will also have direct access to their entire Internet connectivity/peering partners in the USA and this is great for marketing blag and the overall efficiency of the iaxis Internet backbone.

My management (Wacko and his vice president), want me to call them 'ASAP', to bring them up to speed on our potential Internet capacity swap deal, so I'll call Wacko tomorrow morning.

Lucia also informs me that their Big Cat corporate lawyers are going to be drafting up the contract and it should be ready for us next week. However, I have to tell her that we'll get back to her when we can. The next few weeks could be "hectic" as iaxis is going through a "very challenging" time...

The chief entertainment officer has sent our Big Cats away 'touring' for a couple of weeks. They have a few meetings (shows) with some very important creditors. The Big Cats have got to go along and put on a display and hopefully win them back over. Wacko (whose department spent all the money building the network) will be there cracking the whip over them and telling them to stand on their heads! The chief fire officer will also be there, on standby (Red Alert) just in case a big fire-eating stunt by one of his young Dodgers goes tragically wrong... In the past, these performances have been so spectacular that Suzie is now taking advance bookings. And for next week's shows, the Ciena board have asked if they can bring all their kids along!

Not that I tell Lucia any of this.

It turns out Lucia knows quite a few of the big players here as well, as she's been in the Internet since the early nineties. And although I am very new to this Internet crowd, a few people here have actually heard of my name from all my Internet backbone connectivity/peering requests that I've been blasting out. (If I don't get a response within, say, four days, I'd send another. And then another... Eventually they'd crack and connect with iaxis for an easy life.)

So far this evening, after I've introduced myself, the reply is usually 'iaxis huh? So what do you guys do?' Or if they have heard of us the reply is often 'Ah yeah! I remember you. You're that guy that used to keep sending me all those goddamn peering requests! So what's happened with this big ISP customer who was going to buy a huge amount of Internet capacity on your backbone?'

'Well, it's now in their hands and it's gone to their board for approval.'

'Shit! That must be a big one buddy. Here, let me buy you a drink.'

'Cheers!'

Later on, as we're relaxing in the hotel bar, I confide in Lucia about my lack of knowledge in the industry and how I chose her company for an Internet capacity swap. At least she's got a sense of humour as she finds it hilarious that I just phoned her up after a random search. If I made a phone call on Lucia's name, I would have used a very different approach. I might not have even phoned her at all. But I certainly would not have phoned her at 5:30 a.m. and started speaking about her dog! Hopefully we'll get the contract sorted out soon and then the swap can be done in the coming weeks. This swap could save us over three hundred thousand dollars on our North American business plan.

But then again, Psycho was throwing knives in the dark when he hit on those figures!

However, I am under no *illusion* that I got very lucky and I am even making her laugh, despite being on my best behaviour. For professional reasons, I have to make a good impression on this lady as this swap is important to us. But that's not to say my imagination isn't overheating while we have several long eyelocks and a few smiles throughout the evening.

At 1:30 a.m. we say goodnight in the hotel lift and she even gives me peck on the cheek. Nathan has drunk so much beer with those two Dutch girls he now thinks we're in Prague as he staggers off to his room!

I set my alarm for 9:15 a.m. ready for the peering talk at 10:00 a.m. After a hot shower, I drift off into a deep sleep thinking about Lucia, white sandy beaches and *wolves*.

As I wake up, I realise that it is a good job I set the alarm for this morning, as I would've slept right through the morning and would've probably missed lunch as well. My head feels like Kong has been playing basketball with it. (Which I think I did dream about.) But a good blast of water soon brings me back to my senses. There are no clouds in the sky and the sunshine is going to be on full volume all day long.

After some breakfast I walk over to the conference hall and get there just in time for the talk. And I see everyone's coming out. And nobody is waiting to go in. The peering lady from Level 3 sees the confused look on my face as I try to figure out what is going on and she kindly helps me out.

'Steve, the talk started at 9 a.m.'

(*'Do'h!!'*)

I see that Nathan missed it as well as I catch a glimpse of him staggering towards the restaurant. I am told that there's a printout of the technical issues that were discussed in this seminar, so I rush down to the front and grab a couple of copies. It's about thirty pages thick and looks "very complex and challenging" ["...absolutely terrifying"]. Nathan can go through it with me when we get back to London.

'Hi Steve! Did you sleep in?' a familiar-sounding voice asks as I turn around and see Lucia standing behind me, smiling warmly and looking remarkably fresh this morning.

'Yes, I'm afraid so. I set my alarm for the wrong time.'

'I thought so. I was looking out for you, but I couldn't see you. What are you doing this afternoon?' she asks, looking over to some people who seem to be waiting for her.

(I am going to lounge about outside in the sun, have a swim in the pool and drink some cold beers all day on expenses. But then again, I don't want to tell her this as she may think that I can be a bit of a slacker from time to time!)

'Well...er, I've got my laptop and I was going to write a report on the Internet community and wade through all my Internet peering emails,' I say convincingly, as I remember that there's probably an email from Kong in my Inbox, with a coded death threat telling me that 'you are fucking dead now boy!'

'Steve, you can do your report and peering work this morning. Let's sit up by the pool, say 2 p.m. and have a couple of drinks,' she asks, touching my arm, not really expecting me to say no.

'Er... yes. That would be great,' I say while I struggle to contain my big smile.

I am also thinking just how sad it is that Nathan has got to go to a couple of seminars on 'C Programming Language (MP-220)' and 'SUN Usage (MP-109)' this afternoon.

'Excellent, I've only got a couple of hours spare and then a conference call with my New York office. So I'll see you at 2 p.m. by the sun terrace.'

'Look forward to it. See you later,' I say, as she walks off with some of the players.

In the restaurant, I tell Nathan that I'll meet him on the sun terrace at 10:30 a.m. He looks shredded, so I go and fetch him a two-litre bottle of water, which he soon finishes. His body is back in Budapest this morning.

Back in my room I log on and check my emails. The Inbox is full of death threats from Howard, Wacko, Old Boy, Seamus and Gibbsy. Thankfully both McGowan and Merlock are offering me their "close protection" services. But at five hundred pounds a day (each), this isn't cheap.

There are no messages from Kong.

While I am online, an email arrives from Sasha and I hit that one immediately. She tells me that last night she found out one of her other friends had sent her the flowers. And she has now put the word around to everyone. I let out a huge sigh of relief as all bets are off, and that's me off death row. I also hear that Kong and Charlotte have taken the day off work…

Relaxing by the pool, I call Wacko who's pleased to hear that the planned Internet capacity swap with Lucia is still on course and looks likely to go through. However, next week's meetings are going to be more severe than we thought. Wacko thinks that Gas Line could close down the German part of the network after his meeting with them in their boardroom (the Cooler). But this 'Cooler', he assures me, was hotter than hell after they turned the 'flame-throwers' onto them all. They apparently didn't like the numbers stunt detailing how little we would like to pay them and then putting it off for as long as possible.

The meetings with Ciena and the rest of our creditors are all now going to have to be more expertly planned if we're going to keep them onside and delay payments for as long as possible, until we find a buyer for iaxis. The stakes are now very, very high indeed. If the team fails, it is curtains for iaxis.

Nathan wanders up and slaps some factor thirty-three sunblast protector on himself. I tell him about Wacko's 'flame-thrower treatment' at the hands of Gas Line and how severe things are looking with all the planned meetings that are going down next week. I also tell him the latest news on Sasha's flowers…

He reckons she sent them to herself just to piss off Kong. (I'll give her the benefit of the doubt. She's far too sweet to engage in office PSYOPS and do that.)

After finishing a three-course lunch, Lucia meets me on the sun terrace and we chill out with a couple of gin and tonics and catch some sunrays. This is a great way to wind down and beats sitting in an office in central London, even if we are talking politics. But Lucia sitting by the pool really does look fantastic.

It turns out we are both well up to speed on our world politics. Only she is far more informed than I am and has a very *interesting* background. She did her degree in politics at an Ivy League university. More importantly, she did her Internship with *Voice of America's* 'Radio Free Asia'. These simple few words gain her my overwhelming attention, and for once I find her mind even more interesting than her body.

I ask her a few very informed questions on China and *"democracy"* ["...the free trade of microchips, credit cards and Coca-Cola..."] in the run up to the end of the "Cold War". Thankfully, she is also relaxed and chilled out enough to share a few thoughts and basically confirms what I already knew from my own well-informed *"friends"* from various places here and there...

In December 1988, Dr Henry Kissinger ["...when he was also a member of President George Bush Sr's Foreign Intelligence Advisory Board"] of Kissinger Associates Inc, set up China Ventures with an office in Beijing. The sole aim of "the enterprise" was to promote the business interests of American multinationals, including [*"his* life-long mentor David Rockefeller's Chase Manhattan Bank"] the Coca-Cola and American Express corporations, with the Chinese Government in the years *after* 1989 [*"...*when David Rockefeller was also Chairman of the **Trilateral Commission** "].

In the first six months of 1989, the student protests for "Democracy in China" just took off ["... and so did the 'mechanics' of other planned covert activities"]. In 1989 the Voice of America (VoA) was part of the US Information Agency. It is now part of the U.S. State Department. However, during the years of the "Cold War" and in particular towards the end, it also "serviced" other US government agencies as part of an information warfare (IW) tool. At the time of the Tiananmen Square student uprising against the Chinese Communist government, the Chinese infrastructure of VoA/Radio Free Asia was used as a "vehicle" for America's covert activites and PSYOPS warfare throughout mainland China.

In May 1989 thousands of fax machines all over China suddenly started to receive "Democracy updates" from "nowhere". They all received them at the same time across China ["...the 67th Intelligence Wing of the NSA are currently home to the leading information warfare experts in the 'free world'..."]. Also, in the same month, the VoA's radio programming in Mandarin was "ramped up" to eleven hours a day and had over three hundred and seventy million listeners. Then at the start of June 1989, over two thousand Chinese satellite dishes, including all the Chinese military installations, mysteriously started to receive Voice of America's first TV news broadcasts...

While VoA broadcasts were going live in China, on the ground in Peking, Shanghai and other cities were teams of "unknown persons" from a Hong Kong-based "news agency". This *"shadow"* news agency was actually incorporated in Panama and was funded through Austrian Sparbuch bank accounts. The operators on the ground were acting as "frequency management units" tasked with coordinating and managing the Chinese "freelancers" who were leading the peaceful operation.

The "frequency management units" ["...or Tactical Covert Units..."] were also involved in distributing printers, fax machines and other communication devices to the Chinese "freelancers". This featureless equipment was made and assembled in a huge factory in a European country and was shipped through third-party countries. It finally ended up at the harbour in Shanghai in early 1989 ["...when David Rockefeller was now the Honorary Chairman of the Board at the **Council on Foreign Relations**"].

In Peking, the forward operations base for the operation was a basement in a downtown hotel and the command and control centre was situated in a numbers station in Hong Kong. This covert facility was used for the sending of signals to co-ordinate the operators deep inside Communist China. They survived by handsets designed and manufactured by a *"Company"* with a large office in Reston, Virginia.

["...All was going to plan for the envisaged 'New World Order' the following decade. However, a few days before the massacre, the Cryptographic Liaison/Operations Unit (N9), operating under the Naval Security Group at the National Security Agency's Misawa Cryptologic Operations Centre in Japan, picked up and decoded some valuable PLA radio transmissions. The SIGINT was the full orders and timing for the use of lethal military force to end the students' peaceful democracy demonstrations throughout Mainland China. For this 'technical achievement', N9 was awarded the NSA's 'Travis Trophy for Cryptologic Excellence', the top prize for those personnel who 'Serve in Silence'."]

Within a few hours of the SCI ["Secret Compartmentalised Information..."] being received in Fort Meade and the *Product* being delivered to *"The Consumers"* in Washington, a KG-encrypted signal was sent from the numbers station in Hong Kong ordering the "frequency management units" to abort and pull out. Some operators in Peking just vanished into the regular news media camp as "technicians", while others flew out as tourists with their "partners". Most Chinese "freelancers" had a good head start for the 'exfil' out of China. The editorial offices of *China Perspective*, which published the *Chinese Intellectual* were moved quickly and quietly back to its origins in New York City. And certain officials from the 'Fund for the Reform of China' ["...which was established and funded by Mr George Soros in

1986 and had received nearly three million dollars in funds by 1989,"] kept a very low profile.

Sadly, on June 4th 1989, the armoured personnel carriers from the PLA's 27th Army Group moved in and opened fire on the unarmed and peaceful students and massacred them.

["…Their dead bodies were later incinerated along with their twisted bicycles, and the Foreign Denial and Deception Committee (FDDC) at Langley went into full spin…"]

The 'exfil' plan for the "freelancers" was either overland to Hong Kong, or to Shanghai, where a cargo ship would take them out of China. The vessel was owned by a "*Company*" with a regional office in Taiwan and was under a bareboat charter to a freight forwarding "*Company*", which was based in Hong Kong ["incorporated in Panama…"]. "*The Company*" was secretly funded through Austrian Sparbuch bank accounts to support its "*activities*" in the region.

The brave ones who "missed the boat" were shot dead. A token few were used for public show trials and then sent to prison for some "re-education" that would take years to teach. The lucky ones who made it to the boat found a new life in Taiwan or Hong Kong, or they went back to their universities in the USA. Their familes, who were left behind and who were not protected by "ring fencing" supplied from third-party governments, are also dead.

["…Henry Kissinger's China Ventures was later 'dissolved'. The corporations of 'America Inc' saw that 'the enterprise' was not going to be as successful as it was originally envisaged. And so after a relaxing evening dinner with George Bush Sr, James Baker III, General Brent Scowcroft and Dick Cheney to discuss these 'events', Dr Henry Kissinger felt it would be honourable to pay the American corporations their deposits made to his China Ventures back in full. And in the future China would have to be handled very differently by the Council on Foreign Relations and the 'chairman of the board' of '**America Inc**'."]

The boat later *vanished*. (And I might write a second book.)

Lucia also tells me that she is missing her dog. The neigbours have sent her an email saying Bosco can't stop howling. She shares this with me as I rub some sun cream on to her shoulders and back and order two more gin and tonics, feeling quite pleased that she's not missing anybody else.

I am also told that there is a career for me within USAT2, the Internet company she works for, and I'd be based in California. She says she likes the way I think, which I find rather surprising, because I haven't shared any of my real thoughts with her.

In the evening is the formal dinner of RIPE 36. I check the seating plan and I'm not sitting next to Lucia or Nathan. I get to my table and there's a sweet-looking familiar face on it. It's Anna, whom we met last night. The only trouble is that my name-tag is at the other side of the round table. Or it is until I casually switch it around, so I am now sitting next to her. At least this tickled her sense of humour.

During the meal Anna tells me that she's looking forward to going back to Amsterdam tomorrow as she's missing her husband-to-be. I try my best to put a smile on her face, as I tell her how wonderful she looks in her Prada evening outfit. Some other giveaways to a woman of wealth are the Boucheron gold watch and jewellery from Chopard. They could be fakes, but her natural grace and elegance implies otherwise. (And Nathan found out that her family owned a publishing house.)

I know I don't stand a chance with Anna, but Lucia, who is on another table and in perfect eyeshot of us both, doesn't know this. Nor do the passing waiters: as far as they're concerned, the lovely Anna and I make a really good couple. But my will-power is stretched to the limit not to look up and meet those very frequent glances I can feel coming my way from two tables across to my left.

I pour Anna a glass of Chateau Cantemerle 1996 and she of course doesn't believe me as I tell her, yet again, just how stunning she looks. The wine is well chosen and the meal is superb. Just as the dessert is about to be served I can feel my ears burning.

'So where are you going for your break next week?' I ask Anna, just as the strawberries and cream arrive.

'Well, we are both going to my family's chalet in Davos, Switzerland for a week's walking in the Alps. It's lovely to do some walking this time of year,' she says, as I remember I am going mountain biking with Wacko around Taplow this weekend.

'Davos! Do your folks live there?' I ask, showing lots of interest.

'Yes, and also in Monaco and Spain. I don't see them very often and I don't really get on with them. I'll see them once a year if that,' she says, as her mood turns a bit low.

'Why, what have you done to them? You seem perfect. You haven't gone on a spending spree with your father's pension cash pot have you?' I ask, trying to humour the truth out of her.

Anna forces a little smile, but there is something written on her face and behind her dark eyes that obviously troubles her. And my posture drops as I think I've now upset her.

(Shit!)

She finishes her last strawberry and I notice just how slender her arms are as she takes a sip of her black coffee.

'It's the family business. I detest it,' she says, calmly as she looks me in the eye while I focus on her sweet face.

I look perplexed and she picks up on this immediately.

'None of my colleagues knows about my family. But I'm so ashamed,' she continues, as her eyes do an intense scan of my face, eyes and character. She looks at my sympathetic expression, while inside I'm so pleased it's not me that's made her upset. I can suddenly feel more glances on me as Anna and I now look quite intimate. Anna glances around the room and decides to take me into her confidence and share what's on her mind with me.

'My family owns and runs one of the biggest pornography empires in Europe.'

I somehow stay calm, while inside I want to jump up and shout, 'Hey Nathan, fucking hell!! Get over here and listen to this mate!'

'Pornography empire?' I ask quietly, as a large dark cloud of black smoke continues to pour out from my ears.

'Yes,' she says, still watching my reaction for any signs of utter disgust at her family.

'Is it profitable?' I ask, trying really hard not to show any signs of enthusiasm.

She laughs slightly. 'Yes, it is very profitable. The business has profits of tens of millions of dollars every year. And after my parents retired three years ago, they gave me twenty per cent joint ownership of the company.'

There is no way I can cover it up as I use a napkin to quickly wipe away a thin bead of sweat that made a dash for it and escaped out of my forehead! 'All that from magazines?' I ask, as my throat goes dry and I mentally try and work out how much Anna is worth.

'Yes, but that's only a small part of the company now. Most of the revenue comes from film production, websites, voice calls, books and a few shops. But they are looking at putting the whole thing online. They already have several websites, but they want to put live feeds online so people can see live sex shows from Amsterdam, while they're at their PCs in, say, Tampa, Florida.'

'Did you say looking to move online?' I ask quickly, as I take a mouthful of black coffee and sober up in just under two seconds.

She looks around herself very carefully. 'My family have been on to me to get my company involved, but I've told them not to contact me about it.'

I try and hide my natural entrepreneurial streak, but it just slips out.

'Look Anna, I'm sure iaxis will help them out. We've been very discreet with our Internet marketing. Nobody knows us in the Internet world. But we've got one of the best European Internet backbones and we could fill it with live feeds and high resolution images.'

She considers this for a short while. 'Okay. I'll give you my brother in-law's contact details. He's their Chief Commercial and Technical Director. My sister now runs the company.

'Yes, that would be great. We'll make a direct approach with your introduction.'

She takes out her business card from her small matching Prada bag and discreetly gives it to me. I take it from her and slip it into my pocket. I laugh slightly at her moral stance. Although she hates the family firm, she loves spending their money. Absolute quality.

'You'll have to move quite quickly, I think they are already negotiating with Concert and UUNet for web-hosting and Internet transit capacity,' she says, as she sees me drawing the mental revenue curve in my head.

'How much capacity are they looking at taking?'

'An STM-4.'

'Shit!' I say, as my revenue curve hits the fucking ceiling. (This is a monster size of Internet transit capacity with millions of dollars in revenue for iaxis.)

'Can I speak with him over the weekend?'

She looks at her watch.

'No, he's in Moscow until Sunday evening. They're looking for new stars,' she says, with a sad and sorrowful look of disgust in her eyes. 'But I'll email him and let him know you are going to call.'

'That would be great. But give me a few minutes. I'm going to have to run this past my management to see if it's okay. And Anna, it's just a thought. But, there's no illegal material on there like underagers and stuff are there?' I ask her very quietly.

She laughs, but appreciates my concern as she shakes her head.

'None at all. My family has been in this business for over thirty years. They have a good relationship with the authorities,' she says, as I suddenly feel a lot better. But I know iaxis will do their own checks. There are some very well connected people around that glass table. And our *"Fire"* insurance costs are getting very steep as it is.

I look at my watch and the pubs will still be open back home. I quickly excuse myself while I make a phone call to London, in order to get the run-down on if I should proceed here.

I dial the *hotline* (Wacko's mobile) and he answers it after four rings. It turns out Wacko is in Centros and he has just been Buffalo'd. In the background there's an iaxis bender going down. I tell him to go outside on to Gray's Inn Road, as all I can hear is noise. Wacko tries to steady his handset as someone has just given him a shot of tequila to down in one gulp.

'Wacko, I've just been with the daughter of one of Europe's biggest pornographers and she says her family wants an STM-4 connection for Internet transit capacity, for live feeds, a whole range of websites. And…er, will iaxis look at doing porn?'

Wacko thinks about it for approximately three nanoseconds.

'Fucking yes Steve!!... And we want free live feeds in to the NOC on an hourly basis!'

'I thought it would be okay!'

'Shit, that's a lot of revenue… *now get that fucking deal!'* shouts Wacko, showing no signs of containing his enthusiasm as he knocks back the tequila.

'Wacko, please go and check with the CEO. Just to be really sure. I don't want to get into trouble here.'

He starts to calm down.

'Okay, that's not a problem, I've just been chatting to them all. We're having a few drinks at the bar.

'Excellent. Who's all there with him?'

'Fucking everyone: the CFO, the finance raiser, a few of the Dodgers, Psycho, the CTO (chief technical officer/*'chief trapeze officer'*) and er… Scary Spice (Emma from vendor management).'

'What's going on? It sounds a bit heavy.'

'Yeah, they're all shitting themselves about these meetings next week, that the shareholder board want organising. And everyone else is just getting hammered. Look, I'll call you back in two minutes, Steve, don't go away for fucksake!' he says, as he hangs up and runs back in to Centros.

While waiting on Wacko, I have a laugh to myself as I can just picture that scene at the bar.

The shareholder board ('entertainment committee') has sent the chief entertainment officer to brief the chief fire officer, Hellraiser, the chief trapeze officer and all of the iaxis Dodgers about a new and highly deadly stunt called the 'Fireblast'. *It is, the chief entertainment officer assures them, a possible, but highly dangerous fire-eating display involving an explosion, lots of fire, a blindfolded knife thrower, several flying Dodgers and a large cannon (bought by Wacko)!*

This performance, he says, will earn them all a standing ovation at next week's shows and this will hopefully keep iaxis on the road… However, the chief fire officer will now have both of his hands up to his head and will be shaking it away in total horror at the thought of this deadly, high altitude, flying firebomb act. But Hellraiser will be smiling broadly and rubbing his hands together, while Psycho will be sharpening up at least a dozen knives. Scary Spice from vendor management will be up on a table doing her famous belly dancing routine, waving her blindfold about, while the iaxis Dodgers and the CTO will all be gripping onto the bar rail in Centro's looking absolutely fucking terrified!

My phone goes off, while I am thinking how lucky I am to be out here!

'Steve, you've got clearance. The CEO says iaxis has no problem with porn content. But check that there are no underagers or minors on their stuff, we don't want the fucking nonce squad raiding us!'

'It's okay, I've already asked and she said there's none whatsoever.'

'Excellent, then go for it!... And get as much free stuff as possible!'

'I'll see what I can do. But I'll call you tomorrow when I get back.'

'Nice one! says Wacko, as he starts shouting at a Dodger telling him to get back inside the bar.

'No probs mate.'

'See you later, Steve!' he shouts, as he clicks off.

I get back to the dinner table as I make a hand signal to Nathan, who is at the bar, asking him to get me a drink as well.

Anna smiles as I return to my seat.

'Yes, iaxis will approach this very discreetly and with total professionalism. We can easily look after the family's business online,' I say, as I try my hardest not to laugh about flying Dodgers, *fire* and belly dancing!

'If your company is serious about getting into that market there are several big porn industry conferences and exhibitions coming up in New Orleans and Las Vegas. There are lots of telecoms and Internet companies that have stands there. I'm sure my sister will be able to give iaxis the registration details and even help get a stand if you want,' says Anna, looking a lot more relaxed.

I start laughing as I see Nathan at the bar struggling to get served.

'What's so funny?' Anna asks, looking concerned that I'm laughing at her.

'Look Anna, if iaxis had a stand at a porn conference, there would be over a hundred people from the office in the queue outside to get in. One would be updating (making up) his CV and someone called Nick would fly out, become an organiser and blag them into bringing it forward by three months!'

She just laughs and tells me Nathan did a good job of bring her up to speed on the antics of iaxis personnel in the bar last night.

Nathan sends me a hand signal that tells us he can't get served here so it's back to the hotel.

Back at our hotel we say goodbye to Anna. She's got an early flight and after last night's session with Nathan, she wants to get some sleep. As we say good night, I ask her for a postcard from Davos.

'You'll get it next week. Check your emails and I'll put you in touch with my sister,' she says, as we kiss goodnight.

Nathan's mouth is suddenly wide open.

'Is she fixing you up with her sister?' he asks, as we wing it double quick over to the bar. Two vodka and Red Bulls arrive on my room tab and I put him out of his suspense as I have one of the biggest grins on my face.

'You are not going to believe this mate, but her family has one of the biggest porn empires in Europe and her sister is running it.'

'Fucking hell! And she's looking for a boyfriend, yeah?' he asks, looking impressed.

'*No!* She's looking at putting all the material on new web servers and running Internet feeds for their live shows. I've already checked with Wacko, who checked with *"entertainments"* and iaxis has no problem with putting porn on our Internet backbone.'

'How much capacity are they talking about?' he asks, as he tries to work out just how much capacity will be involved.

'An STM-4 of Internet Transit,' I say, having a big mouthful of my drink.

'Fucksake! Just before Christmas, when the Internet backbone was being built, we discussed Internet porn in a management meeting. About fifty per cent of the total volume of traffic on the Internet is hardcore porn. It takes a shit load of capacity to download porn images and even more for the downloading of moving images in a live feed,' says Nathan, as he takes a mouthful of his Red Bull mix and lights up. 'But an STM-4, shit, the network will be paid for in a few years! We should've been targeting the porn industry all along,' he says, with hindsight.

'Do we have any contacts in the porn industry?' I ask him, as I look around and see Lucia at the bar. She catches my eye and waves hello.

'No, just this one you've found. But from next week, could you and Old Boy get on the case and start surfing all the porn sites and target them with an online email marketing blag telling them how fantastic the iaxis internet backbone is?'

'Yes, sure! What do we have to do?' I ask, as I see Lucia talking to some people at the bar.

'Just go on to the porn websites and look for their email contact and postmaster details. They will all be somewhere on their web page. Once you've found that, then email them all our iaxis Internet marketing blag material which Old Boy has spent hours putting together.'

'Look Nathan, we might be late. I think they're already speaking to Concert and UUNet.'

'Shit. I might've known they'd be there already. They shift loads of porn on their Internet backbones as it is. And it's all legal stuff,' he says, as Lucia walks up to us both.

'Hey what's up? You two look like you're planning something. What's going down?'

'Oh, it's just a spot of office politics, but we've got it sorted.' I say to her as I glance back at Nathan.

'Oh yeah, what's that then?' she asks, as if she might be able to help us out with her own years of experience.

'Well it's all sorted out now. But basically Nathan is responsible for managing our Strategic Internet Marketing Campaign,' I say, looking at him and lifting up my very nearly empty glass and raising a couple of eyebrows.

'Excellent!' she says, as Nathan takes the hint from me and propels himself to the bar to get in another round.

'Do you have a Palm Pilot, Steve?' Lucia asks discreetly, looking around.

'Yes, it's here.' I tap the inside pocket of my suit jacket.

'Good, take it out and I'll beam you contact details of my database in the Internet and telecoms industry. It is very extensive.'

'Are you sure? You must have loads.'

'Well yes, there's quite a few, in fact there's over one thousand two hundred names on it. It contains the names and numbers of the world's leading Internet and telecoms players. It's a very comprehensive list of the industry,' she says, as she looks at me in a way I take to be rather affectionate as my heart starts to beat faster.

I take out my Palm Pilot and we connect the beam and it slowly absorbs all her database.

'This is really kind of you. Thank you very much,' I say, as I swallow hard. I know this information is top-drawer material.

'It's a pleasure. But please don't go calling these people on their home numbers and get them out of bed! It's just a little present for you,' she says, laughing at our little memory as the technology transfer goes down.

I hold eye contact and I have her total attention. 'I really do appreciate this and for all the time you spent introducing me to the players.'

'You're welcome,' she says, as she looks at her watch. It's 12:30 a.m.

'Who was that lady you were sitting with at dinner?' she quietly asks.

'Oh, she's new to the industry as well,' I say, trying not to smile.

'I thought so. I knew the people sitting next to her. The company she works for is quite a small outfit. She's not a player.'

'Yes, I know that, but she doesn't want to be one. She's just enjoying the ride. And she's got a big heart and she laughs at my jokes!' I say, as Lucia smiles.

Nathan brings back some drinks and shows fantastic initiative by getting Lucia a vodka and Red Bull as well.

'Cheers! Here's to the capacity swap,' she says, as she runs her hand through her blonde hair and she clicks my glass.

'Cheers!'

'Regarding the legal paperwork Lucia, I think my management and the lawyers are going to be rather busy in meetings next week (with Ciena, K-Net, Gas Line and Nortel) and they might not have time to read your contract as quickly as your company would like.'

'It's okay, don't rush it. I'll pass it on to my company's legal team,' she says, not looking too concerned. But Nathan looks concerned as he thinks about these meetings and his iaxis share loan. If the meetings don't go well, our creditors could take us to court and effectively close us down since we owe them well over two hundred and fifty million dollars.

…I start to laugh as I picture the chief fire officer being put under sedation as Wacko ('the Fire Master') gives a morale-boosting talk to the Dodgers: 'Look, it works, I've seen it being done before so stop fucking crying!'

'We'll be fine. The iaxis team is the best in the business,' I say, to a tired-looking Nathan, who totally agrees.

…We both know just how high the stakes are in this high altitude fire-eating stunt. However, if the stunt goes wrong, Wacko was only following orders when he bought the cannon. Psycho was wearing a mask and gloves and their vice president was unaware of any such activities and was overseas at the time. The CEO and the CFO were both under orders from the shareholders to come up with a good performance and hopefully sell iaxis on to the highest bidder.

The main shareholders all invested money in iaxis through funds from several Cayman Island trust companies. And these trustees all take their orders from the trustees of another company that is registered in the Bahamas, and these trustees all take their orders from another brass plate company which is incorporated in Atlantis and registered somewhere inside the Bermuda Triangle!

So right now in the glass boardroom, the only piece of clarity from around the glass table is that everybody knows nothing about everything to do with anything as to the origins of 'The Fireblast', which is soon to be launched from seven floors high…

'You guys are in trouble,' says Lucia, with a slight hint of knowledge.

'What makes you say that?' asks Nathan, yawning, as I look unfazed at her knowledge.

'You missed your high-yield bond and there's no chance of floating on the NASDAQ in the future market climate,' she says, sadly.

We agree with her.

'But I do think that you guys will be bought out in a couple of months. My company's also been looking at buying you out, but your debts are too high. And bandwidth in Europe is going to be hugely oversupplied,' she says, with confidence.

Nathan's had too much to drink to flinch.

'Yes, I know that your company has already been in to see us,' I say, as I try and catch her off-guard.

Nathan flinches. Lucia doesn't. She just has another sexy eyelock with me. But her senses are *pinged*.

'How do you know that, Steve?' asks Nathan, as he was, until now, totally unaware of her company's interest in iaxis.

Lucia watches me like a hawk.

'I've got my *"friends"* old boy.'

'Come on, who let you in on that?' asks Nathan, trying to work out which member of the board it was.

I'd never blag him so I tell him the truth. 'Nathan, it was Charlotte on reception. She keeps me up to speed on which companies the CEO and the board are presenting to in the boardroom.'

'No way!' says Nathan, shaking his head as he lights up.

Lucia laughs quietly as Nathan learns a trick that they don't teach anyone who's doing an MBA at Harvard.

Lucia has other ideas...

'Steve, the *Voice of America* is always looking for good people to work overseas. The *Office of Engineering and Technical Operations* is actively recruiting and you'd be good at *"frequency management"*. Just give me a call,' she says, with an informed smile.

'What! Steve knows jack shit about engineering and he hates techie stuff,' says Nathan truthfully, while trying to get his bright Cambridge mind around Charlotte on reception and a connection with a potential job offer in the VoA's 'Office of Engineering and Technical Operations'.

...I look down at the murky-looking cold cappuccino that has been left behind on the table, which nobody seems to care about.

'Yes, Nathan's right,' I say, as images of Terry Waite and Ian Spiro flash before my mind.

Lucia seems unconcerned, and Nathan decides to call it a night and gets up. He says goodbye to us both and staggers off to the lifts.

'What's up Steve?' she asks, noticing that I look a bit serious.

I motion for Lucia to come closer as I look around the bar. She leans her head very close to mine and she is so close I can smell her Issey Miyake perfume. And it smells great on her.

'Lucia, what is USAT2's current policy on Internet pornography?' I ask, very quietly.

'Why do you ask that?' she asks, looking surprised (as you do), but with an interest in my answer.

'Well, after dinner I took a call from London and iaxis might be signing a major porn company for web-hosting and live feeds.'

'That's great! USAT2 has got one of the biggest porn companies in the USA on our Internet backbone. Every company in the Internet needs to have a big-ticket porn player on their backbone just to bring in the revenues. Porn content on the Internet is just over forty-six percent of all the total Internet capacity. See, this Internet capacity transit swap really is going to benefit our two companies!' she says, as we click glasses.

'Look Steve, there's an Internet peering conference in New Mexico in a few months' time. Try and come over to it. It would be great to see you there as well,' she says, as she looks at her watch.

'I'd love to, but I'll have to run it by my boss first and let you know,' I say, as the Internet porn conference in New Orleans will soon be on everyone's minds.'

'Please do,' she says, as we both stand up and leave the hotel bar to catch the lift upstairs.

As we are walking out of the bar, I notice that she folds her arms and glances around as we walk slowly towards the lift. My heart is thumping wildly as we look at each other while we're getting into the lift with a few other people she knows. Lucia replies to their small talk as the lift doors close.

The lift goes up all too quickly and I get to my floor and the lift door opens. She moves to kiss me gently on my lips. And for such a brief kiss, her lips are so warm and tender. I feel her hand briefly squeezing mine as we look into each other's eyes and say goodbye.

I walk the short distance down the corridor to my room and all I can think about is Lucia. I walk into my room and I am unable to get the tenderness and smell of her out of my mind. I take off my jacket and quickly throw the few clothes into my bag. It takes less than a minute to pack and I sit on the bed trying to think what she would say if I went up to her room. I lie back and look up at the ceiling for some inspiration and I close my eyes. Her room is only two floors above mine, and the only logical thought going through my mind right now is the look in her eyes as we said goodbye. And this sexy look is now pulling me up and into her room as I get up off the bed to go upstairs.

As I walk towards the door (which is now less than two feet away from me) the silence within my room is broken by a quiet double knock on the door. I look through the spyhole and my heart beats even faster. I open my door and Lucia is standing in front of me in the hallway and is smiling warmly at me. I look in her eyes as she moves towards me; we embrace each other and start to kiss. As I pull her into my room, she manages to close the door behind us and within moments I feel her warm hands on my skin, slowly pulling my shirt away from me.

The next morning I feel completely drained and my very tired eyes don't even notice the British Airways cabin crew as we board the plane to fly home.

THE FINAL CHAPTER

The noise of 'The Fireblast' has woken up every single wolf in the forest.
They are now being spotted far more frequently as the pack runs through the
thick trees past the cabin. In the woods, the air is so cold the wolves can see
each other's breath as they start to howl away. And soon other wolves in the
forest also find the cabin. The iaxis staff cannot hear the wolves just yet, but
the 'entertainment committee' can and they're not laughing at all. The
wolves can smell blood and their howling keeps them awake all night long...

We get the introduction email from Anna first thing on Monday morning, so
I contact her brother-in-law at around eleven. He says Moscow was great and
sounds business like and very busy. I wasn't sure what to expect from him,
but the rest of the quad are watching and listening intently to this
conversation.

Sadly, it transpires that Anna's family firm has already signed the deal
and it was done just seven days ago. And therefore iaxis has missed out on a
lucrative contract to some of the main telecoms players in the Internet porn
industry. We could have made over three hundred thousand dollars revenue
per month if they'd taken this amount of Internet capacity from us.
(Everyone is gutted. But I think that is more to do with the free live feeds we
would have got, rather than the cash revenue stream.)

However, because of the family introduction, Anna's brother-in-law
would like to keep in touch with iaxis. He says that next year, demand for
online porn feeds will go skywards and they are going to be looking for four
times this STM-4 capacity (STM-16). Everyone is rubbing their hands
together at this staggering amount.

Almost immediately, Old Boy and myself have been given total clearance
to surf all the Internet porn sites we can find and then send the iaxis Internet
marketing blag email to them. Our Internet backbone is technologically
perfect for live feed material out of Europe.

During the course of a day's porn-surfing there are sometimes as many
as six females around our desks at any time. Most are 'just over for a look to
see what it's like...' which is what they said yesterday as well.

Suzie has also been told to stay at her desk and do some work (take bookings). She was round our desks all the time and we couldn't get rid of her. We are, however, under strict instructions to forward any 'Grade-A' websites on to her, which we of course do on an hourly basis! In any other company this would get Old Boy and myself escorted off the office premises in handcuffs. Neither of us is particularly bothered at the current workload. It is a good laugh for everyone, but after a while all the sites look pretty much the same. I go about it in a professional and dedicated manner as I tell myself someone has to do it. But pulling in a big-ticket Internet porn live feeder would make me enough commission to buy a two bedroomed flat in Fulham. This has been keeping me very focused.

Anna's sister has also sent over the registration details for the Internet porn conferences and exhibitions coming up in New Orleans and Las Vegas. But unfortunately all business travel is cancelled, unless it's essential. Despite protests pointing out the potential future revenue and developing international business opportunities, this business jolly to a porn conference is not deemed essential. However, we go on to the organisers' website and get the list of companies that are registered to go. There are quite a few famous telecoms, Internet and new media companies registered with stands. (There's also a good few leather bondage and rubber strap-on manufacturers registered as well.) You can even book online for all the after-conference parties in the hotel if you want.

Not surprisingly the whole quad (and quite a few others) want to go even more now, but iaxis has no money to send a few people over to the USA and brass it out at a porn convention. Besides, Old Boy has got more chance of seeing his pet puppy being flown to Mars than his lovely *Soundblast* allowing him go on an iaxis business jolly over to a porn convention in Las Vegas!

After a few days of surfing for new business opportunities on the porn sites, Old Boy breaks the silence.

'Blaady hell!' he yells, as he jumps back from his screen.

Whilst doing some porn prospecting he has just clicked on to a box called 'Bad Puppy'. It was the logical thing to do as he forgot to feed his puppy last night and it bit him on his nose nearly taking his pecker off. But this particular Bad Puppy has taken him to a hardcore gay porn site.

'Look Old Boy, you've got to contact them. Gay porn is a massive industry.'

'Fuck off!' he says very quickly, as everyone cracks up.

While Old Boy and I are surfing all these filthy sites, we find, by accident, a real gem: an Internet chatroom for genuine porn stars to communicate with each other and to offer their services to film production companies. We learn that in the summer of the year 2000, the going rate for a group sex scene is about three and a half thousand dollars per day. We of course tell this to Suzie who begs us to give her the email address so she can put her details up there , as she was wondering what to do with her forthcoming two weeks off! However, Old Boy and I suddenly become concerned about her welfare if we expose her to this potentially dangerous environment, so we refuse to give her the website details. She then goes off in a sulk and books a two-week holiday in the iaxis villa in Marseilles. (Nick will be there to look after her…)

But, no matter how hard we try, we cannot let this opportunity pass us by. After a couple of beers we decide to email the bulletin board the personal details of one of the most spectacular Dodgers called 'Beelstar'. This Dodger enjoys a good laugh, but even he is shocked when he receives an email from a film production company in NYC offering to pay him over two thousand dollars *'just to test how tight his ass really is!'*

This keeps us entertained for the rest of the week!

The revenues for porn companies on the Internet are counted in billions of dollars and how it all works is rather simple. A person in, for example, Texas, will pay the porn company online with his credit card to watch an online live sex show taking place in Amsterdam. It costs a lot of money (via punters' credit cards) to download the still and moving images. And there are millions and millions of people getting their kicks out of this stuff. But what they don't tell you is that National Security Agency surveillance software ["which is far more advanced than the FBI's 'CARNIVORE' computer Internet surveillance system at Building 1203, Fort Monmouth…"] monitors commercial transactions and private emails over the Internet. Emails going through the world's Neutral Internet Peering Exchanges are all intercepted in real time up to 128 bits by the National Security Agency's global electronic surveillance system.

And how this massive global surveillance works is even simpler… The viewing, transaction and choice of book you buy online from (for example) Amazon.com is monitored globally and processed at the NSA's Tordella Ops site in Fort Meade. Here on Ream Road, just one of the NSA's CRAY and IBM supercomputer systems can do billions of calculations every single second. The NSA has quite a few acres of these CRAY supercomputers deep underground ["…helping the 694th Intelligence Group, 704th Military Intelligence Brigade and USAF Cryptologic Operations at 9800 Savage Road all carry out their worldwide 'national security' duty…"] at Fort Meade, Maryland, USA.

["…The NSA's HQ at Fort George G. Meade consists of over 1,400 buildings, covering several thousand square acres. The NSA is one of America's biggest employers and it is the most sensitive part of the US Federal Government. And in order to 'protect freedom', it does not appear on any maps in the 'free world' or anywhere else..."]

These CRAY supercomputers are the codebreaking and raw data processing systems of the NSA's massive global surveillance network of everyday communications. This surveillance system is correctly known in the media as ECHELON. ["... The NSA's National Cryptologic School at Fort Meade even has a few courses that describe ECHELON in great detail. The modules are called, EA-048 Transmission Media, EC-124 Introduction to COMSAT, EA-049 Global Telecom Networks, EA-040 Communications Signals and TM-101 Overhead Collection Management..."].

Today, via ECHELON, the NSA can decode and read all voice, fax and email data ["and Wall Street and Frankfurt share transactions..."] sent in real time from anywhere in the world. Once the communications data has been intercepted, it is then electronically read by countless NSA CRAY and IBM supercomputer systems, which are then specifically programmed to look for key words in over one hundred different languages through the various electronic 'Dictionary' monitoring systems. This might be "old news", but it is none the less important. *And true.*

["...'The Beast', has a huge appetite for raw COMSAT data, and the 'ten horns' of the ECHELON network are located at Sugar Grove, Yakima, Menwith Hill, Leitrim, Shoal Bay, Geraldton, Waihopai, Morwenstow, Sabana Seca and Misawa..."]

ECHELON data is stored in a colossal processing system that can store seven trillion pages of population information. The NSA's 'Mass Storage Executive Committee' is reponsible for the current filing system and it is light years ahead of the *"Digicom System"*, which the NSA helped develop for the Argentine secret police in 1977. It was this system which made it more efficient for thousands of innocent civilians to be murdered during President Ford's CIA-backed *Operation Condor*. And this covert policy for South America was [" ...'quietly approved' by David Rockefeller's board at the Council on Foreign Relations"] secretly sanctioned by the White House and "overseen" by the "40 Committee" when Dr Henry Kissinger was its chairman.

["...Operation Condor was flying high when Benson Buffham was Deputy Director of the NSA and George Bush Sr was running the CIA... There was NO hiding place in South America. The CONDORTEL had linked up the secret police comms of Chile, Bolivia, Uruguay, Paraguay, Brazil and Argentina,(others were targeted for assasination in North America and elsewhere) and hundreds of thousands were tortured and killed in places like Videla's Naval Mechanics School or the 'closed' Ford Motors plant at Pacheco. Operation Condor was also covertly coordinated from CIA/DoD and thousands of tortured bodies were dumped into the icy South Atlantic by Argentine military cargo planes. This was while the NSA *listened* and the Vatican "institutionally" turned a blind eye and a *deaf* ear to the mass genocide of its South American 'flock'. Got a clean conscience for the afterlife Karol? Sleep well do we, Messers Gerald Ford, Donald Rumsfeld, Vernon Walters, Dick Cheney, Brent Scowcroft, George Bush Sr, Lew Allen Jr, Henry Kissinger and **David Rockefeller?**"]

Apart from being used for mass population and economic surveillance [" with CIA's National Resources Division"], ECHELON is also used for identifying and tracking cells of ["the once CIA-trained"] Osama bin Laden and his al-Qaida terror network. This is in order to monitor terrorists via their logistics, financial and communication network ["with close and ongoing HUMINT from Pakistan's ISI and Saudi Arabia's Istakhbarat…"], with a hope to penetrating al-Qaida's overall infrastructure.

["…It is also known as 'peeling the onion' in the trade. During the eighties, Osama bin Laden was a CIA asset after being personally forwarded to the Agency by Prince Turki al-Faisal, then head of Saudi intelligence. At a time when Claire George was DD/O at Langley and Charles Cogan and Christina Rocca were co-ordinating the CIA's secret Afghan offensive, Osama bin Laden was the chief financial officer and logistics manager for Sheikh Abdullah Azzam's Peshawar-based Mekhtab Al-Khidemat or the Office of Services, later known as al-Qaida or 'The Base'. From Rawalpindi and Khost, Osama bin Laden was CIA trained, then tasked and coordinated by CIA Islamabad via General Fazle Huq of Pakistan's ISI to carry out 'Disruptive Action' against the Soviets. This was the sharp end of US covert foreign policy after President Reagan's National Security Decision Directive 166 and 270 (Afghanistan) which George Bush Sr, George Shultz and Richard Armitage know all about… Lt General William Odom's NSA provided the comms for this covert policy and John McMahon's CIA and Saudi Arabia's Istakhbarat secretly funded the entire $3 billion anti-Soviet Jihad through banks like the BCCI and also a few heroin shipments by Mr Gulbuddin Hekmatyer. However, after the Gulf War fraud, the later owner of Wadi al-Aqiq Ltd, with help from ex-US Army Sergeant Ali Mohamed turned the Jihad on to America, and BCCI's secret money network from BCCI Miami to Karachi was shut down. And overnight the old Jihad's 'black network' for money transfers ceased to exist. And so did quite a few other little secrets from the **George Bush** 'Centre of Intelligence', all carried out under the Stars and Stripes, in the name of **God Bless America.**"]

Today, terrorists who use email, mobile and SAT phones to communicate, search online for terror books written by Islamic fundamentalists via Amazon.com and then transfer money through Western Union are all carrying out actions that are being "picked-up" by the NSA.

["...The NSA's CRITIC System and the C-TC/CIA have never been so busy, as the past might have been 'a different country', but it always catches up with *The Present,* dear boy."]

Not suprisingly, the US government gets very sensitive when terror groups conspire and carry out terrorist attacks against American embassies and battleships ["by using their old CIA training manuals from Afghanistan for making bombs"]. These terror groups now communicate via email and "all necessary measures" are in place to intercept their communications ["...and everybody else's, including foreign governments and corporations"] in order to "protect" US national security ["...Beyond All Boundaries..."] on a global basis well into the new century.

Federal Law in the USA does not encourage US multinational corporations to have data encryption systems that the NSA cannot decode in real time. However, you will be reassured to know that Motorola, Novell, MITRE Corp, Oracle, Texas Instruments, IBM, SAIC, Lockheed, Verison, Dell, SAR International, Lotus, ITT, National Semiconductor Corp, Xerox, AT&T and Microsoft do not break any US Federal Laws on encryption. In fact they are all aware of the '*Spock Program*' and even work with the NSA on super-classified networks like NSANET and the JWICS or *Joint Worldwide Intelligence Communication System.* ["...Motorola works with the NSA to help develop mobile phone encryption systems such as the KIV-14 and Cipher TAC."]

Needless to say the NSA has "fully approved" the encryption devices for AOL, Hotmail and Microsoft's Window's system. Today it is simply a matter of *perception*: you can look *out* of 'Windows' and you can also look *in* through them. *And when you know what to look for, the view you are looking at is as clear as* glass...

Yet already the National Security Agency's supercomputers are out of date. To keep up with the huge numbers of people online and using mobiles, the NSA is currently upgrading its computer and codebreaking system with the most advanced supercomputer the 'free world' has ever seen; it is known as the CRAY SV2.

I recently met up with Kathryn who also provided me with a little insight into this highly advanced supercomputer system. This new CRAY SV2 will be the "leading edge" of next generation's intelligent supercomputer technology. It will be vastly more powerful than any other computer ever used in the US Federal Government. Just one CRAY SV2 will be capable of billions of intelligent calculations every second of the day, while helping to break foreign codes ["via the ...NAVSECGRU"]. And it will be able to handle all the anticipated growth in global Internet, land and mobile phone traffic with ease. There will be no other supercomputer more advanced than this system anywhere in the world. The CRAY SV2 will crack foreign governments' codes and also read and process raw data intercepted through the ECHELON system quicker than ever before. And the total number that the NSA has ordered remains highly classified. It is going to be ready for operational service in the year 2002.

["...Perhaps this is all uncomfortable reading?"]

On the Internet, whether it is porn, e-banking or just chat, *nothing* is private. It never has been and it *never* will be. Just remember how and *why* the Internet was built. *And whom it was built for*. So when you read your morning's emails, always be aware that the NSA has already read your 'postcards' in real time before they are delivered into your mailbox. And if you have been woken up by the 'delivering' of this 'message', then sorry. But you can always roll over and go back to sleep...

Over the last four decades the Pentagon's Defense Advanced Research Project Agency (DARPA), which spearheaded the development of the original Internet for the Pentagon, has been designing not only "Hubble-Bubbles" ["...to bug submarine communication cables"], but also advanced electronic warfare and global Internet and telecoms surveillance systems for the NSA. The DARPA is a world leader in these highly secretive and specialised fields ["...as is Raytheon, General Dynamics and Applied Signal Technology"] and the NSA is its biggest customer. So when you use a phone, buy stocks and shares, go online to shop, surf and communicate via email, bear in mind that the National Security Agency's ECHELON network is very possibly the *"ten horns"* on top of *"the beast with seven heads"*. And in the new millennium, one of these *'heads'*, *"The Jimmy Carter"*, is having £666 million worth of electronic warfare and 'electronic intelligence' (ELINT) surveillance gear built into it...

...iaxis also has its fair share of problems right now, but the good news for iaxis is that the 'meetings' with our creditors have gone very well and Teleglobe are going to buy us. And it is all looking like it might just be good. The creditors were all 'pleased' with the recent 'shows' the CEO and Wacko came up with and they have all given us some breathing space on our payments for the next few weeks. The reason this was given was that they were all simply told that iaxis has got no money (*'The Fireblast'*). This was always going to be the most terrifying part of the latest *"iaxis Experience"*.

However, 'The Fireblast' *was soon followed by a Flaming Dodger, who was doing a free-falling fire-eating stunt on a bungee, while displaying to them that Teleglobe were now going to buy us out. The Flaming Dodger's performance also told the creditors that this will give us several million dollars and you (big creditor) will get some bills paid. And if you put us under you will get two cents in the dollar.*

...And by all accounts 'The Fireblast' really was a highly spectacular show, that saw some 'spectators' having to be carried home and members of the Ciena board all receiving "Third Degree" burns to their eyebrows. The daredevil, fire-eating Dodgers all conquered their fears of flying and heights and blinded them with a spectacular flying fireball stunt. The Big Cats also did a few somersaults and safely landed back on their high chairs. Even Psycho's blades managed to hit the right future revenue figures, which were being displayed by flying Dodgers. And this was fantastic considering he was actually blindfolded!

In fact they have all been so amazingly spectacular that the chief entertainment officer has got Red Adair wanting to have a word in his ear and the chief fire officer has suddenly developed shellshock, vertigo and a fear of fire!

And Wacko has gone out and bought another cannon...

My twenty-ninth birthday finally comes around on *June 29th 2000 A.D.*. At around mid morning I wander up to Sasha's desk and casually remind her that it is my birthday (she'd 'completely forgotten', of course). Later on at twelve noon she playfully hands me a birthday card and present: an interesting-looking book called *The Bible Code* by Michael Drosnin. Today Sasha's radiance is brighter than ever and Kong is not far behind her, as they are now together (I know it's hard to believe!). As Sasha gives me a little birthday kiss, Kong proceeds to look at me as if he's a bouncer at the Met Bar whose body language and stare tell me that there's no chance of me being allowed in here whatsofuckingever! I must remember that stunt he pulled with Charlotte. He obviously read Sasha well... *the boy has Wisdom after all.*

Later on in the day we head down to Wacko's flat. He lives on Gray's Inn Road where he has a roof garden. This has become a favourite spot where the quad can walk down to and soak up the afternoon sun, when the office is quiet. (And sitting on the roof garden, soaking up sunrays with Wacko, Nathan and Old Boy knocking back a few drinks, listening to '*Heaven's Earth*' by Delerium, beats sitting in the office any day of the week, birthday or not.)

We are having a laugh about the fact that the ex-chairman is still going on about this Med fibre optic cable project. A while ago he chartered a forty-million-dollar yacht for three days and moored it up just off Monaco for the Grand Prix weekend. Nick travelled up from Marseilles and about eight girls from the office also went down to the boat. The ex-chairman took these people down to Monaco as a thank you as they were his friends, which was really very decent of him. The iaxis staff also did a good job of drinking ninety-five per cent of the champagne.

Some very wealthy people from the Middle East and a few other places were also on the boat. At a cost of nine hundred million dollars, some of this Med project has to be sold to these rich international players. Once the funding from these sources comes through, the venture capitalists will start to get interested. However, on the yacht they couldn't even watch the Grand Prix because the TV was broken. They could only listen to the sound of Jackie Stewart's car engines.

'Well that just about sums up the whole crapness of the project,' says Wacko, while he gets some more cold beers out of the ice bucket and hands them around.

'So how did Nick get on in Monaco?' I ask, as information is hard to come by. What happened on the boat stays on the boat…

'Well, he was in his cabin most of the time with that sexy admin coordinator (Miss 'triple-x').'

'But wasn't Jemma down at the Monaco Grand Prix as well?' asks Nathan, who's recently been brought up to speed on office relationships.

'Yeah, Nick had the two of them in his cabin at the same time!' says Wacko.

'Blaady hell!' says Old Boy, who is laughing away at the antics of some iaxis personnel.

Nathan seems unmoved while he lights up his spliff. 'I'm thinking about giving up smoking and joining a gym,' he says, looking serious.

'Here Nathan, have another drink mate!' I say, as the other two crack up. (Last week's attempt ended after three hours when his body went into multiple spasms. As for this gym idea, I'll have the paramedics on standby.)

'Did you hear what happened to the CFO's office while the Monaco Grand Prix was going on?' asks Wacko, who is now bringing us up to speed on even more recent events going on behind all the smoke and mirrors.

'No,' say three blank faces.

'Somebody entered his office and stole his C-drive with all the iaxis finance history on it. It was a professional job. They had a pass to get into the ITN building, knew which office was his and went to work. Everything else was untouched. But they unscrewed his C-drive and vanished into thin air with it. And nobody knows who contracted the lifting.'

'Fuck! That's a bit hardcore,' says Nathan, who's just finished drawing on his spliff.

'So what's going to happen about it?' I ask Wacko, who's nearly finished his drink.

'No idea, but the CFO's okay. He's completely clean. But anyway, how's this corporate chick in LA, Steve?' asks Wacko, rubbing some E45 burn cream on to his head after his recent meetings.

Nathan looks at me and is grinning away. He's been ear-wigging a few phone conversations recently and has started playing 'LA Woman' by The Doors every other day, just for a laugh.

'Well, their lawyers are now dragging their feet…'

'Not the contract! The sexy corporate chick; Nathan says she was very tasty and you spent the afternoon by the pool with her and spoke about China!'

'She's fine. We speak every day and her dog says hello to you all as well!'

Wacko takes another call on the *hotline*, which saves me from further tacquestioning. Not that I would have cracked so easily today.

'Be careful old boy, or else she'll have you over to California to walk Bosco along the beach,' says Old Boy, as he now has to walk his 'blaady' dog everywhere.

'That thing will be taking me for a walk!' I say quite confidently.

'Are you really thinking of moving over to work for USAT2?' asks Nathan, as he rolls another spliff.

It looks like Wacko might have to manage a fire-eating display later on, as there are flames coming out of his phone…

'Well, I've thought about a move to California to work for them. I like Americans, but I couldn't handle all the corporate bullshit over there. Besides, they only give you two weeks' holiday a year and are gobsmacked when you take it!' I say, shaking my head at the lack of future backpacking travels open to me if I worked in the USA.

'Yes, that's right!' says Nathan, looking up at the blue cloudless sky.

'I think I'm going to stay in London and get some more experience in the industry. But the future is in China and India. European telecoms and Internet companies are going to be on their knees next year,' I say, as I wipe my shades clean.

'Why India and China?' asks Nathan, as he looks at his watch. It's just gone past 3 p.m. on this hot afternoon.

'India will be the world's leader in Internet software developments within five years. And the Chinese will try and copy whatever they can get their hands on, including the odd Stealth bomber technology shot down in the

Balkans,' I say, with "informed knowledge" at the sharp end of international relations ["...after the 'Cousins' went and deliberately balanced the books in Belgrade"].

'Yes, you're absolutely right there, old boy. And every second person in those cultures understands the software technology,' says Old Boy, who has just put on 'Aurora' by Ordinary World.

'But Europe's finished. There's more fibre optic cables than telephones,' I say, as I finish my drink.

Wacko clicks off the *hotline*.

'Shit. Teleglobe have pulled out.'

'That is bad news,' says Nathan, now rubbing his eyes at the thought of the loan for his iaxis shares he's got to pay off with his overdraft.

'So why have they pulled out? They were real contenders,' I ask, as we'd all been on the Teleglobe website this morning seeing what jobs were available.

'Well, that's the *"18th Degree"* question. I guess their board didn't like our debts, but we don't know why.'

'So what happens now?' I ask Wacko, as he jumps up and dumps a few empty bottles in the bin liner.

'Well, there's a new buyer who's just come on the scene, so we've got to get back to the office,' he says, as I can just picture several vultures all starting to circle high above 200 Gray's Inn Road.

'Who's that?' I ask as the ghetto-blaster is switched off.

'Gary Klesch.'

'Never heard of him.'

Blank looks from Nathan and Old Boy.

'Me neither, but apparently he's got huge interests in German Cable TV and he wants a big fire-eating display,' says Wacko who's now smiling and rubbing his hands together.

We land back at the office and all hell has broken loose with an email that has been sent to the iaxis Hotmail account. It is from Claire in Personnel. She's just found out about the love triangle involving her 'friend' Jemma and her relationship with Nick. And she is not happy. There is laughter everywhere as people are getting up to go over to the pub to wash this one down.

Back at our desks we all rush to log on to Hotmail...

...Take it from me, Claire has gone fucking mental and shared her thoughts and experiences with everyone in iaxis.

Wacko, Nathan, Old Boy and myself are all stunned. Nathan puts on the

TV theme to Channel Four's *Big Brother* show while he reads the email for the third time.

'Steve, what the fuck is chlamydia?' he asks, looking and sounding a bit shocked.

'I haven't got a clue mate. I've never heard of it before. But just going by the name it sounds deadly, almost as bad as *smallpox*.'

Nathan gets up and wanders over to Merlin, who knows everything. And a short while later he gets back to the quad with the run-down on the disease.

'Shit, you're right. It is deadly. If untreated it can make a woman infertile and a bloke can lose his testicles.'

'Blaady hell! yells Old Boy, as I look over to Merlin who's just smiling at all the carry-on.

Nick is currently 'at work'. Or rather he's lying on a beach in the South of France, laughing at all the fuss. The email is being sent to other people in the industry and beyond as we get up and join everyone else at the pub for a good laugh.

As the summer goes on, iaxis is a very surreal environment in which to 'work'. There is nothing to do and yet the management does not want people to leave. If people start to leave, this will reduce the value of the company. The people who built up and manage the iaxis network are a highly sought-after commodity, but sadly we no longer have much of a sales force as they've all resigned. They were not able to sell any new fibre-optic circuits because of the provisioning problems with Ciena. The sales people who have not left are being asked to help concentrate on selling Internet capacity with Old Boy and myself. However, the market prices for selling Internet transit capacity have also fallen at a vertically steep rate. But iaxis addressed this problem with relative ease.

'Howard, our Internet transit costs are too expensive.'

'What makes you say that, Steve?'

'Well, this is what Level 3 are offering for Internet transit capacity in London and er, here's our prices. We are forty-five per cent more expensive.'

'Okay, well fuck it Steve. Just match Level 3's and use some initiative!'

'Thanks Howard.'

Despite reducing our prices, we fail in our attempts to get a single porn customer or any other customer on the iaxis Internet backbone. The porn websites have all signed up to the big telecoms and Internet companies whose stocks you can buy on the NASDAQ. However, these stocks have already fallen in value by seventy-five per cent or more, and are continuing to fall further.

As Moby's 'Porcelain' track is beating out of my desk speakers it doesn't make what I'm looking at any easier to swallow. All the shares I bought with my redundancy money have crashed. Fayrewoods and Robotic Technology are down by forty per cent. The worst by far is Fyffes. The graph displaying their share performance closely resembles a trace left by someone who has just done a bungee jump. Only the rope snapped and the poor Dodger just kept on going down...

...However, whether or not iaxis has the same fortune is hanging by a piece of fibre optic as thin as the hair on our heads. That is unless your name is Wacko. He lost all his hair due to several 'firebomb displays' he pulled off around Eastern Europe in the years before he joined iaxis. These stunts were so deadly it would only be on a very special occasion that they could ever be staged in the UK. And they'd never be shown on TV!

I check my Hotmail as I try to take my mind away from my losses and there's an email from someone responding to my advert in LOOT, which I placed online to sell my widescreen TV (Fantastic!). I could do with one thousand five hundred pounds in my current account. We agree a time of 9:30 p.m. on Sunday for them to come and see it. They are getting a bargain and they know it. I'm meant to be mountain biking, so I should be back in time for them.

These days there is no great hurry to get to work before 10 a.m. Well, apart from the Dodgers that is; these daredevils are stretched to their limits. And the heat is intense. After all the dodging of payments to our suppliers the total iaxis debt figure could easily be up to three hundred million dollars. And we've only been in business for fifteen months! However, we still don't know the full amount, as we can't find a calculator with a screen that is wide enough. Right now Wacko is busy working out the *fire-eating* display for Gary Klesch & Co and he is speaking to the iaxis 'Financial out-of-Controller' (the Draft Dodger).

This South African Dodger is a world leader in the art of 'Dodging'. A few years ago he dodged the military draft and had the South African Defence Force on his case before the amnesty for all draft dodgers. Now he's safely at iaxis, the Draft Dodger is famous for saying 'the worst case scenario is...'. This is incredibly amusing, because his 'worst-case scenario' tends to get worse every single day. And the Draft Dodger has still retained an unnatural habit of looking over his shoulder every three minutes. He has also got a top sense of humour, as displayed when the Bullet Dodger joined iaxis.

The Bullet Dodger is a Palestinian who has dodged everything shot and thrown at him. On his first day at iaxis the Draft Dodger told him, in all seriousness, that we work in a glass building and he wasn't to start throwing stones in here.

But overall, following the recent terrifying shows, nothing frightens these fine young Dodgers now and they all have wild, starey eyes, which frighten all the young secretaries... Then, without any warning, the emergency fire alarms for the ITN building go off.

Shortly afterwards a voice announces to the office that there's a suspected terrorist bomb alert outside the ITN building. There's also a softball travelling at high speed around the office as Old Boy is teaching a couple of South African and Aussie Dodgers how to play cricket.

'Come on, let's go over to the pub. I'm thirsty after all these numbers,' says Wacko, grabbing his mobile as I pick up the softball and throw it at some Aussie slacker still holding a cricket bat.

Outside we have to go up to the third emergency meeting point (Duke of York). The police have sealed off the street and are a waiting for the bomb squad to arrive and blow up a black taxi. It has just been left empty with its engine running right outside the ITN building and the taxi driver is nowhere to be seen...

Wacko gets a couple of drinks in as Nathan and Old Boy go and get some fags just in case the newsagent gets wiped out in the blast.

'So how long have we got until it's over?' I ask Wacko, as I look around to see who else is here: it's all iaxis staff.

'Fuck knows, it's not over until the fat lady sings, but she's getting close.'

'And how close is that?'

'Well she's so fat she can't get out of the limo! But the mikes and amps are all set, so you might as well get your CV up to date,' he says, laughing at his mental image of "her".

'It already is, thanks.'

'Good, well start winging it out as anything can happen now.'

'Yes, I've been looking, but I'm not really sure what I want to do. I might look at a career in advertising if I decide to leave the Internet.'

'Yes, but you might still have to go in at graduate level on shit pay.'

'We'll see. What about you and Eastern Europe, do you fancy going back there?'

Wacko shakes his hairless head.

Shortly afterwards Nathan joins us both just as Wacko is telling me about one of his old colleagues recently getting shot dead in the lobby of a Moscow hotel.

'You know, that bomb scare's just been cancelled.'

'Why?' asks Wacko, disappointed, as we were both waiting for the sound of the controlled blast.

'The taxi driver went to the massage and kinky sauna shop further up Gray's Inn Road for a quick session!'

'What a complete tosser,' says Wacko, as we go back in to the pub.

'Can you remember what was going on this time last year?' Nathan asks Wacko.

'No, we weren't here, what happened?' asks Wacko, as his eyes look around the bar for a familiar voice he thought he heard.

'Well it was about this time last year the network was lit and iaxis went live.'

'I bet that was a good bender!' I say, as I remember I was getting ready to go off to Kenya and Tanzania about twelve months ago.

'It was a big one all right. The ex-chairman and senior VPs all had a race to see who could buy the biggest bottle of champagne in London. An hour or so later two bottles, four foot tall, turned up, and everyone finished them off, then

we went over to the pub opposite the Aldgate office and got even more slaughtered.'

'So did iaxis have any money at that point?' I ask, with a big grin on my face, as I'm almost sure that the answer would be 'no'...

'Did we fuck! The money arrived two weeks after the network was completed. We used that money to get started on the next couple of networks we had planned.' Wacko looks at his TAG 2000 watch and laughs out, 'one year is a long time in this industry!'

'But the best laugh was that when this initial payment actually came through it was on the same day that Ernst & Young were going through our books,' laughs Nathan.

'Shit, that was lucky,' I say, as I see Hannah walking about the far side of the bar.

'Too right it was lucky. The auditors all dropped their pens and calculators, came down the pub and got pissed with everyone else. They were sweating away and said they needed a good few drinks after seeing the books!'

'So where do you think it went wrong, Wacko? I ask, as he looks up all the ingredients that go into a can of Red Bull and is twisting up his face.

'It's easy, it was when the shareholders backing iaxis started to play politics and removed Bear Stearns from the original high-yield bond issue. We lost valuable time and Greenspan *crucified* us by causing the capital markets to shift against us,' he says, as he empties the remaining contents of that Red Bull can into his vodka and downs it regardless. 'And then the "endless summer" really ended when the NASDAQ dived a couple of months ago,' says Wacko, as he suddenly sees the whites of both my eyes…

Hannah walks up to him from behind and firmly grabs his bottom.

'Ahhhhhhhhhhh !!!!!!!'

The whole pub hears him yell as if he's just been electrocuted. Wacko turns around and gives Hannah one hell of a frightened, freaked-out stare as his body and soul twitches away.

Hannah is just about to suggest something to Wacko and as a sign of sheer good fortune his mobile rings. The call is from his vice-president telling him that Klesch loved the *fire-eating* display and he's going to be making a formal offer to our shareholders to buy iaxis.

Wacko bolts it out of the pub and escapes… Later I go back to the office to get some more money out of my desk drawer and I see Wacko saying 'Well done!' to all the young Dodgers.

The weekend arrives and I get back from mountain biking just in time for the people to view my widescreen TV. They like it, buy it, and the following morning I pay the Halifax Building Society banker's draft in to my Royal Bank of Scotland account on my way in to work.

Not so good is the Internet capacity swap with Lucia's company, USAT2. This has now fallen through. Quite simply, her company has now started to axe people and she has left. No new contracts are being signed and there is a total freeze on all developments. It is a good job I didn't fly over and join USAT2 or else I'd now be dog walking with Bosco (him chasing me from one end of the beach to the other!).

And then the news hits us.

The shareholders have turned down Gary Klesch's attempt to buy iaxis.

(Fuck!)

Mr Klesch is top drawer when it comes to making money. His appetite can digest very large figures. He's already spent over two million dollars in lawyers fees on us. The future revenue potential with Klesch's German Cable TV interests and our fibre optic and Internet backbone would have made perfect business sense as we would have had a huge customer base in Germany connected to our network. This is the best plan we have seen. The CEO is furious when the shareholders bin Klesch and reject it outright. He is then paid *another* one million dollars to leave iaxis quietly.

In April the shareholders paid him 1.2 million dollars to stay on and help sell iaxis.

The CEO is a good bloke who certainly had vision and was really well liked around the office. And he's now made nearly two and a half million dollars out of iaxis in just a few months. But the iaxis shareholders he reported to in America don't really understand the sheer 'meltdown' facing the European telecoms market. This is putting the situation very diplomatically. The Ciena board in Delaware do and they are calling us from their holiday vacations in the USA.

...However, it is no laughing matter that the '*chief entertainment officer*' has moved on and the '*entertainment committee*' has sent in a new replacement to run iaxis. His name is "Mr Lynch" ('*The Magician*') and this little fella doesn't look very funny at all. But everyone at iaxis has been told that he is one of the best in the business and he is going to attempt to make all the iaxis problems disappear and find a buyer for iaxis. And this planned '*magic show*' will be brilliant if he pulls it off.

In no time at all the creditor and supplier writs are starting to get served on us. The iaxis reception has now got a special intray for them all. It's called 'a big fucking filing cabinet.' And sadly, we can feel that iaxis is now in free-fall.

...And back at the old cabin in the middle of the forest, the whole pack of wolves is now looking down on to it from their vantage point. Inside, Psycho is manning the 'grim-reaper' and is pointing it outwards towards the thick dark trees. His finger is firmly gripping the trigger as sweat drips into his eyes. His nerves are being steadily worn down by the sound of the wolves as they howl away without mercy through the cold darkness ...

A couple of days later, over a quiet drink in the Blue Lion, a senior member of iaxis management tells Nathan, Old Boy and myself about the inner workings of '*The Magician's*' proposed '*magic show*'... We are told that '*The Magician*' has plans to make the iaxis headcount shrink by one hundred and ten persons as part of his performance. And it is going to take place within the next forty-eight hours.

We are all stunned.

This is an absolutely *horrific* show to pull off. However, it can be stopped. There is only one thing to do and that is for Old Boy and myself to bring Nathan up to speed on office PSYOPS.

Rule No 1 in covert warfare is to always use a third party.

["...And never, ever forget this, dear boy."]

So after a very basic briefing, Nathan goes up to the lovely Sasha (when Kong is asleep) and tells her everything he has learned about the proposed '*magic show*'. Nathan of course tells her 'in strictest confidence and she's to tell no one about it...'

And after forty minutes or so, as the three of us get back from a couple of beers in Centro's, the word is already round the office. And the secrets of '*The Magician*' and his '*magic show*' are now known to all.

In this situation, the environment is now ripe for ramping up and planting even more rumours.

One of the best ones we come up with is 'everyone who wants to come in to work next week for '*The Magician*' will have to pay him a five thousand pound deposit.' Plant this with the right person ('*Fookin hell!*') and it will take off and develop a life all of its own!

Now the objective has been met and all within iaxis know the *illusion*. The management is now refusing to pay '*The Magician*' for his planned show since the iaxis staff all know his inner *secrets*. And much to everyone's relief the '*magic show*' is cancelled. '*The Magician*' simply puts his axe back into his hat and, before our very eyes, disappears back behind the smoke and mirrors. And we never see him again.

…And there are no "comebacks" for the three of us.

I wake up with a raging hangover. I can't even listen to the *Today* programme as I climb out of bed at 8:30 a.m. with my head pounding. After a hot shower I throw on my Alexandre pinstripe suit and get ready to leave.

Then the post arrives. Two letters: a letter from my bank, the Royal Bank of Scotland, and my Visa card statement. I recently bought some new summer gear from Ralph Lauren and my statement has probably got a few teethmarks in it from that Saturday afternoon. My bank statement should be healthy after selling my TV.

I open the Visa card statement first and I feel light-headed as I see FedEx has billed me for six hundred pounds. This, I am told, is for a VAT payment they squared up with "HM Customs and Intimidation". It was for my camera gear that I bought online and imported last year from the USA. It must've got lost in their system. And it certainly got lost in my mind over this past year. But despite the hefty VAT bill, it still worked out cheaper than going down the High Street.

Then I open the letter from my bank and I nearly have a heart attack as I learn that the Halifax Building Society banker's draft (which I received as payment for my Sony widescreen TV) has turned out to be a fraud. It was a good fraud and the Royal Bank of Scotland apologises for crediting my current account with the amount. However, they have now debited the one thousand three hundred-odd pounds from my current account and they advise me to contact the police and report this fraud. They are also acting within their legal rights in fleecing me of this amount without a single phone call first. However the banker's draft passed their fraud system and they cleared it to enter my account.

As I do a number display in my head I am unable to move for a few minutes until my heartbeat slows down. This is too serious to think about. Two thousand pounds is a lot to lose before you leave the front door to go to work in the morning.

I leave the flat feeling punch drunk as I slowly walk through Fulham to Putney Bridge tube station.

I get in to work looking and feeling rough. Wacko, who was having a laugh with the Big Cats *(teasing them with Fire)* walks in a few minutes later.

'Steve, you look like shit!'

'Thanks.'

'So who's the interview with?' he asks, as I slowly munch away at my sausage bagel while I call directory enquiries for Fulham police's number.

'FLAG Telecom.'

Wacko laughs.

'What's up with FLAG?'

'Our senior management is round there all day. FLAG is interested in buying iaxis. If you see the board just say hello.'

'I've had better starts to the day you know.'

I start dialling the number for Fulham police to report my fraud. They log the details and are very sympathetic. However, the chances of tracing them are zero. I put them in touch with my bank as I try my best to get over it.

After downing two cans of Red Bull, I walk to Mount Street for my interview with a couple of senior executives from FLAG Telecom. It has been a really shitty morning and I need to look sharp and pay attention during this interview. These two respected industry names are genuinely smiling as I walk in. They ask what is going on at iaxis, because they've had over sixty CVs in the last two days from people in iaxis. I tell them that everyone is looking for 'new opportunities'. They don't give away the fact that FLAG/iaxis takeover negotiations are going on upstairs. And neither do I.

Over the next few days, the negotiations with FLAG to buy iaxis take off and they are very serious. We've also had some of FLAG's grey-haired suit brigade come in to do a tour of our office. When they walked into Biz Dev they were appalled at the sight that greeted them: Biz Dev was playing the Dodgers at softball cricket in the office!

But what did they expect? The iaxis staff can now hear the wolves and we know the cabin can't survive past next week and will be overrun. That is unless FLAG move on us very soon. And this is looking very good. FLAG are very serious about buying us.

We all have to submit ourselves for interviews with a senior management figure from FLAG. These take place in our office and this will help FLAG to decide if they want you or not. And it will give them a chance to learn as much as possible about iaxis.

In my interview I speak about "Project Oxygen", a cable deal that was going to link the continents of the world with fibre optic cables. This suit knew all the players from "Project Oxygen" and their eventual shipbrokers, Derrick Offshore. We spoke about ships and the good old days for about thirty minutes. Wacko, who sat in on the interview, said afterwards that he felt like there was not a dry eye in the house.

Afterwards we all go over to the Duke and end up sitting outside comparing stories while we knock back a few drinks... When Dodger No.6 was interviewed she was asked what she likes so much about working for iaxis and she replied truthfully, 'the iaxis culture is really fantastic'. To which this grey-haired American corporate suit glowered and spat out, 'You know, I'm fed up hearing about this goddamn culture thing in this office.' And he was serious.

Americans do have a lot to learn about other people's cultures.

Dodger No.6 is my favourite Dodger. She's an Aussie ('Sheila'). On her first day at iaxis some of the other Dodgers all summed up her new employment terms and conditions for her: 'She was a temp, an Aussie and a woman which means that she had no rights whatsoever whilst working for iaxis!' She of course, turned her mouth into a flamethrower and terrified them all. (I buy her the odd bottle of sherry just to remind her of life down under.)

Her Aussie husband Grant (*Strewth!*) is a famous crocodile-wrestling champion back home in the Northern Territories. Well, that's what we all believed after he came out with us and drank a few pints of XXXX. But over here he works for a BT offshoot in their WAP Division. He's a senior manager responsible for *'Technical Asset Resource Allocation Management'*. Which when translated into the everyday English language basically means that he's technically responsible for setting fire to huge piles of money.

But everyone in the pub is very buoyant at the thought of FLAG buying iaxis. Our European telecoms backbone is perfect for their UK to Japan sub-sea fibre optic cable. We know they've got huge development plans. And they've also got well over one billion dollars in hard cash sitting in their bank accounts. Everyone at iaxis is rubbing their hands together at this tidy sum.

... iaxis could spend most of that for them by Halloween and save the rest for Bonfire Night!

McGowan and Merlock go out and buy some new dark shades and leather jackets. With all the potential overseas network developments that are going to happen, FLAG are going to need these two enforcers. But FLAG have to move fast as iaxis is losing key staff and several co-location buildings in Madrid and Barcelona. This is because we can't pay the deposits. However, the iaxis villa is relatively safe. All the numbers on other villas in the street have been removed and so have the street names. Nobody will find that place in a hurry. Nick is still sunbathing on the beach and is being kept fully up to date through his mobile.

... But during the night the wolves never stopped howling and when the sky began to fall in, Psycho cracked. In sheer terror, he squeezed his finger on the 'grim-reaper' and all the rounds disappeared into the blackness of the cold dark forest. Soon afterwards all the wolves moved in on the cabin. They all howled like never before as they scratched mercilessly away at the old wooden door trying to get inside for a feed...

The following morning I am listening to Katcha's *'Touched by God'* as the whole office gathers for an announcement telling us that FLAG are going to buy us. I turn down the volume of my music, which is now *'Moments of Ambience'* by Odessi (on the Euphoria *Chilled* album) and I have a sudden eyelock with Sasha. She raises her eyebrows at me and we both telepathically say 'Hello!' to each other from twenty feet away. Kong just stares at me and telepathically tells me not to come any fucking closer.

Seamus has got his back to the wall and Howard is standing next to him looking seasick.

Nathan is clutching a packet of fags and is already looking at his watch wondering how long this is going to go on for.

Old Boy is rubbing his ears and Jemma and Claire are at opposite ends of the room, not looking at each other.

Mr Nice is on his mobile to Nick.

Hannah, who is sitting on someone's desk, tries to look fondly over to Wacko, just as he moves himself out of her angle of vision.

Stalker is chewing a pen and considering his next move.

Merlin looks happy at the level of understanding customer services have suddenly acquired in nuclear physics.

Merlock and McGowan are wearing their new leather jackets and shades and are waiting in anticipation for the next overseas job, which might just be a longhaul one.

Suzie is juggling her boobs at Swampy.

TTT is tucking in his creased SINET- Sun SPARC 10 T-shirt.

The Big Cats are all sitting on their chairs waiting to be told what to do.

Hellraiser can only see fire and is playing with some matches.

The Draft Dodger is looking over his shoulder and the Bullet Dodger is crouching behind a filing cabinet. And all of the other young Dodgers are just staring wildy at visions of *fire* as the iaxis chief operations officer stands up to tell us all about FLAG becoming our new employer.

… And we are all very relaxed, just waiting to hear these lovely few words.

He takes a deep breath and begins. *'There is no easy way for me to say this to you all, but last night FLAG's main shareholder, Verizon, rejected FLAG's plans to buy iaxis. Sadly, this leaves the iaxis management board with no option but to place iaxis into Administration…'*

Everyone thinks he's joking. But nobody is laughing. And he's not joking. Wacko is looking down at the floor and he can feel my eyes now tapping him on his head. He looks up at me and just nods solemnly.

Sasha catches my eyes and we hold eyelock, both connected by sheer disbelief. Everyone who invested their money in the iaxis "millionaire" share dream scheme has just lost it. And it is not their fault that iaxis *"missed the boat"*. The shareholders got dizzy up on the high wire and lost their footing looking for one billion dollars.

…In *hindsight*, the offer, which iaxis received for five hundred and seventy-five million pounds a few months ago, was really quite a nice sum.

Then the wolves finally scratch their way in to the cabin… Only these are not snarling away and frightening everyone to death. The big wolf, followed by his pack, comes forward and introduces himself to us as Mr Steven Pearson. He is a partner in PricewaterhouseCoopers (PwC). And instead of savaging everyone and eating us all alive, he comes across as one of the most professional and respectable people you could ever deal with. He and his fellow *'wolves'* now closely resemble a team of professional and dedicated surgeons who are going to preserve the life of the iaxis fibre optic telecommunications network with its Internet backbone. And then try to sell it.

But sadly, the Jammy Dodgers, Swampy in the NOC and a few people in network support are all that are required for this plan to keep the iaxis network alive. The rest of us get ready for our next career moves as everyone at iaxis has a contingency plan. In fact most members of staff have about four job offers.

I go into my office drawer and get out my contract of employment and all my share options and then empty the lot into the bin. I then pick up my Cross fountain pen and *black umbrella* and get ready to leave the office for the Blue Lion for the last time.

As I walk out of reception, I see that Charlotte is finally turning off a CNN state sponsored lapdog who is presenting the American news to the rest of the world. (Well someone had to do it.)

The day after, it is all over. And so we all move on to our next challenges.

Nathan went to work for Enron in content distribution and Old Boy went into the property business.

Howard and Seamus went on to work for a large co-location company.

Gibbsy went on to do product marketing for an Internet software company.

McGowan and Merlock both joined a co-location company doing implementation work and started frightening everyone there as well. Stalker also ended up going to the same co-location company.

Sasha works in sales and marketing for an Internet company.

Merlin joined a start up company specialising in software for Internet Virtual Private Networks (VPNs).

Scary Spice went to work in vendor management for a co-location company.

Suzie went to work in the "illegal" department of a global telecoms company and was told off for porn content distribution on her first day!

Hannah also went to work in a global telecoms company, where she was assured there were lots of young men…

Beelstar stayed out of the film business despite Old Boy and myself offering him really fantastic terms to be his movie agents!

Hellraiser went to work for Ciena.

Psycho went and did some contract work and Porn Star just disappeared!

And finally Nick: he managed to land a job with an American Internet company and blagged it out and persuaded them to keep him based in the Med.

…However, Wacko *('the Fire Master')* and the *'chief fire officer'* have both stayed on to manage the team of Dodgers to help find a new buyer for iaxis. They waste no time at all and go to work on the iaxis fibre optic customers who have had to pay twenty, or even thirty million dollars upfront for bandwidth capacity. These telecom companies have just been told that they need to pay iaxis (in administration) a few million pounds for a couple of months or else the network will be switched off. If this happens, then all their customers' traffic will be lost. A big telecoms company cannot afford this 'worst-case scenario,' so they all cough up the necessary millions with ease just to keep the iaxis network alive.

Within a very short space of time there is one final spectacular show for Wacko to manage. Dynegy Inc. of Texas, USA, has turned up... And they want to buy iaxis! *'The Fire Master'*, who is managing this final display, quickly gets to work. All of the creditors must agree to Dynegy buying iaxis, so he pulls in some of his mates who are all hardened veteran Dodgers from PwC whom he knows from way back. Altogether they have years of experience and they are going to be working alongside the iaxis Dodgers for this final 'display' called the *"Mars Experience"*.

Everyone is now actively involved in planning this deadly fire-eating act. And because this is a truly frightening display to pull off, all of the Dodgers have each been paid twenty thousand pounds in 'danger money' to stay on and do this one last death defying performance. And with all the tickets pre-booked and sold out, the banks, the creditors and all the main shareholders in the glass outfit on the Seventh floor of 200 Gray's Inn Road will soon see that this is the most terrifying display they have ever witnessed... *And on the day of the show everyone takes to their seats and waits for the performance to commence... As the curtain goes up, the Fire Master lights all the cannons and flamethrowers, and soon the spectators are gasping and find it hard to breathe as the free falling, fireball and rocket-eating extravaganza begins...*

Within minutes, all of the spectators' knuckles start to turn white with sheer terror *when without any warning at all, the* "Mars Experience" *suddenly takes off... And after only a few seconds everyone begins screaming for their lives when the Fire Master pulls off a high altitude flying wall of fire which simply defies the laws of physics and leaves everyone in the front rows suffering from fireblast, shellshock and* "33rd Degree" *burns.*

...Shortly after the "Mars Experience" *had finished, both Merlin and the chief fire officer said that even they could see all the flames and fireballs going off, and they were sitting twelve rows back and had both their hands covering their eyes.*

After this one amazing display, the creditors all accept Dynegy buying iaxis for one dollar. And Wacko is made managing director for Dynegy Communications Europe and walks away smiling.

The End *of iaxis.*

'Time moves very fast in here and never forget that anything can happen.'
iaxis: April 1999 to September 2000.

EPILOGUE

The blacker the smoke, the clearer the hindsight.

COMMENTS

Here are some words from people who kindly proof read first drafts to ensure the accuracy of technical details.

Wacko: 'Nice one. But there's not enough fire and alcohol in it. We drank more than that.'

Nathan: 'My ears popped and I needed another fag after reading it!'

Old Boy: 'It's a blaady good effort for a *first* book.'

Chief Financial Officer: 'Very good Steve, I like your writing style. We fought fires every single day.'

Seamus: 'Brilliant, ye wee fooker.'

Aussie Jen (Dodger No.6): 'This is so true I cried. It is excellent.'

"*Friend*": ["An 'interesting' little book…"]

Gibbsy: 'Strewth, what a good read mate!'

Merlock: , 'Really excellent. You don't want to buy a leather jacket, hardly used, do you?'

Chris Harper: 'I stayed up untill 4 a.m. reading this, it's brilliant.'

Natasha: 'You are still one jammy bastard!'

Kathryn: 'A brilliant read young man. You'd better go and buy yourself some Burberry earmuffs as you've managed to piece together the overall puzzle. You've probably upset the vanity of a few political figures and the historical memory of others, but that's your democratic right to do so. However, don't expect the trustees of the *American Enterprise Institute*, or the founders of *A New American Century* to put it quite like this. Just keep a low profile and you'll be fine. Washington will probably say that there's 'no evidence', or it's 'a conspiracy theory', 'pure fantasy' or 'just plain speculation'. But these are all pretty standard and well-used responses to kill stories that challenge the official line. However, regardless of what CNN and FOX tells the world, we both know that the CIA and NSA are not paid to tell the truth to the public. They are paid to *steal* a foreign nation's communication secrets, carry out covert and *Black Ops,* which overthrow foreign governments who act against our national interest. That's the job the US Intelligence Community does on behalf of the White House and the President, twenty-four hours a day, *every single day of the year*.'

However...

Sasha went to the Med and created one of the hottest summers a certain Greek island had ever seen, so I never got a chance to show the script to her. *But she knew it all already...*
Kong was always in the gym.
Mr Nice keeps a low profile.
Jemma and Claire just *vanished.*
Soundblast became pregnant, so Old Boy is now preparing to deal with two sound bombs!
Merlin had his hands full...
McGowan works in "The Dam" and has bought a GPS for his nights out. But I couldn't find him and he said his GPS was fitted with the wrong microchip, which caused problems when we tried to meet...
Lucia went overseas.
Bosco went for the neighbours and is doing hard time in the dog pound.
Psycho is getting treatment for an irrational fear of dogs.
Nick, the lucky old devil, is still with the American Internet company and blags it out in the hot Med, where he has far too many distractions...
Hannah could not be reached. *She has now fallen in love.*

Afterthought...

[*"Wine is Strong. A King is Stronger. Women are the Strongest. But Truth Will Conquer Over All..."*]

The meeting between Saddam Hussein and April Glaspie, the US Ambassador to Iraq, took place on the 25th July 1990. All the operational files and cables from the NSA and CIA to Kuwait, Iraq and Saudi Arabia before and after the Iraqi invasion of Kuwait are still classified at Top Secret/COSMIC level. These and many other CIA/NSA files connected with issues raised in this book are all currently withheld from any *full* Freedom of Information Act releases under the grounds of US National Security.

Location: Presidential Palace - Baghdad: 25th July 1990

U.S. Ambassador - I have direct instructions from President George Bush to improve our relations with Iraq. We have considerable sympathy for your quest for higher oil prices, the immediate cause of your confrontation with Kuwait (pause). As you know, I lived here for years and admire your extraordinary efforts to rebuild your country. We know you need funds. We understand that, and our opinion is that you should have the opportunity to rebuild your country (pause). We can see that you have deployed massive numbers of troops in the south. Normally that would be none of our business, but when this happens in the context of your threats against Kuwait, then it would be reasonable for us to be concerned. For this reason, I have received an instruction to ask you, in the spirit of friendship - not confrontation - regarding your intentions: why are your troops massed so very close to Kuwait's borders?'

Saddam Hussein- As you know, for years now I have made every effort to reach a settlement on our dispute with Kuwait. There is a meeting in two days; I am prepared to give negotiations only this one more brief chance (pause). When we (the Iraqis) meet (with the Kuwaitis) and we see there is hope, then nothing will happen. But if we are unable to find a solution, then it will be natural that Iraq will not accept death.

U.S. Ambassador- What solutions would be acceptable?

Saddam Hussein - If we could keep the whole of the Shatt-al-Arab - our strategic goal in our war with - we will make concessions (to the Kuwaitis). But, if we are forced to choose between keeping half of the Shatt and the whole of Iraq (including Kuwait) then we will give up all of the Shatt to defend our claims on Kuwait to keep the whole of Iraq in the shape we wish it to be (pause). What is the United States' opinion on this?

U.S. Ambassador - **We have no opinion on your Arab-Arab conflicts, such as your dispute with Kuwait.** Secretary of State James Baker has *directed* me to *emphasize* the instruction, first given to Iraq in the 1960s, that **the Kuwaiti issue is not associated with America.** (Saddam smiles).

["Saddam invaded Kuwait eight days later. And the winner, dear boy, always writes the 'history'..."]

Some fine British journalists were also in possession of this transcript as early as August 1990. At the time, April Glaspie declined to make any comment on their most important question. She climbed into her limo and drove away, while in Washington, *National Security Directive* 45 had recently been signed and the "overall strategic objective" in the Persian Gulf was only just beginning to take shape...

["...And the whole world was sold a White House lie."]

In the months following the Gulf War "victory" against Saddam, the "overall strategic objective" of NSD-26 was successfully achieved as the US government sold Saudi Arabia and various other Gulf States tens of billions of dollars worth of US military weapons. This, along with US military bases on Saudi soil, was to help "protect themselves from further aggression" in the region.

In 1991 the 41st President of the United States of America, George Bush Sr, awarded his Defense Secretary Dick Cheney, Secretary of State James Baker III and National Security Advisor General Brent Scowcroft the US Presidential Medal of Freedom. This was for their "services" to the Bush administration ["and also to **Mr David Rockefeller**..."] in securing the "overall success" of the Gulf War ["...for the future corporate oil and defence interests of '**America Inc**'"]. These awards were given when the world, and the American people, did not know about *National Security Directive* 26, which President George Bush Sr had signed on the 2nd October 1989.

Today, in the year 2001, the US government's strategic national interest in the Persian Gulf is secured, as a significant amount of the oil supply in the region is now effectively in America's hands and oil-rich Gulf States continue to buy American military weapons on a vast scale. Yet eleven years on, Saudi Arabia is still repaying the cash debt to America for the overall cost of "defending Saudi Arabia" from Saddam's "imminent threat" and for the Washington led Gulf War to "liberate Kuwait".

"Nothing is hidden that will not be made known or secret that will not come to light."
Yehoshua ben Joseph.

THE END *of the book.*

Steve Goddard
9th Sept 2001.
(first draft)

The *Epilogue*

'For ye shall know the truth and the Truth shall set you free.' John 8:32

APPENDIX

National Security Directive 45 signed by President George Bush on 20th August 1990 states: 'US interests in the Persian Gulf are vital to the National Security... On Thursday, August 2, 1990 the government of Iraq, *without provocation or warning*, invaded and occupied the State of Kuwait, thereby placing these vital US interests at risk... To protect US *national interests* in the Gulf and in response to the King of Saudi and the Emir of Kuwait, I have ordered US military forces deployed to the region... to deter and, if necessary, defend Saudi Arabia and other friendly states in the Gulf region from further Iraqi aggression... US forces will work together with those of Saudi Arabia and other Gulf countries to preserve their national integrity...'.

'I left here some 22 years ago after a limited tenure (Director of the CIA) and my stay here had a major impact on me. The CIA became part of my heartbeat back then, and it's never gone away...' Ex-President George Bush Sr speaking at the 'George Bush Centre for Intelligence' at the CIA HQ Langley 26th April 1999.

["Theca ubi res prestiosa deponitur..."]

'All warfare is based on **deception**.' *The Art of War* by Sun Tzu.

'**The truth shall set you free**.' The motto of the *Central Intelligence Agency*.

'Wine is Strong, a King is Stronger, Women are the Strongest. But Truth Will Conquer Over All.' **Rosslyn Chapel**, Scotland.

["...Si tatlia jungere possis sit tibi scire posse."]

'GOOD MORNING AMERICA'

[" 9/11 OIL: Near East blowback and the 'Grand Chessboard' of 'Middle Earth'..."]

It should have been a normal working day in the office. *But it wasn't.* Shortly after the 'President's Daily Brief' and 'DITSUM' were delivered, thousands of people were massacred when terrorists from Saudi Arabia and Egypt hijacked commercial airliners and crashed them into New York's World Trade Centre towers, live on daytime TV.

["...Buy the book *The Grand Chessboard: American Primacy and its Geostrategic Imperatives in Central Asia'.* It is written by Zbigniew Brzezinski who, with the CIA, created bin Laden's Afghan Mujahideen. The book was drafted as an 'agenda' for the Council on Foreign Relations in 1997... **Read it very carefully, dear boy.**"]

September 11th 2001 was also the day the Carlyle Group hosted their annual investor conference ["...a year in which Carlyle invested one and a half million pounds for the Saudi bin Laden family"]. It took place at the Ritz-Carlton hotel in Washington DC. Those in attendance included the former US Secretary of State James Baker III and others from the 'old guard' Bush administration in 1991 who were party to George Bush Sr's *National Security Review 1* (Afghanistan) - 7th Feb 1989 and *National Security Directive 3:* 'US Policy towards Afghanistan' - 13th Feb 1989. Who knows what was said as events unfolded live on CNN? War is also good for corporate defence profits...

Eleven years previously on the 11th September 1990, following Saddam Hussein being labelled the *"New Hitler"* to the rest of the world, the 41st President of the United States of America, *George Bush Sr* made his famous *"Towards a New World Order"* speech to the US Congress. In it he said, *"...Iraq must withdraw from Kuwait... A new partnership of nations has begun and we stand today at a unique and extraordinary moment. The crisis in the Persian Gulf (with Saddam) as grave as it is, also offers a rare opportunity to move toward an historic period of cooperation... Out of these troubled times a New World Order can emerge. A new era free from terror, stronger in the pursuit of justice and more secure in the quest for peace..."*

Congress gave him a standing ovation... And after the horrific attacks ["...on the 'beacon of freedom'..."] eleven years later, his son announced to a stunned and horrified world that what took place was an "Act of War".

["...Nothing was mentioned about George Tenent, Richard Armitage and ex-CIA man Porter Goss's prior 9/11 meeting with Pakistan's ISI chief, Lt General Mahmud Ahmad who had just sent one hundred thousand dollars to Mohammed Atta... Also silent was a 1995-7 UNOCAL-Afghan pipeline involving Henry Kissinger, Zalmay Khalilzad and the Taliban. Then, the CIA and ISI-backed Taliban were guests at UNOCAL in Sugerland, Texas in Dec 1997..."]

...Whilst Osama bin Laden was hiding in his cave, Saddam Hussein was virtually the only leader in the world who did not condemn the attacks. Instead, he released the following statement after the "twin pillars" of New York City had collapsed and the *Pentagon* was still on fire:

"*Brutal America, suffering from illusions of grandeur, has inflicted humiliation, famine and terrorism on all of the world's countries and today it reaps the fruits of its arrogant and stupid policy...*

...America needs wisdom, not power. It has used power, along with the West, to its extreme extent, only to find out later that it doesn't achieve what they wanted. Will the rulers of America try wisdom just for once so that their people can live in security and stability?

...Americans should feel the pain which they have inflicted on other peoples so that when they suffer, they will know the best way to treat it... In the name of God, Most Gracious, Most Merciful."

["...The CIA was 'explicitly' warned by 'several foreign intelligence services', and the Taliban, of airline suicide attacks on NYC in early September and it did *Nothing*. The FBI knew who Mohammed Atta was and it did *Nothing*. The NSA, monitoring Saudi-Pakistan-Afghan terror communications and financial transactions did *Nothing*, And the NSC and the President also did *Nothing*... Then on 9/11 bin Laden's old 'Bojinka Plan' of 1995 was tragically achieved... Osama made the first move on '*The Grand Chessboard*', and the 'War on Terror' with the 'direct external threat' had began... with the King '*exposed*'."]

Following the "attack on democracy" ["with money wired directly from *Mr Ahmed Umar Sheikh* all under the eyes, ears and noses of the CIA and NSA..."] this is what some newspapers said:

'DAY THAT CHANGED THE WORLD' *The Sun* 12/09/01

'WAR ON THE WORLD' *The Mirror* 12/09/01

'WAR COMES TO AMERICA' *The Times* 12/09/01

'A DECLARATION OF WAR' *The Guardian* 12/09/01

'*APOCALYPSE*' *The Daily Mail* 12/09/01

'DOOMSDAY AMERICA'	*The Independent* 12/09/01
'AMERICA BURNS'	*Al Iraq* 12/09/01
'THE TOMB'	*The Daily Mail* 13/09/01
'TEARS FOR AMERICA'	*The Daily Mail* 14/09/01

The first rule in all warfare is to always *"know your enemy"*: Osama was once CIA trained and is a religious and terror fanatic... Saddam was also CIA trained and is 'poisoned' with revenge... And the **George Bush Sr** 'Centre for Intelligence' is working towards a "One World: America Inc" agenda on behalf of the "chairman of the board": **Mr David Rockefeller** and His quest for "American global primacy".

Maybe in the future, I would prefer to read about Posh and Becks after all...

Oil-for-Food... **GOD BLESS AMERICA**

["...When you know what to look for, the view you are looking at is as clear as *glass*."]

<u>CHECKMATE</u>

Printed in the United States
20630LVS00002B/150

9 781843 750697